Midnight
at the
Blackbird Café

Center Point
Large Print

**This Large Print Book carries the
Seal of Approval of N.A.V.H.**

Midnight
at the
Blackbird Café

Heather Webber

CENTER POINT LARGE PRINT
THORNDIKE, MAINE

This Center Point Large Print edition
is published in the year 2019 by arrangement with
Tor-Forge Books.

The text of this Large Print edition is unabridged.
In other aspects, this book may vary
from the original edition.
Printed in the United States of America
on permanent paper.
Set in 16-point Times New Roman type.

ISBN: 978-1-64358-331-0

The Library of Congress has cataloged this record
under Library of Congress Control Number: 2019943642

For everyone who wishes they could
eat a piece of blackbird pie.

1

"Why don't you start at the beginning?"

"The beginning? Well, I reckon that was the funeral. The funeral turned into a damned circus when the blackbirds showed up." Blackberry sweet tea sloshed over the rims of two mason jars as Faylene Wiggins abruptly slapped her hand on the tabletop. "Wait! Wait! You can't print that. My mama would wash out my mouth with her homemade lemon verbena soap if she knew I cursed for the good Lord and all the world to see in your article."

The reporter flipped the pages of his yellow steno pad. "I thought you said your mother was dead?"

"You're not from these parts, so you're excused for not understanding. Wicklow, Alabama, isn't any old ordinary town, young man. Goodness, I wouldn't put it past my mama to rise straight out of the ground and hunt me down, bar of soap clutched in her bony hand." With a firm nod, she jabbed a finger in the air and added, "Now that you can print."

Anna Kate

Commotion loud enough to wake the dead was never a great way to start the day.

Startled out of a deep sleep, I sat up. It was a quarter past five in the morning, and for a moment I didn't know where I was. It was a familiar feeling, almost as comforting as the worn quilt I'd carted from town to town my whole nomadic life long.

As I rubbed tired eyes, clearing out sleep, the events of this past week slowly came back to me. Wicklow. The Blackbird Café. The funeral. The birds. The neighbors.

My God. The neighbors.

Drawing in a deep breath, I eased back onto the pillows. I didn't know what it was that had woken me, because all I heard now was the air-conditioning rattling through the vents, the tick of the hallway clock, and melodious birdsong. Nothing out of the ordinary.

If there was any mercy in this world, the noise hadn't been a tearful Mr. Lazenby banging on the café's front door—for the third morning in a row. He was a sweet, mournful old man who simply wanted his daily piece of pie, but all I wanted was to pull the pillow over my head until my alarm went off half an hour from now.

Instead, I came fully awake at the sound of unintelligible shouts, a mumbled roar that seemed like it originated from directly beneath my second-floor window. Confused, I tossed the quilt aside and slid to the floor. I knee-walked across dusty pine boards to the window. Dawn brightened over the mountains on the eastern horizon, promising a sunny and undoubtedly humid spring day.

Looking downward, I saw a small group of men and women gathered in the side yard. About twenty strong, they wore big hats and sensible shoes, carried binoculars, and were lined up along the iron fence, staring into the backyard. I didn't recognize a single one of them.

Not that I had met *everyone* in town since I arrived from Boston, but it sure felt like I had.

It had been an intense week, starting with the fateful call that my grandmother Zora "Zee" Callow had passed away unexpectedly of natural causes. I'd made a whirlwind trip down here to Wicklow, a rundown small town nestled deep in the mountain shadows of northeast Alabama, to make funeral plans and meet with Granny Zee's lawyer. I then went back to Boston to pack my few belongings and forfeit the room I'd been renting in a quaint old colonial only one T stop away from UMass Boston, where I'd recently graduated.

I'd loaded my car, mentally prepped myself for a seventeen-hour drive, and headed south. I temporarily moved into the small apartment above the Blackbird Café. Buried my beloved Zee. And unsuccessfully evaded most of my kind yet nosy new neighbors who wanted to know anything and everything about Zee's secret, mysterious granddaughter, Anna Kate Callow.

Me.

There had been an endless stream of visitors these past few days, and I'd never seen so many zucchini loaves in all my life. Each neighbor had arrived with an aluminum foil–wrapped loaf, an anecdote about living in Wicklow, a long story about Zee and her café, and relentless queries about my age, my upbringing, my schooling, my mother's passing four years ago, and my father's identity. I hadn't minded the stories of Granny Zee at all, but I dodged most of the personal questions, especially the ones about my father. I wasn't ready to go there quite yet.

It had been an exhausting, emotional week, and I didn't want to even look at zucchini for a good long while.

Now this daybreak meeting. Who were these people?

A wave of muggy, warm air slapped me in the face like a wet towel as I pushed the window sash upward. It creaked in protest against the swollen wooden frame. "Hello? Hello!"

At the sound of my own voice, my head throbbed, pulsing sharply against my temples. I'd spent most of yesterday with Bow and Jena Barthelemy, the café's only employees, readying the café for its reopening this morning. The energetic duo had given me a crash course in running the place, everything from ordering to inventory, tickets, and the point-of-sale system. I'd prepped dishes and familiarized myself with the menu and kitchen layout. The day had been nothing short of overwhelming, but Bow and Jena swore up and down that I'd catch on quickly enough.

Now, on my knees at the crack of dawn, craving strong coffee and utter silence, I questioned for the umpteenth time this week why on earth I'd moved, even short-term, to this tiny, two-stoplight Alabama town. I didn't belong here. I should be back in Boston, finalizing my plans for my move an hour west to Worcester, where I was going to start classes at UMass medical school in mid-August.

Then I remembered.

Zee.

More specifically, Zee's will.

"There, there!" someone shouted from below as he gestured into the backyard. Then he added in a somewhat shamed tone, "Never mind. It was a crow."

A chorus of grumbles echoed.

"Hello!" I shouted again.

No one seemed to hear me.

Grabbing my robe, I quickly covered up my knit shorts and tank top and ran a hand over my unruly hair. The stairs creaked as I hurried down them. The pine treads were polished in a dark satin finish that came from decades of use. I could easily imagine Granny Zee zipping up and down these steps, which was strange considering I'd never seen Zee do so. In fact, I had never even set foot in the Blackbird Café—or Wicklow, for that matter—until earlier this week.

Wicklow had always been forbidden territory, a family commandment created by my mom, Eden, the moment she left this town at eighteen years old, vowing that we would never return. That had been twenty-five years ago, when she had been just six weeks' pregnant with me. While growing up, every time I had asked about Wicklow, Granny's café, the blackbirds, my paternal grandparents, whom she hated with her whole heart, and, of course, my father's tragic death, Mom stubbornly clammed up.

Not that I could wholly blame her silence—after all, she had lost a lot here in Wicklow, including the love of her life and almost her freedom when she'd been accused of murder. Yet it had always seemed to me that the thing she'd lost most was herself.

The double refrigerator hummed as I glanced at the soffit above it, to the stenciled words that flowed from one side of the café to another.

Under midnight skies, Blackbirds sing, Loving notes, Baked in pies, Under midnight skies.

Zee had taught the verse to me as soon as I was old enough to speak full sentences, much to my mother's dismay.

Once, when I was seven years old, the two of them had a huge argument when Mom had come home from work to find Zee teaching me how to make her café's famous blackbird pie. Mom had sent me straight to my room, but I easily overheard the fight over me, Wicklow, and yes, blackbird pie, of all things, which wasn't made of actual blackbirds at all, but fruit. Heated, bitter words from my mother. Pleading ones from my grandmother.

"I don't want you talking about the blackbirds to Anna Kate anymore," Mom had said. "*Promise me.*"

Mom meant business if she asked for a promise. Callows prided themselves on not breaking promises. Not ever.

Granny had sighed loudly. "You can't keep the truth from her forever. She needs to know. She deserves to know. It's her *heritage.*"

"She's not ever going to step foot in Wicklow, so she doesn't need to know a thing."

"You and I both know that's not true. One day she'll end up in Wicklow, same as you. Your roots will pull you back where you belong."

"Not if I can help it."

"But darlin' girl, you can't stop it, no matter how far you run."

"Promise me," Mom repeated, the words tight, sharp.

It took Zee forever to answer before she said, "I promise not to say another word about the blackbirds."

My mother had come by her stubbornness

13

honestly—she'd learned it straight at the knee of Zee, who wasn't one to back down when she believed in the strength of her convictions.

Later that night as Zee tucked me into bed, she offered to tell me a bedtime story.

"This story stays between the two of us, Anna Kate, y'hear? Promise me you won't tell a soul."

I'd promised. It had been the first of many secrets we shared, all of which had been kept to this day.

Taking my hand in hers, she started the story. "Once upon a time, there was a family of Celtic women with healing hands and giving hearts, who knew the value of the earth and used its abundance to heal, to soothe, to comfort. Doing so filled their souls with peace and happiness. Those women held a secret."

"What kind of secret?"

"A big one." Her voice dropped low, her southern accent wrapping around me like a warm blanket. "The women are guardians of a place where, under midnight skies, spirits cross from this world through a mystical passageway to the Land of the Dead."

"The Land of the Dead? Is that like heaven?"

"It's exactly like heaven, darlin'."

As Zee had spun the tale, I suspected the story wasn't the least bit make-believe, despite how fantastical it seemed. Guardians and leafy passageways and messages from beyond delivered through pies. It should have been absurd, utterly laughable. Instead, it had sounded like history.

Heritage, even.

To Zee's credit, she never did mention "blackbirds" again to me, but that was only semantics. In her story, she'd called the birds "tree keepers," describing them as black as twilight. She'd told me all I needed to know about the blackbirds and their mission—an education that was supplemented over the years by our nature walks and her cooking and life lessons.

It was as though Zee had been prepping me for this day, when I'd be blindsided into taking over the café for two months. She had known I'd come to Wicklow, just like she had told my mother all those years ago.

Shifting my thoughts away from Mom, Zee, and the blackbirds, I let out a breath, unlocked the back door, and then pushed open the screen door that led onto a long, weather-beaten deck. The door snapped shut behind me, a sharp thwack of wood against wood.

A late May sunrise colored the sky in a burst of bright orange and striated pinks while birds chirped and the fresh scent of morning filled the air, tinged with undertones of mint and basil.

I glanced around at the intertwining gravel pathways, raised stone beds, and mix of herbs, vegetables, and flowers, and could practically see my grandmother's heart in this yard, imprinted on each and every leaf rustling in the mountain breeze.

I couldn't help giving the evil eye to the duo of puny, drooping zucchini plants in a bed by the deck stairs as I headed for the assembly line of strangers along the fence in the side yard. Several people offered smiles as I approached, but it was an older man standing front and center at the gate who spoke up as I approached.

A floppy beige bucket hat shaded his eyes as he said, "Good morning, ma'am."

Ma'am. I'd been called ma'am at least two dozen times in the past week, and despite learning the term was a southern courtesy used on *any* woman, it still set my teeth on edge. Unless you were geriatric, no one used "ma'am" up north.

The man looked to be in his sixties, and was dressed in cargo khakis and a long-sleeved tee that had the words "Bird Nerd" on it. On his feet were hiking boots that seemed better suited for the trails of nearby Lookout Mountain than the grassy yard of a rural small-town café.

"Good morning," I said, noticing that the fresh air had taken my headache down a notch. "I'm sorry, but the café doesn't open until eight."

Wobbly beads of sweat sat on the tip of the man's bulbous nose. "Oh, we're not here to eat."

I tucked my hands into the pockets of my robe. "No? Then why are you here? In this yard? At the crack of dawn?"

Eagerness filled his voice as he said, "We're with the Gulf Coast Avian Society from Mobile, and we're here for the *Turdus merula*. Have you seen one?"

"The turd *what?*"

"The common blackbird?" He enunciated clearly as if deciding I was a slow learner, and then held up a cell phone with an image of a blackbird on it. "A flock of *Turdus merula* has reportedly been seen near here, at the cemetery a few days ago? One of the locals said that the blackbirds nest in those there mulberry trees."

I glanced over my shoulder at a pair of red mulberry trees that stood protectively at the rear of the yard.

One particular family of guardians came from overseas a century ago, drawn to a small southern town. There, a passageway is marked with large twin trees. Where their branches meet and entwine, a natural tunnel is formed—and at midnight, that tunnel spans this world and the heavenly one.

As the group gathered closer, clearly waiting for me to answer, I realized I should have antici-pated something like this happening. When the blackbirds swooped through town on the way to Zee's funeral, several tourists had freaked out at the sight, needing repeated reassurances from the locals that a Hitchcockian onslaught wasn't immi-nent.

I hadn't blamed the tourists for reacting the way they did. In normal people's lives, a flock of birds didn't appear at funerals to pay their respects. Let alone blackbirds that didn't even belong on this continent.

The locals hadn't really thought much about the appearance, other than the odd hour at which the birds were seen. The blackbirds had been part of Wicklow since its founding—and were as familiar to the townsfolk as the courthouse, the scenic vistas, and Mr. Lazenby's bow ties.

It had taken outsiders to question the oddity of their existence.

"Ma'am?" he prompted. "Have you seen any blackbirds?"

"I've seen them," I finally answered. "Well, females. They're slightly lighter in color than the male pictured on your phone."

The group let out a whoop. A few pulled out cell phones and started making calls.

"Where there are females, there are males." He smiled as he wagged a finger at me.

Fighting the urge to wag a finger back at him, I kept quiet. There were no males, a fact that Sir Bird Nerd would discover for himself if he stuck around long enough.

"How many of them do you think there are?" he asked. "Estimation?"

Twenty-four in total, black as twilight, Zee had said. "Two dozen."

More whoops went up.

I noticed a man step out of the big house next door—Hill House, appropriately named, as it sat atop a small hill. He leaned against a porch column and offered a hesitant wave.

Gideon Kipling, Zee's lawyer. He'd been nothing but kind to me since I'd arrived, and seeing as how he hadn't foisted a zucchini loaf on me at any point during the past week, I liked him. I waved back before focusing on the group of birders.

"Do the blackbirds nest in those trees?" the birding ringleader asked.

I hedged. "Not so much nest, no. But they perch there from time to time."

Like from midnight to one in the morning—just long enough to sing their songs. The blackbirds only made daytime appearances on the rarest of occasions. Like funerals.

His bushy white eyebrows furrowed. "Are you sure they're blackbirds? Not redwings or cowbirds or ravens or crows? The *Turdus merula* are extremely rare. They've only been spotted a handful of times in this country, most recently on Cape Cod a few years ago."

I could have given him the exact location on the cape if he'd asked—it was where we'd been living when my mother died. Instead, I said, "I'm pretty sure. You are at the Blackbird Café, after all."

Skepticism skipped across his face, narrowing

19

his eyes and pushing his lips out in a dissatisfied pucker. "Do you mind if we stay here and keep watch for a while?"

I couldn't see the harm in letting these bird-watchers stay. No matter how long they watched, they'd never see the blackbirds for what they truly were.

"Ma'am? Is it okay if we stay?"

I gritted my teeth. "On two conditions."

"Name them," he said.

"Stop calling me ma'am and stay on that side of the fence. The café will be open from eight until two if you get hungry."

"Thank you kindly, ma'—" He coughed. "Thank you kindly."

"You're welcome."

I headed back to the deck, but stopped first to apologize to the undeserving zucchini for my mean look earlier. It was then that I noticed a dark gray cat with light eyes watching me intently from its seat on a white stone bench in the center of the garden.

If Zee had had a cat, I thought it a tidbit someone would have mentioned during one of the many, many visits I'd endured in the past couple of days. But it was also possible the neighbors were so caught up in trying to discover who my father was that they didn't think to mention a pet. I didn't see a collar as I smacked my lips, making kissing noises. "Here, kitty, kitty."

The cat stiffened, then bolted, disappearing into a flower bed. I smiled. It was rather refreshing to know there was at least one creature in this town who didn't want to meet me.

As I climbed the creaking deck steps, I fought the sudden urge to also hide in the garden, and instead went into the café to face the day head-on.

2

Natalie

If my mother knew where I was going, she'd undoubtedly clutch her signature double strand of pearls, purse her lips, and vociferously question the heavens above as to where she had gone wrong raising her only daughter.

Seelie Earl Linden had often interrogated the heavens during my twenty-eight years of being on this earth.

The heavens, to my knowledge, never replied. That only served to vex Mama even more than *I* did. Quite the feat.

My grip tightened on the handles of the stroller as I walked down Mountain Laurel Lane, Wicklow's one and only main street. The wide road was lined on both sides with painted brick shops, offices, houses, and a few restaurants. An oval-shaped median with a high curb ran the length of the street, starting at the church with its jutting white spire at the north end of the block to the stone courthouse at the south.

Nearly a century ago, Wicklow had been established as a charming artists' colony that boasted of its eclectic population. Old, young. Rich, poor. Offbeat, average. Country, gentility. All had come together for a shared love of the arts and the magical mountain air. Between the natural landscape with its breathtaking vistas, the unique shops and artisans, and the undercurrent that this town was different, *special,* Wicklow quickly became a day-trip hot spot for tourists.

Now, I reflected, Wicklow wasn't so much as lukewarm.

As I walked along, I couldn't help noticing that in the four years I had been gone from my hometown, a dozen more shops and restaurants had been boarded up and those that remained open looked mighty tired from carrying Wicklow's fiscal burden.

I knew bone-weary exhaustion when I saw it.

The housing recession a decade ago had caused the town to fall on hard times with a resounding thud. A lot of the artists and craftsmen had moved along to more lucrative, populated locations like Fairhope and Mobile, abandoning their houses and shops. By the time the economy rebounded, the damage had already been done. Wicklow had struggled ever since. Recently, however, a committee had been formed to try and rejuvenate what was left.

Revitalization seemed an impossible task, though I saw the committee's fingerprints on the overflowing flower baskets hanging from lamp-posts, the new wrought-iron wastebaskets dotting the sidewalk, the patched sidewalk cracks, and the colorful posters touting the annual July 4th celebration. It was going to take a lot more than some pink petunias and trash cans to bring this community back to life, but I had to admire that the committee was *trying*. Determination was rooted deep in this mountain town.

Glancing down, I checked on my daughter. Ollie was happy as could be in the stroller, playing with the buckle strap, babbling away. She was an easygoing baby, and I often envied her contentment. She was too young to understand the chaos and heartbreak of my world, and for that I gave thanks.

Pivoting, I crossed again in front of the Blackbird Café. The café was one of the lucky ones that had survived the economy's downturn. It was a favorite among locals, not only because of its legendary pies, but because, many had said, Zee put her heart and soul into the restaurant—and shared that with those who ate there. How it would survive without her, I didn't know, but it, too, was trying.

I'd walked past the entrance three times already, trying to work up the nerve to go inside. All I wanted was a piece of blackbird pie before it sold out for the day. Yet . . . I hadn't been able to bring myself to open the door quite yet. Every time I tried, the image of my mother's face swam in front of my eyes and I chickened out, walking straight on past.

It had been a long time since I had set out to antagonize my mother on purpose, and I was trying my best to put those days behind me. To start fresh. To make peace, for Ollie's sake.

And maybe a little for my sake, too.

Mama had frozen me out of her life for a long time now, but during the past week or so, she had started to show signs of thawing. A kind glance. A slight smile. I didn't want to ruin that progress . . . but I really, really wanted that pie. If what people said about the pie was true, I *needed* it—and the answers it might provide—so I could get on with my life.

"Natalie Linden Walker! Is that you? If this don't beat all. It's good to see you, girl! It's been too long."

Oh no. Not Faylene Wiggins. *Anyone* but Faylene. If there had been a prayer of my mother not learning of this pie escapade for a good while, it just went out the window. "Good morning, Faylene."

Faylene, a retired high school art teacher, was a talker. For as long as I had known her, she rambled on fast-forward, speeding through a conversation, barely stopping to breathe, let alone wait for a response. Tall and plump with a sassy pitch-black bob, she had to be in her early sixties, but had more energy than I did at less than half her age.

"I didn't know you were back in town, Natalie!" She gave me a quick side hug. "Are y'all headed for the reopening of the café? Have you already met Anna Kate? Does your mama know you're here? Here at the Blackbird, not here in town. I assume she knows *that*." Faylene tittered. "Where are you staying? Back at home? Are you just visiting or planning to stay for a while?"

I ignored most of the questions, praying Faylene would forget she asked them, as she often did, and said, "We're set up in my parents' guest house for the foreseeable future." Lord help them all.

The little house, as it had been nicknamed, was a two-bedroom, one-bath, seven-hundred-square-foot cottage that might be entirely too close to my mother for my comfort, being that it was in her backyard. It had free rent, however, and was the perfect place to try to pick up the pieces of my life.

"Doc and Seelie must love having you home! Oh! And this one, too! Is this here Olivia Leigh?" Faylene's arthritic knees popped as she bent down in front of the stroller. "Why, aren't you a beauty! Look just like your mama, yes you do. How old is she now?"

Ollie glanced up at me with a bewildered expression in her big brown eyes. Faylene had that effect on people. Even toddlers. I smoothed one of Ollie's wayward curls and said, "She's a few months shy of two, and she mostly goes by the nickname Ollie."

"Ollie? Well, if that isn't the sweetest thing I've

heard in a long while. When did you two get back to town? You were living down in Montgomery, right? Must not have been long, since I haven't seen you at church or around town. How long had you been gone, Natalie? Four years now? Five? Your mama and daddy must be thrilled you're home. I'm surprised they're not singing from the rooftops."

The older woman quieted, smiled, and cocked her head. I realized she was actually waiting for an answer to one of those questions. I chose the easiest.

"I've been back a few weeks now." I had begrudgingly driven into town three weeks ago that very day, dragging my muffler and pride up Interstate 59. Both were beyond repair at this point.

"What's your mama think of Anna Kate?" Faylene wiggled her dark eyebrows.

"Who's Anna Kate?"

Faylene's jaw dropped open, then snapped closed. "Anna Kate Callow? You haven't heard . . . ?"

I was sure I'd met Eden Callow at some point, but I didn't remember her. I'd been only three years old when Eden left Wicklow. Her name, however, had been brought up often enough while I was growing up—as it was being cursed to the rafters. I knew Zee, but in passing and reputation only.

28

The Callows—and the café—were off-limits to any and all Lindens.

Which was why my trip here to the Blackbird Café was A Very Big Deal.

"Heard what?"

Faylene glanced between the café and me, and I could practically see a war being waged behind the woman's blue eyes. Redness climbed her throat, making her skin splotchy.

I glanced at the café. I'd heard my parents whispering about a long-lost family member of Zee's reopening the restaurant, but I hadn't thought too much of it. Honestly, I hadn't cared. All I wanted was blackbird pie. I hadn't dared go inside to order a piece while Zee had been alive—that would have been an unforgivable sin in my mother's eyes, but now?

Just a minor sin.

Or so I hoped, for the sake of that tenuous peace.

I also hoped there was pie left by the time I screwed up some courage to order a piece. I hadn't expected a crowd for the reopening. Locals were jammed inside, elbow to elbow, and there was a large gathering of people I didn't recognize on the side lawn. With each of my passes in front of the restaurant, more and more people had arrived with cameras and lawn chairs.

Faylene pressed a hand to her flushed neck. "It's just, ah . . . I think that she's . . . Well, *the whole town* thinks that she's your . . ." She coughed, then wrinkled her nose. "It's probably best you meet Anna Kate. See her for yourself."

"All right," I said noncommittally. If I was going to eat a piece of the forbidden blackbird pie, I might as well meet a Callow while I was at it. Get all my transgressions out of the way in one fell swoop.

I simply needed to go inside and get it over with. Repercussions be damned.

After a querulous conversation with the heavens, my mother would get over it.

Eventually.

Maybe.

Though Mama's deep freeze would likely return in full glacial force.

I held in a sigh at the mere thought of it. Seelie Earl Linden's preferred method of punishment was stone-cold silence. Truth be told, the frostiness was more effective than swatting me on the back-side ever would have been. I'd like to say I had become immune to my mother's usage of the silent treatment over the years, but that would be a lie, and I didn't like liars.

If only I'd known I married one.

Ignoring the sudden ache in my chest, I picked an invisible piece of lint off the wide strap of my sundress.

"Good, good." Then, as if reading my mind, Faylene said, "I was right sorry to hear about

30

your Matthew. Such a tragedy." Large hoop earrings swayed as she shook her head. "*Such* a tragedy. So young." She *tsk*ed. "How have you been coping since he's been gone? What's it been now? A year since the accident? Eighteen months? Thereabouts?"

This was precisely why I'd been in hiding the past three weeks. I didn't want to talk about Matthew.

Or the tragedy of it all.

Or the accident.

If it even had been an accident.

But this was Wicklow. People were duty bound to offer condolences and speak their minds. They wanted answers about what had happened. Answers I didn't have.

Yet.

Faylene rocked in her wedge sandals and tipped her head again. She was waiting for a response.

I flexed my fingers, forcing myself to relax my iron grip on the stroller. Still, my teeth clenched and my jaw ached as I said, "It's been one year, seven months, three days, and two hours. There-abouts."

Faylene's eyes widened. "Well . . . *bless your heart.*"

Throwing an arm around me, Faylene dragged me close for a tight hug, squishing me against large breasts. I was suddenly enveloped by a lemon verbena scent and kindness.

Faylene patted my head. "You poor thing. I've been in your shoes. My Cyrus has been gone for a good many years now. If you ever need a shoulder to cry on, honey, just holler. If it's one thing I've got, it's good, strong shoulders."

Tears stung my eyes, but I blinked them away. I'd sworn off crying the day my house had been foreclosed on, almost a year and a half ago. It was just . . . this woman had offered me more compassion and solace in five minutes than my own mother had in nineteen months. All Mama had given me was a floral arrangement on the day of Matt's funeral.

"Thank you, Faylene. I appreciate that." I did my best to extricate myself without fully losing my composure—something I'd worked hard on maintaining since Matt died.

"Sure thing, honey. Sure thing. If you ever need anything, you let me know. I'm happy to help." She bent down to Ollie's level. "I'd love to have this adorable little bit play with Lindy-Lou— that's my grandbaby. She turned two last month. You remember my daughter Marcy?"

"Of course I remember Marcy." It was a small town. Everyone knew everyone. And most of their business as well. Like how I knew Faylene had gone into a deep depression when Marcy decided to go to college in California, far away from her mother.

That Marcy left was no surprise whatsoever. If

anyone needed a break from Faylene, it was her only daughter. However, most were shocked to their souls that Marcy had actually come home after she graduated college.

I wasn't.

It seemed to me that all Wicklow girls tended to return to their roots—and their mothers—at some point or another. It simply took some more time than others.

"Lindy-Lou is Marcy's little one. I keep her a couple days a week, and one more ain't nothing, if you're needing some time to yourself, Natalie. I'm the best babysitter around, you can ask anyone."

Ollie stared at Faylene, wide-eyed and completely captivated. I suspected I looked the same. Faylene was a good reminder of why I moved back here. I wanted Ollie to have this kind of supportive community, and if that came with prying questions, so be it. It was worth the pain. "I can't thank you enough for the generous offer, Faylene, but right now I don't get out much."

"You'll get out more and more, I'm sure of it. There's a lot of good you could do around here. Many of our committees are floundering—it isn't any wonder why the town is too. We need some young blood to spice things up. The whole town could use an influx of youth. Doc mentioned once that you were on all kinds of committees and organizations down in Montgomery."

I had been. Everything from the historical

society and the Daughters of the Confederacy to the Junior League and church ministries. I'd dropped a lot of it when I finally got pregnant—something that had taken a good four and a half years of trying—and I wished now that I hadn't cut myself off so completely. Hindsight was always bittersweet.

"You just holler when you need me," Faylene said. "I'll be here. Now, if that isn't the most darling headband Ollie is wearing. I need one of those for Lindy-Lou. She's cute as a button, but nearly as bald as old Mr. Lazenby."

I had just finished Ollie's headband last night. It was embellished with a coral peony made of satin and chiffon petals. Delicate yet fanciful. "I'd be happy to make one for Lindy-Lou."

Faylene's eyes flew open wide. "You made that headband? Of course you did. You surely inherited Seelie's knack for sewing. That woman is magic with a needle. Her quilts are to die for. I'd love for you to make Lindy-Lou a headband. No, two headbands. Three. Yes, three. Different colors, of course. How much are they?"

"I couldn't charge you . . . they'll be a gift." It's the least I could do after that hug.

"Nonsense! I insist." She narrowed her gaze, studying my face for a good, long moment. "How about this? You throw in the first one as a freebie, and I'll pay for the other two."

I wondered what Faylene had seen during

her intense examination. The tattered shreds of my pride? The laughable amount in my bank account? Whatever it was, I was happy for the compromise. "That's a deal."

"Excellent." She steepled her fingers under a big smile. "I can't wait to see them on Lindy!"

"I can have them to you in a couple of—"

"Dog!" Ollie exclaimed. She leaned so far forward in her stroller that she almost toppled straight out onto the sidewalk. "Dog!"

I turned and saw a tall man walking toward us, a fancy camera with a long lens hung around his neck. At his heels was a beautiful brindle-and-white dog, some sort of Sheltie mix.

Faylene clapped her hands. "Oh! Lookie here. Cam Kolbaugh, as I live and breathe. You are a sight for these eyes! I haven't seen you since what? Christmas? Give me some sugar!"

"You saw me last week at the movie on the courthouse lawn." He kissed both her cheeks. "And you know it."

"Oh! That's right, I did see you there. My *mistake*." She elbowed me while wiggling her eyebrows. "Gotta get in what kicks I can, you know what I mean? Cam is such a looker, I just can't help myself."

"Faylene, come on now," he said. "You're going to make me blush."

"Not that we'd be able to see it," she returned. "All that handsomeness hiding under those whiskers. It's a shame. A damn shame. When are you going to shave that beard?"

I smiled at the sheer displeasure in Faylene's voice. I kind of liked the man's beard, not that I'd ever say so.

Ollie saved him from answering when she squirmed excitedly and shouted, *"Dog!"*

The man crouched and spoke directly to Ollie. "His name is River. Do want to pet him?"

"Careful now," I cautioned.

"Oh, don't worry none. River's gentle," the man, Cam, reassured.

"I wasn't so much worried for Ollie as I was for River. Ollie doesn't know her own strength sometimes. She's almost snatched me bald a couple of times."

Cam stared at me for a moment, then laughed as he rubbed River's ears. "He'll be just fine."

The dog licked Ollie's hand, and she squealed as she reached out to tap River on his head. "Dog, dog, dog!"

"Look at that. Fast friends already." Faylene faced me. "Do you know Cam, our resident mountain man?"

"No, I don't think so."

"Silly me! You wouldn't, since you only just moved back. Cam moved down here from Tennessee 'bout a year ago."

He stood up and stuck out a giant, callused hand. "Cam Kolbaugh."

"Natalie Walker." His hand swallowed mine, and I was surprised at his gentle handshake, considering his strength. It was as if he were taking extra care not to crush my fingers. "And this is Ollie."

"Aka Olivia Leigh," Faylene said to the man. "But ain't Ollie the cutest nickname you ever did hear? Natalie is Seelie and Doc Linden's girl. She's a widow, Natalie is. Lost her husband, Matthew Walker, a little more than one year, seven months, and three days ago. Thereabouts. A tragic boating accident."

"I'm sorry to hear that." Cam's thick dark eyebrows dipped low. "My condolences."

I glanced around for a manhole I could fall into. Head first. "Thank you."

He nodded and bent to pet River, who was still being loved on by Ollie. Fortunately, the dog didn't seem to mind toddler kisses one bit.

To me, Faylene said, "Cam is Marcy's brother-in-law. Her husband Josh's brother. Big bear of a man, Josh is. You have to meet him. Despite him being one of Wicklow's finest policemen, he has the sweetest disposition you ever did see." She leaned in close. "Don't tell him I said that. And Marcy runs the gift shop"—she spun and pointed to a storefront across the street, Hodgepodge—"over there. You need to drop in to see some of Cam's photographs. He's a wildlife photographer. Marcy sells his photos on consignment. They're

37

gorgeous. Stunning. No one can take a picture like Cam. He has quite the eye."

I watched Cam's face as Faylene gushed on, and was amused by the look of utter embarrassment sweeping across his features, tugging the fine lines around his hazel eyes and deepening the furrows on his forehead.

Looking back at the shop with its bright yellow awning, I wondered if Marcy was hiring. Top of my priority list, just beneath getting that blackbird pie, was finding a job. The shop was closed at the moment, but I made a note on my mental to-do list to stop by later on.

Faylene added, "Best you hurry, though, seeing as how Marcy's not sure how much longer she can keep the shop open. She thought summertime would bring more visitors up this way to hike and bike, but it's been slim pickings so far."

"I'm sorry. Is there anything I can do to help?" My stomach ached with a sinking feeling as I crossed Hodgepodge off my list of potential employers. Talk about slim pickings— job openings around here were scarcer than touists.

Faylene patted my hand. "You sweet thing. We surely appreciate your offer. We'll get by, we always do."

Cam straightened. "It's been a pleasure, ladies, but I should probably get going. I'm on assignment."

"Oh? Do tell!" Faylene rubbed her hands together.

Cam wrapped River's leash around his hand. "There's been a sighting of some rare birds behind the café, and the news is spreading like wildfire through the birding community. A bird-watching friend of mine contacted me to snap some shots. No big deal, but I should be on my way. The lighting's good right now."

"You mean the blackbirds?" Faylene asked. "Shoo, you've got time. They're not usually out in the daytime. Come back a bit before midnight to set up."

"You know of these birds?" he asked.

"Cam," Faylene said with a cock to her hip, "everyone in Wicklow knows about the blackbirds, not counting you, obviously. You really need to come out of the mountains a little more often."

He glanced at me, and I said, "The blackbirds have been here all my life. Midnight till one in the morning. They sing the prettiest songs you'll ever hear."

Suspicion laced his tone. "That's not normal—the midnight thing, not the songs."

Faylene said, "Sugar pie, the blackbirds are normal around here. I can't hardly believe they're causing such a fuss after all these years." She stood on tiptoes. "But I say, never look a gift horse in the mouth. Or birder, in this case. I best let these visitors know that Hodgepodge will be opening at eleven."

"Ollie and I should really get going, too," I said, eyeing the café. "It was nice to meet you, Cam. See you soon, Faylene."

"Yes, yes!" Faylene said. "Very soon. And you should get together with Marcy sometime, with the girls. Your little one and Lindy-Lou will be fast friends in no time flat."

Friends would be nice. I had suspected coming home would be difficult but thought I'd adjust fairly quickly. Fall into old patterns. Routines. Go back to the way things had been before. Go back to the way *I* was before.

I should have realized that was impossible.

Pain changed people.

I couldn't go back to the way I'd been, because I wasn't the same person who'd left.

All of which reminded me of that piece of blackbird pie that was so important. I needed the answers it would give me. The peace. Not only for my sake, but for Ollie's, too. I wanted to be the best mother I could be to my little girl. That meant I needed to find a way to heal my troubled heart and mind, so I didn't turn out like my own mother, who'd been lost somewhere in a haze of anger and grief for decades, oblivious to anything but her own pain.

Reaching down, I tucked one of Ollie's loose

fawn-colored curls back under the headband. "Say goodbye, Ollie."

"Bye! Dog!" Ollie cried out, waving madly.

Cam offered a wave and River thumped his tail.

I spun the stroller around, took a few steps toward the café, and froze.

I needn't have worried that Faylene would blab my whereabouts to my mother. Because Mama was *here*. Arms folded, she stood rooted in front of the café, staring inside.

Maybe if I backed up slowly, I might be able to make a clean getaway . . .

Mama's head came up sharply, then snapped to the right as if sensing my presence.

Busted.

I tried to mask a wince as Mama marched over. Seelie Earl Linden looked perfectly put together, as always. Flowy linen slacks, a crisp white blouse, leather sandals, a large white sunhat that covered most of her shoulder-length wavy white hair that was shot through with strands of her original coppery color, dark sunglasses, and her double strand of pearls. "Olivia Leigh's eyes are simply precious when she squints just so, and her skin is turning such a lovely shade of brown, don't you think?"

Mama never used Ollie's nickname, claiming it a ridiculous name for a girl, and that people were going to think she was a boy.

As if that were possible with her long hair,

bow lips, arched eyebrows, and button nose. Not to mention the skorts she wore, the pink lace-trimmed shirt with her monogram on the pocket, and matching pink sandals.

"Gamma! Hihi!" Ollie said, waving.

I didn't bother mentioning that I'd lathered Ollie in sunscreen or that she had flung her sunglasses to the ground six times already before I gave up and tucked them into the diaper bag before they broke. It wouldn't matter. By the end of the day, a wide-brimmed toddler-size sunhat would be delivered to the little house along with the expectation that it be used.

"Hello there, sweet pea." Mama bent down to grasp Ollie's outstretched fingers, then kissed her forehead.

My heart wrenched at the affection Mama bestowed upon Ollie. It was something that I hadn't experienced from my mother in a good, long while. While the truth of that stung, I was thankful Ollie didn't know her grandmother's coldness.

And she never would, if I could do anything about it.

Peace, I reminded myself. *Peace.*

Mama said, "You're out and about early."

Even though the statement was directed at Ollie—and wasn't a question—Mama lifted her head, clearly expecting a response from me.

"We're . . . off to the library." Not quite a lie.

Ollie and I *had* planned to go to the library this morning. After the pie. "I'm surprised to see *you* here."

In all my years, I'd never seen my mother within a hundred-foot radius of the Blackbird Café. Mama took great pains to avoid this section of the street, going acres out of her way so as to not even lay an accidental glance on the old stone building.

Mama's hand flew to her pearls. "I was passing by on my way to a Refresh meeting and stopped to see what was causing the racket."

It was a good story, but I didn't buy it. Though Mama *was* the chairwoman of the restoration committee designed to revitalize the community, nicknamed Refresh, the meetings were usually held at Coralee Dabadie's house, two blocks away. "Passing by" here required quite the elaborate detour. Besides, Mama hadn't said one word about my proximity to the establishment. Highly suspicious.

She gestured to the crowd on the café's side lawn. "What *is* going on? Who are these people? Surely they're not here for the reopening."

Amid the chaos of the packed café, a stranger stood out, weaving among the tables with a tray in hand. A woman, about the same age I was, give or take a couple of years. A stranger, yet familiar. Was that Anna Kate Callow? She didn't look much like Zee, who'd been a tiny blonde with straight hair usually tied into a braid, and who'd had an affinity for flowy skirts, long scarves, and dangly earrings. Anna Kate was tall, maybe as tall as my five-foot-eight, and had chestnut-colored curly hair. She wore jeans, cuffed to mid-calf, and a plain purple T-shirt. Not an earring to be seen. "It's the blackbirds. The birding community is fascinated with them. Supposedly, they're rare. The birds. Not the birding community."

I was rambling. Mama had that effect on me.

She glanced inside the café, and her slender fingers whitened as she tightened her grip on her pearls—the pearls that my brother (with Daddy's financial help) had given Mama for her very first Mother's Day, more than forty years ago.

Sadly, I didn't remember Andrew James Linden, golden child, the pride and joy of my family— and Wicklow. I'd been only three when he died at just eighteen years old in a car crash. Some had called me an *oops* baby, a surprise my parents hadn't been expecting so late in life. Apparently Mama had been over the moon at the news of my impending arrival, even though everyone around here knew Seelie Earl Linden didn't care much for surprises.

It was a happiness that vanished forever the day AJ died.

Mama scoffed. "The birds? Foolishness."

"Seelie! Knock me over with a feather, seeing you here at the café!" Faylene said brightly as she approached. "I suppose you heard the rumors . . . Quite shocking, isn't it?"

With a brittle closed-mouth smile, Mama stared at Faylene. "I'm not sure what you mean."

Patches of red appeared on Faylene's neck again. "The rumors about Anna Kate . . . ?"

Mama kept staring, her lips pressed into a thin, frigid line.

Faylene glanced between Mama and me, me and Mama. "I, ah, need to be going." She pointed left, then right. "Good to see you both."

"Do give my best to Marcy, won't you?" Mama said, saccharine sweet.

"I surely will," Faylene called over her shoulder as she scurried off.

"What was that all about?" I asked as soon as she was out of earshot.

"You know I abhor gossip, Natalie," Mama said dismissively.

Baffled, I glanced around. It seemed like everyone stared at us, including the people in the café.

Mama said, "I'm leaving. Are you coming with me? The library is on the way to Coralee's house."

I swallowed hard. Choices. I could either stand my ground, go inside, and get the piece of pie and answers I craved . . . or keep the fragile peace in my broken family.

"We're coming," I said, stifling a sigh.

Peace was worth leaving with my mother right that minute. But come tomorrow morning . . . I would be back for that pie.

Maybe then I'd also figure out why everyone was so interested in Anna Kate Callow.

3

"When did you first notice the blackbirds?" the reporter asked.

Bow Barthelemy kicked out long, thin legs. "They've been here as long as I have."

"How long have you worked for the café?"

"Twenty-five years, but the birds have been here longer. Nearly a century, I've heard."

The reporter rolled his eyes and scribbled a note. "Are there always twenty-four birds like in that old nursery rhyme? 'Four and twenty blackbirds, Baked in a pie—' "

" 'When the pie was opened, The birds began to sing.' " Bow finished the quote. "I know it. Zee once said those birds were probably relatives."

"She was obviously joking. Right?"

"Zee never joked about the blackbirds."

Unsure what to say to that, the reporter tapped his pen, then gestured wide. "You don't find all this strange?"

"Not at all, but what's strange to me could look mighty different to you." He stood up, pushed the chair in. "I need to be gettin' back to work. You want a refill on that blackberry tea?"

"Yes, please. Best damn tea I've ever had."

Anna Kate

"I heard tell you're heading off to medical school soon, young lady," Mr. Lazenby said. His bottom lip pushed outward and his jaw set as if bracing for a fight.

Skirting his chair, I picked up empty plates and gathered discarded silverware from a nearby table. I wasn't surprised by his nosiness, as it seemed to be a community-wide affliction, almost as prevalent as the lack of respect for personal space. People had been giving me hugs all morning, my stiffness not the least bit of a deterrent. Did no one have boundaries around here? "That's right. Classes start in August."

It had taken me seven long years to complete my premed undergrad. Between switching schools twice, taking time off after my mom's death, and running out of tuition money . . . it was a miracle I'd graduated at all. Truthfully, I'd have quit altogether, except for a promise I'd made to my mother a long time ago.

"Hmmph," Mr. Lazenby said, staring long and hard at me.

It looked like he had dressed for a special occasion this morning, wearing pressed trousers, a crisp white button-down, and a red-and-white checkered bow tie, but I'd come to recognize it was his normal, everyday attire.

He'd been here since the doors opened at eight

and didn't look like he planned to leave anytime soon, even though it was now well after ten. Sitting prim and proper, with his back ramrod straight and his napkin on his lap, he glared at his fork.

"Something wrong?" I asked.

"This pie doesn't taste right."

"Otis Lazenby," Jena Barthelemy called out from the kitchen, "I know you're not insulting my cooking. That's Zee's recipe for apple pie, and I'll have you know it's a ribbon winner."

Jena apparently had bionic hearing, because I wasn't sure how she'd heard him over the hum in the room.

"It might be Zee's recipe," he said, "but this pie don't taste like the pies Miss Zee made."

"We can't be changing the fact that Zee's gone to glory, can we?" Jena walked over to us. "God bless her soul. Times are changing, and we need to change right along with them, don't we?"

"But I'll still dream tonight, won't I?" he asked, panic threading through his high voice.

"I don't know. Time will tell, won't it?" Jena said.

A wave of anxiety washed over me.

While on earth, it's the job of us guardians to tend to the trees, nurture them, and gather their love to bake into pies to serve those who mourn, those left behind. You see, the bonds of love are only strengthened when someone leaves this earth, not diminished. Some have trouble under-standing that, so it's the pie that determines who's in need of a message, a reminding, if you will; it's the love in the pie that connects the two worlds; and it's a tree keeper who delivers the message.

Yesterday, Jena had taken on the task of making the blackbird pies, and I should have known they wouldn't be quite right. A *guardian* was supposed to bake the pies. Now that Zee was gone, making the pies fell on me as the only surviving Callow. Unfortunately, I didn't think Mr. Lazenby would get the message he longed for, but I was hoping by some miracle that he would.

"Hmmph." He pouted at the fork before shoving it into his mouth.

"Now tell all, Anna Kate. Did you always want to be a doctor?" Pebbles Lutz asked.

Pebbles, her white hair piled high, sat across from Mr. Lazenby at the ten-seat communal table that took up most of the dining room. This morning, I'd seen her cast more than one longing glance his way, but he seemed oblivious to her attention . . . and affection.

"For as long as I remember," I said, dodging the heart of the question, the *want* part, as I collected more plates.

The café had once been a carriage house. A long time ago, Zee had converted it into a restaurant downstairs and living quarters up. A glass door and big bay windows at the front of the café let in an abundance of light. The floors were the same dark pine as the stairs, and the walls were covered

50

in whitewashed pine, as was the ceiling. With a fairly open layout—only a half wall separated the cooking and dining areas—it felt as though this were a family kitchen rather than a business.

The whole space was light and bright and airy, but right now it felt more than a little claustrophobic. All eight tables were full, every seat taken. Several people stood near the door outside, waiting to come in. Some I recognized as neighbors. Some I didn't, such as the young woman with the baby who kept passing by, staring inside forlornly.

Hands full, I headed back to the kitchen, to drop the dishes at the sink and take a minute to simply breathe. It was overwhelming to be the focus of so much attention.

"You're doing fine, just fine," Bow said from his spot at the stove. His normally pale face was infused with redness from standing over the stove all morning, and concern flashed in his light blue-gray eyes.

"Especially seeing as you have no restaurant experience," Jena added. "I'm impressed."

I decided she impressed easily, because I was a hot mess. I knew my way around a regular kitchen—cooking and baking were second nature to me—but I knew nothing about working in a commercial kitchen or waitressing.

I'd already broken three plates, spilled more water than I cared to admit, and was limping—my feet burned like the devil. "Is it always this busy?"

"It's a sight busier than usual." Bow pulled a basket from the double fryer. "Between the bird-watchers and . . . you. People are curious."

There was a slight arch to his back, and I wondered if that's where his nickname had come from. His body looked like a bow missing its arrow. He emptied the basket onto a paper plate. Crispy hash browns spilled out, glistening and steaming, and I dashed them with salt before they cooled.

"I know they are." I'd expected a crowd. But not quite one this size.

Bow flipped a row of pancakes on the built-in griddle on the top-of-the-line six-burner gas range. It was clear Zee had recently done updates to the kitchen and had spared no expense.

"We can close up early if you want," Jena chimed in. "You're the boss. Nobody's going to argue." Hope sparked in her brown eyes as she cut biscuits from thick dough. She stood at the marble-topped prep island, which was covered in a thin coat of flour. Jena, too. The white powder dusted her dark, plump cheeks and thin, straight eyebrows. Black hair threaded with silver was pulled into a high, coiled bun.

"That's okay. I can handle it." At least I could for another four hours.

Jena dusted off her hands. "You've got Zee's spunk, that's for sure."

Jena and Bow Barthelemy had welcomed me to the Blackbird Café with wide open—if not

52

floury—arms. While they seemed to know everything about me and Mom, they tended to reveal
their past to me much like they cooked. A dash of
this, a dollop of that. A light-handed sprinkling
of history. They were in their midfifties and both
had worked here for decades, coming on board
after my mom left town. Their job titles were
a bit vague, but it seemed to me that they were
everything. Cooks, cleaners, gardeners, servers,
cashiers, and maintenance.

I glanced out the double windows over the deep
farmer's sink, across the yard to the mulberry
trees. Fluttering leaves made it look like the trees
were fanning themselves in the morning heat.
Mulberries, still pale and unripe, hung from thin
stems. Bow referred to the fruit as the blackberry's
skinny cousin—they shared the same pebbled skin
and coloring. Never having eaten a mulberry, I'd
picked a pinkish one a few days ago and had winced
at the sourness. According to Jena, the berries
wouldn't be fully ripe for another three weeks
or so, when they turned fully black. Only then
would their sweet yet mild flavor shine through.

"Zee would be right proud seeing you in here,
working your tail off." Jena's smile was bright
against her dark skin as she glanced over at me.

She had a slow, melodious way of speaking that
I found slightly mesmerizing. Swallowing back a
sudden rush of emotion, I said, "Thank you for
that."

I tended to keep people at arm's distance because it was easier—emotionally—for me when I had to eventually leave them. It seemed as though Mom and I had always been packing up our lives and moving on. But somehow, in the short week I'd been in Wicklow, Bow and Jena had already slipped past my defenses. Maybe it had been the way they'd welcomed me whole-heartedly, or perhaps the kindness in their eyes, or their endless patience as they taught me to run the café. Or maybe it was me, too spent with grief and the mental toll of having to run a business I knew nothing about, in a place where I knew no one, to put up much of a fight where affection was concerned. They were the closest thing I had to family right now.

Jena made a noise that sounded like a trill as she put a tray of biscuits into one of the wide double ovens. "I call it like I see it, sugar."

I appreciated that. Taking a moment to collect myself, I breathed in the various aromas spicing the air. The dark-roast coffee, vanilla, green onion, lemon, cinnamon, thyme, and a hint of yeast underneath it all. The scents reminded me of Zee and soothed my aching heart.

Pulling back my shoulders, I grabbed a fresh pot of coffee for top-ups, and headed back to the dining room and into the line of fire, trying not to slosh coffee all over the customers.

Faylene Wiggins had come in while I'd been

in the kitchen and now sat next to Mr. Lazenby. I had met her at Zee's funeral and guessed her to be in her late fifties or early sixties. She had short dark hair, inquisitive blue eyes, and a way of speaking I wasn't sure I'd ever get used to. At Zee's funeral, she kept close to me, fending off the nosiest of questions from others, and had gifted me with not one but three zucchini loaves.

She held out her mug to me and said, "It's so strange. I've known Zee Callow my whole life long. We grew up together, us two. I've seen her through an ill-fated marriage with your grand-daddy, her opening this café, her birthing your mama, and probably saw her most every day of my life . . . yet she never said a word about you." She looked at me expectantly.

I topped off Mr. Lazenby's mug, not sure if there had been a question to answer, but I noted that she was the first person to mention my grandfather. He'd been a traveling salesman who'd stopped in town to hawk insurance plans. Zee claimed she'd been swept off her feet by his charm and good looks, and it hadn't been long before they drove up to a chapel in Gatlinburg for a quickie wedding. It had taken only a few weeks for the enchantment to fade, however, which happened to coincide with his itch to hit the road again. He'd given Zee an ultimatum: him or Wicklow. He'd left town soon after the divorce was finalized, never to be seen again. By that time, he'd known that my mother had been on the way but had driven off anyway.

Zee had often said my mother's desire to travel the world was in her DNA, but insisted her roots were here, in Wicklow, and that this town was where she belonged.

Anna Kate darlin', promise me you'll never marry a man who doesn't respect the importance of your roots. For where your roots are, your heart is.

"It's strange, isn't it, Anna Kate?" Faylene said. "That we didn't know about you?"

I knew exactly why no one in town, other than my mom and Zee, had known of my existence. The Lindens. Instead of answering, I shrugged.

She frowned. "If you don't mind my asking, honey, where've you been hiding all these years?"

That I could answer. "A little bit of everywhere across the country, mostly up north," I said, refilling mugs as I went around the table. "I moved around a lot growing up. Mom was a traveling nurse."

A lot was an understatement. I'd moved at least twice a year from the time I was born until I turned eighteen and started college. After that, it stretched to a year, a year and a half. Mom had tried to stay put many times, create a home, but old habits had been hard to break. Endlessly restless, she wasn't one to ever sit still for long.

"Up north?" Pebbles said, her lips pursed. "Bless your heart."

I wasn't sure why it seemed like she was offering condolences. "I've been in Boston for the past two years," I added. It was the longest I'd ever lived anywhere, even though I'd changed my living situation four times during that time. "Finishing up my degree."

In-state tuition fees were the only reason I was still in Massachusetts, or I would have moved on by now. I'd yet to find a place that felt like home, something I wanted very much.

"I heard that," Faylene said. "I thought you'd have more of an accent, truth be told. I fully expected you to sound like a Kennedy. I always did like them Kennedys. Especially that John-John. He was just the cutest thing. Those eyes . . ." She sighed. "But you don't talk anything like them."

The disappointment in her voice amused me. "I've never stayed long enough in one place to develop an accent of any kind."

Pebbles said, "My sympathies on Eden's passing, Anna Kate. It was a sad day around these parts when Zee shared the news. A blood clot, I heard."

That's what the doctors had said, but I always suspected that Mom's broken heart had finally given out on her. It was honestly quite amazing it had lasted so long—I suspected a big part of it had died along with my father that fateful day so long ago. The rest of it finally caught up.

A round of murmured condolences swept across

the room, and I tightened my grip on the coffee pot. "Thank you all."

"I'm not the least bit surprised Eden became a traveling nurse," Pebbles said, sipping from her mug. "She always had wanderlust in her heart, that one, even when she was a bitty thing. She forever had her nose stuck deep in travel guides."

Faylene said, "True enough. Everyone around here knew she wasn't long for Wicklow. She and AJ had such big plans for their future . . ." She slid an appraising look toward me. "No one was shocked when she left town so soon after the accident."

"Ooh, especially with the way Seelie Linden behaved toward her," Pebbles said, *tsk*ing loudly.

My heartbeat kicked up, and I fought the urge to pull out a chair and sit down. All my life, I'd longed to know the real story behind my mother's leaving this town. The juicy bits. The gossip behind Seelie accusing my mother of *murder*. All the things my mom—and Zee—would never tell me. Whenever I pressed them for more information, for details of why Seelie would make such an accusation, all I ever heard was the crash had been an accident and that was that.

It didn't help matters that my mother had no recollection of that day at all—she'd suffered a head injury in the accident that had wiped out her short-term memory.

But—and it was a big *but*—I always noticed

on the rare times my mom talked about my dad and the accident, she always had a distant look in her eye, and the corners of her lips would tip downward, like they did when she wasn't quite telling me everything.

I suspected there was more to the story of the crash, and now that I was here in Wicklow, I realized I wanted to know the whole truth of what happened the day of the wreck.

Most of all, though, I wanted to know more about my father. Mom had kept a lot of him to herself as well. It had been too painful for her to share much, and I'd never pushed hard, because seeing her cry tore me apart. But now? Now, the time had come.

"Order up," Bow called out, thumping his hand on the countertop. He preferred that method to using a bell, a sound he claimed to despise.

"Excuse me," I reluctantly said to the table.

I picked up the plates Bow had set out and turned to see an older woman outside the door, staring in. Big hat, sunglasses. She didn't look like she planned to come inside—even though she blocked the entrance. She simply gawked.

Probably another local, curious to lay eyes on the mysterious Anna Kate Callow. It seemed I had my own rubberneckers. I bit back a smile as I set plates in front of a pair of birders, who'd come in for a snack.

"What kind of doctor are you thinking to

become, Anna Kate?" Pebbles asked as I passed by. "A family doc, like your granddaddy?"

I wiped my hands on my apron. "My grand-daddy?" I asked as innocently as I could manage.

She forked a piece of ham slathered in red-eye gravy and said, "Doc Linden? One of the finest doctors this town ever did see. It'll be a darn shame when he retires."

A hush fell over the restaurant, except for the table of birders who seemed oblivious to everything except their eggs and sweet potato hash.

Pebbles suddenly turned ghostly white and dropped her fork. "I, ah, I mean . . ." She glanced around, obviously looking for someone to take the foot out of her mouth.

According to my mother, I was the spitting image of my father, Andrew James Linden, with my curly dark ginger hair, wide downturned eyes, and deep dimples. It was no surprise at all that everyone here saw the resemblance too, especially the older folks who would have known him personally. My likeness to him was one of the many reasons Wicklow had been off-limits my whole life long.

"I'm not sure what I'll practice just yet. I have some time before I need to decide," I answered, dancing around the massive elephant in the room. Everyone might suspect I was a Linden, but I wasn't ready to confirm the rumors quite yet. Not until I figured out how to deal with the Linden

60

family, something I'd been worrying about all week long. I still didn't have a plan.

When my mother left Wicklow, she packed everything she could fit into her car, including an all-consuming hatred for the Lindens. We'd carted the animosity from town to town, unpacked it, and lovingly tended it until we moved again. After she died, I started carrying the load for her.

As much as I was curious about my father's side of my family—and I was—I couldn't simply forget how they had treated my mother. Of how they had accused her of *murder,* even after the car crash had been ruled an accident. How they had shamed her. How they had barred her from my father's funeral, not allowing her to say goodbye to the only man she'd ever loved.

And how she had vowed the day she left Wicklow that they'd never hurt me the way they had her. Which meant no contact with me. Not ever.

But now, I was here.

Avoiding the Lindens while I was in Wicklow these next couple of months wasn't feasible, considering this town was roughly the size of a postage stamp. I had tried to imagine what I'd do or say when I finally ran into them, almost to the point of driving myself crazy. Finally, to save my sanity, I decided I'd wing it. Because there was simply no way to prepare for a meeting like that.

Mr. Lazenby banged a hand on the table. "But what about this place? The café? As Zee's heir,

61

you're the new owner, am I right to think?"

Everyone—including the birders—watched me expectantly.

I didn't quite know how to answer him. I wasn't the heir . . . yet.

Not waiting for a reply, he kept talking. "What's going to happen to the café if you're headed off to become a doctor?"

A sorrowful Mr. Lazenby had awoken me at the crack of dawn these past few days while the café had been closed, yearning for blackbird pie. As I studied him, I was grateful not to see oceans of tears in his rheumy eyes, but there was no mistaking the apprehension lurking in the murky blue depths as he worried about the future . . . and the sweet connection he had to his wife, who'd died more than a decade ago.

"Will there still be pie?" he asked, running a handkerchief over his bald head.

My chest ached. I simply didn't have the heart to break the news to him that I planned to sell the place as soon as my mandatory two months of running the café were up and put any proceeds toward the cost of medical school.

"Well?" he demanded.

"I don't know if there will be pie." I hadn't thought that far ahead.

Mr. Lazenby narrowed his cloudy gaze on me. "Are you sure you're Zee's granddaughter? I'm starting to have my doubts. You didn't even bake the pies!" he said, his words harsh and cutting.

Jena rushed to my side, a pot of coffee in hand. "Where're your manners, Otis? Hush now. Let the girl alone for a minute. All these questions have my head spinning and they aren't even directed my way. Anna Kate, why don't you take your break now? Get off your feet for a bit, get some fresh air." To the table, she said, "Who wants more coffee?"

"Hmmph." Mr. Lazenby crossed his arms over his chest.

"Thanks, Jena." Fresh air was exactly what I needed to clear my mind, to remind myself why I was here and putting myself through this torture. I headed for the garden.

Bow held open the back door for me. "You want a snack? I can whip something up real quick."

"No thanks, Bow. I'll be right back. I just need a minute to myself."

"Take as long as you want. Jena and I can hold down the fort."

Stepping outside, I closed my eyes and leaned against the screen door frame.

The scent of mint was strong, undercut with another fragrance I didn't recognize at first. Then it came to me: honeysuckle. Strange only because I hadn't seen any growing in the yard.

Puzzled, I opened my eyes and nearly jumped out of my skin when I spotted a young woman sitting on the deck steps.

She jumped too, leaping gracefully to her feet. "Sorry, ma'am! I didn't mean to scare you."

Not the damned "ma'am" again. My God.

"Are you one of the bird people?" I asked. I didn't think so—not with the way she was dressed in threadbare Daisy Dukes and a black tank top, her feet bare and caked with dirt.

Tall and thin as a willow, she stared with big blue eyes from a deeply tanned face dotted with freckles. Long dark hair was pulled back, braided along the crown of her head. The rest hung in loose waves down her back. Cradling a twig basket in her skinny arms, she held it as if it were a fragile newborn. An embroidered tea towel was tucked protectively inside the basket.

Those impossibly big eyes blinked in confusion. "The bird people?"

I guessed her to be fifteen or so as I gestured to the side yard. "They're birders, watching for a glimpse of the blackbirds."

She turned, and I realized the honeysuckle scent was coming from her. A lotion or shampoo.

"Oh! No, ma'am. I'm not one of them." She glanced toward the mulberry trees. "I'm so sorry about Miss Zee." Tears pooled in her eyes, but she blinked them away. "She was a good friend to me."

"Thank you . . . ?"

"Oh! I'm Summer. Summer Pavegeau."

"I'm Anna Kate Callow," I said, though I had a feeling she already knew exactly who I was.

I motioned to two rocking chairs on the deck. "Come sit. My feet are killing me."

She followed me to the rockers, her sure footsteps soundless on the rotting deck boards. Carefully, she sat, still embracing the basket. "Your flats are cute, but probably not the best if you're going to be waitressing. Zee wore Crocs. Swore by them."

I made a face. "I am not going to wear Crocs."

Summer smiled. "Did you pack tennis shoes, at least?"

I'd packed everything. "I have an old pair somewhere. I'll pull them out."

"Good idea."

It was my turn to smile—because it had been *her* idea. "How long have you known Zee?"

Summer's fingers, I noticed, were purple. Blackberry stains. On one of our secret excursions, Zee had taken me blackberry picking one summer when Mom and I lived in Ohio. There had been no hiding those stains from Mom, but much to my surprise, she hadn't made too much of a fuss when she caught us purple-handed. Probably because blackberries were her favorite fruit. Instead, she'd smiled and asked Zee if she'd make cobbler with the berries we'd collected.

It was the best cobbler I'd ever eaten.

"All my life. Eighteen years now. I was born and raised here in Wicklow."

Eighteen? I'd never have thought that old—

something I didn't mention. No teenager wanted to know she looked years younger.

"I helped Miss Zee tend her garden a couple of days a week during the warmer months. She told me how much she missed you and wished you could come here."

I raised an eyebrow. "She talked about me?"

"All the time. Showed me pictures, too. Oh, don't worry! I never told another living soul about you. It was mine and Zee's secret. You have her smile—she was right proud of that, claimed it was her best feature." She stared at her dirty feet. "I always thought her best feature was her big heart, but no one asked me."

I studied her, catching the quiver of her chin as she fought to keep her emotions in check. Summer Pavegeau must have been a very good friend for Zee to share such a secret. "Just so you know, I agree with you."

She gave a short, firm nod.

"What have you got there?" I gestured to the basket, hoping desperately it wasn't a zucchini loaf.

Carefully she pulled back the tea towel, revealing a dozen brown eggs. "Miss Zee was a regular customer, but I wasn't sure if you were needing any for the café."

Although there were two crates of eggs sitting on the kitchen counter, I didn't hesitate to say, "Of course. We can always use eggs. What's your going rate?"

"Two dollars a dozen and a piece of blackbird pie."

The addition of the pie caught me off-guard, and I looked more closely at her. That's when I saw the familiar look of grief trying to hide in her eyes. "That's a bargain if I ever heard one."

I pulled a stack of ones from my apron pocket—tip money—and peeled off two singles. As much as I wanted to hand over the whole wad, I didn't. Instinctively I knew Summer wouldn't have taken the money for nothing.

She tentatively reached out with her stained fingers and said, "Thank you, ma'am."

My teeth clenched. "Please don't call me 'ma'am.' I beg of you. Anna Kate is just fine."

"Do you think you'll be needing another dozen tomorrow . . . Anna Kate?"

I ignored the fact that she sounded physically pained to say my name instead of "ma'am," and said, "If you've got them, I'll take them. I see you've been working with blackberries. I could use some of those, too, if you have extra." Suddenly, I wanted to make cobbler.

A shimmer of excitement flashed in her eyes. "How much are you wanting? A pint? Quart? Gallon?"

"A quart is fine. I'm willing to pay top dollar, considering the thorns and snakes."

"Oh, the snakes don't bother me none. I like them more than people sometimes."

Summer might look young for her age, but it was becoming clear to me that there was an old soul behind those big blue eyes. I stood up. "Let me get your pie. I'll be back in a second."

I turned to find Bow standing in the doorway. He had a piece of pie already boxed, as if he'd done this before. He handed the box to me, then said, "I didn't want to interrupt, but you've got a visitor insistent on seein' you."

The cautious look in his eyes made me nervous. "Who is it?"

He ran a hand down his trimmed beard. "Doc Linden. You ready to see him?"

Was I ready? No. No, I wasn't. Why the hell did I think winging it was a suitable idea?

"Anna Kate?" he said. "I can send him away if it's too soon . . ."

I didn't think I'd ever be ready, so I might as well get it over with. I sucked in a breath and let it out slowly. "It's okay. Can you send him out here, please? I don't really want an audience hanging on our every word."

"Sure thing."

My nerves were running wild as I turned around to say goodbye to Summer and to give her the piece of pie.

But she was already gone.

4

Anna Kate

I sat down. Stood up. Set the cardboard pie box on the deck railing. Wondered why Summer had run off. Plucked a mint leaf, crushed it between my fingers. Nerves twisted my stomach into an acidic knot.

I should've known I'd need to deal with the Lindens sooner rather than later. Of course the rumors of my existence had already reached them. News spread fast in small towns.

Heat radiated upward in waves from the splintered deck planks as I paced them. Try as I might, I couldn't stop picturing the constant pain in my mother's eyes. Pain that seemed to become more pronounced every time we moved, as if the hate she carried around chafed at her compassionate nature and rubbed her soul raw.

I dropped the mint leaf and wiped my hands on my jeans as I heard the screen door squeak open. It snapped shut with a sharp bang of inevitability that made me jump.

Bracing for a rush of rage, I steeled my shoulders and clenched my hands and jaw. Slowly, I turned around to finally face the lifelong enemy I'd never met.

My grandfather, Dr. James Dawson Linden.

I didn't know what I'd expected to see. Devil horns, maybe. At the very least, I'd pictured him as a stereotypical old-money southern society gentleman. Air of charming superiority undercut with smugness. Seersucker suit. Slicked-back hair. The scent of pipe tobacco hugging him like a second skin.

At first glance, there was none of that. There was a humble air about him with his casual clothes, dip of his chin, tilt of his head, and his layered white and silver hair that covered large ears. He wore khakis, a periwinkle blue button-down, and scuffed brown loafers. Standing with his hands tucked into his pockets, he stared at me as if trying to memorize every line of my face, every curl of my hair.

He was just a man.

A man with downturned brown eyes that looked burnished from a lifetime of sorrow.

I honestly don't know how long we stood there, taking each other in, trying to find familiarity in the face of a stranger. It was easy to see that I had his eye shape, his dimples. I even had the same cowlick at my hairline that forced my hair toward the right side of my face.

Bitterness burned my throat as I tried to picture what this man would have looked like in his youth, because I imagined, except for the hair color, that my dad had been the spitting image of *his* father.

I broke eye contact and tried to get past the overwhelming awkwardness. Chattering from the bird-watchers in the side yard rose and fell, a steady thrum that drowned out actual birdsong. A small brownish gray bird landed at my feet to investigate the crushed mint leaf. A phoebe, I believed. The ornithology class I'd taken in college had been a favorite.

"Do you mind if I sit down?" he asked, swaying enough to catch my attention.

Deck boards creaked under our feet as I guided him to a chair. He had paled and broken into a sweat. "Are you okay?"

"I'm fine, thank you." He waved away any concern. "The heat . . ."

I didn't believe him. Nor did I think his reaction had been born from emotion at meeting me for the first time. In his distress, his face had lost its normal color, revealing a sallow undertone that had been hiding beneath a deep tan. A faint yellow tinge colored the whites of his eyes as well. Something was terribly wrong. His liver, I guessed.

My gaze went to Zee's flower garden, straight to the yarrow, its white flower clusters making it easy to spot. Her secret teachings over the years hadn't been in vain. She'd given me an education I treasured. From it, I'd developed a love of herbal tea—creating my own blends wasn't so much a hobby as an obsession.

71

Yarrow tea wouldn't cure whatever ailed Doc, but it might help some, given its beneficial properties for the liver. Then I gave myself a good mental shake. He hadn't asked for my help. He didn't *deserve* my help.

Yet I couldn't help myself from saying, "Let me get you some water at least."

I wasn't a monster, for crying out loud.

"No, no. No need." He swiped his brow and upper lip with a handkerchief he'd pulled from his back pocket. "I'm not staying long. Please sit."

Reluctantly, I sat. If the man didn't want water, I wouldn't force it on him.

"I'm real sorry about Zee," he said. "She was a good woman."

I studied him, looking for insincerity, but found none, which made me even more uncomfortable. I'd been raised believing the Lindens despised the Callows and vice versa.

Yet here sat Doc with compassion in his eyes. And then, the more I thought on it, I realized I never once heard Zee speak ill of the Lindens.

It had been only my mother who'd openly despised the family.

The realization threw me off-kilter, tilting the world as I knew it. It occurred to me that my mother had painted me a very specific picture of the Lindens—but how much of it was an *accurate* portrayal?

Suddenly tongue-tied, I was unable to mumble even a thank-you for his sympathy.

"Do you have any regrets in life, Anna Kate?" He rolled the cuffs of his shirt to his elbows. A worn leather watch with a scratched face glinted in the sunlight.

"Don't we all?" I asked.

"Big ones, I mean. Ones that fester deep in your soul?"

A breeze kicked up and the bird hopping around the deck tipped its head as if also waiting for my response. "Just one," I admitted, shoving away the memory.

I caught sight of Bow peeping out the kitchen window. He pointed at Doc, then hooked his thumb over his shoulder. In charade language, I interpreted that as him asking if I wanted Doc thrown out.

I gave a subtle shake of my head, and he gave me a thumbs-up. I wanted to hear what Doc had to say, since something was clearly weighing on his mind.

"I have many." Doc twisted a gold wedding band around his finger. "Too many. You get to be my age, and you start counting regrets at night instead of sheep." He cracked a joyless smile.

He looked to be in his early to midseventies. Barely old age these days. I supposed he could be older than he appeared. I didn't know any Linden family history. Mom had made it clear that any and all questions about *that* side of my family were off-limits, and she'd been so resolute on the matter that I'd respected her decision.

As he dabbed at his forehead again with the handkerchief, I said, "I imagine being in ill health would also cause someone to take a good look back at their life."

One of his dark, bushy eyebrows rose. "I reckon so."

I was completely unprepared for the sadness that poured over me like it had been dumped from a bucket held over my head, soaking me to my bones. I shouldn't care about this man or what was wrong with him. Fighting the stinging in my nose, my eyes, I looked away, focusing instead on watching the bird as it pranced around. One of its wings hung at an angle, as if it had once been broken. Poor little thing.

"We didn't know about you," Doc said after a drawn-out pause.

Thankfully, he didn't try to deny that I was related—something, I admitted, I had feared. Though I'd gladly take a DNA test if need be. "I know."

"Why didn't Eden tell us?"

"Do you really need to ask?"

His gaze went to the bird hopping around the deck, pecking at splinters, and he rubbed his thumb over the watch face. "Your mother had to have known how much a grandchild would mean to us. We would've liked to have known you. It was our *right* to know about you."

"Are you serious?"

"You only know one side of the story, Anna Kate."

There was an ache in his voice, a strain that once again made me question everything I'd ever known about the Lindens.

Gripping the arms of the chair, I said, "Did you falsely accuse my mother of murder? And refuse to let her attend the funeral of the man she loved more than life itself? Because I'd say those things qualify as a forfeiture of any *rights* you may have had. End of story."

"It's not that simple, Anna Kate."

"I think it is." I jumped to my feet. "I need to get back inside." I started for the door. The bird lifted off with a startled twitter toward an open window on the second floor and flew inside. I frowned—I didn't realize a window had been open. Great. Now there was a bird in the house.

"Wait, Anna Kate. Please."

With a sigh, I stopped, faced him, and tapped my foot as I waited for him to come up with something—*anything*—that could explain the unexplainable.

Doc glanced at the mulberry trees with a wince. "I've decided regret is like cancer. It eats you from the inside out, just the same. I have to accept the fact that I can't change the past. I

75

can't. No one can. What's done is done, and I'm truly sorry for it."

Clenching my fists, my nails dug into my palms. I swallowed the words I wanted to speak, and they burned bitterly as they went down. It was a little late for apologies, but . . . I wasn't so heartless as to not hear the sincerity in his tone. I only wished my mother had been the one hearing it instead of me.

"You're wrong about this being the end of the story, Anna Kate. It could be a new beginning if we let it. If *you* let it. We can't go back." He shoved his hands into his pockets and rocked on his heels. "But we can go forward. I'd like to get to know my granddaughter. My hope is that you'd like to know me . . . and all your father's side of the family. We have Sunday supper at four. If possible, I'd like you to be there this weekend to meet the family properly."

"Thank you for the invitation, but I simply can't." I reached for the handle of the screen door and inside saw at least a dozen faces staring my way. All immediately looked away.

"You know, Anna Kate," he said, "I understand that you may not want to get to know us, but what of your daddy? Don't you want to get to know him as we did? We have dozens of scrapbooks and photo albums. You'd barely have to talk to us at all . . ."

Your daddy.

I froze, my hand still on the door handle, immediately recognizing that Doc was manipulating me, managing to see straight into my heart and what I wanted . . . to get what *he* wanted.

Learning more about my dad, getting a better feel for the person he'd been, meant more to me than I could ever express. I wanted to bury myself in those photo albums for hours on end, to hear *all* the stories over and over again. But I had to stay strong. For my mother's sake. "I'm sorry," I said tightly. "I won't be able to make it."

With that, I rushed inside and let the screen door slam shut behind me.

5

"Have you ever eaten a slice of the blackbird pie at the café?"

"Yes, indeedy," Mr. Lazenby said. "Every day for thirteen years, give or take a day here and there when the restaurant was closed up. Quite tasty, the pie."

"The pie isn't really made of blackbirds . . . ?"

"No, sir. It's regular pie." His old eyes twinkled. "Usually fruit."

"No other specific ingredients?"

"It's a Callow family secret recipe. If you're needing the ingredients, you're plumb out of luck."

The reporter thumbed a drop of condensation from his mason jar. "Do you believe the local legend that the pies will make you dream messages from dead loved ones?" He scoffed. "That blackbirds actually sing those messages— *notes*, as the writing on the soffit indicates—into the pies?"

Mr. Lazenby stood up, straightened his bow tie, and set his hat firmly on his head, pulling down the brim. "You haven't had a piece of pie yet, have you, sonny boy?"

"No. Why?"

"If you had, you'd know the answer to your

own question and wouldn't be wasting my time. We're done here."

Anna Kate

"That bird must have gone out the same way it came in," I said, coming down the stairs into the kitchen. It was the third time I'd done a search. "There's no sign of it anywhere."

"Probably so," Bow said as he lifted a chair onto a table in the dining room. "Birds are such curious creatures."

Jena slid a mop across the kitchen floor. "The saying is that curiosity killed the *cat,* not the bird."

What looked like pain flashed in Bow's eyes, darkening the murky blue to almost black. His salt-and-pepper beard was cut short and neatly trimmed, but he repeatedly dragged a hand down the side of his face toward his chin as though smoothing stray hairs. "Sometimes it almost does both, doesn't it?"

"Sure enough," she said with a wan smile.

As I grabbed a rag and a bottle of cleanser, I glanced between the two of them, wondering about the strange tension in the air. It was almost like they were sharing a memory, one tainted with sadness. "Do you two have pets?"

We'd already tackled the prep for tomorrow and were finishing up the kitchen chores. As soon as we were done, I wanted to track down Summer Pavegeau. I owed her a piece of pie, and it was a debt I didn't want hanging over my head. I knew what the pie meant to her.

Whether that pie would bring Summer any comfort tonight when she dreamed, I wasn't sure. I hoped so, but I just didn't know, what with Jena having baked the pies. Tonight I'd take over the task.

"Not unless you count the fake coyote in our vegetable garden," Jena said with a smile. "Keeps away some of the dumber critters."

"Where do you live? Is it close by?"

"Not far," Bow said. "A couple of blocks away."

"It's a small two-bedroom cottage near the bridge over Willow Creek," Jena said. "It's not much to look at, but the land is beautiful and the burble of the creek at night is like a lullaby."

Her voice had softened to the point that *it* felt like a lullaby. "Sounds peaceful."

"Most times, it is." Jena reached up on top of a shelf for a roll of paper towels and let out a soft groan, dropping her arm back down.

"Are you okay?" I asked.

"Fine, fine," she insisted. "Just an old injury that never healed quite right. Sometimes I forget, is all." She reached up with her left arm and grabbed the paper towels.

"Maybe you should see a doctor. It's possible something can still be done . . ."

"Said just like the wonderful doctor you're gonna be someday. But I'm fine, sugar. I learned to live with this little foible of mine a long time ago." She massaged her right shoulder. "I'm sure the Lindens are real proud that you're going to follow in your daddy's footsteps, to continue the Linden legacy."

"*Jena,*" Bow sighed.

"What?" she said, tearing off a paper towel. She wiped a spill on the side of a cabinet. "Everyone knows AJ Linden was going to be a doctor like his daddy and granddaddy. By the way, how did your time with Doc go today, Anna Kate? I haven't had the chance to ask."

My mother had strongly encouraged me down the same path as my father. It made sense. Healing was in my blood, after all, and following his lead made me feel connected to him in a way nothing else did. I wanted *him* to be proud of me. But I didn't want to think about what the Lindens, Doc and Seelie, thought of my career choice. I certainly didn't want to *care*.

I rubbed at a spot on the counter with a rag. "Doc invited me to Sunday supper. I said no. I had to say no."

"You don't think you made the right decision?" Jena asked in that gentle trill of hers, obviously picking up on my conflict.

I added more cleaner to the counter, and a lemon and lavender scent filled the air. "Were you guys around when the accident happened?"

Bow dropped a chair, and the crack when it hit the floor sounded like a gunshot. "Butterfingers," he said. "Sorry. The chair's fine."

Jena pushed the mop back and forth. "We'd arrived in town shortly before the accident," she said. "Why do you ask?"

"My mother was always a little dodgy when talking about the accident and its aftermath—probably trying to spare my feelings. But I want to know what truly happened."

"Well, I can fill in some of it," Jena said, making her way toward me with the mop.

"Jena," Bow warned.

"Hush up," she said. "Anna Kate has the right to know."

"Know what?" I asked.

Bow sighed and picked up another chair.

Jena's dark eyes were full of light when she said, "To hear tell, Eden and AJ had been fighting like cats and dogs that summer, with him heading off to school down at Alabama. Eden didn't want to be left behind. She was itching to leave Wicklow, and she always thought she'd be leaving with AJ. But they couldn't figure out how to make it all work, between school and expenses and Zee wanting Eden to stay here—they'd been at each other's throats too, over Eden wanting to leave."

I'd known that last part, because that tension between them had never fully ebbed.

"Finally," Jena said, "Zee relented for the sake of Eden's happiness, and even offered up a small loan to help get the lovebirds on their feet. A plan came together. Eden and AJ would rent an apartment in Tuscaloosa. After getting settled, Eden would find work, eventually enroll in a nursing program, and start planning a wedding. And after their schooling, they'd go wherever their whims took them, see the world together before the winds of destiny brought them back to Wicklow."

"Back to Wicklow?" I asked, eager to hear more. To hear it *all*. "Why?"

"You see, AJ was destined to take over his daddy's practice. And your mama, well, her destiny is here, with the blackbirds. It was why Zee was willing to let Eden go and fly free for a while. She knew Eden would come back. That she *had* to come back or her soul would never be at peace."

I glanced out the back windows, toward the mulberry trees.

No matter how far a guardian roams, she will always return, and while away she will never be settled, as her soul is tethered to the roots of the trees. She'll never be truly content until she's home among the roots, comforting and healing once again.

Jena leaned on the mop. "But Eden and AJ's plans were derailed before they could even rent an apartment."

"Why?" I asked.

"Seelie."

Why was I not the least bit surprised?

"When Seelie caught wind of the plans, she threatened AJ, saying she wasn't going to let him play house on her dime. She wanted him to join a fraternity and not tie himself down to Eden so young. Seelie gave him an ultimatum. College or Eden."

I couldn't imagine the pressure he'd been under, having to make a choice like that. Forced to pick between his dream of becoming a doctor—and the family expectations that goal carried with it—and the woman he loved.

Jena dunked the mop in a bucket. "AJ and Eden were on their way back from a tour of the Alabama campus when the crash happened. Seelie believes AJ told Eden he'd chosen college over her and that Eden, in a fit of madness, drove off the road."

"Seelie's the only one who believes that," Bow added quickly as he set another chair on a table.

It was the first time I'd heard any of this, and I ached with the knowledge, feeling a depth of sadness for my parents. "Do we . . ." I took a breath. "Do we know for sure that had been his decision?"

"No, ma'am," Bow said. "Not since Eden couldn't remember anything from that day. Thankfully, the police declared the crash an accident, but Seelie still insists to this day that it happened her way."

I forgave the "ma'am" in this situation. "But the police cleared my mom. Why can't Seelie let it go?"

Jena said, "Technically, the police didn't have enough evidence to charge Eden. And while Seelie's voice carries a lot of weight in this town, a good portion of the community backed Eden. Everyone with eyes saw how much she and AJ loved each other. As soon as it was announced that no charges were going to be filed, Eden left town. Many expected she'd be back one day, destiny being what it is, but then, they didn't know about you. It's clear now why she stayed away."

Absently, I nodded. "I think I might stop by the library after I go to the Pavegeaus' . . . It's inside the courthouse, right?"

"Yep. Second floor. Are you going to look at old newspapers?" Jena asked, eyebrow raised.

I smiled at how well she could read me. "Guilty." I wanted—needed—to know anything and everything about that accident. Old articles were a good place to start.

"Best you hurry, then," Jena said. "The library closes at five. We've got the rest of the chores covered."

"Are you sure?" I asked.

"Positive," she said.

I tossed the rag in the laundry room and put

away the cleaner. "I don't know how you two do this day in and day out. All this work is exhausting."

Bow said, "For one, it's not usually this busy."

"For another," Jena added, "Zee always hired day help when we needed it most. It's something for you to consider."

"I'll think about it." Hiring someone right now seemed a daunting challenge. I'd wait a few days, see if the birders stuck around, before putting a sign in the window.

Bow finished with the chairs. "You've got that map I drew to the Pavegeau place?"

"I do." I pulled it from my back pocket and stared at the squiggles, trying to pretend they made sense.

"You sure you don't want me to show you the way? It can be tricky," he said, offering for the third time.

"I'm sure. Thanks. I need to start finding my way around here on my own."

Jena leaned the mop against the pie case. "The Pavegeau place isn't exactly on the beaten path, tucked off in the woods like it is."

"I'll be okay. And this is a great map," I lied as I headed for the front door. "I'll find my way, no problem."

Jena said, "Be sure to announce yourself loud and clear when you get there, so you don't get your head shot clear off."

I looked back at her to see if she was joking.

She wasn't.

"People 'round here are real protective of their land." Her dark eyes were wide with reverence. "And Aubin hasn't been quite right in the head since his accident. He used to be real social, but he's become a bit of a loner, practically going off-grid. I can't imagine he's too keen on drop-in visitors, especially strangers."

"Aubin? Accident?" I asked.

"Summer's father," Bow said. "The family was in a bad wreck six winters ago. Hit an icy patch and slid down the mountain. Not a scratch on Summer, but her mother, Francie, died from her injuries. Aubin was banged up pretty badly. Head and internal injuries. Mangled leg."

"How horrible." I quashed my own grief for the father I'd never known, which tended to pop up at any mention of fatal car accidents, and glanced at the pie box in my hand. I was more determined than ever to get it to Summer.

"Terrible time." Jena *tsk*ed.

"Is Aubin okay now?"

"Mostly," Jena said. "But no denying he's a changed man. Quiet when he used to be the life of the party. Cautious when he used to throw caution to the wind. He doesn't come into town much except to visit his wife's grave. He's at the cemetery every day come four o'clock, rain or shine."

"Does he work?" I asked, thinking of Summer selling me eggs this morning.

"Used to." Bow pulled a trash bag out of its can. With a flick of his wrist, he tied off the bag and set it aside. "He was a mail carrier. Went on disability for a while after the accident, then was reassigned to a clerk position since he had trouble driving with his bad leg and all. But he up and quit after a month or so."

Jena tapped her temple. "Mentally he hadn't been ready to go back to work. Nowadays, he makes do with what he and Summer grow on their land and by selling handmade soaps and the like at craft fairs. They get by okay."

Bow put a new bag in the trash can. "It'll take me but a minute to finish up here. Let me go with you, Anna Kate. I can make introductions."

"No, no," I insisted stubbornly. I didn't know why Summer had hightailed it out of here earlier, and I didn't want to spring more people on her than I had to. "I'm used to figuring out things on my own. I'll be all right."

"But sugar," Jena trilled. "You have us now to help you out."

"Thanks all the same. You two have done so much for me already," I said, trying to reassure them. "Speaking of, thanks for everything today. I couldn't have reopened the café without your help." I pulled open the front door.

"You're welcome, you sweet thing," Jena said.

"Please don't get shot dead. I've become mighty fond of you."

"I'll do my best." I gave them a wave and let the door close behind me. I'd made it two steps before looking at the map and realizing I was heading the wrong way. I turned around, glanced into the café, saw Bow shaking his head, and waved again.

I'd barely taken two more steps when Sir Bird Nerd stepped in front of me.

"Sorry to bother you, ma'am," he said. "I just wanted to say thank you for sending out the cold water and tea sandwiches earlier. Very kind of you. Most of us hadn't planned to stay here the whole day long." He held his hand out. "Zachariah Boyd."

I shook. "Anna Kate Callow. You're welcome, and I thought we discussed the ma'am thing." I'd rather share the food than see it go to waste, and as the day had gone on, the birders seemed to wilt in the heat. I didn't want any of them passing out in the side yard.

His cheeks colored. "Right. Sorry about that."

"Now if you'll excuse me, I have to go—" I eyed the map, looking for landmarks I recognized.

"Before you do . . ." he said.

"Yes?"

"I heard a rumor the blackbirds don't come out until midnight. Is that true?"

"Yes, that's true."

His double chin jiggled as he glanced toward the mulberry trees, which were barely visible from this spot. "But blackbirds don't come out at night."

"Some things can't be explained, Mr. Boyd. The birds are out for an hour, from midnight until one."

He frowned at his watch. "Thank you kindly, ma'—" He cut himself off and walked back toward the fence line, where he'd used a folding chair to stake out a prime viewing spot.

The yard was crowded with people, chairs, blankets, cameras, and scopes. It seemed to me the numbers of birders had tripled during the day. Even as I stood there watching, two more people arrived, bucket hats and binoculars in tow. As I walked away, I decided it would probably be a good idea to bake a few extra pies tonight.

As I walked past the courthouse, which had a playground occupying one corner of its vast grounds, I saw a woman playing chase with a young girl. I recognized them as the pair who'd crisscrossed in front of the café a dozen times that morning—but never came inside.

"Mama's going to get you," the woman said, using exaggerated stutter steps as she rounded a gleaming silver teeter-totter.

I couldn't help smiling as the toddler ran across the playground as fast as her stubby, stiff legs could carry her, her arms open wide for balance. She squealed in sheer delight. I couldn't remember what it was like to not have a single care in the world like this little one, but for a moment it felt as though she were sharing her joy with me. A gift I gladly accepted as I pressed onward, looking for the next landmark on Bow's map.

"Hey! Hello! Wait up! You with the pie box! Anna Kate!" a voice yelled out.

I stopped and slowly turned around. The woman held the little girl in her arms and was trotting toward me.

"Hi," she said, slightly out of breath.

The girl's cheeks were flushed bright red, a mix of heat and exertion. Dirt smudged the delicate skin on the toddler's knees and the tiny toes that peeked out of sturdy sandals.

Strands of the mother's hair had come loose from the knot at the nape of her neck, curling loosely around gold stud earrings that glinted in the sunshine. Her pink cheeks gave her a healthy glow, and her rose-colored lipstick wasn't so much as smudged. There wasn't even a speck of dirt on her yellow dress. How she could chase a toddler and still look so . . . put together was beyond me.

"Hello?" I said back, unsure why she had called out to me.

"Hihi!" The girl flapped an arm.

"Hi," I said to her. "I like your flower."

Her dirty hand went to her head, where a floral headband held back damp, sweaty hair. "Pink!"

"It's *very* pretty."

"Hihi!"

I smiled and looked at the woman. "She's adorable."

"Thank you. She's a hot mess right now in desperate need of a bath. I am, too. Playgrounds aren't for the faint of heart, especially on a hot day like today."

"Ba!"

"Yes, bath," she said to her. To me, she added, "I'm Natalie, by the way. Natalie Walker. And this is Ollie. Well, Olivia Leigh, but she goes by Ollie. Thanks for stopping. I didn't mean to sound so . . . manic. I saw the pie box and had a *moment*. I really want a piece of that pie. Is that one available?"

"Sorry. It's earmarked for a friend. Didn't I see you pacing in front of the café this morning? Why didn't you come inside?"

Natalie shifted her daughter from one hip to the other. "Long story. Can I ask a favor? Beg one, really?"

"What kind of favor?" I asked, suddenly suspicious.

"Down!" Ollie wriggled like she had ants in her pants.

It was becoming clear to me that she didn't

speak in anything other than exclamations.

As Natalie set her down, I was relieved to see that the pale pink polish on one of Natalie's toenails was chipped, and that a fine layer of dust had settled on her white sandals. Maybe she *was* human and not some sort of Stepford mom.

As Ollie toddled toward a stroller parked near the teeter-totter, Natalie said, "Will you save me a piece of blackbird pie tomorrow? My mother keeps Ollie on Fridays, and I won't be able to get to the café until after nine. I'm afraid you'll sell out before then."

In her eyes I saw a flash of desperation and something else that made me take a step back. "Are you . . . a Linden?"

"I am." Her head tipped in confusion. "Natalie Linden Walker."

I noted with interest that she didn't sound pleased by the fact.

"What gave it away?" she asked as she kept close watch on her daughter.

Ollie had plopped herself in the dirt and was happily pushing it around with a toy backhoe while making *vroom*ing noises.

"The shape and color of your eyes. I saw almost the exact same pair a couple hours ago when Doc Linden came by the café. How are you related to him?"

It was her turn to take a step back, her expression turning wary. "I'm his daughter."

"Daughter?" Why hadn't anyone ever told me I had an aunt? Feeling a mix of confusion and anger, I added it to the other secrets that had been kept from me, tossing it like an old bone onto a growing pile of family perplexities.

The look in her brown eyes reminded me of a startled doe as she said, "He went to the café to talk to you? Why?"

I broke down the conversation to its most basic element. "He invited me to Sunday supper."

"To Sunday supper," she repeated woodenly.

She opened her mouth, closed it again. Put her hand on her chest, muttered something about Mama and stroke. She looked away. Looked back at me.

"To be perfectly honest, I'm beyond confused, Anna Kate. It's been a *day*. First my mother was lurking at the café, then my father actually went *into* the café? And a supper invite . . . ?"

My palms began to sweat. "Your mother was at the café?"

"Yes, peeking in like a stalker, when she's refused to even look at that place for decades. Sorry," she said, suddenly giving me a sweet smile. "I'm rambling. It's just that you took me by surprise. Sunday supper is reserved for family only. Always has been, at least. Inviting a Callow is—"

She shook her head as though unable to finish the thought of exactly how unheard of it was.

95

Then her eyes flew open, and her cheeks slowly turned from pink to red.

Smoothing an invisible wrinkle from her dress, she said, "I've made a mess of this situation. I'm terribly sorry if I made you feel unwelcome, Anna Kate."

I'd have laughed if she didn't look so miserable at the thought of hurting my feelings. "I said no to the invitation, if it makes you feel any better."

"It doesn't. I know better than to blather on like that."

"Like you said, you were surprised."

Nodding, she said, "Exactly. Surprised. Confused. Take your pick. Thank you for understanding."

It was obvious she had been kept out of the loop as well. She had no idea I was her niece. Natalie and Ollie Walker might be the only two people within a ten-mile radius who hadn't been clued in that I was AJ's daughter, and I wondered what rock they'd been hiding under this past week.

I could see a dozen questions written on Natalie's face, but it was clear she thought better of asking any of them. I should've said it was nice to meet her and then been on my way, but I was sick to death of secrets, and she deserved to know the truth. "What do you know about me?"

"I don't know anything, really, other than your name and that you're a relative of Zee's who's taken over the café. Why?"

"I'm Zee's granddaughter."

Dark eyebrows shot upward. "Her grand-daughter? I didn't know she had a granddaughter."

I took a deep breath. "I'm Doc and Seelie's granddaughter too."

"You're . . . wait. *What?*" Natalie's mouth fell open.

"My mother—Eden—was pregnant when she left Wicklow."

With laser intensity, Natalie studied my face. Her eyes widened, and she gasped. "Oh. My. Lord. I've got to go."

Without another word, she rushed over to Ollie and started tossing all her playthings into a backpack hooked on the arm of the stroller. But before I knew it, Natalie had picked up Ollie and jogged back toward me.

"Hihi!" Ollie said as they neared.

Natalie threw her free arm around me and squeezed me tightly in an awkward hug. Ollie joined in, setting a chubby arm on my shoulder. I didn't quite know how to react, so I stood there, uncomfortable with the affection.

Natalie smiled and said, "I forgot to say welcome to the family, Anna Kate."

Stunned, I said, "Thank you."

Natalie pulled back. "Now, I really must go have a word with my mother. Bye!"

Ollie flapped her arm in my direction. "Bye!"

I finger-waved.

Welcome to the family.

All I'd ever wanted growing up was to have a normal, stereotypical life. Two parents, a pet. Sleepovers at my grandparents' houses. A house that had a growth chart penciled on a doorjamb, marking height milestones from toddlerhood to teenager. A garden that didn't need to be planted in a container on a small balcony because apartments didn't have yards. Sunday dinners with generations gathered around the table. Big family holidays, with everyone gathered around, laughing and squabbling and loving.

My childhood had been so drastically different from what Natalie had undoubtedly experienced, and I couldn't help the envy that came over me. Not to say that my childhood had been bad—it hadn't. I was loved. Clothed. Fed. I'd seen many places, learned to take care of myself. But it had always felt as though I'd been cheated out of something everyone else tended to take for granted.

As Natalie buckled Ollie into the stroller, she yelled, "Don't forget to save me a piece of pie! See you tomorrow." And off she went, half walking, half jogging down the sidewalk.

As I turned toward the foothills, I took a deep breath, and tried to ignore the fact that I was starting to regret not accepting Doc's invitation.

6

Anna Kate

I was lost.

Truthfully, it wasn't the worst place to lose one's way. I stood in the middle of a rutted golden-orange dirt-and-gravel lane riddled with fissures that resembled cracks on an overbaked gingerbread cake. A breeze swooping through the valley cut the humidity and brought with it a burst of pure, clean air swirling with pine scent.

Soaring oaks, pines, and black walnut trees cast long shadows. Butterflies skimmed colorful wildflowers standing brightly among the tall weeds and grasses that hugged the lane. I often found peace in the woods, thanks to Zee. For as long as I could remember, whenever she would visit, she'd find a way to sneak me out to the woods to teach me the magic of nature. She lovingly shared how plants, shrubs, trees, and flowers offered alternatives to traditional medicine—all things my mother had also forbidden.

"Callows have always been healers and nurturers, Anna Kate, but you *must* remember that there are many ways to doctor people, physically and emotionally."

It was a sentiment she drilled into me whenever

I saw or spoke to her. My mom had shied away from holistic medicine, which had caused endless strife between mother and daughter. It was a conflict that had begun before I was born, but I'd been caught in the middle of the emotional tug-of-war between their differing philosophies.

A hawk climbed high, rising on an updraft, and a chickadee chirped a warning call from somewhere in the dense woods.

"Birdie," I called out. "Calm down. I'm just passing through."

My assurance did little to soothe the bird. In fact the *dee-dee-dee*'s seemed to grow louder.

Using my wrist, I wiped sweat from my forehead and checked the map again. I'd passed the stand of six mailboxes that leaned shakily to the right as though ready to fall over if burdened by a heavy letter. I'd turned right at the black walnut tree, split down its middle from a lightning strike. I'd gone past two dirt lanes on the right and two on the left that snaked up the hillside. I turned onto the fifth lane, on the right, which should have been the Pavegeau's long driveway. But after walking twenty minutes, and taking two forks, backtracking, and taking the other options, there still wasn't a house to be seen.

There hadn't been any signs of human life, either, except for deep tire ruts that I'd come to suspect were made by a four-wheeler.

Flecks on black rocks in the path sparkled in

patches of sunlight as I trudged along, hoping something would look familiar soon, but it seemed to me the further I walked, the more everything began to look exactly the same. Every bush, every tree, every rut in the dirt.

My gaze caught on a barberry shrub, and I eyed its ashy bark, knowing it could be used in a tea to help with jaundice, which started me thinking of Doc Linden again. With a sigh, I told myself to stop worrying about him, and continued on my way, leaving the bark behind.

The chickadee's cries kicked up in their intensity, and I suddenly picked up the sound of rustling and the awareness that it hadn't been *me* causing the bird's distress. I stopped dead still, peering into the woods. I backed slowly away from the tree line. Whatever was making the undergrowth shudder was bigger than the squirrels that had been racing around, keeping me company for most of my hike.

Waving away a black fly from my face, I walked backward, trying to distance myself as I braced for the worst. A rabid raccoon. A wild boar. Did Alabama have bears?

I'd freaked myself out so well that when a gray cat leaped gracefully out of a patch of thick fern, I jumped and screamed.

I took a moment to enjoy the hilarity of my overdramatic reaction and realized the cat, with its charcoal-gray coloring and milky blue eyes,

101

looked like the one who'd been sitting in Zee's garden this morning.

The cat, as if it didn't have a single care in the world, sauntered toward me and passed on by without so much as twitching a whisker in my direction.

About ten feet from me, the cat stopped. Sat. Looked over his shoulder. He took another few steps. Sat. Glanced back. *"Reow."*

It could have been my imagination, or perhaps heat exhaustion setting in, but I could have sworn there was a hint of impatience in the cat's voice.

As I took a tentative step toward him, he took one away from me. We repeated our odd dance until he finally stuck his tail in the air and strutted off down the dirt lane.

I dutifully followed, and twenty minutes later, the path widened, flooding with sunlight. Ahead, I caught sight of asphalt.

The cat had led me back to the road I'd come in on.

"Well, okay," I said to him. "Thank you. I should probably head back to town at this point." Considering I knew where *that* was.

Instead of turning left, toward town, the cat went right. A few steps away, he stopped, sat. Waited. His ear twitched, and I noticed it had a notched scar, probably a long-healed battle wound.

"All right, I guess we're not going back to town. Lead on."

As we walked the berm of the road, in my head I ran down the warning signs of heat exhaustion. Confusion and hallucinations *were* two of the symptoms, but I wasn't dizzy, and I didn't have a headache. My heartbeat was fine once I realized I wasn't under attack from a wild boar. Still, I didn't rule out the condition at this point.

After all, I was letting a cat lead me around.

If that wasn't confused, I wasn't sure what was.

We'd gone only a short way when the noise of an oncoming car sent the cat darting into the woods. The rumble of an engine grew, along with the thumping bass of a loud stereo. I stepped to the side as a dust-covered red pickup truck came up the hill. The music quieted as the truck rolled slowly to a stop beside me. I recognized it immediately. It belonged to my neighbor, Gideon Kipling—he'd been the one who'd picked me up at the Birmingham airport nearly a week ago.

The windows were down, and Gideon leaned toward the passenger side. "You okay, Anna Kate? You look a little . . . flustered."

I could only imagine how I looked. Hair and T-shirt sweat-plastered to my body. Flaming red cheeks. Alternating expressions of bewilderment and defeat. "I was lost for a while, but . . ." I glanced toward the woods. No sign of the cat. "But now I'm not. At least I don't think so."

A smile twitched the corners of his mouth. "If

you're looking for town, you're going the wrong way."

"I was looking for the Pavegeau place? I have a piece of pie for Summer."

"Want a ride? It's not too far from here, but it is hard to find if you don't know where to look."

An understatement if I ever heard one. "Sure. Thanks."

Reaching over, he opened the door from the inside, and as he pushed aside an iPad and several jars of honey, I climbed in. I buckled up, wiped my forehead with the back of my hand, and let out a breath. "Is it always this hot and humid?"

He put the truck in gear. "Nine, ten months of the year, it is. It's actually a little cooler up here in the mountains than it is downstate."

"Cooler? You're kidding. How do people survive? My skin feels like it's trying to melt off my bones."

His accent, which wasn't all that pronounced in regular conversation, thickened when he said, "Some around here will feed you lines about hydratin' and usin' air-conditioning or fans, but the simple truth is . . ."

I enjoyed the way he played up his Southern. "Is what?"

"We survive on sweet tea and complaining, plain and simple. Mostly the sweet tea, if I'm tellin' it to you straight."

My mom had given up a lot when she left Wicklow, but she hadn't left behind her love of sweet tea. It had been a staple in our house, all year long. "I'll keep that in mind."

The cab of the truck had a small backseat that was covered with assorted fishing gear, a box of zucchini, a couple of folded shirts and pants, and two pairs of shoes—one a pair of sneakers, the other dressy—and a dusty black satchel.

"How did your first day with the café go?" he asked.

I thought of the last time I was in this truck. Gideon's low, smooth voice telling me the terms of Zee's will. Of how, in order to inherit her estate, I had to live in Wicklow and run the café for a full sixty days. After that time was up, I'd inherit. From there I could do what I wished with the property, and I'd already asked Gideon to start putting out feelers to real estate agents.

I still couldn't believe the terms Zee had laid out. What if I had already been in school? Or had a full-time job? Had she really no qualms about expecting me to put my life on hold for two months?

I laughed inwardly. Of course she had no qualms. Zee had been trying to get me to Wicklow for as long as I could remember. Through her will, she'd made sure it would happen.

Zee was anything but a quitter.

"It had its challenges," I said, thinking of Mr.

Lazenby's tirade and of all the dishes I'd broken, "but overall, it went well."

"I imagine it'll get easier over time."

"By the time I get used to it, it'll be time to leave."

"I wouldn't be so sure about that. Wicklow has a way of holding on to you once you're here."

Why did that sound like a warning of some sort? One I didn't need. I was starting medical school in August. My deposit had been paid. An apartment had been rented—my move-in date was August first. My destiny, as Jena would call it, was all mapped out. It wasn't a confusing hand-drawn map from Bow, either. It was Garmin-worthy, even though I'd taken an unplanned detour through Wicklow along the way.

"That's what happened to me," he said. "I came over from Huntsville six years ago to do some mountain biking, and Wicklow didn't let go."

Up close, I could see he had some age on him. I guessed early to midthirties. Shallow crow's feet spread from the corners of his eyes even when he wasn't smiling, and strong lines bracketed his mouth under the hint of a five-o'clock shadow. His hair was short, sandy blond with a patch of silver near his right temple, and his eyes were nearly the same color as the amber honey sitting between us.

"I heard Doc Linden stopped by to see you earlier. So he knows about you?"

I didn't even pretend to be surprised Gideon

had already heard. I knew how fast news traveled in this town. "He knows." I held up a jar of honey to change the subject. I didn't want to think about Doc, let alone rehash the conversation. "Do you keep bees?"

He slid an assessing look my way. "No, a client does. She pays me by way of honey."

Grateful he hadn't pushed the Doc subject, I turned the jar, warm from the heat of the day, examining the way the sunlight played on the color. "It's not going to pay the bills, but it's a form of payment I wouldn't mind. It's beautiful."

"Take a jar. Two. I have plenty. Do you need any zucchini?"

"No! I mean, no thank you. Zee's garden has a couple of plants."

The blinker ticked as he turned right onto a dirt strip nearly hidden by sweetgum branches arching across the driveway. I wasn't sure I would have seen the turn even if I had made it this far up the hill.

"No one had a green thumb like Zee."

Branches scraped the truck's roof as we bumped along the lane, and I swallowed back the sorrow that bubbled up, thick as the honey I still held. "True."

A dog's bark carried into the truck, and he said, "That's Ruby. She's sweet but also a jumper, so brace yourself."

The driveway stretched into a clearing, and a

milk chocolate–colored dog bounced around. I'd been expecting a small cabin and was surprised to see a rather large cottage with a wraparound porch and a pitched metal roof topped with solar panels. A man stood on the front steps, a fancy, hand-carved walking stick in one hand. No sign of a shotgun. Thank God.

"That's Aubin. Have you met him yet?"

"No, but Bow and Jena told me a little about him."

"I'll introduce you." Gideon cut the engine. "Do you want me to stick around to give you a ride back to town?"

"You don't have to do that—I'll find it easy enough now that I know the way."

"I wouldn't want you melting into a puddle on my account."

I pushed open the door. "I'll be okay. Thanks."

"All right, then." He hopped out of the truck and Ruby made a beeline for Gideon, jumping all around him. He gave her a good petting, and then came to stand by my side.

Aubin spoke around some sort of stick in his mouth. "Wasn't expecting you, Gid." He glanced toward me and gave a firm nod. "Ma'am."

I bit back a sigh at the salutation and nodded back.

Ruby rushed toward me, sniffing and bouncing. I kept the pie box out of reach and tried to keep her from knocking me over.

Aubin took the stick out of his mouth, tucking it into his back pocket as he whistled sharply. Ruby immediately ran to his side and sat. Her tail swished the ground, stirring up a cloud of dirt.

"Hope you don't mind us dropping in. Anna Kate is looking for Summer." Gideon made quick introductions before saying to me, "You sure you don't want me to wait?"

I turned to him. "I'm sure. Thanks for the rescue."

"Anytime, Anna Kate." He gave Aubin a wave and hopped in his truck. Ruby took off after him as he drove off in a cloud of dust.

Aubin studied my face with light, troubled eyes. "Come up on the porch, out of the sun."

I'd been picturing Aubin Pavegeau as an old man for some reason. His name, maybe. But by the looks of him, he was midforties at most. A shock of dark, thick hair drooped onto his forehead. A head taller than me, he was lean but muscled, wearing a tight blue tee. His jeans seemed extra baggy, and I wondered if he'd lost weight recently or if he preferred a looser fit because of his damaged leg.

"Your name is Callow?"

I followed him up the steps. "That's right."

"How old are you?" he asked.

I could practically see the mental math he was doing as he pieced together the truth of who I was. "Twenty-four."

"I see."

He walked steadily and surely despite a marked hobble. Part of the porch was screened in, and he held open the door for me. I went ahead, noting the small tears in the screen, the blistered, peeling paint on the frame, the sagging ceiling panels, and the loose deck boards. A small wooden table was flanked by two white rockers, not a speck of dirt on them. On the table was a library-loaned cookbook, a pitcher dripping with condensation, half-filled with purplish-red tea, and a mason jar full of ice.

"Have a sit-down. I'll be right back—I need to grab another glass."

A set of hand-carving tools were lined up on a workbench pushed against the wall. An assortment of walking sticks and canes in mid-production leaned against one of the porch columns.

Aubin returned a moment later, a tall glass clutched in the palm of his big hand. He set his cane against the house, then sat and went about pouring the sweet tea.

"Beautiful work," I said, motioning toward the carvings. One cane had a handle that looked like Ruby's face.

"Thank you. My father taught me. He was a woodcrafter, had a shop in town before it became too pricy to keep open. He's been gone a few years now."

"I'm sorry."

He tipped his head in acknowledgment, and handed me the glass he'd just filled.

I glanced around. "Is Summer here? I have a piece of pie for her—she accidentally left it behind at the café this morning."

"She's out picking blackberries this afternoon."

"Oh. Then I'll leave this with you if that's okay and let you get back to your day." I set the box on the table.

"No need to rush off," Aubin said, motioning to the glass in my hand. "That sweet tea isn't going to drink itself, and you look like you could use some hydration."

I could probably drink a whole gallon of water right now and still be parched. "Thanks." I took a sip, unsure at first what I was drinking, and then I decided I'd never tasted anything so good. "Blackberry? It's delicious."

"Took me nearly a month to perfect the recipe."

"Worth every minute." I took another sip, trying to deconstruct the flavors. "Is there honey in there?"

"Yes, ma'am. But what gives it that extra something," he said, listing forward and dropping his voice, "is grenadine."

I took another sip, and now that I knew what I was looking for, I could taste it. "I wouldn't have thought to use grenadine. It's a perfect complement."

"I have a few pomegranate trees out back, and I

make my own syrup. Out here in the woods, you tend to use what you have on hand." He pulled the stick from his pocket and started chewing on it again.

It was a sweetgum twig, I realized. Nature's toothbrush, Zee had once said, but it seemed to me Aubin's chewing was more habit than anything.

"I should be taking notes. I'd love to serve something like this at the café."

"You've taken over the Blackbird, then?"

"For the time being. I'm going to medical school soon back in Massachusetts."

"Medical school. You don't say," he said, not sounding surprised at all. He peered at me over the rim of his glass. "You've got your mama's eyes. The coloring, that bright green is all Eden."

"You knew my mother?"

He broke eye contact, turning his attention to Ruby, who was galloping across the yard. "A long time ago, I did. Knew your daddy, too. No denying you look like AJ."

I held on to the glass tightly, its chill seeping into my palm. My parents, if they were alive, would be forty-four years old this year. Aubin, if I figured his age right, would be about the same. "How well did you know them?"

"AJ and I grew up together. When he and Eden started dating, we three would hang out from time to time."

"So you were close friends, then?" I would love to find someone who knew them well, who could share stories with me. Someone other than the Lindens. I wanted to get to know the people my parents had been.

"What is friendship, really?" His voice was strained, and he wouldn't look my way. He just sat there, running his hand along the thigh of his bad leg.

I saw pain in his eyes and wondered where it originated—in the past or with his injury—but I couldn't bring myself to push for an explanation. Feeling suddenly bereft, I set the tea glass on the table. "I really should get going."

Aubin didn't seem the least bit sorry to see me go. He grabbed his cane, walked me to the screen door, and held it open.

"Thank you for the tea."

I was barely off the porch steps when Aubin said, "Anna Kate?"

My chest ached as I glanced back at him, standing there leaning on his beautiful cane, his eyes looking like dark reflecting pools of remorse.

He said, "You . . . Did you grow up happy? Was your mother happy?"

I didn't want to think too hard about the answer to those questions. But my voice gave away my emotions, nearly breaking flat open as I said, "What is happiness, Mr. Pavegeau, really?"

7

"Some people don't want anything to do with the pie," Summer Pavegeau said. She tucked a strand of hair behind her ear. "My daddy, for instance. He tells me all the time it's best to leave the past in the past."

The reporter took note of her blackberry-stained fingertips as he said, "But you don't think so?"

She glanced out the window, looking toward the mountains as though searching for something only she could see. "No," she said, "but I find comfort in the past. All he finds is pain."

He capped his pen. "Why's that?"

Her gaze snapped back to him. "I thought you were doing an article on the blackbirds?"

Smiling, he said, "I seem to have gotten a little sidetracked."

Summer nodded. "Wicklow has a tendency to do that to people."

Natalie

I'd rushed straight home from that enlightening encounter with Anna Kate Callow for naught.

Neither Mama nor Daddy had been home. Since it was growing late and they were hardly night owls, they would most likely return any minute now. This time of night, they liked winding down with cocktails and dessert on the patio, a nighttime ritual of theirs as habitual as the setting sun.

I'd wait them out. Although it was past Ollie's seven o'clock bedtime, I wasn't ready to give up on getting answers regarding Anna Kate. How long had they known about her? By Mama's strange behavior at the café this morning, I assumed not long. The way she had acted now made perfect sense—she had been trying to get a look at Anna Kate while keeping me in the dark. It was a familiar pattern—Mama often kept me in the dark on important matters.

While I understood why Mama fought so hard to protect me from anything physically or emotionally harmful, her rigidity on the matter had ended up making *her* my biggest threat. I wasn't sure she fully understood the damage she'd done. Or perhaps, she simply hadn't cared as long as I was safe.

As for Anna Kate, I was thrilled to discover someone else hanging off my mother's branch of the family tree—surely, she would take some of Mama's pressure off me. If that someone happened to be a young woman, close to my age, all the better. When I was younger, friends had been hard to come by, being that they all needed the Seelie Earl Linden stamp of approval. I had long since learned to close myself off from

116

potential playmates, just to save the ultimate embarrassment of telling someone that I couldn't come over that day.

Or ever.

I threaded my fingers through Ollie's velvety soft hair as I read her a book, and she shifted to lean against my chest. Curled up together on the overstuffed sofa, I took a moment to inhale the sweet, lingering scent of her baby shampoo. This was actually my favorite time of day with her. It was our downtime, when she was extra loving and snuggly.

It had been hours since we'd arrived home, and after getting Ollie fed and bathed, I'd spent most of my time reading books, building blocks, playing trucks, and occasionally checking to see if any of the lights were on in the main house. Or the big house, as I'd called it growing up, seeing as how it felt like a jail.

Ollie blinked slowly, her eyelids growing heavy at the cadence of my voice, and I took a moment to appreciate the miracle that was my daughter. To enjoy the warmth of her tiny body, to feel her heartbeat against my arm, to soak in her innocence and sheer joy at simply being alive.

Dressed in lightweight shortie pajamas decorated with excavators, loaders, and dump trucks, she burrowed even deeper into my side, resting her head on my chest. She was going through a construction phase and had been over the moon when she'd spotted these PJs in the boys' section at the department store. While I didn't have a lot of money for extras, there was no way I could pass those pajamas by. But I hadn't completely lost my senses—I bought them a size up, to last her a long while.

Growing up, I never would have been allowed to wear pajamas like these. Until I was a teenager, I had owned only monogrammed cotton nightgowns, ones with scalloped hems or ruffled cuffs. I hadn't been allowed prints with Disney princesses or fluffy cats or anything cutesy or what Mama would consider tacky. And God forbid if I had worn pajamas designed for *boys*. A bolt of lightning might have struck my mother dead on the spot.

Ollie's breathing deepened, and I quietly closed the book and set it aside. I wrapped my arms around her body and held on tightly, resting my cheek against her hair.

It was times like these that Matt most often slipped into my thoughts. Ollie had been only a few months old when he'd died, and I hated that he was missing out on these moments—even if it had been his choice to do so.

My chest tightened, thinking about him choosing to leave us on purpose.

Had he? Or hadn't he?

I forced myself to breathe evenly, a trick a therapist down in Montgomery had taught me to keep anxiety from blooming into a full-blown panic attack. Breathe in, hold. Breathe out, hold. After a minute, the ache in my chest eased some, pinching instead of crushing.

I'd have the answers I longed for soon. If legend was true, the blackbird pie would tell me all I wanted to know. I'd eat the pie tomorrow, and tomorrow night I'd receive a note from Matt in a dream sometime after midnight.

A note that would hopefully explain everything about his death. With it, maybe I could finally put the past to rest and find the peace I craved. Until then, I'd keep breathing deeply and taking one day at a time.

It was hard for me not to see Matt in Ollie. In her infectious laugh, and in how outgoing she was. Ollie was part of him, and I wished more than anything that he could see the wonder we'd created together. What our love had created.

I watched Ollie sleep and marveled at how little it took to make her happy. Construction pajamas and a new book from the library, and she was the happiest girl in the world.

A yawning pit grew in my stomach, as it always did when I thought about happiness. I would do anything to make sure Ollie stayed this way—perfectly content and oblivious to the hurtful world around her.

Which was why I was here, wasn't it? A grown woman, essentially living with my parents. I was thankful for their help, yes, but also mortified my life had come to this.

Before I fell down a rabbit hole of regret, I forced myself to stop thinking about things I couldn't change. All my life, I'd let others take care of me. My parents, then Matt, then my parents again. I needed to stop dwelling on my deficiencies and start figuring out how to become a self-sufficient, *independent* woman—for Ollie's sake. She didn't need a milquetoast mother, but one who was strong. Capable.

Which was all so much easier said than done.

With that thought, the ache in my chest started to grow once again.

As I sang the ABC's in my head—another trick my therapist had taught me to refocus my thoughts—my gaze fell on the big box near the door that had a note in my mother's handwriting taped to its top. I had brought it inside and dropped it near the door, not wanting to deal with it straightaway. Besides, I knew what was in it: a sunhat for Ollie. Seeing as how Mama would expect a thank-you when I saw her next, it would probably be a good idea to have laid eyes on the hat in case she gave me a pop quiz on its color, size, or adornment.

I lowered Ollie gently onto the couch, and tucked a throw pillow next to her in case she rolled. I set the box on the raised counter bar that divided the open living room from the kitchen and pulled the note free from its tape. My mother had old-school looping penmanship and took pride in its beauty.

Natalie,
Stacia Dabadie will arrive promptly at nine a.m. Please have Olivia Leigh ready at no later than eight forty-five.

—M

Soon after we'd moved here, Mama had offered to keep Ollie on Friday mornings. Special one-on-one time. So far, they'd had a teddy bear picnic in the park and driven down to Fort Payne for a children's theater production. While grateful for some time alone, I had also dreaded those mornings. I didn't like letting Ollie out of my sight for long and I didn't want Mama smothering her with rules, either.

It had crossed my mind more than once this past week to sit down with my mother to put an end to the outings. I hadn't yet found the strength to do so, however, because I knew stopping the excursions would hurt Mama's feelings and disrupt the progress we'd made with our truce.

Since I wanted peace in the family, I'd bitten my tongue.

But what did Stacia Dabadie, Coralee's grand-daughter, have to do with tomorrow? Using a butter knife, I cut the tape on the box and opened it. Inside there was a frilly pink sunhat, a pink bathing suit, a pink beach towel printed with hearts, and a bottle of sunscreen, SPF 50.

Bile crept up my throat as I set each item on the countertop. My hands went clammy, then ice cold, when I recalled Mama mentioning during last week's Sunday supper that Stacia Dabadie had taken a summer job as a lifeguard at the pond of the local state park and wasn't that lovely?

I, of course, had changed the subject straight-away, believing Mama just hadn't been *thinking* to bring up something like that.

I should have known better.

Oh, how I should have known.

Seelie Earl Linden rarely spoke without thinking.

As my stomach rolled, I spread the towel out on the counter, folded it in half, then quarters, then eighths until it was too bulky to fold anymore. I set it back in the box. The swimsuit was folded in half, in quarters, in eighths, then rolled into a pink rope. I set that in the box. The hat went next. I carefully set the sunscreen bottle on top of the obnoxious pink pile and went about closing the box, overlapping the flaps until it was secure. I picked up the box, opened the front door, stepped out onto the narrow front porch, and flung the box as far as I could. It flew over the iron safety fence that surrounded the swimming pool and tumbled to a stop on the stamped concrete patio, inches from the shimmering water subtly lit by underwater lighting.

As I turned to go back inside, I noticed the lights on in the big house and could see my parents moving around the kitchen.

With my current mood, it would serve me best to go inside, close the door, and bolt it.

Instead, I peeked in at Ollie, who was still peacefully asleep on the couch, and instantly decided to leave her be. I'd be gone only a few moments. Just long enough to let my mother know, plain and simple and to the point, about my position regarding swimming lessons.

I quietly closed the door, and marched myself along the stone pathway that cut through the manicured lawn, past the tea roses, and up the three stone steps of the back porch.

In my anger, all thoughts of Anna Kate Callow had fled my mind, but they came rushing back as soon as my mother's voice floated through the open patio doors.

"I couldn't even get a good look at her for all the busybodies at the café, not minding their own business."

"You could have gone inside," Daddy said, his tone flat, as though exceptionally tired.

"Don't be ridiculous."

"Putting off the meeting is only going to make it harder, for both of you."

"I'll not be put on display for the whole town to

talk about for years to come. I simply wanted to see if what everyone said is true. That she looks just like AJ."

A cabinet closed with a thud. "She does, indeed. I stopped by to see her myself this morning."

My mother's tone took an icy turn I knew well. "You *what?*"

"I spoke with her and invited her to supper on Sunday."

There was a stretch of frosty silence before Mama said, "Why would you do such a thing? We don't know who she is, what she's like, or her intentions. She could be after our money."

"She is our *granddaughter,*" he said, his voice tight. "There is no doubt in my mind."

"How naïve of you. I won't believe it until I see DNA evidence."

"All it takes is one look to know the truth. The DNA is evident in the shape of her eyes, the dimples in her cheeks, and the color of her hair. She has your hair, by the way, only curlier."

There was another stretch of cool silence. "If it is true, *if,* damn that Eden Callow! How dare she steal that girl from us, sneaking out of town like a thief in the night without anyone even knowing she was with child."

"Enough!" Daddy shouted.

Something slammed. A fist on a table, maybe. I froze on the deck, then tiptoed toward the door. I'd never, in all my years, heard my father raise his voice. He had a calm demeanor about him. He showed displeasure with the lift of an eyebrow, a cool glance, or a pucker of his lips.

"Don't you dare raise your voice to me, James Linden. I'll not stand for it."

"I am *done,*" he said, heat in his tone. "I'll not hear another word against Eden Callow. She's not to blame in this situation."

Mama laughed bitterly. "Who is, then, pray tell?"

"We are," Daddy said. "We might as well have bought Eden the one-way ticket out of Wicklow with the way we behaved after AJ died. No wonder she kept that child from us."

Mama sucked in a breath. "You've lost your senses, yes you have."

"No," he said. "I'm finally seeing things with clarity. Eden did nothing but love our boy, and we were ready to hang her from the nearest tree. She was grieving, same as we were. You know as well as I do that AJ loved her just as much. They were planning to get married! I pray he doesn't know how we treated that poor girl after he was gone. It makes me sick to think I let him down."

"She *killed* him," Mama said, her voice so cold I actually shivered.

"We don't know that," he insisted. "No evidence was ever found to support anything other than the crash was an accident."

Mama scoffed. "There were no skid marks at

the scene. That should be evidence enough. Eden didn't try to stop the car. She didn't brake."

"It's flimsy evidence at best. Anything could have happened to prevent braking. She was pregnant. She could have passed out from low blood pressure or any other early pregnancy symptoms."

"I *know* it was murder."

"What if it wasn't, Seelie? What if you're wrong?"

I held my breath. I was certain my mother believed she hadn't been wrong a day in her life. She was always right. Always.

Mama's voice practically dripped icicles as she said, "Cold-blooded murd—"

"Stop it!" he yelled. "I won't have it anymore. Do you hear me? We lost AJ. Are you willing to lose his daughter, too? Because I'm not. It's why I invited her to supper, an invitation I'm disappointed to say she declined."

"Thank the Lord someone has some sense around here," Mama said.

Daddy let out a long sigh. "I'm going to keep asking until she says yes."

"You most certainly will not."

"I most certainly will. It's past time to stop blaming and start healing." He quietly added, "I suggest you look deep into that guarded heart of yours, Seelie, to see what's truly important in life. Now, I'm going to bed. I have a headache."

I heard fading footsteps, and imagined him heading off toward the back staircase. His parting shot echoed in my head, especially the part about Mama's heart.

For most of my life, I'd believed Mama hadn't a heart at all, just a hard, spiky shell, like a dried-up sweetgum ball. It wasn't until I witnessed the interaction between her and Ollie that I suspected there was something warm in her at all.

"Natalie Jane," Mama snapped. "What are you doing out here?"

I'd been so lost in thought that I hadn't heard her approach.

She looked around. "Where's Olivia Leigh?"

"Sleeping."

Mama's eyebrows snapped together. "Then I suggest you get back to her. I cannot imagine what was so important that you'd leave her alone."

I'd been angry before the jab at my mothering, but now fury buzzed through me, starting at the bottoms of my feet and working its way upward. "I came to tell you that Ollie won't be available in the morning. Or any morning you try to sneak in swimming lessons."

"How dramatic. Sneak? I don't think so. I told you plain as day last weekend that Stacia would be coming over."

Mama always knew how to twist my words. "You did not ask me about the swimming lessons. I know, because I would have said no.

127

You need to call Stacia and cancel. Ollie won't be participating. Not tomorrow. Not the next Friday. Not ever."

"Yes, Olivia Leigh *will* be participating."

"No, she won't." I pressed clenched fists to my thighs. "I would have thought you of all people would understand my position on the matter."

"Natalie, it's *because* I understand that I hired Stacia. Teaching Olivia Leigh how to swim is the only way to ensure she doesn't drown."

Nausea churned in my stomach. "Matt knew how to swim. It didn't stop him from drowning, did it? Keeping Ollie away from water will make sure she doesn't drown. No water, no drowning."

"And what happens if she slips past you? Finds a way into the pool? Or a neighbor's pool? Or Willow Creek behind the house? It's best for her to know how to save herself."

"You do not know what's best for her. I do. She won't slip past me. She's never out of my sight."

"Is that so?" Mama's self-righteousness was in full bloom as she looked pointedly at the little house, then tipped her head and pursed her lips.

I turned. Ollie was coming up the pathway. Oh Lord.

"Hihi, Mama! Hihi, Gamma!" She waved her whole arm as she toddled along, her smile bright in the twilight.

My stomach ached something fierce. "We'll finish this some other time."

128

"No. We finish it now. My house, my rules, my pool. I will not take a chance with Olivia Leigh's safety. She *will* take swimming lessons with Stacia, starting tomorrow morning. If you have a problem with that, Natalie, you don't have to stay here, on this property. But you already know that, don't you? You're real good at running away."

I couldn't even speak. I turned, scooped up Ollie, and took her back to the little house.

I was halfway down the path when I heard Mama say, "Eight forty-five, Natalie."

Holding in a scream of frustration, I jogged up the steps of the covered porch and threw open the door, and it took everything in me not to slam it closed. I didn't want to scare Ollie.

It took another half hour to get her resettled and tucked into bed for the night. My emotions were all over the place as I paced the living room, trying to keep a panic attack at bay.

It was true—my first instinct was to run. It always had been. To get as far away from my mother's oppression as possible. But until I married, I was never gone for very long.

Down in Montgomery, I'd been a happy home-maker, living in a secluded bubble, just Matt, me, and then Ollie. My father visited regularly, but my mother had little to do with me after I married a man she hadn't approved of. I had seen her maybe ten times in all the years I'd been gone, and one of those times had been at Matt's funeral.

It wasn't until after he died, and the dust settled, that my blinders came off. I suddenly realized exactly how isolated I had become . . . from everything and everyone.

The last thing I wanted was that kind of isolated life for Ollie.

When I moved back to Wicklow three weeks ago, I'd told myself I wouldn't run anymore. That I'd do anything to make peace in the family, to give Ollie a solid foundation.

But I couldn't live like this. With this feeling of . . . suffocation.

I just couldn't.

There had to be a middle ground.

After much pacing and consideration, I hatched a plan that I hoped would be an ideal solution. I'd start looking for an apartment in town, which I considered self-preservation rather than running away. I'd still be in Wicklow and Ollie would still have the family and community I wanted for her, but I'd be out from under Mama's thumb.

First things first, I had to find a job. I needed money. Unfortunately, until I had enough saved up to move out, I had no choice but to play by my mother's rules and allow Ollie to take those damned swimming lessons.

Bitterness burned my throat as I crept outside, stealthily hurrying along the dimly lit pathway leading to the pool. A small brown bird with a crooked wing sat on an iron post watching me intently as I unlatched the gate. Frogs croaked and crickets chirped loudly as though tattling on me as I retrieved the box I'd hurled over the fence earlier.

As I carried the box back to the house, it took everything in me to ignore the overwhelming desire to wake up Ollie, pack what little we owned, load our junky car, and get out of this town.

And never, ever come back.

Anna Kate

Out on the side lawn, there had to be at least fifty people waiting for the blackbirds. Maybe more. Tiki torches were lit, a few people had portable grills set up, and excitement hummed in the air.

I'd taken a quick break from rolling pie dough to watch them a minute. I sipped hot tea, my favorite homemade blend of chamomile and mint that I usually drank before bed. The food dehydrator on the counter held today's clippings from Zee's garden: lemon balm, echinacea, and mint. Once dried, I'd store them in an airtight container until I concocted a tea recipe that perfectly captured their flavors and health benefits.

As I went back to the dough, Doc Linden and his sallow coloring kept slipping into my thoughts, along with Natalie, and Ollie with her tiny backhoe. Mostly, I thought of my mother, as I tried to put myself in her place twenty-five years ago.

By eighteen she'd already had a hard life. She'd lost the man she loved and was accused of killing him. She'd walked away from this town, away from everything familiar. But as I stood here in this kitchen with the scent of flaky, buttery pie crusts surrounding me, I couldn't help wondering if leaving had hurt her more than if she'd simply stayed put.

As soon as the thought came, it went. Because as much as my theory might be true—that my mother would have been happier here despite living near and dealing with the Lindens—she hadn't left town because of her own pride or embarrassment or even *wanderlust,* as Pebbles had called it.

She'd left this town because of *me,* determined to keep me away from people she truly believed would cause me harm. Not physically, perhaps. But mentally. Emotionally.

Fighting a yawn, I pushed away the image of Doc Linden's sad eyes and tried to focus on the task at hand. It was closing in on midnight, and I'd purposefully stayed up late to hear the blackbirds sing their songs, and I was more than a little anxious.

As I slid the rolling pin over the pie dough, stretching it, shaping it, I heard Zee's voice in my head with each pass. I had been ten years old when she finally taught me how to make piecrust from scratch.

"Careful now, darlin'. Too thick and the crust won't cook all the way through. No one wants a soggy-bottomed pie. Soggy bottoms are *always* unfortunate." Her hands, soft and sure, had covered mine on the rolling pin, guiding my strokes. "Too thin, and the crust will burn, and no one wants to taste charcoal when they're expectin' something sweet."

"Granny, how do you know when it's right?" I'd asked.

She'd smiled at me, her teal eyes twinkling. "You're a Callow, Anna Kate. And Callows know pie. That knowledge is deep inside you. You'll know. You'll see."

I felt a teardrop snake down my cheek, and I swiped it away with the back of my hand, unwilling to let emotions get the best of me tonight. I'd already made six pies but, still restless, decided to make one more with the abundance of blackberries I'd found in a bucket on the back deck earlier this evening.

I finished rolling two crusts, knowing they were about as perfect as they could be. There was something in the weight of the dough, its stretch, its texture, that told me as surely as if it could speak that it was ready to be baked.

Gently, I folded one of the crusts in half, then in half again and draped it over a glass pie dish.

I unfolded the dough and pressed it against the glass, molding it to fit the dish perfectly, leaving a bit hanging over the edge. I dipped a spoon into the bowl of blackberry filling I'd already prepared, and though it was good, I thought it wasn't quite *right*. It was a nagging feeling, one I'd had with each of the pies I'd made. Something was off.

It didn't help that Mr. Lazenby's voice was echoing in my head.

This pie don't taste like the pies Miss Zee made.

The pie hadn't—I'd sampled it myself. I'd eaten enough of Zee's pies to know. Whenever she visited, she'd bake me special miniature pies, all my own, lovingly showing me how to make each one. Apple, blueberry, peach, cherry. Endless combinations.

None of mine tonight had tasted like hers.

I grabbed a clean spoon and took another sample of the filling, letting it roll around on my tongue. Something was missing—a flavor I couldn't place.

"Now turn your back," Zee would say before we added the top crust to those miniature pies.

"Why, Granny Zee?"

"I need to add the secret ingredient."

"Secret? What is it?" I'd asked eagerly.

She leaned down. "I promised your mama I wouldn't tell, but you already know what it is."

"No, I don't! I swear I don't."

"You do. You'll put it all together one day, Anna Kate, when you're older."

"And if I don't?"

"There'll be a whole flock of women there to help guide the way, that I can promise you."

"Give me a hint? *Pleeeeease,*" I added over-dramatically. "It's not something silly like love, is it?"

She'd bopped me on the tip of my nose with a floury finger. "That's exactly it. The secret ingredient is love, darlin'. The purest kind of love there is. Now, turn around, and remember—these pies are our little secret from your mama."

I may have been young, but I'd clearly heard a telltale pop of a sealed lid each and every time I turned. A sound anyone would recognize if they'd ever opened a full jelly jar. *Love* shouldn't have been so noisy. Besides, Zee wouldn't have broken her promise to my mom, so I knew that she'd been pulling my leg about the whole love thing.

Frustrated, I ventured into the deep pantry off the kitchen to search the spice and extract shelf. My gaze skipped over cloves, allspice, nutmeg, vanilla, almond, and lemon.

"What did you put in those pies, Zee?" I asked, poking around.

It couldn't be a common ingredient, or I'd have been able to place it easily. I had a decent palate. I closed my eyes, recalling the unmistakable *pop* of a seal being released. The mysterious ingredient, I realized, couldn't have come from a tin or twist-off bottle.

I turned away from the spices and searched among the jarred goods, most of which Zee had canned herself. Plums, grapes, tomatoes, cucumbers, corn, raspberries, beets, rhubarb, peas, okra. All were in tall glass canning jars, but I was looking for smaller containers, a size that Zee could have hidden from me in a skirt pocket, something along the lines of a baby food jar or a jam sampler.

It was a futile search.

Ignoring the feeling that I was doing something wrong, I finished the blackberry pie and put it in the oven. The other pies had already cooled and were in the pie case, waiting for tomorrow's diners. I checked the clock as I cleaned up and washed dishes. It was just past eleven.

If all went as it should, in less than an hour the blackbirds would emerge from the tunnel between the mulberry trees and sing songs—messages from the Land of the Dead—to those who ate pieces of pie today. While those people slept, they'd dream the message meant for them, sent by people who'd loved them.

At a minute shy of midnight, I opened the back door, and the energy of the excited crowd pulsed through the room. I shut off most of the lights, leaned against the marble-topped island, and waited with anticipation. Right at midnight a loud whoop from the birders went up when the blackbirds emerged.

Unbidden, tears sprang to my eyes at the reaction of the strangers, and I watched with a watery gaze as the birds soared upward in a tight formation. They swooped low as they circled the backyard, garnering *ooh*'s and *aah*'s from the crowd, then they landed, one by one, on the branches of the trees.

Four and twenty blackbirds.

Out the side window, I spotted multiple smartphones glowing in the darkness. The birders had gone eerily silent as they watched the blackbirds, as though expecting something more. Most likely, they'd heard of the songs sung at midnight and were waiting.

"Come on," I urged under my breath. "Sing."

The birds remained silent, sitting, watching. I could feel their gazes on me, even through the darkness.

The longer they kept silent, the sicker I felt. Minutes ticked by. The birds would be gone soon, back into the leafy tunnel. "What am I doing wrong?"

But even as I asked, I knew. Instinctively, I *knew*.

The missing ingredient.

I needed to figure out what it was.

You'll put it all together one day, Anna Kate, when you're older.

I was quite a bit older now and still had no idea. My eyes stung with frustrated tears as I watched the birds take flight, soaring, then dipping low to return the way they'd come.

The birders applauded.

Bone-weary, I climbed slowly up the steps and planned to go straight to bed, not even bothering to brush my teeth, but as soon as I came into my bedroom, I noticed that the window was slightly ajar.

I thought I'd checked all the windows earlier when searching for the trespassing phoebe, but I must have missed this one. I walked over to the window and looked out. The birders were holding strong in the yard, their animated chatter filling the air. As I started to slide the window down, I sucked in a breath when I saw two blackbirds sitting on the sill.

I hadn't yet seen any of the birds up close—they rarely left the area around the trees. Suddenly shaky, I knelt down to get a closer look at them as the bedtime story Zee told me long ago echoed in my head.

It's not until one of the guardians in the family passes over that she becomes a tree keeper, taking with her only the color of her eyes. Twenty-four in total, black as twilight, the keepers fly between the two worlds. They collect messages from those who've crossed and pass them along to those who mourn through sweet songs, songs that are too otherworldly to be understood in anything but a dream state.

Immediately, I was taken aback by the birds' unusual eyes—a thin band of color rimmed dark pupils. I couldn't make out the exact shade in the dim lighting, but I suspected one had green, the other teal. My mother's and grandmother's natural eye colors.

Tears pooled along my lashes, and I was beyond grateful that Zee had shared with me that bedtime story of my heritage. The Callows were guardians and gatekeepers of something incredible. All twenty-four of the blackbirds were my ancestors—generations of women protecting something amazing.

There'll be a whole flock of women there to help guide the way, that I can promise you, Zee had said.

She hadn't been exaggerating.

"What am I doing wrong with the pies?" I asked the pair.

The birds bobbed their heads and watched me with somber eyes, and then lifted off, soaring into the backyard to join the rest of the keepers.

I knew full well they couldn't tell me—they couldn't speak. Only sing. And I'd never receive a message in my sleep, either, even if I ate a dozen pies. Zee had told me once that one of the drawbacks of being a keeper was that they couldn't sing messages of their own. Only notes from others. Even so, I thought perhaps they could have given me some sort of hint or sign, but as they disappeared out of sight, I was left with only a pit of sadness in my stomach and tears blurring my eyes.

Grief was a capricious companion. Sometimes distant and aloof. Sometimes so overwhelming it was hard to think a straight thought. Its mood changed at whim, making it emotionally exhausting to keep up.

There were times, like right now, when it felt as though I'd been grieving my whole life long.

Probably because I had been.

I sat there on my knees for a good, long while, hoping they'd return, before slowly standing up. I closed the window and climbed into bed, feeling like the weight of the world anchored me to the mattress.

I pulled up my quilt, tucking the worn fabric next to my face, and closed my eyes. I could hear the birders chattering loudly about the black-birds. I fell asleep the same way I'd woken up that morning. To the sound of a ruckus outside my window.

8

Natalie

I'd slept in fits and starts and woke to a dulcet female voice insistently saying my name.

"Natalie. *Natalie.*"

I stirred, then stiffened in fear that I wasn't alone in my bedroom.

"Natalie, your father is dying."

I bolted upright in bed and blindly reached for the baseball bat I kept next to the headboard. My heart pounded as my eyes adjusted to the early morning light streaming in through the windows, which were open only wide enough for the mountain breeze to ruffle the sheer curtains. The screens were in place. No one had come in that way.

Throwing the sheet off, I slid out of bed and hurriedly checked Ollie's room, right next door. Her blanket was on the floor, and she was fast asleep in the toddler bed, her small hands thrown above her head. Her gentle, rhythmic breathing set me at ease for a moment.

I checked her closet, the only possible hiding spot, and found nothing out of the ordinary. Doubling back, I searched the little house top to bottom. There was no one.

Loosening my grip on the bat, I leaned against the wall, letting the adrenaline settle. I gave myself a moment, then went back into Ollie's room.

I knelt down and retucked the quilt—her blankie, or *bankie* as she called it—around her, and watched her breathe for a moment.

I let my fingers linger on the quilt. It had been a gift from my mother to Ollie, crafted from remnants of her baby clothes. Mama had made many quilts in the same fashion, including AJ's, which had gone missing after the car wreck that killed him, and she'd made many for friends and family.

But never one for me. She'd been working on it when AJ died, and in the aftermath, like most everything else in her world, it had ceased to exist.

My fingers drifted across the fabric, lingering on a soft terry cloth square in the corner. The image came easily of Matt holding a newborn Ollie in the crook of his arm like a football, her tiny head resting in his big hand. She'd looked like a little pink peanut against his muscled arm as she blinked up at him.

"She's looking at me like I've done something wrong," he'd said.

"Probably she's wondering what in the hell just happened to her."

He gently kissed Ollie's downy head. "Don't worry, sweet girl. Daddy's here now."

My heart hurt as I withdrew my fingers from the scrap of fabric cut from the outfit Ollie had been wearing that day.

Shoving the memory aside, I went back to thinking about the voice I'd heard. It had sounded so real. It couldn't have been, though, as there was no one inside the house.

Inside.

Was it possible someone had been outside? Speaking through my open window?

I slipped on a short summer robe and a pair of sandals. A bold sunrise set the horizon aglow as I crept down the porch steps to check the perimeter of the little house for any sign that someone had been out there recently.

Several lights were on in the big house, including the kitchen. Not surprising, since my parents were early risers. If they'd seen someone trespassing, however, Daddy would have been out here with his shotgun long before now.

I considered for a moment that the voice had been my mother's, then dismissed it almost as soon the thought came. The way the words had been spoken reminded me of Snow White's singsong way of talking. Mama didn't singsong. Not ever. Not even when she was actually singing. She had a gunfire way of punctuating lyrics that perfectly matched the tightly controlled way in which she lived her life.

Thick dew soaked my feet as I made my way

toward my bedroom window. Crickets silenced. The wet grass showed no footprints other than my own, and the mulch bed beneath my window was undisturbed, covered in spots with sparkling spider webs. Dew droplets clung to the leaves of the boxwood shrubs and fragrant rose bushes.

Satisfied that there had been no intruder other than an eight-legged variety, I rolled my neck to ease the tense knots in my shoulders. I must have dreamed the voice. There was no other explanation.

"Natalie?"

Jumping, I spun around quickly, baseball bat at the ready. I let out a breath of relief as I came face-to-face with my father.

He threw his hands up. "Whoa, slugger!"

"Sorry." I lowered the bat and willed my heart rate to slow. "I was lost in thought and didn't hear you coming."

"What's going on?"

Looking fresh from a recent shower, he was already dressed for work in his crisply ironed pants and baby-blue button-down. Combed back off his forehead, his damp brown hair looked black in the morning light. As it dried, the hair would flop forward, its waviness winning out over a forced taming.

"A noise woke me up," I said. "I wanted to make sure no one was out here lurking."

Your father is dying.

My voice cracked as I added, "But I think I was just having a bad dream."

While I'd been focused on finding a potential intruder, I'd been holding in the emotional deluge caused by the mysterious message I received. Of course it had been a bad dream. My father dying? No. Not possible. He looked . . . I studied him closely. He looked the same as always. Thank the Lord.

Absently, I pointed at my footprints in the wet grass. "No one's been out here but me."

Putting an arm around my shoulders, he started walking me toward the front door. "Seems like that nightmare still has you shaken up. You should have called me—you shouldn't be out here alone looking for a bogeyman."

I allowed myself to be drawn toward him. When I was younger I'd spent a lot of time glued to his side as he read me books, one after another after another—it was our favorite thing to do together, to disappear into the pages of another world. I'd always considered the crook of his arm to be the safest place in the whole world. "Daddy, if I called you for every bad dream I had, you'd never get a good night's rest."

As soon as I said the words, I wished I hadn't. Even though I spoke the truth, I didn't like exposing my emotional baggage to others. Especially him. My problems were mine, and mine alone. I didn't want him worrying.

He stopped walking. "What can I do to help, Nat?"

"You've already done more than enough to help me . . . and Ollie, too. You and I both know I need to learn to be strong enough to stand on my own two feet, and if that means chasing after bogeymen at the crack of dawn, so be it."

After Matt died, I'd found a job that allowed me to work at night from home. No doubt about it, being a home-based support representative for a local department store had been a lousy job, but I could stay with Ollie and it had paid some of the bills. The rest . . . that's where my father had stepped in.

Over the past couple of years, he'd paid what I couldn't, and all he'd ever asked in return was for us to spend time with him—he'd often come down to Montgomery to take me and Ollie out to lunch or dinner, which, if I were being honest, was simply one more gift he'd given us, not the other way around.

There had never been any mention of Mama during all those years of him visiting us—and even now I wasn't sure if she knew how much he'd provided after Matt died.

I suspected not.

"Asking for help doesn't mean you're weak, Natalie. It's a sign of strength."

"That's sweet of you to say, Daddy." It was just like him to try to make me feel better about my flaws. "But I can't keep asking. I already can't repay you for all you've done for me."

"They weren't loans, Nat. I wanted to help."

"I know, but I still feel like I owe you more than gratitude."

He was silent for a moment as though mulling my words. "I have an idea of how you can repay me."

We climbed the porch steps. "I hope you're not going to say money, because I don't have any. Unless you count the kind that's in Ollie's toy cash register. And if that's the case, I hope you don't mind that it comes with bite marks. Those plastic coins are some of the best teethers around."

He smiled. "I don't want money."

"What, then?" I'd do just about anything for him.

"Same as always. I want *time*. Stick around here for a while. Six months. A year. Give yourself the chance to get to know this place again. A chance for this place to get to know you again."

There was only one reason he'd be asking that of me this morning. "You heard Mama and me having words last night."

"Hard not to."

I longed to say she'd started it, but I bit my tongue instead, not wanting to get worked up all over again.

"Time is what I want, Natalie. Can you do that for me?"

He knew me too well—and how my first inclination would be to run. My gaze cut to the big house. Mama's face was clearly framed in the kitchen window above the sink—she was watching us.

"You know I don't—and can't—make excuses for your mother," he said, "but she was on edge last night and took it out on you. She has a lot going on right now."

"With Anna Kate. Yes, I know."

Surprise flared in his eyes. "You know about Anna Kate?"

"While I rather wish it was either you or Mama who told me about her, yes, I do know. I met Anna Kate yesterday at the park. She seems nice."

"I'm sorry. We were waiting to tell you until we knew for certain."

"There's no denying she's a Linden." It had taken me a moment to see the resemblance, but that was because I hadn't been looking. The possibility that I had a niece out in the world had never once crossed my mind. AJ had been only eighteen when he died.

"Yes, I knew the minute I saw Anna Kate in person yesterday." Daddy's chin lifted slightly as he glanced off in the distance. "Your mother and I were going to discuss it with you today."

I tapped the head of the bat on the top of my foot. "Now you don't have to. I already know. For the record, I think asking Anna Kate to supper was a nice gesture."

"You and I might be the only ones to think so. Anna Kate turned me down flat."

I twisted his words and threw them back at him. "Give Anna Kate the chance to get to know this place. A chance for this place to get to know her."

By *place,* we knew we both meant Mama.

"I'm sure Anna Kate is overwhelmed right now," I added. "She needs time to adjust to the idea of us."

Sadness haunted his eyes. "I'm not sure time is going to help in this situation. What happened in the past . . . She thinks the worst. Justifiably so."

In all the years I'd heard Eden Callow's name cursed to the heavens, I never really stopped to think whether my parents had been right to persecute the young woman. I'd simply believed their truth that Eden had killed AJ and gotten away with it.

Their truth. But had it been the *whole* truth?

After overhearing their conversation last night, I now questioned all I ever thought I knew about Eden. I kept tapping the bat against my foot. "Overcoming the past is a challenge, especially since it looks like you and Mama were wrong about Eden and treated her badly. The key to it all, I think, is that you need to show Anna Kate who you are now, because your relationship with her isn't about what happened back then.

149

It's about what happens from here on out."

He glanced away, toward the big house. "If only it were that easy, Natalie."

As his head turned, the sunrise caught his face just so, highlighting deep shadows beneath his eyes. Had those been there before? "No one said it was going to be easy."

His chin came up, and he faked a smile. "I best get going. I'll see you later on?"

"I'll be around."

"And tomorrow?"

It took me a moment to understand why he was suddenly so interested in my whereabouts. "Then, too. I'll stick around for a while, Daddy. I promise."

"A year?"

"Don't go pressing your luck. I'm not putting a time frame on it."

He hugged me. "All right. I'll take what I can get."

"Thanks for coming out here and checking on me." I squeezed him more tightly than I normally would and frowned. Had he lost weight? Breathing in the smell of him, I picked up the hint of soap and mint . . . and something else I couldn't quite identify. Something sharp, bitter, and completely unfamiliar.

"Anytime. I'm always here if you need me."

He released me, and I suddenly felt chilled. "Have you been feeling okay lately?"

"What makes you ask?"

Your father is dying.

"Just making sure. Since I'm going to be sticking around for a while." I tried to make light, but I could hear the strain of worry in my voice coming through loud and clear.

He jumped off the porch with a flourish, kicking his heels up to show off. "Do I look like a man who's feeling puny? Don't you worry about me, Natalie."

As he walked off, I noted that he hadn't actually answered the question. I kept watch over him until he disappeared through the patio doors of the big house before I turned to go inside, wake up Ollie, and get on with the day.

As I swung the baseball bat onto my shoulder, I told myself not to let the worry take root—that I'd had a bad dream. Nothing more. He was fine. Just fine. Absolutely fine.

If my father were dying, I'd know it . . .

Wouldn't I?

Anna Kate

Early the next morning, I woke up before my alarm went off. Today, all was quiet outside, and I knew exactly where I was.

In Wicklow with the blackbirds.

I should have been exhausted after the day I'd had yesterday, but I felt oddly rested. Sitting up,

151

my first thoughts were of coffee. Although I was slightly obsessed with herbal tea, I always kick-started my days with coffee. But soon I started thinking about the blackberries Summer had dropped off. Zee's cobbler sounded like a perfect breakfast treat—I hadn't had a chance to make it yesterday, but I had the time now.

I hurriedly showered, dressed, and pulled my hair into a sloppy bun. Before I went downstairs, I made the rounds of the small apartment. Zee had been a minimalist, and it showed in her sparse furniture and lack of knickknacks. Her artistic flair wasn't lacking, however. The walls were painted eggplant purple. The deep sofa was mint green, and the floral upholstery on the single armchair was a riot of colors. The small kitchenette was bare-bones, and I figured that was because Zee mainly cooked downstairs. Her room was painted summer-squash yellow. Crisp white curtains and bed linens added to the bright, sunny atmosphere. I closed the door and went down the hall for my shoes. My bedroom was painted a serene green that reminded me of a mint leaf, and it had the same white, light fabrics as Zee's room. The whole apartment, while color-ful, reminded me of nature. It felt like Zee.

I opened the curtains to check on the birders. Most had gone, but there were a few who remained behind in sleeping bags. I spotted Sir Bird Nerd milling about, his binoculars in hand,

and I was surprised he hadn't headed back to Mobile.

It wasn't until I turned to go that I saw something green on the other side of the window, on the corner of the stone sill. Puzzled, I slid the window upward, knelt down, and saw that the green belonged to a leaf. It was held in place with a small stone.

Smiling, I carefully picked it up. I realized the blackbirds had given me a clue after all. When they'd bobbed their heads last night, it had been toward the corner of the sill where this leaf sat. Between the darkness and my tears, I hadn't seen it.

I gently turned the brittle leaf over in my hand. It had five lobes, the tips of which looked like hearts. This leaf was browned along its edge as if in distress, and something deep within me responded to its call for help.

It was a mulberry leaf.

I quickly slipped on my sneakers and went running down the stairs, through the kitchen, and out the back door, which thwacked behind me. I hurried across the lawn toward the mulberry trees, immediately noticing that some of the unripened fruit had dropped overnight. White, green, and pink berries littered the ground beneath the trees. Leaves had started to brown and curl inward.

I bent and pushed my finger into the ground beneath the trees. Their distress wasn't from lack of water—the earth was dry but not parched.

Confused and a little nerve-wracked, I knew the blackbirds had given me that leaf for a reason.

You'll put it all together one day, Anna Kate, when you're older.

As Zee's voice rang in my ears, I calmed. I closed my eyes and tried to recall any part of her bedtime story that had to do with the trees.

It's the love shared between the two worlds that allows the passageway to remain open, Anna Kate, darlin'. Without the love, the trees will wither and die.

The love. The phrase echoed in my head as I stood under the trees, looking upward at the sad leaves and drooping berries.

While on earth, it's the job of us guardians to tend to the trees, nurture them, and gather their love to bake into pies to serve those who mourn, those left behind.

Gather their love to bake into pies.

I reached up, cupped a cluster of berries.

The secret ingredient is love, darlin'. The purest kind of love there is.

I dropped my head back and sighed at my thick-headedness. Zee had been right—I knew exactly what the secret ingredient was—it had just taken me a little while to put it together. "Sorry!" I called into the leafy tunnel. "It's been a long week."

As I pulled the cluster from one of the

trees, however, it took only a moment for my excitement to wear off. These berries were hard, greenish pink. Unripe. I couldn't possibly put them into a pie as they were—the pies would be inedible. I debated whether I could cook them down to a syrup, adding extra sugar to make the berries palatable.

It was worth a try.

But that wasn't the end of my worries. My gaze swept over the trees—while there were still a lot of berries, there wasn't enough to make a month of pies, never mind a year's supply.

How had Zee done it?

Then I recalled the *pop* of the secret ingredient she'd added to the pies she'd made me.

Of course! She'd processed the berries. I ran back into the café, still clutching the cluster of unripe berries. I waved to Sir Bird Nerd, promised the zucchini some TLC, and ran up the steps and into the kitchen. I checked the pantry, the freezer, and all the cupboards. There was no cache of preserved mulberries.

Hands on hips, I clenched my jaw, and took a deep breath. I'd figured out the hard part—I'd ask Jena and Bow what they knew of the mulberries when they came in later on. For now, I'd start the mulberry syrup to use in the pies I planned to bake later today.

Unfortunately, the pies I made last night were simply regular old pies, and I winced at the thought of dealing with Mr. Lazenby's disappointment. And mine, too, when I realized the blackbirds would have no songs to sing tonight, either.

Tomorrow, however, everything would change. Suddenly I couldn't help but wish the day away, even though it was barely six in the morning.

I went about making coffee, remembering Bow's instructions on how to use the fancy coffee maker that held three pots.

Once the coffee was brewing, I washed the mulberries and set out to remove their stems, which might have been the most tedious job I'd ever undertaken. So dreadful, in fact, that I ended up setting the bunch aside to work on later. After I was caffeinated.

I poured a cup of coffee and gathered together the ingredients for the blackberry cobbler. In a saucepan, I heated sugar, cornstarch, blackberries, lemon zest, and vanilla and let it thicken as I worked on the cobbler's topping.

As I measured flour, I heard a tap on the back door and saw Gideon Kipling's face outlined in the window above the sinks.

I waved him inside. "You're out early. The birders aren't bothering you, are they?"

"Not at all," he said, peering out the window into the side yard. "They're dedicated, aren't they?"

"They're something. What have you there?" I gestured to his hand.

He held up a jar of honey. "I saw you were up and thought I'd bring you some of that honey you were drooling over yesterday."

"I was *not* drooling. I was too dehydrated to drool."

He laughed. "Fair enough. If you don't want it . . ."

I dusted my hands on my apron and lurched for the jar. "I might be drooling *now*." I admired the color. "It's beautiful. Thank you."

"I have the feeling you'll put it to good use."

"I most definitely will. Coffee's hot. Want some?"

"Absolutely." He crossed to the shelves where the mugs were stored and grabbed one. Then he backtracked to the fridge for the cream, knowing exactly where it was located in the double-wide refrigerator.

I stirred the blackberry mixture and turned off the heat before grabbing the coffee pot. I motioned with my chin to the mug and creamer he'd set out. "You come here often?"

Putting his hands on his hips, he looked astounded, as if only now realizing what he'd been doing. "Sorry. Habit. I used to have coffee with Zee a few times a week before the café opened for the day." He glanced around, his gaze eventually going upward, lingering on the blackbird quote on the soffit. "I've missed it."

Surprise rippled through me as I filled his mug. "I didn't know you two were that close."

"Zee was a good friend to me."

"I'm sorry. I didn't know." Grief ballooned in my chest.

With a nod of acknowledgment, he said, "You couldn't have."

But for some reason, I felt as though I should have known. About him. And about Zee's relationship with Summer, too. It stung, this feeling of exclusion, which seemed strange to me since I'd never minded being left out of Wicklow before now. I'd always accepted that this was a forbidden place I'd never see, with forbidden people I'd never know, and that was that.

Only, it turned out it wasn't.

Pushing those thoughts out of my mind, I topped off my mug. "I'm glad you said something. I like knowing you and Zee were friends. It's . . . comforting."

"Really? Then why the sudden frown?"

"Oh, it's nothing about you and Zee, I promise. It's only that for a second there I was overcome with the deep need to bake you a zucchini loaf."

Laughing, he added cream to his coffee but didn't bother stirring it through. A white cloud bloomed in the dark liquid as he said, "See, Wicklow's already getting a hold on you. I told you it would."

"Not hardly." I went back to making the cobbler's batter, adding sugar, salt, baking powder, and, lastly, buttermilk to the flour and butter.

He leaned against the sink apron. "This coffee is good. Reminds me of Zee."

"It should. Jena taught me Zee's way of making it." I'd been happy to carry on one of her traditions, but it was another thing that made me feel strangely left out.

"What're you cooking up over there?" he asked.

"Blackberry cobbler."

"Did you know you smile when you measure ingredients?"

I glanced at him. "I do?"

"With every ingredient. I noticed because I think it's the first I've seen you smile since you've been in Wicklow. Which is a shame, because you have a nice smile."

I ignored the sudden flustered feeling that nearly made me drop the wooden spoon I was using to mix the batter. "Cooking and baking make me happy."

"Runs in the family, then?"

"It does. I learned from the best." I assembled the cobbler, stuck the eight-inch square pan in the preheated oven, set the timer, and faced him. "Are you hungry? How about an omelet?"

"Thanks for the offer, but I should get going. I'll be forever indebted if you save me some of that cobbler, though."

"That's a fair price for the honey."

He finished his cup of coffee, rinsed the mug,

and set it in the dishwasher. "When you have some extra time, I need—"

His words were cut off by someone pounding on the front door.

Mr. Lazenby had his face pressed to the glass, which only seemed to highlight each and every frown line. "Miss Anna Kate! I need to be talkin' to you!"

I let out a breath.

"What's wrong with him?" Gideon asked.

"The pie," I said, heading for the front of the café.

"The pie?" I heard Gideon mumble behind me.

"Miss Anna Kate," Mr. Lazenby said as soon as I opened the door, his color high, "the pie is broken. I didn't get a dream."

"I know. Come back tomorrow."

"What about today's pies?" he asked, eyes wide.

"Broken too. There actually won't be any pie sold today," I said, making a spur-of-the-moment decision. "Everything will be back to normal tomorrow. See you then." I forced a smile and closed the door.

I turned back to Gideon, only to hear pounding on the door again. I spun around.

"But I'm hungry," Mr. Lazenby said pitifully through the glass. "And something smells real good."

I hesitated only a second before pulling open

the door. It was the least I could do for the sorrowful old man.

"You're a nice girl," he said, passing me by, heading straight to the island where Gideon was already pouring him a cup of coffee.

They said their hellos, then Gideon headed for the back door. "Thanks for the coffee. I'll talk to you later, Anna Kate."

"But wait. You were saying something earlier . . ."

"It can keep."

"You sure?"

He nodded. "Don't forget to save me some of that cobbler."

I followed him to the screen door and leaned against the jamb. "Gideon? I know I'm not Zee, but I'll be down here most mornings around six if you want to come on by for some of her coffee."

Sunshine glinted off his eyes. "I just might take you up on that."

With that, he was off, down the deck steps and walking across Zee's garden toward the back of the yard.

I turned to face Mr. Lazenby and rubbed my hands together. "Now, while we wait for that cobbler, how about we pass the time destemming some mulberries?"

9

"What initially brought you to town, sir?"

"A report of a rare sighting of *Turdus merula*," Zachariah Boyd said, proudly puffing out his chest to show off his Bird Nerd T-shirt. "I'm the president of the Gulf Coast Avian Society. We welcome new members."

The reporter carefully wrote down the name of the group and its website, noting it would make a good inset for his article. "How long do you plan to stay in Wicklow?"

Mr. Boyd scratched his chin, which was covered in a neatly clipped white beard. "Don't rightly know. I came for the blackbirds . . . but I'm staying for the pie."

Natalie

I hadn't stuck around to witness Mama gloating her way through Ollie's swimming lesson. I'd headed straight out the moment I'd handed my cheerful daughter over to my also-cheerful mother for the day.

The town was jumping. There was a group of people walking around, hanging flyers about the Fourth of July carnival, which was still more than a month away. I recognized them as being from

Mama's Refresh group and went out of my way to avoid contact. The last thing I wanted was to run into Coralee Dabadie and have to make small talk about Stacia giving Ollie swimming lessons, something I didn't like to think about, never mind discuss with a woman I hadn't spoken to in years.

Cars were backed up along Mountain Laurel Lane and many of the diagonal parking spots were taken. There was a vibrant hum in the air that hadn't been here yesterday, and an even bigger crowd in front of the Blackbird Café, where I was headed. I'd eat my piece of pie, check around town to see if anyone was hiring, then head home.

Staying behind to watch Ollie's lesson would've been sheer torture. Taking a deep breath, I reminded myself that she was in good hands. Mama loved Ollie and wouldn't let harm come to her.

Not willingly, anyway.

But accidents happened.

No. I refused to go *there*. Between Mama and Stacia, Ollie was *not* going to drown.

She was not going to drown.

I struggled with the need to race back to the pool, grab my daughter, and never let go. Suddenly dizzy, I latched on to a light post for balance as Matt's bloated, ghostly white face floated in and out of focus, then came sharply into view, in the finest possible detail, the scar on his cheek almost translucent. His blue eyes opaque. His skin puffy.

I'd barely recognized him enough to identify his body, freshly pulled from Lake Martin, where he'd been missing for two days. I closed my eyes against the memory, clenched my jaw, and willed myself not to throw up right here in the center of town, all over the purple and pink petunias along the sidewalk.

I was still clinging to the pole when I felt something wet and slimy on my hand and heard a throaty whimper. Alarmed, my eyes flew open. River, the Sheltie mix, was at my feet, staring upward. His wet nose nudged my arm and he gave my hand another lick.

"He has a knack for finding people in distress," the mountain man, Cam Kolbaugh, said. He ducked his head to look me in the eye. "You okay?"

"Oh, fine." I coughed, trying to clear the lingering anxiety from my throat. I patted the light post. "Just checking to make sure this thing's sturdy. It is."

"Good to know. You can probably let it go, then."

My head swam. "I'm thinking I should keep on making sure it's not going anywhere for a bit longer. Another minute or so should do the trick."

Cam knelt down, pulled a backpack from his shoulder, and riffled around inside it. He brought forth a canteen and held it out. "Water. Full. None of my cooties on it yet."

"I'm not thirsty. Thanks, though."

He sat back on his haunches, then suddenly pulled out his camera and took a shot of me.

"Why'd you do that?"

He studied the image for a moment, a deep frown causing his eyes to narrow. He stood and showed me the camera's screen. "You've lost all coloring. I've never seen someone go so white in all my life."

"Count yourself lucky." I stared at the picture of myself and couldn't argue that I looked ghostly. And ghastly. And that I was almost the same color Matt had been on the shore of the lake. Just like that, his face was back, staring blankly at me. I wobbled.

Cam grabbed my arm. "Hey, now. Come on. I've got you."

He led me to a nearby bench, sat me down. River set his chin on my knee, not taking his doleful eyes off me. When I started shivering uncontrollably, Cam inched closer, then placed his right arm around my shoulders, pulling me close, anchoring me to him, as if he did it all the time. He took his other hand and reached in front of me, gathering up my left hand to hold it tightly in his enormous callused palm. The contact should have felt like a confining invasion of my personal space—he was practically a stranger, after all. A big, overpowering stranger. Instead his heat and his strength seeped into me like a soothing balm.

I focused on breathing. In, out. One breath at a time, just like the therapist had taught me when I'd first started having panic attacks. It took a good few minutes, but the shaking stopped. The nausea was still there in the pit of my stomach, but under control. My head throbbed but was no longer fuzzy.

Cam let go of my hand and rubbed River's ears. "How's the bench doing? Sturdy as the lamppost?"

I managed a weak smile. "I don't think it's in danger of collapsing anytime soon."

He caught my eye. "Good to know."

"Thank you for watching out for me," I said.

"You're welcome."

"Oh, I was talking to River."

Cam laughed, long and hard. "I should've known." As casually as he'd draped it around me, he removed his arm. He fussed with his backpack and his camera.

"And thank you, too." I tried to explain what had just happened, without going into the gory details. "I get . . ."

"You don't have to go explaining anything to me. Traumatic events leave emotional wounds that're hard to heal. Everyone has their own way of getting through it." He stood up, held out his hand.

I slipped my hand into his and looked up. "What's your way?" I asked, because instinctively I knew he spoke from experience.

"I hide in the mountains."

"I like your way better."

"Took me a long time to find a method that works. You'll find yours. Now, where're you off to? I'll walk with you."

I wanted to argue that I'd be fine on my own, but truth was I liked his company. He had a calm strength about him I envied. "To the Blackbird Café."

We started off in that direction. He said, "It's a hot spot today. Loads of people showing up because of the blackbirds."

"I suppose I'm going there because of the blackbirds, too."

"But you know they won't be out until midnight. They're a sight, too, let me tell you. I've never seen anything like it in my life. I got chill bumps when they appeared, practically out of nowhere."

River walked a step ahead of us, his tail wagging as he sniffed people who passed by. I wished Ollie were here—she'd have loved this time with the dog. "Oh, I'm not going to *see* the blackbirds. I'm going because I need their help. To heal."

He glanced at me, confusion filling his hazel eyes. "Their help?"

"You haven't heard about the pie, then."

"The pie?"

"The blackbird pie? It's . . . well, it's something special. And I'm counting on it to help me get rid of a ghost."

Anna Kate

My quiet, peaceful morning hadn't lasted long. By nine thirty, the Blackbird Café was jam-packed. Every table was full and there was a line out the door and down the block. We couldn't cook or serve fast enough, and at one point I thought we might run out of food. I couldn't even offer up pie, as I'd handed it out among the early-birders before the café opened.

I dropped a plate of home fries at a table, then went around the room to refill coffee cups. Other than Mr. Lazenby, Pebbles, and Faylene, I didn't recognize the rest of people in the café, but by their discussions I'd picked up that they were only in town to see the blackbirds.

Mr. Lazenby had been here for close to three hours now, and each time I passed by him to refill his mug or drop off a plate, he grumbled about mulberry stems. You'd think I'd asked him to destem a whole tree instead of a small bunch of berries.

I'd talked to Bow and Jena about the mulberries earlier, but they didn't know too much other than that Zee looked forward to harvesting them each year. They had never seen her preserve, process, or freeze them, or do *anything* other than gather them when ripe. She never made mulberry pies, either, which I thought was strange.

"Order up!" Bow thumped the countertop.

I hurried into the kitchen, dropped off the coffee pot, and picked up two plates laden with johnnycakes, a type of cornmeal pancake, according to Bow, topped with brown butter apples, the day's special. "Thanks, Bow."

"You holding up okay out there?" he asked.

Surprisingly, I was. Maybe because there were more birders than locals, and I wasn't the focus of everyone's undivided attention. I'd fielded only a few questions about my life, so word must be getting around town on its own. And I'd dropped only two plates and one mug. "Better today than yesterday."

Jena bit back a yawn as she set another sheet of biscuits in the oven—she'd been yawning all morning, saying she'd woken up earlier than usual to tend to a friend. It didn't help that she'd been pulling double duty this morning—helping in the kitchen and the dining room. "And tomorrow will be better than today, just you wait and see. You fit right in here."

I didn't know about that, since I'd had no idea what a johnnycake was, but it was nice not to feel like a *complete* outsider.

As I delivered the plates, I spotted Natalie out-

170

side in the crowd. She waved when she saw me, and I pointed to the back door. She ducked out of line and disappeared around the side of the café. I dreaded telling her that there would be no pie today.

"Was that . . . ?" Faylene stood up, then sat back down. "I'll be. It *is* Natalie." She turned to me. "You know Natalie?"

A hush fell over the locals, but the chatter from the birders kept steady, covering the sudden awkwardness. "I met her yesterday. At the park."

I glanced at Mr. Lazenby, and even he seemed on the edge of his seat. "What did she have to say?" he asked.

"Yes," Pebbles said, leaning in. "Do tell."

I wiped my hands on my hip apron. "Well, not all that much. She asked me to save her a piece of pie."

"Pie? Oh." Faylene pressed her hand to her heart. "The dear, dear thing." She turned to the table, including all the strangers, and said, "Natalie's husband passed away one year, seven months, and four days ago, thereabouts. A tragic, tragic accident. Drowned in Lake Martin, and search and rescue didn't find his body for two whole days."

A sad murmur echoed down the table, and my eyes stung with tears, though I hadn't even known the man. Then I realized that I wasn't hurting for him—I was hurting for Natalie. And little Ollie. Especially Ollie. I knew what it was like to grow up without a father.

Mr. Lazenby straightened his green-striped bow tie. "I'd forgotten about that."

Pebbles said, "I didn't know Natalie was back in town. How long is she planning on staying? How old is her girl now?"

"Just under two, and I'm not sure," Faylene said. "Unless Natalie's relationship with Seelie has changed, I'm guessing they won't be here long. Like oil and water, those two, especially when Natalie was a teenager."

"She's going to be mad about the pie," Mr. Lazenby said, as if his brain had only now caught up to that part of what I'd said. Then his eyes brightened. "Hold up now, Miss Anna Kate. You said the pie would be fixed tomorrow—will you put aside a piece for me? I'll pay extra."

Behind him, Pebbles shook her head so vigorously I thought for sure she was going to end up with whiplash—she wasn't the least bit sorry he hadn't been getting his heavenly messages from his dearly departed wife.

"Sorry, Mr. Lazenby," I said, not feeling too badly. I knew he'd be waiting at the door at dawn—there would be plenty of pie for him to choose from. "First come, first served. Café rules."

Indignantly, he sputtered, "But you were going to save a piece for Miss Natalie!"

"Family members are exempt from that rule," I said, then walked away. But not before I heard a squeal out of Faylene.

"*Family?* Did you hear that! Anna Kate *is* a Linden. I knew it. I just knew it."

"We *all* knew it," Mr. Lazenby said grumpily.

I smiled as I strode to the back door to greet Natalie—she was coming up the steps of the deck.

"Come on in," I said. "Excuse the madness. It's a little busy."

"A little?" Natalie said. "It's a nuthouse."

Bow said, "Who're you calling nutty?"

"Hi, Bow." She gave him a big smile.

He came over and gave her a bear hug. "Never thought I'd see you inside this place."

"Things change," she said with a touch of sadness in her voice.

"That they do," he agreed solemnly. "It's been too long."

"We sure did miss you," Jena said, edging Bow out of the way with a jab of an elbow to hug her as well. "Where's that sweet baby of yours?"

"Ollie's with my mother for the day."

"Well, isn't that nice?" Jena said.

Natalie said nothing in response—only gave a closed-lip smile and a guttural "Mm-hmm."

Her hair was pulled back the same way it had been yesterday—in a low side knot at her neck—and she wore the same gold stud earrings, and

173

no other jewelry. Her summery floral dress had a boat-neck bodice, a thick belt, and a loose A-line skirt that twirled around her knees. Strappy black sandals looked freshly shined, and the chip in her toe polish had been painted over.

She looked every bit a cultured southern beauty, from her perfect posture to her makeup to her clothing, but for some reason, I suspected it was all surface, and that she was, as she'd mentioned yesterday, a hot mess. At least on the inside.

I said, "The bad news is that there isn't any pie today. I'm really sorry. I messed up the recipe. But the good news is that I know what I did wrong, and there will be pie tomorrow."

I watched emotions play across her face, changing from unhappiness to acceptance to . . . relief?

"Will you save me a piece tomorrow?" she asked.

"Of course."

"Thanks. I guess I should be going, then. I'm hoping to job hunt while Ollie is occupied. Do any of you know someone who's hiring?"

Bow stroked his beard, smoothing it in swift downward strokes, as was his way. "Times are tough right now. I can't think of anyone looking for help."

Natalie winced.

"Maybe down in Fort Payne," Jena said. "The drive's not too bad."

"I'd like something local, if possible," Natalie said, clasping her hands together tightly. "Something walkable."

"Hmm," Jena said, her gaze sliding to me. Her dark pencil-thin eyebrows went up, and her head tipped toward Natalie.

I didn't have anything against Natalie personally, but she was a Linden. I wasn't sure I could face her day in and day out. The emotional toll . . .

But then I saw something in Natalie's eyes, a shimmering desperation that told me exactly how much she wanted—needed—a job.

She needed help. The healer in me, the nurturer, couldn't see that and walk away, even if she was a Linden.

Damn it.

I took a deep breath and said, "As long as the birders are around, we're going to need extra help in the dining room a few days a week, if you're interested. It'd be temporary. Only until the birders finally get their fill of the blackbirds and leave." Or I did. Whichever came first.

Jena grinned ear to ear, and I tried not to roll my eyes at her.

Natalie brightened and pressed her clasped hands to her chest. "I'm interested. I have to be honest, though. I don't have any experience as a server—*but* I'm a quick learner who isn't afraid of hard work."

175

Undoubtedly, she could have said she was allergic to coffee, pie, *and* people, and I probably would have offered the position to her anyway—that's how deeply the call to comfort ran in Callow blood. "Sounds like you're as qualified as I am," I said. "When can you start?"

"Today," she said with a smile. "Right now."

"I don't want to be the voice of doom and gloom, but what of Ollie? Have you checked out daycare for her?" Jena asked. "And . . . Seelie? I can't imagine she'd approve of you working here, knowing how she feels about the café."

Natalie's back straightened, ramrod stiff. "I . . . don't know. I hadn't really thought that far ahead. I know someone who might be able to help with Ollie . . ." Her gaze drifted to the dining room and softened. Then it hardened immediately when she said, "My mother is another matter, but I'm old enough now to make my own decisions."

If her voice hadn't caught on the word "own," I would have bought her Miss Independent act, but it had and now I wondered how much say she had in her own life.

It was none of my business, I reminded myself. More so because Natalie *was* a Linden. My arm's-length policy was more imperative now than ever. Even though I was breaking my resolve not to have anything to do with the Lindens by hiring Natalie, that's where it ended. She was an employee. I'd be friendly. That's it.

Bow whistled low. "Look at you, all grown up. Seems like only yesterday you were just a bitty thing, helping us tend our gardens."

"We all have to grow up sometime, don't we?" she said.

"Some sooner than others." Jena pulled biscuits from the oven as she looked over her shoulder at us.

"How about this," I suggested. "You help out today, see if you even like the job, and then we'll go from there once you've had some time to think on it."

"A good plan," Jena said with a firm nod. She grabbed an apron from the rack near the back door and tossed it at Natalie. "Welcome to the Blackbird. Now get to gettin'. We've got customers waitin'."

"Thank you, Anna Kate, for giving me a chance." Natalie threw her arms around me.

I sighed and gave in to the hug but quickly wiggled free. "You're welcome."

Most of the diners were oblivious to us, but there were a handful watching our every move. Faylene dabbed at her eyes. Between those tears and Natalie's hug, something deep inside me started to ache, a pain I remembered well.

It occurred every time I started making friends in a new place, knowing I'd eventually have to leave them behind. Whether it be a few months or six months or even a year, I always had to leave, for one reason or another, and it always hurt. Once, when Mom and I moved to a small town in Pennsylvania when I was in middle school, I decided I wasn't going to make any friends. I planned to be a loner for six months, to save myself the pain of it all. That had backfired spectacularly, because all I'd learned was that the pain of denying oneself friends was worse than leaving them when it was time to go.

Over time, I developed an arm's-length approach that had worked well for years. Friendly, not friends. It still hurt to leave, but not quite as much. The downside, of course, was that I lived a rather lonely life. It was a small price to pay to protect my emotional well-being.

I needed to be more careful here in Wicklow and not grow too attached. The last thing I wanted was to add to my grief when I left town in a couple of months.

Drawing in a deep breath, I pushed those thoughts aside for now and got back to work. Extra hands made quick work of the lunch crowd. Natalie turned out to be a decent server, personable, strong, and quick on her feet. She dealt with the shock of locals seeing her working here much better than I would have, laughing off the slew of questions with grace.

The most common one wondering if her mother knew she was here.

Between that and Bow's comment about never

thinking he'd see Natalie inside the café made me wonder if the Blackbird had always been as forbidden to her as it had been to me.

Things change, Natalie had said.

I couldn't agree more.

10

Anna Kate

An hour after closing the café for the day, I ventured toward the south end of Mountain Laurel Lane, toward the limestone courthouse that anchored it. Its grounds had a small outdoor amphitheater that hosted concerts, movie nights, plays, and was home to the playground where I'd run into Natalie the day before. According to Bow and Jena, the inside of the courthouse held all of the town's administrative offices, the police station, two courtrooms, and the public library, which was my destination.

There was a trio of people at the amphitheater, setting up a screen for tonight's Movie in the Moonlight event, a showing of *Peter Pan*. A big banner strung across wide wooden doors touted the Fourth of July carnival. There'd be festival rides, abundant food and music, arts and crafts, and, of course, fireworks—all sponsored by something called the Refresh Committee. I noted, too, that the events taking place on the lawn were sponsored by the same group.

Across from the courthouse to the west was a small motel, its lot full, its NO VACANCY sign flashing neon red. It was flanked by several boarded-up storefronts. The only other businesses still open in that strip were a laundromat and an Italian restaurant that many locals had informed me was the town's favorite pizza place. No one had ever mentioned that it also happened to be the *only* pizza place, but that didn't surprise me much. It had become clear in my short time here that the residents of Wicklow tended to focus on what they had rather than what they had not.

To the courthouse's eastern side, there were more boarded storefronts, a small general store, and a hardware and farm store. Most of the houses I could see from this spot were in want of TLC, needing new roofs or fresh paint. Or both. Fences leaned and lawns grew long.

A uniformed policeman came out of the courthouse just as I reached the top of the steps, and he stepped back to hold open the door for me. Tall and brawny, he had a barrel chest, wide shoulders, and a nose that looked like it had been broken a time or two. A gun was clipped at his hip, a shoulder mic rested near his strong chin, and he wore a dark cap that shaded bright blue eyes.

"You're Anna Kate, aren't you?" he said with a smile, then he stuck out a big hand. "I'm Josh Kolbaugh. Faylene Wiggins's son-in-law."

I should have known who he was, simply from Faylene's very apt description of him being a "big bear of a man." He was quite bearish. Practically a grizzly. "Marcy's husband, right?"

He kept on smiling. "Yes, ma'am. You're a quick learner. I imagine you've been meeting lots of people this past week. It's not easy keeping track of names and faces."

The "ma'am"s were killing me slowly. "It helps that Faylene told me all about you and Marcy and Lindy-Lou, not four hours ago." She'd practically talked my ear off, and every time I'd leave to tend to another diner, Faylene would pick up right where she'd left off when I came back. She was making my *friendly* policy really difficult.

"Heck," he said, "you probably know my life story better than I do by now."

"Not quite. Maybe by the end of next week."

"I don't doubt it." Humor flashed in his eyes. "Are you going inside? You need help finding something? It's a maze in there and not well marked."

"The library?"

He pointed. "Go straight this way, turn right at the first hallway, left at the next, up the flight of steps, and around the corner. Can't miss it."

"Straight, right, up, left, around." I stepped through the doorway. "Got it."

Shaking his head, he used his right hand as a directional tool, as if we were playing charades. "Straight, right, left, *up,* then around."

I hoped this excursion didn't turn out like my afternoon outing the day before, or there might be need of a search party. "I'll find it." I sounded more confident than I felt. "Thanks."

"No problem." He tipped his hat. "Have a good one, Anna Kate."

The door closed behind me, and I breathed in the scent of the old building, a combination of wax and dust and history mixed with a touch of mildew. My flip-flops slapped against marble floors, and the sound echoed against mahogany wainscoting. I turned right, then left, and then went up. And sure enough, there was the library. One of the double doors was held open with a plastic wedge.

I stepped inside and immediately felt at ease, as though in the presence of close friends among the many books with their colorful spines, the towering wooden shelves, and the scent of old paper, mustiness, and memories. Growing up, I'd spent a lot of time in libraries—which had been sanctuaries in the hours between school letting out and when my mother came home from work.

A middle-aged woman with pink streaks in her blond hair looked up from the checkout desk as I approached. "May I help you?"

"Hi, yes. Does the library have a collection of old newspapers?"

"Depends," she said, clicking out of a computer screen to give me her full attention. "How long ago? There was a flood in the late nineties that wiped out nearly everything we had. We've been slowly piecing together what we can, but there are a lot of gaps."

"Twenty-five years ago."

She gave me an odd look, then said, "August, by any chance?"

"How'd you know?"

"Wish I could say I was psychic, but sadly that's not the case. Otherwise I'd probably be a lottery winner and not working here at the library. Not that I don't love my job," she added quickly, looking around as though her boss might be nearby. "Follow me."

I followed, wondering if she, too, was related in some way to Faylene—her manner of speaking was quite similar.

She looked back at me over her shoulder, saying, "We're working on digitizing our newspaper collection, but it's tedious work and sadly we have limited funds. The newspapers we've recovered from that year are on microfiche. Are you familiar with the machines?"

"I've seen one. Does that count?"

She laughed quietly. "It's a sight better than some who come in here. They're easy enough. It won't take long for you to catch on."

We wove through a warren of bookshelves, past an aisle devoted solely to DVDs and Blu-ray movies, through the children's section, where it was story time. I smiled at the small, enraptured faces as a woman read with great theatrics about a boy named Eddie who'd lost his teddy. I fought the urge to sit down to have a listen.

During the vast time I'd spent in libraries, I'd discovered they weren't as quiet as people believed. There were almost always librarians speaking in hushed conversations. There were muffled footsteps on the carpet, the crackling noise of pages being turned, and children speaking loudly because they hadn't quite learned how to use indoor voices yet. People coughing, sneezing. The heating or cooling systems groaning. The melody was comforting and soothing.

As we approached a wall of private rooms, which, according to the sign posted on the wall, were used for study groups or community meetings and could be reserved, the chatty librarian said, "You'll have to wait your turn. The film from that month is currently in use." She gestured through a window into a room that held a single microfiche machine, a table, two chairs, and a copier.

I stared in disbelief at the person sitting at the scarred wooden table, peering at the screen before her.

Natalie.

She must have sensed someone watching her, because she looked up suddenly. A red flush crept up her neck as she gave me a halfhearted wave.

"Oh, do you two know each other?" the librarian asked.

"She's my aunt," I said as casually as I could manage.

"Natalie is your aunt?" Her eyebrows dipped. "Are you related to Matt?"

"Matt?"

"I guess not," she said with a small laugh. "Matt is Natalie's husband. *Was.* May he rest in peace." Her head tipped to the side as she studied my face. "But if you're not on Matt's side of the family . . . Oh my God. Are you Anna Kate?"

Small towns never ceased to amaze me. "I am. Anna Kate Callow."

The librarian grabbed my hand—not to shake but to hold. She clasped it tightly. "I'm Mary Beth Sheehan. It's good to meet you. Zee was a wonderful woman, may *she* rest in peace. She was a regular here, and we miss her so. It was such a *shock* to learn she had a granddaughter. I went to school with your mama. No one even knew she was pregnant when she left town." She *tsk*ed. "Such a tragic shame what happened."

I didn't know if she was referring to my mom being pregnant, her leaving town, the car accident, or my mother's or Zee's deaths. It was possible she meant *all* of it.

I tried to free my hand, but Mary Beth held on tight. I disliked the grip more than hugging. "Were you friends with my mother?"

"Not especially. Eden was a quiet sort. Kept to herself a lot. Didn't have any best friends to speak of, unless you count AJ and Aubin. Have you met Aubin Pavegeau yet? He's a bit of a hermit these

187

days." She dropped her voice. "He was in a bad car crash years ago, lost his wife—may she rest in peace—and he never quite recovered. Anyway, he and AJ were thick as thieves growing up. When Eden started dating AJ, it was only natural she became part of their friendship. You have her eyes. Such a pretty color, that *green*. Oh! It's so good to meet you."

"Thank you." I finally freed my hand and hooked a thumb toward the door. "I don't want to keep you when you probably have other things to do, so Natalie can show me how to use the microfiche. I'll come find you if I have any problems."

"Sure, sure." Mary Beth grinned. "You know where to find me. Oh! I am pleased as all get-out that you're in Wicklow. You'll love it here. I just know it. Come see me on your way out, and I'll set you up with a library card." She gave a full-body wiggle of happiness before pivoting and walking away.

Natalie had a wry smile on her face when I finally opened the door and stepped inside. I took a deep breath, blew it out.

"Bless your heart," Natalie said, pure syrup.

"Is Mary Beth related to Faylene? She has to be, right?"

"She's Faylene's first cousin. Their mothers are sisters, though Faylene's mama is passed on a fair time now."

"May she rest in peace," we said in unison and couldn't help laughing at each other.

As I pulled up a chair and sat down next to her, I couldn't remember the last time I'd laughed. It felt good.

I tried to mind my own business, but couldn't keep from saying, "No doubt you heard Mary Beth mention your husband just now, and Faylene did earlier, too, at the café. I'm really sorry."

Her hand fisted, released. "That's kind of you to say so, Anna Kate, but I really don't like talking about it." She wrinkled her nose. "Mostly because I hope he's *not* resting in peace at all."

Pain flashed across her face. It was so unlike everything I knew of her to this point that I immediately knew Matt Walker had hurt her terribly. I hated him instantly. "I see. Then I hope he's rotting to pieces in eternal squalor."

She looked over at me, and ever so slowly, she smiled, a bright smile that filled her eyes with warmth, making them look like melted chocolate ganache. Her shoulders loosened as the tension faded. "That's the nicest thing I've heard in a long time." She let out a light laugh. "And I shouldn't have said what I did. It's just that I've been stuck in the angry stage of grief for quite a while now."

"I understand that," I said. "I've been there myself, but I'm guessing there's a little more to your anger than mine."

189

What was I doing? This was all much too friendly. Yet I couldn't stop from trying to help her through her pain. "If you ever want to talk . . ."

Sometimes being a Callow stunk, plain and simple.

I did not need to help everyone.

I didn't.

Stupid *heritage*.

Oblivious to my inner turmoil, she stretched out her long, tan legs next to the table. She had on sandals with a slight heel but hadn't once complained of aching feet during her shift, even though I could see an angry blister near her left baby toe. I was beginning to believe she was part Stepford after all.

"Thanks, Anna Kate. Maybe I'll tell you about it sometime. Only not today. Or tomorrow. Or the next day."

"Well, you have until the end of July before I move back to Massachusetts for medical school. Plenty of time."

Her eyebrows went up. "Medical school? Family doctor, I'm guessing."

I knew why she'd taken that guess. It was because my father was supposed to have become a family doctor, going into practice with Doc Linden to continue the Linden legacy. "I'm not sure yet." Family medicine didn't appeal to me. Most traditional medicine didn't, if I were being honest. "I'm drawn more toward integrative medicine, osteopathy, or homeopathy." My mother wouldn't approve, but it was the only way I was going to make it through medical school.

Natalie nodded, but I noted her frown and the way the skin pulled together between her eyes.

"What's that look? Do you not believe in natural medicine?"

"Oh! No, *I* do." She pressed her hands to her chest.

I noticed she did that a lot—when she was being earnest.

"Let me guess. Your father doesn't."

"My mother *and* my father. I think the term 'quackery' has been said a time or two about the subject."

"Well, it's good then that it isn't their decision." And suddenly, it made sense to me why my mother had shied away from holistic medicine. I'd bet a zucchini plant that my dad hadn't believed in natural medicine either. She'd denied *her* heritage to give *his* importance.

No wonder she and Zee were always snippy with each other on the matter.

"Very true," Natalie said. "It's important to follow your own path."

She said it with such conviction that I suspected she was saying it more to herself than me. *Mind your own business, Anna Kate,* I told myself, even while biting back a dozen questions. I wanted to know the details of her childhood, how it had

191

been living with the Lindens, how she knew Bow and Jena so well, and, mostly, I longed to know everything, every last detail, about my dad. I needed to change the subject, so I said, "I'm a bit surprised to see you here."

She glanced at the newspaper article she'd been reading. "I feel like a kid who got caught with her hand in the cookie jar."

I glanced at the headline that had been zoomed in on.

CAR CRASH KILLS WICKLOW STANDOUT

Leaning in, I studied the face of Andrew James Linden in a photograph that looked like it might have been one of his senior pictures. Dimples framed a wide smile. Downturned blue eyes sparkled with mischief, and freckles dotted his nose and cheeks. His gingery blond hair was cut short and styled in gelled spikes. "My mother only had one or two photos of him. I've never seen this one."

"I'm surprised she didn't have more. Didn't they date for years?"

"Three years, since the start of sophomore year in high school." I stared at the photo, wishing for things that were impossible. "My mother wasn't much for picture taking. Or having her picture taken. Do your parents have any photos of them together?"

"Not that I've ever seen," she said.

"They probably would have ripped my mother out of them anyway."

After a moment, she said, "Probably so."

I admired that she didn't try to sugarcoat it. "Why are you looking at these old articles?"

She leaned back in the chair. "All my life I grew up believing Eden had gotten away with murder—it's all I ever heard. But last night I heard my parents arguing, and Daddy claimed the crash had been an accident. Mama said it was murder. I don't know much about what happened that day—I was only a toddler—but it was unsettling to know that the crash might have been an accident after all. Since I really don't want to ask my parents for more details, I came here for more information. Unfortunately, most of the articles are generic. Lots of 'the crash is still under investigation,' " she added, using air quotes.

I scanned the article. It had been a sunny day when the car veered off a back road and hit a tree. The passenger, Andrew James Linden, died instantly. The driver, Eden Callow, had been taken to the hospital and was in serious condition. Preliminary reports showed that no drugs or alcohol had been involved and that speed hadn't been a factor in the crash. An interesting tidbit was that it had been my dad's car. So why had my mother been driving?

Natalie said, "Is it true Eden couldn't remember the crash? My mother always said it was convenient amnesia on Eden's part."

"It's true. She only knows what people told her. Do you know why my mom would have been driving the car?"

"No idea. But my mother is absolutely convinced they had a fight about him going off to college and leaving Eden behind, and in a fit of rage, she drove off the road, aiming to kill them both, only Eden survived."

It was the same story Jena had told me. "Mom wished she hadn't survived. If she hadn't been pregnant with me, I think she'd have found a way to join him much sooner than she did. She loved him more than life itself, and because I was a part of him, she loved me enough to raise me until I could take care of myself."

I tried to tell myself that sharing this information wasn't overly personal, that it was our history, but it felt like a lie.

Natalie set a hand on my arm. "She didn't . . . she didn't kill herself, did she?"

"Not purposely, no. But she never went to the doctor, and ignored the warning signs of the blood clot that led to a heart attack. I figured her heart finally had enough grieving and just gave in. But the thing is, she always claimed that she'd never, ever hurt my dad on purpose. That they loved each other and planned to get married. She doesn't remember how that car ended up in the trees, but she knew it was an accident."

"Why did she leave Wicklow so soon after the accident? My mother always said it was because of her guilty conscience."

How I could so despise a woman I'd never even met was a mystery to me.

"She left town because of *me*. What would your parents have done if they'd known she was pregnant with AJ's baby?"

She paled. "They would have tried to get full custody."

"Exactly. They had the money, the resources, the clout, and the emotional desperation . . ."

Natalie let out a weary sigh. "Tell me this, Anna Kate . . ."

I glanced at her, waiting.

"Why are *you* here today? Why did you want to see these old articles?"

Rubbing at an ink stain on the tabletop, I said, "Mostly for the same reason you are. I want more information. My mom rarely talked about the accident, but when she did . . ."

"What?"

"I couldn't help thinking there was more to the story. I think I have the right to know what truly happened that day."

"If anyone does, it's you. So what now?"

"Maybe there's more information on the police report?"

"Probably. But that was twenty-five years ago—long before most police stations became computerized. Do departments keep paper reports that long?"

I looked at my father's smiling face on the computer screen and once again felt a tug of sorrow. "I don't know, but I'm going to find out."

11

"Excuse me," the reporter said to the young woman hustling between tables.

"Can I help you?" she asked, her brown eyes bright with youth, yet dim with a sorrow that told him she'd already had a hard life.

"I was just thinking I might need to stay the night in town, so I can see these blackbirds for myself. I saw the motel was full. Is there any other place to stay nearby?"

"There's a few places taking people in," she said. "Let me check around, and I'll get back to you."

"I'll be here," he said.

Natalie

"Sixty-six, sixty-seven." I stared at the stack of money on the table. I'd earned nearly seventy dollars in tips at the café today, on top of the hourly wage Anna Kate had paid me.

It was a start.

I put five dollars into Ollie's piggy bank, put twenty in my wallet, and tucked the rest into an old metal watch box that I hid in my underwear drawer. Which, I quickly realized, was probably the first place a burglar would look, so I then moved it into the bathroom, under the sink. Much safer there, mixed among shampoo, soap, and bath toys.

I'd done some checking around and found a one-bedroom apartment in town that ran at four hundred dollars a month, not including utilities. I'd need first and last month's rent as a deposit before I could even think about moving out of the little house—and out from under my mother's iron fist. I'd need to eventually find a full-time *permanent* job as well.

Taking a deep breath to quell rising panic, I told myself finding another job was a worry for another day. For now, I'd squirrel away as much money as I could. The thought of building a nest egg appealed to me so much that I took the twenty out of my wallet and put it into the watch box, swapping it for a ten-dollar bill. Then I swapped that for a five.

Ollie sat on the floor of the living room, in the green Tinkerbell costume my mother had bought for her to wear to tonight's moonlight movie. Pushing a dump truck loaded with blocks across the throw rug, Ollie didn't look the least bit tired, even though it was closing in on bedtime.

Taking a moment, I simply watched her play and thanked my lucky stars that there had been no drama with the swimming lesson this morning. According to Mama, Ollie had taken to the water like a fish and had stayed in the pool with her long after the lesson had ended. All of which had been reported with a smugness I could've done without. It had taken every last ounce of maintaining some semblance of peace, as phony as it was, to keep my mouth shut. To simply say "Thank you, Mama, for keeping Ollie all day."

I took another deep breath to settle my suddenly queasy stomach and tamp down my anger. Ollie was fine. Happy. Alive. No harm, no foul.

But how many lessons would it take for me to be okay with Ollie being near water? How long until the paralyzing fear subsided? Because right now, I didn't see an end in sight.

Out the front window, I noticed my father walking toward the little house and suddenly had second thoughts about going with my parents to the movie at the courthouse tonight.

It seemed easier to stay here. Easier, that is, than dealing with everybody's condolences and questions and Mama's frostiness.

I pulled open the door before Daddy could knock. He stepped inside and handed me a plastic grocery bag.

I peeked inside. "What's this?"

"Window alarms. I thought they might help set your mind at ease after this morning." He bent and opened his arms wide, and Ollie went running toward him.

"Gaddy!" Ollie shouted.

It was her shorthand for "granddaddy." I was learning that toddlers were quite inventive at creating words.

"Well, aren't you the prettiest thing I've seen all day," he said to Ollie, fluffing the gossamer petals of her costume's skirt. "You know what's missing, though?" From his pocket he pulled out a hand-carved, scarred green tractor, its finish worn thin from use and time.

Her face lit up. "Tactor!"

He said, "That tractor was mine when I was a boy, then AJ's. I thought it was time to pass it onto someone who would love it as much as we did."

Ollie happily dumped the blocks out of her dump truck, then set the tractor in the truck's bed. She pushed both around the rug, running over the blocks in her path.

My chest swelled with emotion. This was why I'd moved back, I reminded myself. This was what made the aggravation and fights with my mother worth it. For Ollie to have these little connections to my family. If I had stayed in Montgomery, that beloved tractor would have remained a dusty relic on AJ's bedroom shelf. Because Ollie and I had come here, a piece of my daddy and my brother would now have a place in Ollie's heart. In mine as well.

"Thank you," I said, trying to keep my voice steady. "She already loves it, as you can see."

200

He rocked on his heels. A sure sign something was on his mind. I waited him out and he finally said, "Heard you did some waitressing today."

"I'd say a lot of waitressing. The café was packed." I fussed with the stacks of fabric samples I'd laid out on the countertop. I planned to work on Faylene's headband order after Ollie went to bed. "So Mama knows too, then?"

"She received six calls, three emails, and a bouquet of flowers from concerned friends, all before eleven o'clock."

Sometimes I despised small towns. "Yet Mama didn't mention a single word about it when she brought Ollie home earlier."

"Did you want her to?" When I didn't answer, he added, "What are you doing, Natalie? Why are you working at the café, knowing how your mother would likely feel?"

My skin heated. "I went there to buy a piece of pie, but there wasn't any today. I stayed because I need a job much more than Mama needs her pride."

Lord knew there was a time I would've set out to make my mother miserable on purpose, but I was past that. I wanted peace—and was willing to give up a lot to make that happen.

Just not this.

"If you need money . . ."

"I need to earn my *own* money."

"I see," he said after a moment. "And Ollie?"

"I've made arrangements with Faylene Wiggins."
She had been more than generous to take on
watching Ollie a few days a week. We'd argued
for a good five minutes about me paying her—
she'd been set on doing it for free—but finally
she agreed to take my money. It wasn't anywhere
near the going rate for babysitting or daycare,
but it was enough to make me feel like I wasn't
freeloading. "Faylene keeps her granddaughter a
couple of days a week, so Ollie will have a friend
to play with."

"You do know you could have asked your
mother."

I crossed my arms stubbornly. I could've
asked my mother. I probably *should* have.
But I hadn't wanted to. It was as simple—and
as complicated—as that. Instead of debating
my decision with my father, I said, "It's utter
foolishness that someone sent Mama flowers.
Flowers! Good Lord."

He cracked a smile. "The flowers came with a
sympathy card."

"You're kidding."

"Sadly, no."

I couldn't help but laugh. It was either that or
lose my mind. "Honestly, I didn't set out to disappoint Mama yet again, but I don't see anything
wrong with working at the café. Or getting to
know Anna Kate. She's family. This feud with
the Callows has gone on long enough."

Ollie rolled the tractor over our feet, then up the side of the coffee table. She was babbling in her own language as she did so, completely oblivious to the strife around her.

I longed for that kind of peace of mind.

It was he who dodged the debate this time by saying, "You went to the café for a piece of pie? Blackbird pie?"

"That's right," I said, hearing the defensiveness in my own voice. "No need to make a big deal about it."

"Who's making a big deal?" he asked casually.

Obviously, he'd picked up on the defensiveness, too.

Ollie drove the tractor over the back of the couch, and I tried my mightiest to focus on the good in my life.

Daddy started rocking on his heels again. Sticking his hands in his pockets, he said, "I happened to speak to a colleague in Fort Payne this afternoon. She has an appointment available next Thursday if you want it."

Instantly suspicious, I said, "What kind of colleague?"

"A counselor."

"What kind of counselor?"

"A grief counselor."

I clasped my hands together and prayed to the good Lord above for patience. "I've had therapy."

"It might be time for more," he said calmly.

"You said yourself you're still having nightmares. And I heard you had some sort of panic attack in town this morning."

"You've been hearing lots today, haven't you? Who told you?" So help me if he'd received flowers, too.

"Does it matter? Were you clinging to a lamppost, white as a sheet, or not?"

Embarrassment set my cheeks on fire. " 'Clinging' seems a little overexaggerated. I was merely holding on to the lamppost. Tightly."

"When did your panic attacks come back?"

I didn't want to admit that they'd never entirely left, so I shrugged in answer.

He gave me a pointed look. "Also, let's not forget that fight with your mother yesterday . . ."

"Which was about her controlling nature, not anything to do with grief."

"Is that so?"

"The decision about swimming lessons should have been mine to make. No one else's."

"I agree," he said.

"Then why didn't you side with me last night, when you heard Mama and me arguing?"

"Because it *is* in Ollie's best interest to learn how to swim."

Confused, I stared at him. "Whose side are you on? Because I'm getting mixed signals."

"I'm not taking sides. I'm trying to help."

"Well, you're not." I kept my voice low, tame,

204

as to not alert Ollie that there was tension in the air. She seemed oblivious, however, as she stacked blocks only to plow them over with her new toy.

"Don't you see, Natalie? You allowed fear to make the decision. You weren't thinking about what you knew, as Ollie's mama, was best for your little girl, because you *do* know that Ollie learning to swim is a good thing. You let fear take away your voice."

His words, and knowing he was right, cut like a jagged, rusty knife. I turned away from him, unable to look at him a moment longer without bursting into tears. I'd sworn off crying long ago. Tears did nothing at all except make me feel like I was drowning too.

"The blame," he said, "for that argument last night isn't on your mother, and it's not on you. It's on the accident that killed someone you loved deeply. It might be a good thing to talk to someone about that, a bit more in depth."

He reached around me, a business card in his hand.

I stared at it through blurry eyes before taking it.

"Grief can change a person to the point where they become someone they don't know, or even like very much. I don't want that to happen to you. Or to Ollie."

I had the feeling his message was more than

advice—it was an explanation. My mother had changed completely after AJ died, but she had never sought help to deal with her grief. Would life have been different for me if she had? Or was there no turning back after experiencing the pain of losing a child?

He gave my shoulder a squeeze. "You're not going to find healing in a piece of pie, Natalie. The healing's got to come from within you. Make the appointment, please?"

Unable to talk, I nodded. I'd call.

"We'll be leaving in five minutes," he said. "Are you walking over to the courthouse with us?"

If I was going to back out of going to the movie, now was the time to do so. As much as I wanted to stay home, my father's wisdom had hit its mark. What was best for Ollie? My gaze drifted to my daughter, in her Tinkerbell outfit, with that scarred toy tractor clutched in her hand as if it were the most priceless object in the world.

Maybe it was.

I closed my hand around the business card and found my voice. "I need to pack a few things, so it might take a minute. You don't have to wait for us if you need to get going."

"We'll wait for you, Natalie," he said quietly as he walked to the door. "Always have. Always will."

Anna Kate

Saturday at almost midnight, I sipped my hot tea and tried not to stress.

Today, I'd sold four kinds of blackbird pies, twelve in total. I'd increased the pie output because of a tip from Mr. Boyd late yesterday afternoon. He'd mentioned how word of the blackbirds had spread throughout southern birding groups and many were headed here this weekend for a glimpse of the rare birds. They'd arrived in full force this morning, and not a crumb of pie remained by noon.

All those pies had held a secret—a teaspoonful of mulberry syrup, which on its own was pretty terrible, but it was practically undetectable in pie filling to those who weren't looking for it.

The flavor of the mulberry came across boldly to me, as if my taste buds had been searching for it all along, and I hoped the syrup would be enough to get the blackbirds to sing. I had the feeling the proper secret ingredient was a fully ripened mulberry, but I still didn't know how Zee had managed to use them in pies year-round. For now, the syrup would have to do.

Whether the syrup had worked its magic, I'd know tonight.

Looking out the window, I saw that the birders gathered seemed just as anxious as I was—fidgety and oddly quiet.

Unable to stand still, I itched to cook something, anything, but I didn't want to mess up the clean kitchen. I'd already made another twelve pies for tomorrow: apple, peach, blackberry, and rhubarb. They sat in the pie case, their flaky crusts the perfect shade of golden brown.

Instead, I washed my teacup and busied myself by neatening rags in the laundry room, triple-checking inventory, and making sure the restroom was spotless.

Finally—finally—the clock turned over to twelve.

I shut off all the lights inside but kept on the outdoor lights that dimly illuminated the backyard. I stood at the screen door. Crickets, katydids, and frogs vied for volume, and fireflies were like sparks of magic in the garden.

The thick, humid air stilled as the blackbirds emerged from the leafy tunnel, and it seemed to me that they took extra time tonight in the sky, soaring and circling in rhythm like some sort of dance only they knew. An aerial ballet.

The night silenced as the blackbirds landed, the fireflies dimmed, and the blackbirds . . . began to sing.

Tender notes, sweetly melodious. Even with no lyrics, the songs told stories of love, of life, of laughter, of sadness, of hope. Harmonies rose, then fell as if in conversation, the emotional tones eliciting in me memories of my mom and me standing side by side at the sink, doing dishes together as we talked of weekend plans. It reminded me of Zee and me, holding hands as we walked along dense wooded pathways, the air heavy with the scent of the earth.

It seemed as though time stood still as I listened to the ethereal symphony, my chest aching, my throat tightening as my soul found peace for the first time in a long while.

When the blackbirds finished their glorious songs, the birders erupted in applause. I closed and locked the door, and climbed the stairs with tears in my eyes. I waited up for a while longer, hoping for another visit from the two rogue blackbirds, but they never came.

Still wrapped in that feeling of peace, I fell into bed and closed my eyes, and tried not to worry about how hard it was going to be to leave the magic of Wicklow behind.

12

Anna Kate

The following morning, I crouched in the garden, a basket at my feet as I filled it with the day's bounty. "I see you've forgiven me," I said to the zucchini plant closest to the deck steps. I tugged a small zucchini from its stem, its beautiful green skin seemingly more vibrant in the hazy morning light than it would be in full sunshine. "Aren't you pretty? What shall we make with you? Frittatas? Fries?" Anything but zucchini loaves was just fine with me.

I'd decided to nurture the zucchini instead of curse it. The two plants were coming along nicely. In only a few days, they'd lost their sickly appearance and had perked up. They were still on the small side, but I had faith they'd be full and healthy in no time. There were plenty of orange-colored blossoms peeking through the leaves.

As I worked collecting more zucchini, cucumbers, squash, beans, and rhubarb, I tuned out the drone of birders camped in the side yard. Many had come to me yesterday for permission to set up tents, which I allowed, or pop-up campers, which I had not. The yard already looked enough like a campground without any trailers parked there. However, Pebbles Lutz had offered up her back field to recreational vehicles for the cost of only twenty dollars a night. The acreage was already on its way to being full.

I halfheartedly pulled crabgrass as I walked around the garden, noting that I needed to spend some time doing it right. Zee, I decided, must have spent hours out here every day just on the upkeep. I checked on the progress of the tomatoes and two lonesome corn stalks and stopped in front of the yarrow.

Doc Linden had stopped by the café again this morning to reissue his invitation to supper this afternoon. I'd declined, and he said he'd be back in a few days to ask me to next week's meal. He could ask until he was blue in the face. It wasn't going to happen.

I finally made my way over to the mulberry trees and smiled at the leaves, seeing that they were flat, not curled. Some brown tips remained, but hopefully after a few more songs, the trees would flourish once again. I picked a cluster of mulberries—the pinkest ones I could find—to make another batch of syrup. As I headed back to the café, I saw Summer Pavegeau coming up the path from the side gate, a basket on her arm.

"Good morning, ma'—Anna Kate."

"Hi, Summer," I said. "You're up early."

Today she wore a pale blue dress that highlighted her tanned skin and those big blue eyes. Her long hair shone in the morning light, sunbeams glancing off natural highlights. On her feet were a pair of leather sandals, and she looked like she wanted nothing more than to kick them off and go barefoot as she shifted foot to foot.

"I usually come by early on Sundays, before church."

"Makes sense. Thanks for the eggs you've been leaving on the deck these past couple of days. Come on inside, and I'll get your payment. Would you like a piece of pie, too?"

Hope bloomed in her eyes. "Is it fixed?"

She followed me up the steps and into the kitchen. "I think so?" I wouldn't know for sure until Mr. Lazenby arrived. He was my test subject. "The blackbirds are singing again."

I set my basket on the counter and checked the crock-pot. I was making a salve to give to Natalie for her blisters, and using the crock-pot to speed along the process.

A faint sheen of moisture glazed her eyes. "Then yes, ma'am, I'd like a piece, if you have enough to spare."

I let the "ma'am" slide as I glanced over my shoulder at the twelve pies in the case. "I guess that depends on how many pieces you'd like."

She laughed, then looked around. "Why does it smell like marigolds in here?"

"Calendula-infused oil." I motioned to the crock-pot. *Calendula officinalis* was best known as the common marigold. "Marigold petals have great healing properties for skin ailments and injuries." Among many other things. In tea, it helped with digestive issues.

She smiled. "Cool."

I thought so too.

Then her gaze narrowed as she looked in my basket. "You do know that those pink mulberries are going to be sour."

"Oh, I know they are. I'm making syrup with them, using lots of sugar to sweeten them up."

"Syrup would taste better if the berries were ripe," she said slowly, as if wanting to correct my decision without coming off as critical.

"I still have a good week or so before the mulberries will be ripe, and I need them now." I unpacked the rest of the basket, hoping she didn't ask me why. I wasn't sure I was allowed to share the secret ingredient to someone who wasn't a family member.

"Oh, for the pies?"

I almost dropped a zucchini. "How'd you know?"

She smiled, a slow, sly smile. "For one, I can taste them. Also, for the last few years, Zee hired me on to help her gather the berries, remove their stems, and process them." She frowned. "The stems are a nightmare."

"Wait, process them?"

"Sure. Zee has years' worth stashed away in

small jars. They're adorable, the jars, but time-consuming to assemble and steam. I'm surprised you haven't been using those for your *syrup,*" she said, as though I were making cow pies, not something edible.

"There's no processed mulberries. I've looked. Bow and Jena haven't seen any either."

"Oh my word. I'm sorry. I didn't even think— Zee claimed those mulberries were the most valuable thing in the café, and didn't like people knowing about them. She hid them. I should've thought to tell you, seeing as how you're making the pies now. I'll show you where they are."

I immediately thought it odd that Zee hadn't told Bow and Jena of the mulberry cache but trusted Summer with the information. She'd told the couple about me, as she had with Summer, so why not share the mulberries with them too?

I followed her into the pantry, and she closed the door behind us. "Just in case."

Baffled, I went along, not entirely sure why she was taking me into the pantry when I'd already told her there were no mulberries to be found.

"Here, scoot out of the way, Anna Kate."

I ducked in behind her. "I've searched this pantry, top to—"

My words died in my throat as she grabbed the molding on the shelving unit closest to the door and pulled. The floor-to-ceiling wooden shelf swung outward, revealing a secret room.

My jaw dropped. "A hidden door?"

"Yes, ma'am." She went into the darkened space and flipped on a light. "I call this the Harry Potter room for obvious reasons."

I smiled. Because Harry had slept in a cupboard under the stairs. I followed her inside and noticed the slanted ceiling—this room was also under the stairs. Long and narrow, an apartment-size refrigerator stood along one of the walls, but most of the space was lined with shelving. The far wall held canning supplies—empty jars and lids—but the rest of the shelves were stocked with processed mulberries in small jelly jars. I picked up a jar, held it to the light.

Summer stood back as I took it all in. She said, "Each jar has two tablespoons of mashed mulberries in it. The jars are processed with a simple syrup of sugar and water."

There had to be a thousand jars in here. Maybe more. It was hard to tell with the way they were stacked. My eyes suddenly filled with tears thinking of how much *love* this room held.

"Each harvest makes near about five hundred jars. One jar makes six pies—one teaspoon per each since there's three teaspoons in a tablespoon. A teaspoon's worth doesn't seem like enough to me, but Zee always said it was plenty."

I hugged the jar to my chest. "Summer, I can't even tell you what this means to me."

"I'm just sorry I didn't think of it earlier."

"Better late than never," I said, tucking the jar back on the shelf. "Bow and Jena will be here soon, so we should probably close this place back up."

But I'd be back—later tonight, and I'd finally make the blackbird pies the way Zee had intended them to be made.

Summer gave me a quick lesson on how to operate the swinging door, and I hired her on the spot to help me gather this year's mulberries when they were ready.

I was cutting into an apple pie to give her a slice when Bow and Jena came sailing through the back door.

"Where have you been hiding, Summer?" Bow asked as he grabbed an apron from the rack near the door. "Haven't seen you in days."

As he slid the apron over his head, it caught on his hair, tugging it away from his left ear. I noticed he had a small scar along the upper curve.

"I haven't been hiding," Summer said, but looked quickly away.

I slid the pie into a to-go box, wondering about her strange reaction.

Jena tipped her head. "This isn't about Natalie working here, is it?"

It seemed to me her melodious way of speaking had taken on an even softer tone.

Summer glanced at the back door. "I should be going."

"Oh, sugar." Jena shook her head. "Natalie's just Natalie. Give her a chance."

I handed Summer the pie box. "I don't understand . . . you don't like Natalie?"

"I don't *not* like her," Summer said. "I don't really know her."

"You're not the only one who has issues with the Lindens," Jena said to me.

"What did they do to you, Summer?" I asked.

"To me?" she said. "Nothing. To my dad . . ."

Jena said, "Seelie didn't much approve of Aubin, either."

A bright flash of anger went through me. "Does she approve of anyone?"

"A few," Jena said with a smile. "But, Summer, honey, Natalie isn't her mama."

Summer shrugged and looked away.

"Seems to me," Bow said as he went about preheating the ovens, "there's a whole lot of people around here carrying around a heap of pain tied to the past. Might be time to start letting that go and start healing."

Jena said, "I agree."

I crossed my arms. "Letting go is easier said than done."

Summer nodded her agreement.

Jena patted my cheek. "But sweetie, letting go is the only way you can fly."

Her words rang in my ears as I went for my purse to pay Summer before she left. I owed her for several days of eggs and also for the blackberries.

When I handed her the money, she said, "This is too much, Anna Kate."

"No, it's not. That was a huge container of blackberries you left here. Plus, the eggs. Don't argue."

She snapped her lips closed, then smiled. "Thank you. I can use the extra money for college."

"College!" Jena cried. "I didn't know you were leaving us. Where are you going? When?"

"'Bama," Summer said with a shy smile. "In August."

"Roll Tide!" Bow pumped a fist.

"Well, that's just wonderful." Jena beamed. "Good on you! I bet your daddy's tickled."

"He's proud. Prouder than usual," Summer added.

"What will you study?" Jena asked.

"I'm not sure yet. Ecology? Forestry? Something outdoorsy—I can't imagine having a job in an office all day, all cooped up."

I thought back to the first time I met her, with her reddish-purple fingers and filthy feet. Nature was her calling, no doubt about it.

"I have time to decide," she said. "I'll take general-ed courses my first year, then pick a major."

Bow wiped his hands on a cloth. "If you need help moving down, you let me know."

"I will," she said. "Thanks."

She offered her goodbyes and was on her way out when she abruptly turned around. "I almost forgot to give you this, Anna Kate." She handed me an envelope. "It's from my father."

"What is it?" I asked, turning it over to see my name written out in scratchy penmanship.

"Don't know. He only said to make sure I got it to you. Bye, all!" She went out the back door, and it slammed closed behind her.

"I really need to fix that," Bow said, edging closer to me.

"Yes, you do," Jena agreed as she sidled up. "What have you got there, Anna Kate?"

I laughed as they hovered, their blatant nosiness on full display. "Only one way to find out." I slid my finger under the envelope's flap and lifted it. Inside was a lone piece of lined paper, folded in thirds. I pulled it out, not sure what to expect. When I saw what he'd written, I couldn't help feeling like I'd been given a wonderful gift.

A little taste of happiness for you, Anna Kate.— Aubin

Below it, he'd carefully written out his recipe for blackberry tea.

My gaze swept over the recipe as I took in every detail, but my head came up suddenly when someone pounded on the front door.

Mr. Lazenby had his face pressed to the glass.

Jena chuckled. "I think that's for you, Anna Kate."

Taking a deep breath, I tried to read Mr. Lazenby's expression. If the mulberry syrup had worked, the pie he ate yesterday would have brought him a dream from his loved one last night.

I saw that he had tears in his eyes, and my heart sank as I pulled open the door. "It didn't work?"

He ducked his chin, then stepped forward and threw his arms around me in a bear hug. "It worked just fine, Miss Anna Kate. Thank you."

No one was more shocked than I was when I hugged him back.

13

"You live near here, don't you?"

"Up the mountain a bit, in a cabin on Creek Hill," Cam Kolbaugh said.

"Great area for photographing wildlife." The reporter jotted a note.

Cam adjusted his camera strap. "Some of the best."

"Have you managed to get any shots of the black-birds?"

Cam reviewed the photos on his camera. "Haven't been able to capture a clear shot quite yet." He turned the screen toward the reporter.

"Blurry and hazy. Is that because it's a night shot?"

Cam clicked a button, and the screen went black. His gaze shifted toward the back of the café, out the window to the mulberry trees. "I don't think so."

Natalie

"I should just cancel," I said under my breath as I hotfooted it from the little house to my car parked at the far end of the driveway.

It had been a day.

Actually, it had been a *week*.

A week of dealing with my mother's chill because I hadn't asked her to watch Ollie while I worked at the café, which was in addition to her iciness that I had taken the part-time job in the first place.

There had been nonstop guests at the café—people who'd come to see the blackbirds, a phenomenon I admit I thought would fizzle within a few days but only seemed to be picking up steam.

I was already worried about Ollie's swimming lesson the next morning and trying my hardest not to think of her going under the water and not coming back up.

On top of it all, I was dreading the appointment I had with the grief counselor down in Fort Payne this afternoon. I'd almost canceled three times in the last few days and was currently mulling it again.

Even the thought of talking about Matt dredged up emotions I'd rather keep tamped down. It was easier that way. I'd been fending off panic attacks left and right this week, and I was spent from the effort.

If not for my father, I might already have the answers that would bring about peace in my life.

You're not going to find healing in a piece of pie, Natalie. The healing's got to come from within you.

It was one thing to disappoint my mother on purpose, but I couldn't bring myself to do the same with my father, so I tried to take his words to heart. I hadn't eaten the pie, and I'd made the appointment with the counselor. Baby steps.

If this appointment in any way, shape, or form helped me to be a better mother to Ollie, it would be worth it. The last thing I ever wanted was for Ollie to witness one of my panic attacks—something she'd come too close to seeing recently. As much as I hated to admit it, even to myself, I needed help.

The small brown bird that I'd been seeing a lot lately sat on the fence railing next to my car, not looking the least bit disturbed by my presence as it used its beak to clean under its crooked wing. The ribbon of black coloring near its eye made it look like it had drawn-on eyebrows, and the thought of a bird wearing makeup suddenly lightened my mood.

The blooming pink viburnums lining the driveway filled the air with a sweet floral scent, which was a whole lot more pleasant than the perfume of bacon, coffee, biscuits, and chicken-fried steak that I'd worn home from work.

Unwilling to go to my appointment smelling like the café, I'd taken precious minutes to shower. I braided my wet hair, since I didn't have time to style it properly, and changed into a long lightweight skirt and sleeveless blouse. I chose my loosest sandals, ones that wouldn't rub my healing blisters. A salve Anna Kate had given me had worked wonders, but the new skin was still tender.

As quick as I'd cleaned myself up, I was still running late. Since most everywhere in Wicklow was walkable, it had been a month since I'd driven my tiny white hatchback. The neglect showed. The rain that had come through the night before had smeared together the dirt and pollen that encased the car, making the paint job look like it had been done at the hands of an Impressionist. I couldn't remember how much gas I had left in the tank, and then there was the matter of the dangling muffler. Crouching down, I peeked under the bumper and saw that someone—most likely my father—had placed a plastic pan under the car to catch dripping oil.

He was forever cleaning up my messes.

I made the quick decision that the muffler was on its own—I didn't have time to fuss with it. At the filling station on the way out of town, I'd stop to see if someone could add a quart of oil to the engine while I filled the gas tank.

It would all be fine.

Just fine.

Absolutely fine.

I dropped my head into my hands, took a deep breath to pull myself together, and Lord help me, I swore I could still smell hickory-smoked bacon on my fingers.

A quivery female voice came from nearby.

"Don't you cancel that appointment, Natalie."

My head snapped up as I looked around. I didn't see anyone. "Hello?"

Slowly turning in a circle, my gaze swept the area, zeroing in on places where someone could hide. Other than a few birds and some bees, I was alone as far as I could tell.

Chill bumps rose along my skin. The voice, I realized, sounded exactly like the one that had woken me last week.

Your father is dying.

I'd done my level best to forget that unsettling declaration, chalking it up to a bad dream. But now . . . I wasn't sure what was going on. Could be I was overheated and my mind was playing tricks. It *was* hot and humid.

Throwing a wary look over my shoulder, I started wondering if the voice was my conscience speaking. I didn't know what that theory meant in terms of my father and his health, however.

I threw a glance at the big house. I had spent much of this past Sunday's supper studying him, looking for any trace that he was ill. On the surface, he didn't appear to be. If I was nitpicking, I'd say his skin color was a bit off, but I didn't know if that was because he'd been golfing the day before and had a bit of a sunburn, or if it was due to something else.

There were other things I'd noticed—only because I'd been looking. His appetite wasn't near to normal. He'd taken smaller portions and had poked at most of it. He'd seemed a little slower to lift up Ollie as well, as though he were in pain.

When I questioned him, he blamed his lack of an appetite on stress, and the pain on his golf game.

If I didn't know him so well, I'd have sworn he was lying.

But he didn't lie. It was one of his traits I loved most.

Still, by the time I went home that night, I couldn't ignore the pit in my stomach that something wasn't right with him. Whether it was the business with Anna Kate or something else . . . I wasn't sure.

"Git!" the voice said in a high-pitched tone, darn near operatic.

It sounded like it was coming from the driver's side of the car, near the fence, but there was nothing there but the bushes and that fastidious bird.

"I'm *going*," I said loudly, and there was no mistaking the irritability in my tone.

Car keys in hand, I prayed to the good Lord above that the car started. It was looking more and more likely that I'd be a few minutes late for my appointment. Which, now that I considered it, might not be a bad thing. A short initial meeting appealed to me. Get in, scratch the surface of my issues, get out. Nothing too deep or painful.

Leaving the door open to let the car exhale its

hot, stale air, I slid behind the wheel and groaned at the pulsing wave of blazing heat that nearly pushed me right back out. I tossed my purse on the passenger seat and leaned across to roll down the window, hoping a stiff breeze would blow through. Hurricane-force winds seemed delightful at the moment. The window stuck halfway, but I didn't have time to fight with it.

Sweat rose along my forehead as I put the key in the ignition. "Please start, please start, please start."

The engine coughed like an asthmatic at the perfume counter in a department store but didn't turn over. Taking a deep breath, I tried the ignition again, pressing gently on the gas pedal, hoping a little fuel would help the situation.

Unfortunately it didn't do anything other than fill the car with the odor of gas.

After counting to ten in my head, I turned the key again. The engine sputtered, died, and the scent of burning oil filtered through the vents. Cursing a blue streak, I pulled the key. The car would be no good to me at all if it caught fire, and though it probably deserved a quick, flaming death, I didn't want that to happen.

I'd scraped and scrounged and saved the money to buy the used car after Matt's death. Long after our two much-fancier cars had been repossessed. The hatchback was a bare-bones model. No fancy power windows, no radio. Its stick shift tended to, appropriately, stick, and the clutch made ungodly groaning noises. But it was *mine*.

I popped the hood, even though I had no earthly idea what I was looking for. Mama would have had a stroke if she ever caught me looking under the hood of a car, let alone tinkering with an engine. I could practically hear her now making a comment about who'd keep food on the mechanics' tables if we tended to our own cars, and did I want taking food out of babies' mouths on my conscience? Never even mind the grease issues.

As I lifted the hood I wasn't sure what I'd expected to see, but it surely wasn't a hastily formed bird's nest sitting right smack-dab on top of the battery. There was a single speckled egg in the nest that looked a lot like a mottled rock.

Even if I had been able to get the car started, there was no way I could bring myself to remove that nest. Not until after the egg hatched and the baby bird flew away.

My car wasn't going anywhere for quite a while.

Apparently, neither was I.

Closing my eyes, I waited for that singsong-y voice to tell me what to do now, since it was being so bossy this afternoon. Instead, I picked up the sound of barking. Barking that seemed to be growing louder and closer.

I peeked around the hood. Racing toward me

up the driveway was a dark gray cat being chased by—I squinted—River, Cam Kolbaugh's dog. Both animals ran at full speed, one barking, one growling.

"River! Stop! Heel!" I jumped in front of him and tried to grab his collar. He darted around me. The cat, one I recognized as a local stray who'd been around for what seemed like decades, zipped under the car's bumper, hissing the whole way, his ears flattened.

River followed the cat under, dropping his belly to the ground like he was taking part in some sort of army obstacle course.

"No, no!" I looked under the car. "Heel!"

Still yowling, they both avoided the pan of oil—thank God—and emerged on the other side of the car, near the passenger door. The cat took off again, circling around the car, River on his heels.

The noise of it all was about to do me in when screeching tires added to the ear-splitting chorus. Cam had parked his truck at the end of the driveway. "River!" he shouted, breaking into a sprint. "Down!"

The cat made his way back to me and leaped into the car, onto the driver's seat. I quickly slammed the door before River could go in after him.

Still barking his head off, River set his mud-crusted paws on the door and rose up on his hind

231

legs to look through the window. The suddenly serene cat looked quite smug as he watched River slobber on the glass. One ear came up, then the other, which I noticed was scarred. Probably from a run-in with a dog at some point. The cat's head tipped to the side, and he began washing his face, using a paw to stroke his cheek.

I grabbed River by the collar, keeping tight hold as Cam quickly clipped on a leash.

"Down, boy."

River glanced up at Cam, then slowly sat down, inch by inch, as if it were the last thing in the whole world he wanted to do.

"What was that all about?" he asked the dog.

River panted and wagged his tail.

To me, Cam said, "We were driving home when River suddenly jumped out the open window. I don't know what came over him—he's never done anything like that before."

I pointed inside the car. "A cat came over him."

But the cat was gone. I looked around. "He must have gone out the passenger window."

Cam scratched at his beard, and there was confusion in his tone when he said, "River's never gone after cats before."

"I'm sure the cat instigated it, right, River?" I patted his head.

Cam smiled. He had on mud-splattered hiking pants and a blue moisture-wicking shirt, also covered in grime. "Don't go giving him ideas that it's okay to chase cats." He spotted the open hood and said, "Car trouble?"

"If by trouble you mean catastrophe, then yes."

Looking under the hood, Cam whistled. "Looks like a squatter's made herself right at home, and that's the least of the problems."

"Can't say I blame her. The car hasn't budged since I parked it here a month ago."

"This is your car?" The confusion was back in his voice, along with a touch of judgment.

"Yes. Why?" I put my hands on my hips.

"Just making sure," he said quickly.

He leaned in and poked around the engine. "Wait a sec." He reached in and touched the egg. "This is a rock."

"What?"

"It's a rock." He held it out to me.

"How did it get in the nest?"

"Can't say I know, but that bird's going to be sorely disappointed when the rock doesn't hatch." He gently put the stone back into the nest. "But, even with no nest, this car isn't going anywhere without a tow truck."

I sighed. "It's my fault for not checking on it sooner, but I didn't need it."

"And you do today?"

"I have an appointment down in Fort Payne . . . *had*. I was already running late. By the time I track down a car to borrow I'll have missed the appointment altogether."

233

"Well, come on." He hooked a thumb over his shoulder. "I'll take you down. My truck's right here. Let's go."

"I can't let you do that."

"Why not? You don't want to go to the appointment?"

That question hit too close to home. "It'll waste your whole afternoon."

"I have some errands down there I've been putting off. I can get those done while you're busy. You're actually doing *me* a favor, putting an end to my procrastination."

Meeting his gaze, I held it. I wanted to say no thanks, go collect Ollie from Faylene's house, and settle in for the night. But I could also feel the anxiety under the surface of my skin, poking and prodding me to do the right thing. "Put that way, okay, I'll go with you to do your errands."

He laughed as I grabbed my purse from the car, and within minutes we were on our way out of town. His pickup was a newer model with all the bells and whistles, and I couldn't help smiling at the comparison to my junker.

Between me and Cam, River had settled in, his head on my leg, and he kept trying to lick my fingers. I *knew* I'd smelled bacon on them.

"Where are we headed?" Cam asked.

I pulled a piece of paper from my bag and read off the address. "It's a medical building."

He looked over. "You feeling okay?"

I rubbed River's ears, which had flecks of mud stuck to the fur. "Physically, yes."

He gave a firm, understanding nod. "Counseling?"

"I thought I was done with therapy, and I don't particularly want to go back, but . . ." I shrugged, wondering why I was telling him all this. Maybe it was because he seemed to understand what I was going through—something most people couldn't even fathom.

"To my way of thinking, it can't hurt to go back. But it could help, right?"

"Have you ever been?"

"Sure. Unit-mandated, but I continued on my own after I got out."

"Unit?"

"Sorry—I thought you knew. Most people around here seem to, though I don't talk about it much."

"Small towns . . ." I said, my tone sympathetic.

"I was a Green Beret." His eyes darkened with a haze of sadness. River shifted, lifting his head off my leg. He pressed his nose into Cam's thigh.

By Cam's reaction, I should have stopped right there with the questions, but I was curious about this man. How had he gone from being a highly trained soldier to being a wildlife photographer? "How long were you in?"

"Seven years." He petted River's head. "I've been out for three."

There was an emptiness in his voice that made

my heart ache. I could only imagine what he'd seen and done to protect and survive. "Do you regret it? Your time as a soldier?"

He kept his eyes on the road, looking like he was debating answering before he finally said, "I don't regret fighting for the country, protecting the soldiers I served with. But I definitely lost more in those years than I gained. Including good friends in combat and ultimately my marriage."

There was absolutely nothing I could say that would help him in any way—I knew that from my own experiences with grief and trying to get on with life. But, as he showed me the other day, sometimes all it took to provide a little comfort was to just sit and *be* with someone else. "There's a bench I know that's great for sitting and watching the world go by. I'd be happy to sit with you for a while, if you ever feel the need."

"I'll remember that. Thanks, Natalie."

"Anytime, Cam."

We drove in silence for a while, and River eventually shifted his head back to me and my bacon scent. Mud from his ears flecked off onto my skirt.

"Were you two mudding today?" I asked.

"It feels that way, but no. We went down to Lake Martin early this morning to get some pictures of bald eagles—there's a beautiful nest down there. We got a little too into our work, didn't we, buddy?"

I instantly broke out in a cold sweat. My stomach pitched, and my head swirled. I slammed my eyes shut against the image of Matt's bloated face.

"Natalie? Don't hold your breath. It makes it worse."

As I gulped in air, I felt Cam's hand on my arm, warm and firm.

Rocks hit the undercarriage as the truck slowed to a stop on the side of the road. I heard the window go down. Hot, soggy air hit my face.

River whimpered and nudged my leg with his nose as Cam said, "Slow and steady breaths. Easy there. Good. That's good. In. Out."

Trying to focus on breathing, I rocked in my seat and felt Cam's hand on my back, rubbing it in gentle circles.

"Did I ever tell you about the time Josh and I decided to sneak out of our house to go to a party a town over? I was sixteen, he was fifteen, and this party was the talk of school. *Everybody* was going. Somehow our mother caught wind of it and forbade us to go. As a single mom, she gave us a lot of leeway growing up, but for some reason she put her foot down that night."

I opened my eyes—he was leaning in close to me and had a devilish look in his eyes. His hand kept rubbing my back.

"We, of course, were not to be deterred. Mom was an early bird and rarely could stay awake past ten at night. She wears earplugs to bed and sleeps like the dead. Josh and I thought we were golden. At midnight we climbed out a window in the spare bedroom at the back of the house. A buddy of ours picked us up and took us over to the party. We were there for five minutes, tops, when all hell broke loose. Had to be a least a hundred kids there. Fights broke out. Someone started busting windows. The cops came and everyone scattered. The cops caught the friend who drove us there, so Josh and I ran as fast as we'd ever run in our whole lives. Took us four hours to walk back to our neighborhood."

My stomach started to settle and the dizziness faded.

"All we wanted to do was get home, go to bed, and forget the night ever happened. Hell, we hadn't even gotten a beer out of it for all that effort."

I smiled and rubbed River's perked ears, which relaxed under my touch.

"So we finally get home and make to get back inside. Only the window's stuck. Won't open. None of them will. And while we were trying our damnedest to get into the house, a policeman shows up. Someone had reported seeing suspicious characters trying to break in."

I smiled at him—his wry tone was completely captivating.

"Stop me if I already told you how all this ends," he said, his warm gaze feeling like a hug.

I cleared my throat. "You know full well that we only met last week and you haven't told me anything, so don't leave me hanging."

He tugged on his beard. "Oh, that's right. Just feels like I've known you forever. Where was I? Right. The policeman. He doesn't believe Josh and me that we live there. And Mom doesn't answer when he knocks—like I said, she sleeps like the dead until her internal clock goes off at five a.m. The policeman hauls us down to the police station, sticks us in a jail cell. We didn't get offered a phone call, nothing. By noon, Josh is blubbering, certain that Mom was going to kill us on the spot when she found out where we were. I was trying to figure out a way to break out of our cell." Cam pulled his hand from my back, checked over his shoulder, and pulled onto the road.

"And?" I asked, telling myself I wasn't missing his hand on my back. "Did you find a way out?"

"Three ways. But we didn't need 'em, because Mom finally showed up. Didn't say a word to us as we waited to be let out. There was a vent above our heads—escape route number one, by the way—and Mom's voice carried through it."

"She was the one who called the cops on you," I said.

"Hey now, don't go stealing my storytelling thunder. How'd you know?"

I laughed. "Because my mother did the same thing to me once when I was a teenager."

His eyebrows shot up. "You don't seem the type to sneak out."

It was sneak out or be suffocated. "What type am I?"

The corner of his lip twitched. "Oh, I don't know. Prim and proper. You know which fork goes where at a dinner table. I suspect you have monogrammed clothes, a lot of hats, and were a sorority girl—probably a legacy. I haven't seen you wear pearls, but I'd bet you own them. You're loyal and giving and a people pleaser. A *good* girl. Picturing you climbing out a window is as surprising to me as if you said you were from Mars."

What he had said was annoyingly on point, right down to the pearls. I didn't wear them because they reminded me too much of my mother.

"Am I wrong?" he asked.

"That I'm from Mars? Yes, you're wrong. It only feels that way sometimes." Like right now. "It's true that I once *was* that girl. Some of me still is, I guess. Mostly, I'm not sure who I am anymore." I didn't really want to talk about that, so I quickly added, "Let's just say my teen years were . . . challenging. The only reason I wasn't arrested that one time was because my father stepped in before the police officer carted me off. Said I'd learned my lesson." He didn't talk to my mother for nearly a week afterward, using her own silent treatment against her.

"Did you learn it?"

"No. Did you?"

"Yes, ma'am. Never snuck out again. Josh, either. But that's not where *my* story ends."

I shifted to face him. "It isn't?"

"See, you thought I was just telling you a sweet coming-of-age tale, but what I was really telling you is a love story."

"Oh, then please, go on."

He grinned. "The policeman came back the next day to check on Josh and me, make sure we were staying on the straight and narrow after our run-in with the law. And he came by the day after that, too. Eventually Mom invited him to supper, and he pretty much never left. They're happily married and living down in Key West these days."

I pressed my hands to my heart. "*Aww!* How often do you remind her that if you and Josh didn't sneak out that night . . ."

"As often as I can."

"Well. That might be the best story I've ever heard. Thank you."

"My pleasure." He glanced my way. "Do you want to share what set you off a minute ago?"

Not really, but I felt as though I owed him an explanation after all he'd just done for me, talking me down.

Turning, I looked out the window at the passing scenery, then said, "Lake Martin is where my husband drowned after his boat overturned in a storm. His death was ruled an accident, but . . ."

"But?"

"I'm not sure it was."

"You think it was murder?"

River had fallen asleep, and his soft snores filled the space between us. "No, nothing like that. I think it could have been a suicide."

"What makes you think so?"

I liked that he didn't try to console me or talk me out of the notion. He wanted the evidence. It was easier to focus on the details than the emotions. "I didn't know until after his death that he'd been gambling. I had no clue. He'd been keeping it from me for years. *Lying.* He traveled a lot for his job, so it was easy for him to hide it."

"Casinos?"

"Mostly. Some online gambling as well. Got in way over his head, apparently. Our house had a second mortgage on it I didn't know about, and was already in foreclosure. Our savings had been drained. He'd maxed out our credit cards. He'd borrowed money from friends. He'd lost his job the week before his death, and I didn't know that, either. It seemed like every day after he died, something else came to light. I was a fool to let him handle all the finances, but it's how we'd always done it."

Just like my parents had, and theirs before them. I chafed at the reminder that I'd fallen easily into the same gender roles. How had I let that happen? I was more than capable of balancing a checkbook, yet . . . I'd let him do it. I *happily* let him do it while I tended to the house and tried my hardest to get pregnant.

"You're not a fool," he said.

I crossed my arms. "I shouldn't have been so trusting."

"Love *is* trust, Natalie. You had no reason to doubt him, did you?"

Suddenly choked with emotion, I shook my head.

"Did he have life insurance?"

It took me a moment to answer. "Yes. We chose the policies when we bought our house, just one of those things the insurance agent recommended when we met with him."

"Did the company honor the policy?"

"By some miracle, they did. Wasn't near enough to cover Matt's debts, though. The house was foreclosed on not long after the funeral, the cars were repossessed. I sold as much as I could before I finally had to declare bankruptcy to get out from underneath it all."

My father had begged me to come home, but I hadn't wanted to face my mother. Ollie and I had moved into a tiny studio apartment he'd found for us, and I searched for an entry-level job for someone who had never before been employed a day in her life. I didn't have a degree to fall back on either, as I'd quit school two years shy of graduating to marry Matt and keep house.

My mother had fought me tooth and nail to stop the wedding, telling me over and over I was making a huge mistake. That I should finish school. That I should put myself before Matt. That I barely knew him.

But I'd been in love, and nothing she said could have stopped me.

I rambled on. "I know I should accept that it was an accident and move on with my . . ."

"Why was he on the lake that day?"

I jerked my head to look at him. "You're good. Not many people ask that question. He was supposedly fishing."

"He didn't normally?"

"Not alone. Usually he went with a group of buddies."

"Was he acting strangely that morning or the night before?"

I'd thought about that morning a million times. "It was a Friday, early. He said he was going out to the lake, and that he loved me. He kissed Ollie goodbye and left." My voice caught and I cleared my throat. "It was strange only that it was a weekday—he said he had the day off—and that he was going alone. A storm blew up fast, and his boat capsized. He was missing for two days afterward. In that time, the man he rented the boat from said Matt had been there every morning for a week, fishing alone. I just hadn't known . . . More lies."

"The gambling and the debt are red flags for suicide, but he could have also been out on that lake trying to figure out how to tell you he'd been fired and how bad your financial troubles were. I know I take to nature to sort out my problems. How would you have reacted to his news?"

The trees gave way to businesses as we neared the city. "I'd have been hurt, but we'd have figured something out. I took a vow, and I meant it. I'm driving myself crazy wondering if it was an accident or a suicide, because knowing the way he died is the only way to know the truth about our life when he was alive. If he could easily lie to me about the gambling and the money, was he lying when he said he loved me?" My breath caught and my hands clenched. "Was our whole marriage one big lie? I can't get past it, and it makes me . . . so *angry* with him. I don't want to be, but I can't help it."

The truck rolled to a stop at a red light. "Sometimes people lie to protect the ones they love," Cam said.

I narrowed my eyes on him and said sharply, "And sometimes people lie to protect themselves."

He laughed. "Innocent bystander over here."

"Sorry," I said, leaning back. "I can't abide liars, no matter how much the truth hurts."

Cam took hold of my hand, held it tight. "I wish I had answers for you, Natalie. But all I can ask you is this: Did you love him?"

Did I love him? I thought about the first time I looked into Matt's blue eyes and my world lit up, and remembered how my world went dark when I found out he was gone. I said, "So much."

Cam turned into a parking lot and pulled up in front of the medical offices. He let go of my hand to shift into park. "Whatever he did or didn't do that day on the lake doesn't change that fact."

"But it does—"

"No," he said. "It doesn't. You're not angry because you don't know whether he loved you. You're angry because you loved him and he left you. Healing will only come when you forgive him for leaving you. And for leaving Ollie."

What he said hit me straight in the heart, and it hurt like hell. And by the way he said the words, I sensed he knew of what he spoke.

Letting out a breath, I glanced at the dashboard clock and gasped. "I've got to go. I'm late."

"I'll wait here a few minutes, just in case."

River's head came up as I pushed open the door and hopped out. I ran inside the building, found the right office, and wasn't the least bit shocked when the receptionist told me I'd need to reschedule.

I made an appointment for the following week and went back outside. Cam and River were walking on a strip of grass dividing the parking lot.

"Looks like I get to come back next week," I said, holding up the appointment card.

Cam threw an arm around my shoulders, pulling me in for a side hug. "I'm real sorry you missed your counseling session."

So was I. But as I glanced up at him, feeling safe and relaxed at his side, I thought the ride down here with him might have been just the kind of therapy I needed.

14

Anna Kate

By the time Friday rolled around, my days had settled into a comfortable routine. Early mornings were spent in the garden, collecting herbs, vegetables, and flowers, and then Gideon would come by for coffee before Bow and Jena arrived. The café took up most of my day, as I worked from seven until three. Having Natalie in the café part-time had helped immensely—what she lacked in skills, she made up for with her work ethic. I found that I enjoyed having her around. She had a gentle nature that set me at ease, and she was sweet and funny and nothing at all like I thought a Linden would be. I liked her. Summer, I noticed, had taken a liking to her as well—once Jena had enlisted them to help find the gray cat she'd seen sneak inside one afternoon when the back door had been propped open.

Had it been a coincidence that Jena had been the only one to see the cat, who supposedly ran in just as Summer was dropping off eggs?

Or that Natalie and Summer had been *accidentally* locked together in the laundry room for a short while during the search?

I didn't think so.

That Jena was a wily one.

She'd been grinning ear to ear when Natalie and Summer were finally freed and emerged talking about vintage apron patterns.

In the late afternoons, I spent time making pies, tinkering with food and herbal tea recipes using some of the morning's bounty, clearing weeds from the garden, and making the rounds among the birders.

To my amazement, Sir Bird Nerd was still in town. He'd disappeared for a day, but then came back with a small motor home, which he was parking on Pebbles's land. If the blackbirds were a museum, Zachariah Boyd would be their docent. He was the go-to guy for information on the birds' nighttime ritual, a veritable one-man information kiosk. Every birder who arrived, whether it was a quick stop or a multiday excursion, ended up talking to Mr. Boyd. Honestly, I should probably put the man on the payroll, as there had been a nonstop stream of visitors.

The blackbirds were singing regularly, and there would come a time, I knew, that I wouldn't wait up to hear them anymore, but I wasn't there yet. It meant less sleep, but I'd never been one who needed much. The songs were worth any fatigue I felt throughout the day.

I currently had four pies in the double ovens and was outside checking on the mulberry trees before I started weeding. Another day or two, and Summer and I'd lay a tarp down beneath the trees and shake the branches to release the ripened fruit, which was almost black.

I set to work on the weeds, sorting what could be thrown in the compost pile versus what I could use in the kitchen. Dandelions were keepers. Crabgrass could go. I was talking to the zucchini plants, telling them about Doc Linden's latest supper invitation—he, with his sad eyes and unhealthy coloring, had begun stopping at the café most mornings for a cup of coffee to go—when I heard a rustling sound behind me. I turned, hoping I wouldn't find a snake slithering out to enjoy the late afternoon sunshine. I liked most creatures and knew many snakes were harmless, but I preferred to keep my distance.

By a mile or two.

Instead of something slithery, not a foot away, I found the gray cat watching me.

"Hello there." I held out my fingers for him to sniff, but he didn't budge. Up close he appeared well fed, but he had a few scars other than the one on his ear. One ran across his scalp, and there was a long, thick jagged one on his back left leg. "Are you hungry? Thirsty?"

I stood up to find him some water, and he wiggled an ear and strode off toward the back of the yard. He stopped, looked back at me, then took two more steps.

Surely he didn't want me to follow him again. I wasn't lost here in Zee's garden—where could he possibly lead me?

He took another step, stopped.

"Okay," I said, leaving my basket where it was on the gravel pathway, "I'm up for the adventure."

The cat always stayed two or three steps ahead of me as he led me along the fence at the back of the yard, past the mulberry trees, toward the property line I shared with Gideon.

With a graceful leap, the cat landed on the top iron rail that ran horizontally along the fencing. He paused long enough to make sure I was behind him, then continued on his merry way, tail in the air.

I glanced back at the café, at the birders, at my sanity—all of which I'd clearly left behind.

In the rear corner of the yard, he paused. When I caught up to him, I saw he'd stopped at a gate I hadn't noticed before now. It opened into the woods behind the yard. All this time, I thought Gideon had been hopping the fence back here. I unhooked the latch. The gate creaked as I pushed it open and clicked soundly in place when I closed it behind me.

When I turned around, the cat was already strutting through the woods. The scent of wild garlic filled the air as the cat scurried toward the lush green lawn behind Hill House, a two-story wood-framed I-house that was as pretty from the rear as it was from the front. Gideon had given me a full run-down on the architecture when I admired the house earlier this week.

I walked around a screened-in gazebo and along a path flanked with colorful annuals that led to a stone patio shaded by a pergola covered in climbing trumpet vines. Hummingbirds flitted around the vibrant red blooms, and I heard the phoebe singing nearby.

I quick-stepped to keep up with the cat. "I'm pretty sure this is trespassing," I called after him.

"Anna Kate?"

Embarrassed to be caught sneaking around, I froze. "Gideon?"

"Up here."

Shading my eyes with my hand, I looked up. Gideon stood on the edge of the roof. Feeling suddenly woozy at seeing him up there, I said, "Could you back up a step? You're making me nervous being that close to the edge."

"Do you have a fear of heights?" he asked.

"It's not so much of heights as *falling*."

"It is a long way down, isn't it?" He took a step back. "I'm guessing thirty feet at least. I've had some time to consider exactly how far it is, since I've been up here going on an hour now."

"What are you doing?"

"Having a heart to heart with a squirrel. She was trying to make a nest in the chimney, but I talked her out of it and suggested the loblolly behind you would be a better, safer option."

I glanced that way and sure enough, there was a squirrel running along a high branch, leaves in her mouth. "Are you staying up there in case she changes her mind and comes back?"

He laughed. "No. I'm up here because my ladder fell. Don't suppose you could grab it for me? It's on the other side of the house."

I walked around the corner and saw an aluminum extension ladder laying in the grass.

"It's not the easiest to handle on your own," he warned.

I lifted an end, judging whether I needed help. "I think I can manage." It took some doing, but I propped the ladder against the house without breaking anything. The house or me. A small miracle, that.

I held the ladder as he came down, the metal vibrating under my palms. With two rungs left, he jumped to the ground, and wiped his hands on his jeans. His dark T-shirt was soaked to his skin, and his hair was damp with sweat.

"Thank you. You couldn't have come along at a better time. I was just contemplating how much damage would be done if I tried jumping onto the pergola."

"To you or the pergola?"

"Both," he said, flashing a smile.

His face had a bright pink tinge to it. "Looks

like you've got yourself quite a sunburn. Do you have any aloe?"

"I'm sure I do."

"Fresh aloe?"

"I'm sure I don't."

"Zee has an aloe plant in her living room. I can harvest some gel."

He rested his hands on his hips. "Her living room. Not yours?"

I lifted a shoulder. "I think it will always be Zee's, and that's okay. I don't mind being its caretaker for a while."

He opened his mouth to say something, then apparently changed his mind. He'd often done the same during our coffee chats, as though he were holding something back. I didn't want to needle him about whatever it was on his mind—he'd get there in his own time.

He rested a hand on the ladder. "Out of curiosity, what brought you by here?"

I hesitated only slightly before saying, "I was following a cat." Who was nowhere to be seen now.

"A cat?"

"He's big and gray with milky gray-blue eyes. I've seen him a couple of times in Zee's garden. Do you know who he belongs to?"

He smiled. "I think he mostly belonged to Zee. She told me he showed up at the café one night, a long time ago, and never left. He prefers to be outside and tends to do his own thing."

"Shouldn't he have a collar with tags? Has he had a checkup? Shouldn't he be neutered? You know, protect the whole pet population thing."

"Let me guess, you watched a lot of *Price Is Right* when you were younger."

"I watched a lot of everything when I was younger. Books and TV were some of my closest friends." I winced, realizing how much I'd revealed. "I was a latchkey kid. My mom worked a lot."

"Me, too," he said. "And mine, too." As he lowered the ladder, he added, "Zee tried to put a collar with a bell on the cat once, and it didn't go so well. Be careful of his claws if you give it a try."

"Does he have a name?" I asked.

"Zee always called him Mr. Cat."

It kind of fit, though I was starting to think Lassie would work too, considering Mr. Cat seemed to have a knack for rescues. With me in the woods last week, and today with Gideon.

"Mr. Cat it is. I'll start putting some food out for him, and see if I can lure him to the vet." I took a step backward, toward the woods. "I should get going, I have pies in the oven."

He crossed his arms over his chest. "Anna Kate, what are you doing tonight?"

Smiling, I said, "More pies, and I have some aloe to scrape . . ."

"Have you eaten dinner?"

For some reason my palms started to sweat. "Not yet."

"How about we pack a dinner, picnic-style, and take it to the Movie in the Moonlight tonight?"

For a moment there, I was caught up in the way he was looking at me. That deep intensity mixed with a hint of playfulness and a touch of heat.

I swallowed hard. "I don't think that's a good idea. There's probably going to be a lot of people there," I said, thinking arm's length might not be far enough away from that alluring gaze of his. "They'll stare."

"Sure, people might stare a while, since you're a novelty right now. But the only way to get them to stop is to give them their fill. Besides, most everyone has already stopped by the café this week."

Not Seelie Linden, and I wasn't sure I wanted to take the chance of running into her. After all, Natalie had mentioned she was a bigwig with the Refresh Committee.

"Once the movie starts, people won't stop to talk to you. It'd be rude. People around here would rather eat soap than be openly ill-mannered. And I'll be there as a buffer."

He made good points. Still . . .

"*Beauty and the Beast* is the movie tonight. You know you love that library scene."

It was true—I did. My head tipped side to side as if weighing my decision.

"Come on," he said with a big, hopeful smile.

"What's better than watching a movie under the stars on a beautiful summer night?"

I could feel myself being reeled in. A night out, under the stars, did sound nice. Minus the people, of course. I searched his honey-colored eyes, looking for any reason to keep saying no. All I saw was kindness and that touch of heat shimmering in the brown depths. "Okay," I said, relenting to the power of his charm. "But only if you let me pack the basket."

"Nope. I asked, I'm doing the packing. Hope you don't mind cold corn dogs," he teased.

I smiled. "You have to let me bring something."

"Okay, drinks are on you," he said finally.

"I can do that."

"Then it's a da—" He abruptly cut himself off. "Then I'll pick you up at six forty-five."

"I'll be ready."

As I walked off, toward the woods and the way I'd come, his words echoed in my ears.

It's a da—

Date. He'd been about to say date.

He hadn't—and it wasn't a date, I told myself as I slipped through the back gate. It was simply two people going to see a movie together.

I should have been happy about that, considering the arm's length of it all.

But as I headed into the café to check on the pies, I couldn't deny that I was the tiniest bit disappointed.

"Over here! Yoo-hoo, Anna Kate, honey!" In the distance Faylene Wiggins stood on tiptoes and waved her outstretched arms like she was flagging down a B-52.

"I think someone is trying to get your attention," Gideon said, keeping close.

So close I could feel the heat of his body. I'd have stepped away to give myself some breathing room, but there wasn't anywhere to go. The lawn leading to the amphitheater was packed with people in line at the snack stand, for the portable restrooms, and searching for a patch of lawn to stake a claim.

There was still an hour until official sunset, but the sun was already sinking behind the mountain, casting Wicklow into an early twilight. Fireflies—or lightning bugs, as people around here called them—flickered, small bursts of light that made me smile, thinking of how Zee always told me the bugs lit up because they were magical.

I still believed that to be true.

"Plenty of room for y'all!" Faylene yelled, still waving.

I pretended to scan the crowd. "I don't see anyone . . ."

Laughing, he placed his hand on the small of my back and steered me toward Faylene. "I hope you didn't want to sit elsewhere, because I don't think she would stand for it."

"I don't mind." There was a natural effervescence to Faylene, with her chatty personality and her big laugh. She should have been overwhelming, but her boisterous disposition often turned people's attention on her . . . taking it off me. I had the feeling she knew exactly what she was doing, too, and that made me like her all the more.

Trying my best to ignore Gideon's hand at my spine, I held tightly onto a small lunch cooler I'd found in one of Zee's closets. Inside the cooler were two thermoses full of blackberry sweet tea, my first batch made using Mr. Pavegeau's recipe, and a stack of paper cups. The tea was delicious, if I did say so myself. And Aubin had been right—it had brought a taste of happiness.

When Gideon and I reached Faylene's landing zone, she pressed her hands together and smiled brightly. "I'm tickled to see you two here together. Just tickled." She eyed us as though sizing us up for wedding clothes.

"It's a beautiful night for a movie, isn't it?" Gideon said.

I admired the way he completely ignored her innuendo that we were here on a date, though I didn't think Faylene would give up without knowing for certain if we were or weren't.

"Nicest one yet this spring," she said, winking at me.

Spring. It felt like we should be well into

summer by now, with the way it had been so hot. The official change of seasons, however, wasn't for another few weeks.

Faylene then gestured to the group of people behind her, gathered on three overlapping blankets. "Anna Kate, you know Marcy and Lindy-Lou, right?"

"I do." They'd stopped into the café a few times this week.

"And that there hiding behind the camera is Cam Kolbaugh, Josh's brother. He's our resident mountain man and wildlife photographer. Josh went for pizza across the street and will be along soon enough."

I was glad to hear that Josh would be around tonight. I hoped he was just the big bear of a policeman I needed to help me get hold of an old police report. Namely, my parents' accident report.

I said my hellos to everyone and smiled at Lindy-Lou, who was sound asleep next to Marcy, a light blanket draped over her tiny body. She had her thumb stuck in her mouth, and peach-fuzz hair that reminded me of a baby bird stuck up in downy tufts.

"It's a rough life she leads," Marcy said, following my gaze.

"I'm amazed she can sleep with all the noise."

Faylene took the blanket Gideon brought out of his arms. She flipped it open, spread it between her quilt and a magnolia tree, and then bent down to pull the blanket's edges taut. "Haven't seen this place this crowded in decades. It's all them birdwatchers. I suppose they don't have anything better to do until midnight."

Marcy grinned and said to me, "Lindy-Lou's real used to blocking out loud noises."

Faylene's eyes narrowed in confusion, then she let out a laugh. She swatted playfully at her daughter. "You hush now."

"Me, hush?" Marcy said with faux outrage, and Faylene laughed again.

It was clear the two adored each other, and their good humor set me immediately at ease.

"Y'all, sit, sit," Faylene said.

"You've picked a prime spot up here," I said, kneeling down. The sweet scent of magnolia blossoms hovered in the air, holding strong against the popcorn smell coming from the snack stand.

Faylene eyed the basket Gideon carried. "What have you there?"

Gideon lifted the basket flaps and said, "I promised Anna Kate a picnic dinner, and I think I delivered pretty well. Crispy buttermilk fried chicken, flaky hand pies, pasta salad, and shortbread cookies for dessert."

"Wooing Anna Kate right, I see." Faylene laughed. "Seems like you already know the way to that girl's heart and you haven't even known her a full two weeks yet."

Gideon flushed three shades of red as he pulled plates out of the basket. I'd known Faylene wouldn't give up so easily. He could have saved himself a lot of teasing if he'd simply told her we weren't here on a date, but oddly, he kept quiet.

"He's wooing *me* right," Marcy said, craning her neck for a look in the basket.

"Me, too," Cam said. "Did you say fried chicken?"

Gideon handed over a plate. "I brought plenty."

"Good gosh, Gideon. If I wasn't married," Marcy said, picking up a thigh.

Faylene chose a breast. "I'm not going to tell Josh you said that."

"Have you tasted the chicken yet? You can tell him," she said. "He'd probably throw me over for Gideon's cooking in a heartbeat, given that I can't cook a can of beans without burning them."

Cam was in mid-reach for a leg when he froze, his gaze caught on something over my shoulder. I turned to see Natalie threading through the crowd, a stuffed diaper bag draped over her shoulder and Ollie, dressed in a yellow Belle costume, in her arms. I looked back at Cam. He saw me watching him and quickly looked away, completely forgetting the chicken as he suddenly fussed with his camera settings.

"Oh, lookie there!" Faylene said, waving a chicken breast in the air. "It's Natalie! Yoo-hoo! Over here!"

Natalie blinked and then smiled as she veered in our direction. She blew a loose strand of hair off her face. "Can you get claustrophobic outside?"

"I think you can in this crowd," Marcy said. "Do you know Cam, Natalie?"

He looked up from his camera, smiled. "We go way back. Hi, Natalie."

"Hey, Cam." She glanced around. "Where's River?"

"Pouting at home. No pets allowed to this shindig," he said.

"That's too bad." Natalie shifted Ollie from one hip to another. "Does anyone mind if we sit a second?"

"Come on down, sugar. There's plenty of room next to Cam," Faylene said, eyeing the two of them.

There was plenty of room next to Marcy, me, and Gideon as well. Faylene was a matchmaker at heart—I could tell.

Cam shifted, looping his camera strap around his neck, and he smiled as Natalie set Ollie down on his blanket.

"Hihi!" Ollie flapped an arm at him. She had a green toy tractor clutched in her hand.

"Hey, Ollie." Cam waved back. "What're you holding there?"

"Tactor!" she said, proudly showing it to him.

"I couldn't get her to leave it at home." Natalie

sat down, taking care to tuck her dress around her legs. "It's clear who makes the decisions in our house."

Cam held out his hand to Ollie. "Can I drive it?"

She stared up at him, her brown eyes big and round. And then, as if finally deciding he was trustworthy, she handed it over.

He took the toy and drove it up her leg and arm with exaggerated machinery sounds. Her joyous giggles echoed, and I watched Natalie's face as she watched her daughter. The naked emotion made me want to walk over and give her a hug. Arm's length was getting more and more difficult where she was concerned. And little Ollie had won my heart the first time I met her.

On the days Natalie worked, Faylene dropped Ollie off at the café at closing time, and I'd found myself looking forward to her arrival. I'd missed her yesterday, when Natalie had an appointment down in Fort Payne and shared that it was with a grief counselor. It had been such a busy day, there hadn't been a chance to ask her how it had gone.

Faylene said, "If you're hungry, Natalie, Gideon brought loads of food, on account of him trying to woo Anna Kate."

Natalie's gaze flew to mine, and I gave a small shake of my head. She smiled. "Is that homemade fried chicken? Must be he's in love already."

Faylene nodded. "This is what I'm sayin'. It's plain as day to anyone with eyes."

Gideon looked pointedly at Natalie. "Just when I was going to tell you that it's nice to have you back in town. Now I'm not so sure."

It struck me as odd that Gideon hadn't caught up with Natalie before now, but then again, she tended to keep to herself even more than I did, and with his early morning visits to the café, he was long gone well before she started her shifts.

She laughed. "I do like your honesty, Gideon. It's an important quality in a mate, Anna Kate. Top of the list."

Gideon hung his head and groaned.

"I'll keep that in mind," I said, picking at the edge of the blanket.

"Hihi!" Ollie ran forward and flung herself at me.

I was caught off guard, and she nearly knocked me over. "Hi, Ollie." I laughed as she settled herself in my lap, snuggling in close. I set her princess dress to rights and tried to soak in as much of her joy before she flung herself at someone else.

"I'm glad I ran into you, Faylene," Natalie said, unzipping the diaper bag. "I was hoping I would. I finally have those headbands you ordered for Lindy-Lou. Sorry it took me longer than I thought."

Faylene wiped her greasy hands with a wet nap

266

and said, "I wasn't expecting them for another week or two, honey, so don't you worry none." Faylene made quick work of opening the tissue-wrapped package. She gasped. "Oh, Natalie! These are precious. Absolutely precious."

They were. There were three headbands in varying thicknesses, covered in colorful patterned fabric and decorated with large flowers. I recognized the style as one Ollie wore often. It was easy to see that Natalie had a great eye for color and patterns.

Ollie wasn't wearing a headband tonight, however. Her soft hair was down and loose and smelled faintly of chlorine and sunshine. She pushed off me to reclaim her tractor from Cam and then went about driving it over Gideon's head. He didn't seem to mind, which made me like him even more than I already did.

"Ollie," Natalie warned. "Not on the top of his head, please."

Ollie barely broke stride as she shifted to running the tractor over his face instead.

"To be fair," he said, laughing, "it's not the *top* of my head."

Natalie smiled, then asked Ollie to please move her playing to the ground.

Cam, I noticed, had stood up and started taking pictures. Of us, the crowd, the fireflies. Every so often, he'd lower the camera and I'd see his gaze wander to Natalie.

Almost as much as I saw Natalie's gaze wander to him.

Maybe Faylene was on to something with pairing them up.

Marcy took one of the headbands Faylene held. "These are beautiful, Natalie. The craftsmanship is outstanding. Most headbands are flimsy and not nearly full of this much personality. Could you make more of them? I can sell them at Hodgepodge on consignment."

"Really?" Natalie asked. "That would be great."

"Come by tomorrow. We'll work out the details. Oh my word, are these individual petals on this flower?"

With a pleased smile, Natalie looked to be glowing from the inside out. "They are. Adding them piecemeal allows me to mix and match fabrics and textures. Gives it more visual interest, I think."

"I'll say so," Marcy said, eyeing her sleeping daughter as though wanting to try one of the headbands on her right away, but then seeming to dismiss the idea as quickly as it came. "I'll need more for Lindy-Lou as well. They're darling."

Faylene puffed up as she looked between Natalie and her daughter. She pulled her shoulders back and held her chin high, looking like a proud mama hen. "C'mon, let's get you something to eat, honey," she said to Natalie. "I wasn't kidding about all the food Gideon brought."

"She really wasn't," he said over his shoulder. "Help yourself."

Shifting on the blanket, Natalie said, "I wish I could, but I can't stay but a minute more. My parents will be along shortly, and Ollie and I will be sitting with them for the movie."

My stomach went sour at the mere thought of seeing Doc and Seelie. I'd known it had been a risk coming here tonight, but now I wanted nothing more than to run.

"Have you met Seelie yet, Anna Kate?" Faylene asked.

I wiped my hands on my shorts. "No."

I didn't know, upon seeing her, how I was going to react. As much as I told myself to keep any meeting civil, to act distant, cold even, I didn't know if I could do it. There were twenty-four years of bottled-up emotions stuck inside me. Holding back those feelings wasn't going to be easy.

Faylene let out a low whistle and looked around as if sizing up escape routes.

As Ollie continued to zoom her tractor around the blanket, Gideon said, "Do you want to leave, Anna Kate?"

My mouth went dry as they all watched me, waiting for my answer. As much as I wanted to stand up and run all the way back to the café to avoid making any kind of spectacle here tonight, it might be better if my grandmother and I met this way, when I had all this support behind me.

"No," I finally said. "Might as well get it over with, right?"

Faylene coughed. "That's real brave of you, Anna Kate."

"There's nothing to worry about," Marcy said. "I've never met a woman more southern than Seelie Earl Linden. The last thing she'll do is make a scene. Especially with all these people around. She'd rather dig her own grave and throw herself in."

It wasn't Seelie I was afraid of making a scene. It was me. "Maybe we should go," I said to Gideon.

Without missing a beat, he started packing up the basket. Faylene helped. Natalie, too.

My pulse raced as I tugged at the blanket, trying to get it out from under Gideon while he was still sitting on it.

Ollie came over and held her hand out. "Tactor?"

"Thank you, Ollie," I said, crouching to her level. "But you should hold on to it."

Her sweet face crumpled. *"Tactor!"*

I quickly took it from her. "Thank you. *Vroom, vroom.*" I ran the tractor over her feet and she laughed.

For a second, all was right in my world. There was something about Ollie's happiness, her laughter, that brought me peace. I wanted to stay in this moment forever.

But then her eyes went wide at something she saw behind me, and she yelled, "Gaddy!"

"Oh no," Marcy whispered. "Too late."

I looked behind me in time to see Doc Linden lift Ollie into his arms. Seelie stood at his side. I slowly stood up to face, head-on, the woman who'd sent my mother through hell.

Seelie didn't look like I had imagined, either. In my mind, she'd resembled an evil queen from a children's fairy tale. Tall with high, sharp cheekbones, pointed chin, thin lips. Beady dark eyes, dark hair in a tight bun, long bloodred fingernails.

Seelie was none of those things. She was about my height, five foot seven, with white-blond hair that had cinnamon highlights. A heart-shaped face was aging gracefully. Her large blue eyes flew open when she spotted me, and then narrowed on the tractor I held, before lifting to meet my gaze once again. Her hand went straight to a double strand of pearls, gripping them tightly.

My heart pounded as I searched for something, anything, to say and found nothing at all.

Seelie's gaze didn't waver from my face as it swept from feature to feature. She swayed and Doc grabbed onto her arm to hold her steady.

"She . . . *AJ*. Oh my Lord," Seelie said so softly I almost didn't hear her.

"Mama?" Natalie said, coming up beside me.

As Seelie continued to stare at me, she blinked, once, twice, and pools of tears gathered in her eyes but didn't fall. She took a furtive look around and saw everyone nearby watching her. Watching *us*. Abruptly, she turned on her heels and rushed off.

Doc handed Ollie to Natalie and went after his wife.

"Bye! Bye!" Ollie waved her arm.

Stunned, I watched Seelie go, feeling a mix of relief . . . and confusing sadness. I hadn't seen the evilness I'd expected in her eyes. Or any cold, calculating intentions.

I'd seen only the sudden, heartbreaking realization of all she had lost.

And there was nothing remotely satisfying in that.

Because in that moment of locking eyes with her, I suddenly realized all I'd lost, too. It was a devastating feeling.

"Well, look at that," Faylene said with an awestruck sigh as she came up next to Natalie and me. "I didn't think it was possible, but Anna Kate's done it. With just one look, she managed to crack Seelie's steely core flat open. And I'll be damned if there wasn't a heart hiding in there after all."

15

"You've lived next door to the café for five years now, but you didn't know the blackbirds were a rare species not commonly found in the United States?" the reporter asked.

"I knew they were special," Gideon Kipling said. "The former owner of the café protected the birds fiercely. Didn't let anyone close to them."

"Didn't that level of protection strike you as odd?"

"Lots of things strike me as odd in this town."

He tapped his pen. "Let me get straight to my point. Do you think the previous owner was hiding something?"

Gideon folded his hands on the table. "Aren't we all?"

Natalie

I pulled open the front door of the little house late Sunday afternoon. It was just after three o'clock, and Ollie was still napping. "Come in, come in. I thought for sure you'd had a moment of insanity when you called earlier. Have you considered seeking medical attention immediately? Could be you're having an aneurysm or something."

Anna Kate clutched a foil-wrapped platter with

both hands. "Having my head examined might not be a bad idea. I'm not sure what I'm doing."

That made two of us. When Anna Kate had called this morning and asked me to let Doc know that she decided to accept his Sunday supper invitation after all, I about fell over. I suggested she come here first, so we could walk over to the big house together in hopes of taking some of the strain off Anna Kate. "Ollie's still napping, and I'm letting her sleep as long as possible. She's grumpy if she wakes up too soon, and we don't want that at supper tonight on top of everything else."

"Why not? I hear grumpy pairs well with awkwardness and discomfort."

"As tasty as that particular menu sounds, I think I'll let her keep sleeping a few minutes more."

"Cute place," Anna Kate said as she followed me inside. She wore white denim capris and a teal-blue sleeveless blouse that brought out the green in her eyes. I hoped to the heavens that Mama wouldn't say anything about the rubber flip-flops.

"It is that. Mama has good taste. It's the free rent that makes it especially attractive, but I'll be moving as soon as I can."

Light glinted off the copper in Anna Kate's eyebrows as they furrowed. "Really? Where?"

"An apartment in town. Maybe a rental house if I can swing it. Just . . ." I'd been about to say "away from here" but realized it wasn't the whole truth. "I want to be independent, stand on my own two feet. I really envy you, Anna Kate. It's inspiring how you came here and picked up running the café like it was no big deal. I could never do something like that."

"It was a big deal, and yes, you could. Your success at the café is proof—look how you stepped right in without batting an eye. Besides, being independent isn't all it's cracked up to be. I can't tell you how many times I wished to have a normal, stable life growing up. Like you."

"Normal is in the eyes of the beholder, I suppose." I gestured to Anna Kate's hands. "If you're willing to let that dish go, you can set it on the kitchen counter and come sit down. I'm just cleaning up my mess." I'd been working on sewing projects while Ollie slept.

Anna Kate glanced down as if not realizing how tightly she was gripping the platter, then laughed as she set it down. "I guess I'm a bit nervous."

"I have to admit, I am too. Mostly because I don't know what to expect." I knelt in front of the coffee table and went about picking up the notions I had spread out. The lace, ribbon, pearls, and sequins. I'd been crafting items to sell at Hodgepodge. Marcy Kolbaugh had been excited at my ideas for designs to sell in the shop.

Anna Kate sat on the floor on the other side of the coffee table, and rested her hands on her knees. "You and me both. What did your parents say when you told them I was coming?"

"Daddy smiled. He gets this glint in his eyes when he's happy—he was glinting like crazy. I didn't see my mother. She's been in hiding since the incident. He says she's fine, just sorting through her feelings."

It hadn't been surprising to me that Mama had locked herself away—it's what she always did when she couldn't deal with an emotional overload. Only, this was the first time I knew of that she'd done it physically, rather than mentally.

I'd have worried more, but I saw the light burning late into the night in her sewing studio these past two days, so I knew she wasn't completely lost.

Anna Kate hugged her knees. "Do we know that Seelie will even be at supper?"

"Technically, no, we don't. But she'll be there."

"How do you know?"

"I know my mother. She wouldn't want to be seen as an ungracious hostess, especially to family. And I think that when she saw you face-to-face, she realized just that: you *are* family. She'd been in denial up until that point. The truth all but slapped her in the face on Friday night. She had to admit she'd been wrong, and she's never wrong. She has a lot of reconciling to do—mostly with herself. Hand me that glue gun, will you?"

Anna Kate passed over the glue gun and picked

up a piece of rainbow fabric in desperate need of a good pressing. "Is this a bow tie? Mr. Lazenby would be so proud."

"I'm expanding my headband business," I said with a laugh, gesturing to a sewing machine in the corner of the room. "Baby bow ties, bibs, hair bows, booties. I need to either raid my mother's sewing studio soon or get down to Fort Payne for supplies and fabric, because I'm fast running out."

I was leaning toward Fort Payne, since I would be down there at the end of the week for my counseling appointment. Daddy had offered me use of his car, though I wouldn't mind another trip with Cam. I wanted to learn more about him.

"Seelie sews?" Anna Kate asked.

It was hard to describe what happened to my mother when she sewed. It was as though she were replaced with a woman full of life, of passion, of personality and creativity. "Faylene says Mama is like magic with a needle. It's true. The items she creates are works of art. She's been sewing since she was a little girl. She taught me, and one day I'll teach Ollie, if she wants to learn."

It was one of the few heartfelt gifts I'd received from my mother. Something that wasn't bought in a store or with the intention of improving me somehow, like the collection of Clinique makeup and acne treatments I'd been given for my fourteenth birthday. There had been no hidden motives behind teaching me to sew—she'd simply been sharing something that made her happy because she thought it would bring joy to me, too.

It had. Some of the happiest times in my childhood were spent in Mama's sewing studio. Unfortunately, those lessons never lasted long, and then she would retreat into her shell once again, leaving me wanting more of the woman she'd been before AJ died.

"As nervous as I am, I'm glad you decided to come to supper today, Anna Kate. But I admit, I'm mighty curious. What made you change your mind? I heard you were dead set against ever sharing a meal with my parents."

"I can only guess where you heard that."

"People like to talk."

"Gossip, you mean."

Smoothing a finger over a scrap of ribbon, I said, "I'm surprised you haven't realized that means the same as talking around here."

"I *was* dead set against it, because I didn't want to betray my mother. I had such a picture of what the Lindens were like in my head. What they looked like, where they lived, *how* they lived, and the kind of people they were." She laced her fingers. "Since I've been here in Wicklow, I've realized that the picture I had painted in my head wasn't my picture at all. It was my mother's. There have been things I've seen that don't match up. In fact, the only thing that does is how much Seelie hates my mom."

"Hate" was such a strong word, but I struggled to find a replacement. It could be because there wasn't one—my mother *had* hated Eden Callow. Still did. "Is it not still a betrayal, you being here today?" I asked as gently as I could.

"Maybe it is," Anna Kate said. "But on Friday night, when I looked into Seelie's eyes and saw all that pain and regret, I decided that maybe it was time to start painting my own picture. As much as I love my mom, she did teach me to think for myself, so I believe she'd understand." She grimaced. "Maybe. I hope."

I couldn't help laughing. "Like I said, I'm glad you're here. As much as Eden might've disliked my parents, I imagine she'd want you to know more about AJ. You'll probably get an earful today."

Her eyes brightened. "I hope so."

"I know so. Mama, especially, will probably go on and on."

Anna Kate ran a finger along the edge of the coffee table. "What's Seelie like? Truly like? I only know my mother's version of her."

I tightened the lid on a canister of beads, and then set it into the laundry basket I used to store my sewing goods. "I'm not sure I'm the right person to ask."

"But as her daughter, you know her best. Right?"

I tried to evade the question. "It's complicated."

"Why?"

Setting a pair of pinking shears in the laundry basket, I took a deep breath. "To people in the community, she's prim and proper and graceful. She's charitable and driven and stoic. She has high expectations, impeccable taste, and a discerning eye."

"They also know she's quick to judgment and can cut you with a look. But I really want to know how *you* see her. I've heard rumors you're not close. Why is that?"

I wasn't sure I wanted to get into all this, but Anna Kate was family, and she had the right to see all the dirty laundry. "My earliest memories of her are warm and loving. There were lots of hugs and kisses and cuddling. But all that changed when AJ died. I was three. I didn't understand much of what was happening, all I knew was that AJ was gone, and my mother, as I knew her, was gone too. She'd disappeared into someone who looked like Mama, but she wasn't the same. Cold and distant. It was Daddy who started reading me stories at bedtime. Daddy who kissed my scrapes and made my breakfast and picked out my clothes, which was all well and good, but I really wanted my mama back."

Anna Kate picked at a loose string on the seam of her pants. "I'm guessing she never came back?"

I wove a piece of lace through my fingers,

pulling so tightly it hurt. "While I was growing up? No, not really. Every now and again, when she sewed, I'd see her, but it was so brief that I questioned whether it was real or just me hoping she was finally healing. I see glimpses of the old her with Ollie, though, and it gives me hope that she's still in there, trying to find her way out. I hope she does, I truly do, but it doesn't make up for what I lost out on."

My father's words echoed in my head as I set the lace in the basket.

Grief can change a person to the point where they become someone they don't know, or even like very much.

"And I feel terrible for saying that," I admitted, "but it's the truth. I know she was suffering—but she never sought help for it. She tried to stiff-upper-lip it, because she thought mental health was something to be ashamed of, to be swept under the rug and whisper about behind people's backs. I don't think Mama could have withstood gossip on top of her grief."

Mama hadn't come around on the topic of mental health until I'd had my first panic attack and Daddy had insisted I see a therapist. It had taken her seeing my pain to understand that help meant health and there was nothing to be embarrassed by in seeking treatment.

Anna Kate said softly, "Seems like we all lost a lot when my dad died."

"It's kind of astounding, isn't it? How one split second can alter so many people's lives? Dividing our lives into categories of before and after? Before AJ died . . . after AJ died . . . Sorry. I'm getting philosophical."

"It's okay. I think a lot about that kind of thing, too. What if the car hadn't crashed that day . . . ? Would my mother and father have gotten married? Would I have grown up here in Wicklow? Would my mom still have become a nurse? Or would she be running the café? The what-ifs keep me up at night sometimes."

"Same here," I said, thinking of how many sleepless nights I'd had. Not just with AJ and his accident, but with Matt and his drowning, as well. "If AJ hadn't died, would I have been a happier child? Would I be less of a people-pleaser? I spent a good portion of my younger years trying to get my mother's attention. I did everything she asked, going above and beyond to make her proud. Yet my every accomplishment was compared to AJ in some way."

"Like how?"

"Oh, little things. I'd come home with A's on a report card, and Mama would be sure to tell me that AJ always earned A's, too—usually in harder subjects than mine. If I mentioned that I liked the color green, Mama would mention that his favorite color was blue. Foods were the worst. If I said I liked carrots, I'd hear about the time AJ tried carrots for the first time and spit them out on Daddy's tie. He hated them. Not only that, I had a thousand rules to live by, because Mama had become irrationally overprotective."

"I can kind of understand why."

"Oh, I can too, but it didn't make it any easier to live with. By the time I was a teenager, I came to the realization that to get Mama to notice *me*, I needed to do things AJ never had."

Anna Kate's lips twitched. "Oh no."

"Oh yes. I thought bad attention would be better than no attention, so I started rebelling. Small ways, mostly, just to aggravate Mama, because I really was a good kid. Dyeing my hair. Smoking, which only made me queasy. Listening to music she didn't approve of. Running away tended to get the most attention, but I never went far."

I almost laughed, thinking of the times I'd run off—only to wander along Willow Creek and get eaten alive by mosquitos until the wee hours. I hadn't had any best friends to get into teenage mischief with and there certainly had been no boy-friends—no one was ever good enough for Seelie Earl Linden's approval. But when I was located or eventually wandered back home, I always let my mother think the worst. Getting caught, after all, was the whole point of sneaking out.

Anna Kate smiled. "I bet that went over well."

"It backfired, actually. I thought she'd finally start seeing me for who I was, but the more I acted out, the more rigid she became, freezing me out even more. Just when I thought I couldn't take her coldness any longer, I graduated from high school and went off to college. There, I suddenly had all the freedoms I ever wanted, so of course I went and did the stupidest thing possible, at least in my mother's eyes. It certainly got her attention, but it was the final straw for her, and she all but cut me out of her life."

"What did you do?" Anna Kate asked, eyes wide. "Don't tell me you got arrested."

"Worse." A squeak came from the hallway—Ollie was waking up. I threw a look at the clock. And it was time to go over to the big house.

"What could possibly be worse in Seelie's eyes than getting arrested?" Anna Kate asked.

I stood, lifted the laundry basket, and looked at Anna Kate dead on. "I got married."

Anna Kate

"Okay," Natalie said, turning to face me on the walkway between the guesthouse and the main house. Her dark eyes were focused and serious. "If you get too overwhelmed, we leave. Just get up and go." She snapped her fingers. "We should have a signal or code word or something. How about . . . oh, I don't know . . ." She looked all around, up and down, and then laughed. "I can't think of a thing."

284

A sleepy-eyed Ollie lifted her head off Natalie's shoulder, stared at her mother, and then started laughing too.

I loosened my grip on the platter. "How about succotash?"

"As in sufferin'?" She laughed harder, which set Ollie off again.

I smiled at them. "I used to love watching *Looney Tunes*. Sylvester the Cat was a favorite."

"Sufferin' succotash. I haven't heard that phrase in forever. It definitely fits. You ready?"

"As I'll ever be."

She nodded vigorously. "It'll be fine. Just fine. Absolutely fine."

It wasn't the first time I'd heard Natalie say those words in that order, and I wondered how often she used them as a pep talk for herself. A lot, I guessed.

As we headed for the patio doors leading into the kitchen, I wished we could turn around and go back to Natalie's cozy little cottage and pick up the conversation we'd been having. She'd left me on a cliffhanger with the whole marriage thing, promising to tell me another time what had happened.

Keeping my arm's-length policy had crashed and burned where Natalie was concerned. Was it because she wasn't simply a friend but my aunt? I wasn't sure. All I knew was I'd never opened up to someone like I had with her. This wasn't a relationship that would simply fizzle out because one friend moved away from another and lost touch. Family was forever. For better or for worse.

The air-conditioner droned as Natalie led us into a spacious kitchen. Light flooded the room, catching on copper pots hanging from a ceiling rack above a wide island.

A light stone countertop complemented dark maple cabinets and vivid sage-green walls. A potato masher, its wires thick with creamy spuds, rested on a wooden cutting board, and a roasting pan scraped of drippings sat on iron trivets. Bowls and plates were piled deep in the farmhouse sink. Several colorful flower arrangements were displayed in vases on the countertops and the kitchen table.

The air smelled of sweet ham, a hint of rose, and was filled with soft jazz. Plates rattled from the dining room, and my grip once again tightened on the platter.

"Hello!" Natalie called out. "We're here!"

"Hihi!" Ollie said as Natalie put her down and straightened the hem of Ollie's dress.

For the millionth time since I woke up that morning I reminded myself why I was doing this. It would have been easy to keep on minding my own business. To ignore the Lindens and the pain they carried around like an aura.

But as I had gone to sleep last night after hearing the blackbirds sing their soul-stirring song, it was

Bow's voice I heard echoing in my thoughts.

Seems to me there's a whole lot of people around here carrying around a heap of pain tied to the past. Might be time to start letting that go and start healing.

The pain we all shared stemmed from that one moment in the past when our worlds were split, like Natalie had said, into a before and an after.

Twenty-five years of grief and sadness, pain and anger.

It was time to let go. To heal.

I was the link between the before and the after, and I could no longer deny that the job of putting this family back together was mine. As uncomfortable as that may be.

However, as a Callow, healing was my calling, and I was suddenly very much up for the challenge. Or so I told myself, so I wouldn't run out the door and not look back. Nerves were making me question my decision.

Doc appeared in the dining room doorway, and upon seeing us, his shoulders dropped, and he let out a breath. His eyes were, in fact, glinting.

Ollie's dark hair flew out behind her as she went running as fast as her little legs could carry her straight into his arms. He winced as he picked her up.

"You okay there, Daddy?" Natalie asked.

"Went golfing again yesterday, and my old muscles are feeling it." He met my concerned gaze and pasted on a smile. "I am so happy to see the three of you. Thank you, Anna Kate, for accepting my invitation. Welcome. You didn't have to bring anything."

"Anna Kate brought something?" Seelie said, coming into the room.

She had a hand wrapped around her pearls as she kissed Ollie's cheek, then hesitated before pecking Natalie's. She then took a step toward me as if coming in for a hug, then abruptly dropped her arms and took the platter out of my hands.

I wasn't sure whether I was relieved or sad about the hug. Seelie's voice was light, her face neutral. I didn't sense any malice or ill will. Just awkwardness. She wore linen trousers, a short-sleeved sweater, and only the bare minimum of makeup— a little cover-up, mascara, blush, and lip gloss. Her feet were bare, her toes painted soft pink.

I glanced at Natalie, who had a hand pressed to her cheek, and wondered when Seelie had last kissed her.

Seelie bent her head low to the platter. "Biscuits. Oh, they smell divine, Anna Kate. What kind are they?" she asked casually, as if I'd spent every Sunday with them my whole life long.

I threw a look at Natalie, who stared at her mother, as if not recognizing her. It suddenly felt like the Twilight Zone in here. "They're zucchini and cheddar."

"Is that," Seelie sniffed, "thyme I smell?"

"Fresh thyme from Zee's garden and a bit of jalapeño."

Seelie smiled—a smile I recognized as my own—and said, "What a delightful combination. I look forward to tasting them." She dropped the foil on the counter, picked up the platter, and carried it toward the doorway, slowing only to tickle Ollie's leg.

Natalie snapped her mouth closed, opened it again. "What's with Mama?" she asked Doc.

His eyes were still glinting. "I'm not sure what you mean?"

Natalie said, "Is she medicated?"

"Not that I know of," he answered.

"Drunk?" she offered.

He tipped his head as if debating it. "I don't think so."

"Mental break?"

He grinned. "Breakthrough, perhaps."

"What does that mean?" she asked.

Seelie popped into the doorway. "C'mon, now. Supper's getting cold."

Doc motioned for us to go ahead of him.

Natalie dropped her voice and said to me as we shuffled toward the doorway, "Her feet were bare, right? I wasn't seeing things, was I?"

"Bare feet," I whispered. "Blush-pink toenails."

"Mama, where are your shoes?" Natalie asked.

Seelie looked down at her feet. "Oh! Look at that. You'll have to forgive my lapse."

Her gaze slid to my flip-flops, and I saw her lips purse in disapproval before she quickly masked the reaction.

Natalie glanced at me, her eyes wide, before taking Ollie from her father's arms. She headed into the dining room behind her mother.

Doc snagged my arm, pulling me to a stop just short of the doorway. Dropping his voice to a whisper, he said, "I'd appreciate it, Anna Kate, if you didn't mention anything about my"—he paused for a second—"issues with the *heat*."

In the light of the kitchen, he didn't look as ill as he had on the deck of the café the day I'd first met him, but I could still see the sallowness of his skin. I didn't know exactly what was wrong with him, but I knew that whatever caused that yellowish skin tone had nothing to do with the weather. "Heat?" I said, emphasizing the word.

"Yes, the heat."

It hit me suddenly why he was acting suspiciously. "They don't know, do they?"

The truth shone in the depths of his dark, downturned eyes. Neither Natalie nor Seelie knew he was ill. "Promise not to say anything?"

It wasn't my diagnosis to share, but it didn't seem fair to Natalie and Seelie that they didn't know. *I* would want to know. "Only if you promise to tell them soon."

"I will."

"Are you at least under a doctor's care?"

"Many." He sighed.

"What exactly is wrong?"

"It's nothing to—"

"Come on now, let's sit down. What are you two whispering about?" Seelie asked.

Doc propelled me into the dining room and said, "I was telling Anna Kate again how wonderful it is to have her here."

It's nothing to worry about. That's what he had been going to say—I was sure of it. But by the looks of him, I was worried. I had my share of biology and anatomy classes in college, and I was quickly searching my brain for a disease that would cause that kind of coloring. Hepatitis or liver failure jumped first to mind. Treatable, yes, but sometimes fatal.

"It is indeed," Seelie said, raising her gaze to meet mine. She quickly dropped it again, as if not wanting to seem like she was staring. "I hope it becomes a tradition for as long as you're in town, Anna Kate. Our home is your home."

I managed a weak, noncommittal smile. "Thank you."

"Where am I? Are there hidden cameras?" Natalie buckled Ollie into a booster seat tethered to the chair next to hers and looked upward, scanning ceiling corners.

"Don't be absurd, Natalie," Seelie said. "Now let's sit and have a nice meal. What can I get for y'all to drink? There's sweet tea, wine, Coke, and coffee . . ."

Natalie went back to shaking her head in disbelief and gave Ollie a green bean to gnaw on.

I wasn't much of a drinker, but I eyed the wine and wondered if anyone would mind if I drank it straight from the bottle. To play it safe, I opted for tea.

Along with an overabundance of surrealism, the dining room held a farmhouse table, painted matte black. A long runner embellished with embroidered roses ran down the center of the table. Among plates and bowls of food, three small vases held fresh flowers that looked like they'd come from the backyard flower beds. Daisies, black-eyed Susans, white roses, and ferns.

"Beautiful flowers," I said as Doc held out a chair for me.

"Thank you." Seelie put a tall tea glass in front of me, then went around to the other side and handed one to Natalie as well. "James cut them from the garden this morning."

James. Doc. My grandfather. My very ill grandfather.

I fought a rush of sadness and focused on my surroundings. White china sat on thick green cotton placemats that had an intricate floral design stitched into them, and the polished silver flatware gleamed. The artwork tended toward colorful animal prints, watercolors of rabbits, squirrels, and a lamb. Framed family photos were tucked around the room, on the sideboard and on top of a hutch. I wanted to get up to study each and every photo, but I didn't want to be overtly rude.

"Before we eat, I'd like to say something," Seelie said as she took her seat. She looked across the table to Doc.

He gave her an encouraging nod.

Seelie's gaze shifted to Natalie, then me. She inhaled deeply. "Anna Kate, I don't know what happened the day your father died. No one does. I chose to believe the worst, because it helped me deal with the pain if I had someone to blame. It was easier than not knowing the reason why he isn't here. I *needed* someone to blame."

In my lap, my hands were fisted so tightly my short fingernails dug painfully into my palms. "And now you suddenly don't need someone to blame?"

I tried to keep in mind all Natalie had told me, about how the accident changed her mother. Her account had tugged at my heartstrings, because I was human. I couldn't imagine what it was like to live through the death of your child. It didn't excuse Seelie's behavior toward my mom, but it explained it to a certain degree.

However, even knowing all that, accepting it, even, didn't stop the anger simmering within me.

I tried my hardest to tamp it down, to listen, but I could feel it bubbling under the surface.

Healing, I reminded myself. *Healing.*

Seelie held my gaze. "Until I saw you the other night, I couldn't admit to myself that's what I'd been doing. There's an unimaginable pain that comes with burying your child, agony that I wouldn't wish on my worst enemy. Accepting that God simply decided AJ's time was up and took him away . . . I couldn't bear the thought." Moisture shimmered in her eyes. "It was easier for me to blame your mother than accept it was God's will. It was the only way I could go on."

Ollie fussed and Natalie quickly gave her a handful of green beans, a scoop of mashed potatoes, and a sippy cup of milk.

"It sounds to me," I said, trying to keep my voice even, "as though you still haven't accepted it. Do you believe the crash was an accident or not?"

"I don't know what happened," she repeated.

I broke eye contact and pressed my lips together to keep from lashing out.

"Seelie," Doc said, a warning in his low tone.

"Hush up," she said to him. "I'm just being as truthful as I can. Anna Kate, before now I wasn't even willing to *consider* the crash was an accident. Now, I am, but I need more time to fully process it. I need time to adjust to the fact that I could've been wrong for so many years. That I could've caused irreparable damage to others in my quest to see that someone was held accountable for AJ's death. To accept that there might be no reason at all why my son was taken away from me."

Could have. Might be. The words stung, not because she wouldn't blindly accept that my mom hadn't driven off that road on purpose, but because the words needled my conscience. The fact of the matter was that Seelie was right: no one knew what had happened on that road.

But I knew my mom. Knew her well enough to know she wouldn't physically hurt another person. She abhorred violence of any sort. The only times I ever heard her truly angry were the rare times she spoke of Seelie and Doc, and even then she hadn't raised her voice. "My mother would never hurt anyone on purpose. If you'd taken any time to get to know her, you'd know that."

"Of course we knew her," Seelie said dismissively. "She and AJ dated for three years."

Taking a deep breath, I said, "You knew her only as the enemy. You didn't know who she was as a person at all."

"Eden is not an innocent victim in all this," Seelie snapped. "She hurt us by hiding you away, didn't she? Vindictive isn't a pretty look on anyone."

"And there she is. *That's* my mama." Natalie leaned back in her chair. "Thought I'd lost my mind for a while. Bare feet," she murmured.

"Natalie." Doc sighed.

"What?" she asked. "Bare feet. When have you ever known Mama to walk around with bare feet in the house? Never. That's when. Slippers, sometimes. But mostly it's normal shoes. Heels, even."

Seelie looked toward the ceiling and muttered something under her breath before saying to Natalie, "That's enough, young lady. If I want to be barefoot in my own house, then I will."

Natalie rolled her eyes, and I had the feeling they'd been rolled quite a bit under this roof while she was growing up. "Yes, ma'am."

Seelie faced me. Her blue eyes had frosted over, and in them I saw the hard woman Natalie knew so well. "If Eden wanted to punish us by keeping you away, she succeeded. We will never get those years back."

"This isn't getting us anywhere," Doc interrupted.

Heat radiated through my body as my temper flared. "Actions reap consequences. You can try to spread the blame around, but it's your vile behavior that has led us to this point. You know what you've done."

She linked her hands together, set them on the table's edge, and leaned in. "Yes, I do know. I loved my son so much that I wanted what was best for him. Parents want what's best for our children, and if that comes across as harsh sometimes, then so be it. Eden was opinionated and headstrong and came from questionable bloodlines—between Zee's hippie ways and a practically anonymous father . . . Eden didn't fit in *our* world. She wouldn't have been happy," Seelie said. "There are expectations that come with being a Linden. Could you imagine Eden at a Junior League meeting?"

I glanced at Doc. He was shaking his head as though he couldn't believe what he was hearing, but he didn't speak up.

I turned my attention back to Seelie. "You're not seriously trying to argue that you were doing my mom a favor by treating her badly?"

"Of course not. I'm trying to make you understand that we lived in two vastly different worlds. Eden wasn't the right choice for AJ."

I unclenched my fists, then clenched them again. "That wasn't your decision to make. They loved each other."

She kept her hands joined, her fingers laced together so tightly they were turning white. "Can parents make mistakes? Absolutely. We're human. I, however, don't see that I was wrong to think Eden was anything other than an obstacle holding AJ back from his full potential. And I was right. She was driving the car when he was killed. If he hadn't been dating her, they wouldn't have been together, and he'd still be here, wouldn't he?"

"So much for God's will," I said through clenched teeth.

"It must be nice to sit there steeping in your self-righteousness," Seelie said, her tone softening as she leaned back in her chair. "You haven't walked in my shoes." She pointed at Natalie. "Not one word about my feet."

Natalie snapped her mouth shut.

Seelie went on, and in that moment of letting her guard down, I could once again see the imprint of all she had lost. "But let me ask you this, Anna Kate. How do you feel about Eden hiding you away all these years? She undoubtedly believed she was making the right choice for you, because as I said, that's what parents do, but do *you* think she made the right decision keeping you sequestered? Keeping you from people who would have done nothing but love you?"

I looked between the four of them, focusing mostly on Ollie, who was eating mashed potatoes with her fingers. I thought of all the hate after the accident. The hatred my mother had endured. Her hatred toward this family. Hate, hate, hate.

"I thought maybe she *had* made a mistake," I said. "It's why I came here today. I was hoping that we could try to put the past behind us and start over, but now I can't help feeling that the hate runs too deep for me to dig us out. I'd been foolish to even think it was possible." I pushed back my chair and stood up.

"It wasn't foolish, Anna Kate," Doc said, standing as well. "It's what we want, too."

"We're a family, Anna Kate," Natalie added. "The thing about families is sometimes they fight. Especially our family. We get angry and say things we don't mean—and sometimes things we do. It doesn't mean that there's not love beneath the anger. Please don't leave. We can work through this."

The tears shimmering in her eyes nearly did me in. I couldn't bear to see her upset. It was then that part of Zee's blackbird story came back, loud and clear.

Above all else, the guardians must nurture the love. Without it, all is lost.

That those words would resurface now meant I should take them to heart, but I couldn't overcome the sense that I'd be fighting a losing battle. "I don't know how we can. The past can't be changed. There's no getting over it or putting it behind us. It's *become* us. We live it and breathe it, keeping the anger alive, fanning its flames. There's no way to overcome it."

"There has to be a way," Natalie said. "I refuse to give up."

I wanted there to be a way—the healer in me wanted it more than anything. But there was no balm or salve or herbal tea that could take away this kind of pain.

Seelie stood. "No. Anna Kate's right. The past cannot change."

"Mama," Natalie said on a sigh.

Seelie held up a hand. "The past can't change, but people can. The minute I saw you, Anna Kate, I realized how *hardheaded* I'd been all these years. It started me thinking that maybe Eden and I had more in common than I thought. That, perhaps, I'd been wrong about her after all, because if she hadn't been in AJ's life . . . we wouldn't have you. If I could go back and make some changes—and truly get to know something other than your mother's flaws, I would. I can't. I can, however, start making changes right now. I've made mistakes that hurt people, and I'm truly sorry. I hope one day you'll forgive me."

I gripped the back of the chair as I listened. I felt her words, knew she believed what she said, but I wasn't sure I trusted her to follow through. She was seventy-odd years old and had lived her life in such rigid confines that going barefoot was a big deal. Could someone truly change after all that time? "I appreciate that. I do. I'm just . . ." My emotions were too jumbled to make sense of how I was feeling. "I need some time."

Doc said, "Our door is always open, and the supper invitation stands."

My gaze fell on Ollie. Oblivious to the turmoil around her, she grinned when she saw me watching her and flapped her arm, sending a green bean flying. "Annkay! Hihi!"

My heart felt like it was breaking in half. She'd started calling me Annkay when she couldn't

300

properly pronounce Anna Kate. "Hi, Ollie."

As I watched her play with her food, I realized she only knew love and happiness, so that's what she gave people. Even people she didn't know very well. She didn't know hate, and I didn't want her to, especially when it came to her own family.

I was leaving this town soon, but when I left, I didn't have to pack that heavy hatred along with my quilt, like always.

The choice was mine.

I could cut them off completely here and now, or I could start healing, like I had originally intended.

Talking over the catch in my throat, I said, "I'll be back—I just don't know when. I need to sort through all these feelings."

"We'll be here waiting," Doc said, and Seelie nodded.

With that, I practically ran toward the patio door, hoping I'd made the right decision by not cutting them off.

I wasn't sure.

But as I walked home in the bright sunshine and thick humidity, I noticed my steps were just a little bit lighter.

16

Anna Kate

Early the next morning I found myself sitting in the garden at dawn, staring at my feet when I should have been collecting veggies and pulling weeds.

I'd been crouching on the gravel pathway telling the zucchini what went down at the Lindens' house the day before when I'd taken notice of my feet. My blue toenail polish was chipped. My ankle bones stuck out as usual. They'd always seemed to be extraordinarily bony to me, despite the many times my mom had told me that they were perfectly ordinary. Morning dew mixed with garden dirt had left dark streaks on the tops and sides of my feet, and wishbone-shaped tan lines attested to the fact that flip-flops were my preferred summertime footwear.

The phoebe sang from the stone bench in the center of the garden as I slipped my feet out of the flimsy shoes and sat down, stretching out my legs, then drawing them inward to press the soles of my feet together. I held them, closed my eyes, and fought a wave of guilt.

"Anna Kate? Are the weeds so stressful you're meditating?"

My eyes flew open, and I found Gideon looming over me. "How did I not hear you?"

"Either I'm light on my feet," he said, sitting down, "or you were deep in thought."

Looking like he'd just rolled out of bed, his hair was rumpled, his eyes hooded and sleepy. He had on a wrinkled T-shirt, long gym shorts, and sport sandals. Most weekdays, he went for a long bike ride before starting work. "If I was a betting man, then I'd say it was the latter."

He had nice feet, I noticed. Clean with neatly trimmed toenails. "Are you a betting man?"

He studied me. "Today I am. You're not really meditating, are you? If so, I can come back later."

"I'm not meditating. I tried to once, but I couldn't figure out how to shut off my thoughts. It was as though sitting still, breathing evenly, gave my brain permission to run wild. What exactly is high-fructose corn syrup, why is the Earth round, what really happened to Elvis . . . that kind of thing. It was a free-for-all in there." I let go of my feet, stretched out my legs again. "The same goes with yoga. I can't concentrate."

"Maybe you should come with me on a bike ride or a hike sometime. Riding works wonders at clearing my mind."

"Maybe I will," I said.

I looked at my feet again, at that chipped polish, then shifted my gaze to the mulberry trees. Their branches hung low, weighted by morning dew and almost-ripe berries. The blackbirds had come to sing their songs last night, and I'd listened with tears in my eyes, wishing one of those messages could be for me.

"Anna Kate?" He nudged my leg. Light springy hairs covered his legs, and he had a small scab on his right knee. "Are you sure you're okay?"

I wasn't certain what he saw that made him ask the question, since I was usually better at hiding my emotions. The concern in his amber eyes had me blurting out what was weighing on my mind. "I like walking around barefoot."

"Okay," he said slowly, a question in his tone.

"Do you walk around your house barefoot?"

Leaning forward, he rested his forearms on bent knees. "All the time. Why?"

I tucked a zucchini into the basket. The plant's leaves had grown to the size of dinner plates, and I couldn't pick fast enough for what the plants produced now that they were healthy and happy. "I know somebody who doesn't. Who, because of the way she was raised, feels it's improper to go around in bare feet. Even in her own home." I looked at my toes, but all I could see was Seelie's blush-colored nail polish.

"Seems old-fashioned and a little sad in a way, but it's not a big deal. Why is it bothering you?"

It *was* bothering me. A lot. I tried to push it out of my mind, but it kept finding its way back.

I didn't want to think about how the way a

305

person had been raised could influence them throughout their whole life to the point where they were seventy years old and still wearing shoes in the house because they didn't want to break protocol.

Because if I dug deep to see the bigger picture, then I might have to consider that a person who had been nurtured under those kinds of strict rules and archaic wisdoms wouldn't consider getting to know someone they deemed beneath them. Someone like the daughter of a free-spirited café owner, even if that young woman was dating their son. It simply wouldn't cross their minds to care. Oh, they'd be polite. Civil. All surface and no depth. Because that's just who they were. How they were raised. Undoubtedly, they believed their son would tire of the girl he was dating and move on to someone more suitable. Someone from an upper-class background.

Who probably never walked around barefoot.

Shaking my head, I said, "Sorry, I shouldn't have said anything. I'm just . . . I didn't get a lot of sleep last night. I have a lot on my mind and haven't had near enough coffee this morning." I stood up, slipped my flip-flops back on, and held out my hand to him. "Let's fix that, shall we?"

Looking at my hand, he hesitated only a second before putting his palm on mine, and then he wrapped his fingers around my wrist. He rose in one fluid motion, but once on his feet he didn't let go of me. "If you ever want to talk about it, Anna Kate . . ."

"Thanks, Gideon." I pulled my hand free and started up the steps. "Are you hungry?"

"Coffee's just fine." He surged ahead to open the back door for me. I washed up, and we fell into our usual routine.

"What's today's special?" he asked.

Last week, I'd taken over creating the day's specials. I enjoyed coming up with the recipes. So much so that I wished I could spend all my time in the kitchen, but three cooks in here was a bit much. "Sausage and ramps mini-frittatas."

"Ramps? How very southern of you."

"Not true. I simply discovered some growing at the back of Zee's garden and thought I'd try them. They're good. I'm going to start incorporating them more often in my cooking. When, you know, they're in season." I wrinkled my nose. "I wonder if they grow in Massachusetts."

"Next thing you know, you'll be cooking up collard greens and grits."

"I already cook those—my mom taught me when I was little. You can take the woman out of Wicklow, but not Wicklow out of the woman."

Which was especially true for the women in our family.

"It's what I've been telling you," he said. "Wicklow has a way of holding on."

I clutched the handle of the coffee pot. "Yeah,

but it always sounds like a warning when you say it, even when you're joking."

He smiled over the rim of his mug. "Does it?"

"Are you saying it isn't?"

"That depends."

"On what?" I set the pot back on its warmer.

"On whether you want to be held."

Out the side window, I saw that some of the birders were already awake and milling about. Zachariah Boyd, Sir Bird Nerd, was walking around the yard with a trash bag picking up litter. I was starting to wonder if Wicklow had gotten a hold on him, too.

"Do you, by the way?" Gideon asked.

I looked over my shoulder. "Do I what?"

"Want to be held?"

I turned to face him fully, wondering if the flirtation I picked up on was real or if I was imagining it. He looked perfectly relaxed, his hips resting against the counter, his ankles crossed, his hands holding his mug to his lips. It was his eyes that gave him away. There was heat in them, making that amber look like molten lava.

My stomach tightened with a need for something I'd never wanted before. Instantly I told myself to knock it off, because there was no arm's length in *those* thoughts.

He quietly added, "Held by Wicklow?"

"By Wicklow," I repeated, struggling against the disappointment of it all. I busied myself filling ceramic containers with sugar packets. "It doesn't matter much what Wicklow wants. I'm leaving at the end of July."

He set his mug on the counter and started helping with the sugar. "Then a warning it is."

"Noted." I took a sip of coffee. "I wanted to apologize for the other night. It was . . . dramatic."

After the horrifying scene with Seelie, we'd quickly packed up and left the amphitheater. Gideon and I had walked back to the café in silence. Our goodbyes had been awkward. And later, I realized I hadn't even had a chance to unpack the blackberry sweet tea before all hell had broken loose. If it had been a date, then it would have fallen under the "disastrous" category.

We reached for the sugar packets at the same time, our fingers tangling. Our gazes met, then we pulled our hands away.

"What's family," he asked, "without a little drama?"

Family. "You make a good point."

His gaze went up to the soffit again. "Speaking of family, I'm surprised Zee never mentioned me to you."

"She didn't really talk about anyone from Wicklow when she visited. Is there a reason she should have? Mentioned you to me, I mean? Besides your friendship?" Because to my ears, it sounded like there might be something more.

"I thought she would. Considering."

"Considering what?"

He was stopped from answering by a knock on the front door.

"You do have your fair share of early morning visitors, don't you?" he asked, laughing. "I'm starting to think I had it all wrong, and it's you who has the hold on Wicklow."

Smiling, I turned, expecting to see Mr. Lazenby at the door. It wasn't. It was Pebbles.

"I'm going to head out," Gideon said, walking toward the back door.

"You don't want to stay and talk? I'm sure I'll only be a moment with Pebbles."

"I'm sure. There's a bike ride calling my name."

"All right, then."

He went out the back while I opened the front door. Pebbles had a smile on her face. "That Gideon's a cute one, isn't he?"

"Is he?" I asked as innocently as I could manage. "I hadn't noticed."

Pebbles chuckled, clearly seeing right through me. "I suppose you're wondering why I'm here so early."

"I suppose I am. Is everything okay?"

She looked left, then right. "I have a favor to ask."

I stepped aside. "Come on in."

Later that morning, I stopped by Mr. Lazenby's chair at the far end of the community table to refill his coffee mug. He had Faylene next to him and Pebbles across, as usual.

He coughed into a handkerchief. He'd been coughing all morning. I said, "I can whip you up something for that cough, Mr. Lazenby. Help clear out those lungs. A little licorice root tea will do you a world of good."

"I don't be needing none of that," he stated as he tucked away his handkerchief. "I'm fine, just a tickle from the grass pollen. I mowed my lawn last evening."

I eyed his uneaten, yet thoroughly dissected, piece of pie. It had been gutted, its berries mashed, the crust scattered like buckshot. He'd cleaned his plate of scrambled eggs and sweet potato hash, so I knew he wasn't feeling too terribly. "Something wrong with the pie, then?"

He looked up at me, his rheumy eyes swimming with dismay. "Yes, ma'am. The blackbird pie has blueberries in it."

"It's a mixed berry pie. Blueberry, raspberry, and blackberry. It's a new recipe I started making last week, since the blueberries are ripening."

"Well, I wish you wouldn't go changing what isn't broken. I hate blueberries, and I hear tell from Jena that all the other—*normal*—pies are long sold out."

"You aren't goin' to up and die, Otis, from not being able to eat a piece of pie," Faylene said, then glanced my way. "Don't be minding him, honey. You go on and keep that pie on the menu. Everyone else thinks the pie is delicious. Ain't that so?" She stood up and asked again, much more loudly to the whole room, "Ain't the mixed berry pie delicious?"

A concerto of agreement rose to the rafters, and I smiled. Faylene was anything but subtle.

She sat back down, set her napkin on her lap, and picked up her mug. "Told you so."

Mr. Lazenby wore a black-and-white polka-dot tie today with his short-sleeved white dress shirt. "What're you going on about, Faylene? You haven't even had a piece of that pie. You don't know how delicious it is or *ain't*."

Pebbles said, "Well, I ate it, and it's mighty good pie, Anna Kate. One of the best pieces of pie I ever did have."

Mr. Lazenby scowled at her.

"Don't be looking at me like that, Otis Lazenby. A little change never hurt anyone." Pebbles sipped from her mug, her pinky in the air.

"It's hurting me right now, isn't it?" he snapped back.

She set down her mug and glared. "Don't you go takin' your bad mood out on Anna Kate. She's been doing nothing but running herself ragged all morning taking care of everyone, not even having one day off since she opened the café. Where's your *grace*? If you wanted a particular piece of pie, you should have gotten here right at eight, like always, not two hours late, expecting there to even be pie left."

Her head bobbled as she gave him what for, and her beehive hairdo wobbled back and forth. For a second there, I was afraid it was going to topple over, but whatever hairspray she used worked miracles.

Pebbles knew firsthand that Mr. Lazenby wasn't here right as the doors opened, because she had been. And she'd been sitting in that exact chair, nursing a cup of coffee and keeping a worried eye on the door, until he came inside and sat down.

She also knew there wouldn't be any pie left but the mixed berry, because she'd bought every last one of the others and delivered them to the birders camped outside—as a gesture of hospitality, she'd said, feeding me a line of how appreciative she was of the birders for bringing her extra income just as her property taxes were coming due.

I slid her a look, and she blinked innocently at me.

I realized now that her act of kindness had nothing to do with hospitality and everything to do with keeping Mr. Lazenby from his pie. She had to have known he didn't like blueberries and that was why the mixed berry pies were the only ones she didn't buy.

I gave her a pointed look, and she simply smiled at me and sipped her coffee, the sneaky woman.

"Two hours late?" Faylene repeated. "That isn't like you, Otis. Did you sleep in? Did you have an appointment? Did you forget where you put your wallet? Did you lose your way here and end up on the other side of town?"

"That last one only happened once," he said, "and I wish you'd stop reminding me of it. As you know, I had started a new allergy medication that made me lose my bearings."

I turned and filled the mugs on the table behind me, while still listening to the conversation. It had been strange not to see Mr. Lazenby at the door first thing that morning, but I'd been so busy I hadn't had a chance to really think about *why*.

"And that's not what happened today?" she asked.

He sent her a withering look that fell flat. "No," he grumbled, dragging the word out as he shoved plump berries around the plate.

I swapped out my nearly empty pot of coffee for a fresh one and cleared a newly emptied table, a two-top. I wiped it down and reset it fast as I could, so I could keep an ear on the conversation.

"Now you've gone and piqued my curiosity," Pebbles said. "Why *were* you late this morning?"

He set down his fork and sighed. "Not that it's anyone's business but mine, but Rosemarie told me I should come in at nine today."

Pebbles leaned back and sighed. I might have

314

been the only one to see her roll her eyes, because Faylene was already patting Mr. Lazenby's arm while saying, "Well, bless your heart."

"Rosemarie?" I asked, shamelessly inviting myself into the conversation as I cleared the plates from the spot next to Faylene.

"My wife," he said wistfully.

His *dead* wife. "Her message to you from yesterday's pie was to come here two hours later than usual?"

"That's right," he said, his shoulders stiffening. "What about it?"

"I just . . . I thought the messages being sent would be more . . ." I searched for the right word.

"Affectionate?" Faylene offered.

"Well, yes. I always thought they were love notes." I gestured to the soffit. *"Under midnight skies, Blackbirds sing,* Loving *notes . . ."*

"What is love?" Faylene said, reminding me of Aubin Pavegeau.

I hadn't seen him since the day I stopped by his cottage, but I'd become addicted to his blackberry tea.

"Once," Faylene said, "one of my notes from Harold reminded me to pay the county taxes. Another time, he went on and on about the importance of changing the oil in the car after I burned out the engine. If you're asking me, that message would've been real helpful *before* the engine burned out, but who am I to nitpick messages from the dead?" She took a deep breath, blew across the top of her coffee mug. "He sent those notes because he loves me and doesn't want me to lose the house or blow up the car. Taking care of me is how he always showed his love."

"That's kind of sweet," I said. "But I don't think I've seen you eat any pie since I've been here. Do you not want messages anymore?"

"It's been some time now that I gave up the pie. I'd like to fall in love again at some point, and I don't think I'd ever be able to fall for someone else if I'm still talking to Harold all the time, never able to truly mourn him. Sometimes it's best to let the past go, know what I mean?"

"No." Mr. Lazenby thumped the table with a closed hand. "I'm not ready to be lettin' anything go."

Faylene elbowed him. "You don't ever think of falling in love again, Otis? Have someone to share your twilight years with?"

"I have someone," he said. "Rosemarie."

Pebbles groaned softly.

I thought I was the only one who heard her, but then I saw Mr. Lazenby give her the side-eye and wondered if he knew more about how Pebbles felt than he let on.

Mr. Lazenby said, "I know Rosemarie nags sometimes—"

"All the time," Pebbles said, cutting him off. "She nags you *all* the time." Her voice went up an octave. "Get a haircut, weed the flowers, throw out the expired crackers in the pantry, get to church early, watch your cholesterol, eat more vegetables, cut back on the sweets . . ." Pebbles thumbed away a drop of coffee sliding down her mug. "And Otis always does what she says. Always."

Pebbles pressed her lips together as though holding back what she truly thought of the matter of Mr. Lazenby and his wife's messages. It was probably wise of her, considering his hackles were already raised, blinding him to why Pebbles would care so much.

"Why wouldn't I? It's darn good advice." He handed me the pie plate. "Take this away, please. *Blueberries. Blech.*"

Faylene stood up. "I best be on my way. I have a grandbaby to see. Chin up, Otis. There'll be more pie tomorrow." She paid her bill and with a wave, she was gone.

Mr. Lazenby started coughing again, and I said, "Are you sure about that herbal tea? It wouldn't take any time at all to brew."

"I'm sure." He threw his napkin and a ten-dollar bill on the table. "I'm going home. I'd appreciate it if you saved me a piece of apple pie tomorrow, Miss Anna Kate."

Pebbles shook her head vigorously, and the beehive swayed. "Anna Kate only saves pie for family, remember?"

"Daggummit," he said.

He might not be blood related, but for some reason it had started to feel like he was family. A grumpy old grandpa. "That's true," I said, "but I've decided not to sell the pies in bulk anymore, so there should be plenty left when you get here tomorrow, Mr. Lazenby, no matter what time that is."

He beamed. "I appreciate that. See you tomorrow morning."

Pebbles pouted as he left, and I said, "If you want him, you can't trick him. He has to come around on his own."

She stared into her mug. "It's been years. How long am I supposed to wait, Anna Kate?"

Unfortunately, I didn't have an answer for her.

17

The reporter glanced over at the older woman at the next table. Pen in hand, she was focused on a leather-bound portfolio spread open on the table. But she wasn't writing. A full glass of iced tea sat untouched, and condensation slid down the glass into a napkin placed under its base.

There was something in her intensity. The way she stared at the paper as if willing the words to come. The stubborn set of her chin. The white-knuckled grip on the pen. From a quick look, he pegged her as someone who was used to getting what she wanted. She had an air of power about her, evident in the way she held herself. Shoulders low, chin up, back straight.

As though sensing his examination, she turned her head his way and narrowed her icy blue eyes as if perturbed by the disruption.

"Are you writing an article about the blackbirds too?" he asked, trying to cover his nosiness.

"No," she said, some of the ice thawing from her gaze. "If you must know, I'm trying to rewrite the story of my life."

Natalie

Late Thursday morning, I hurried along the side-walk, my ponytail swishing across the back of my neck. I paused to look both ways for a break in the steady stream of traffic before dashing across the street to the grassy median.

I waved to an imposing-looking Josh Kolbaugh as he informed two people that they'd need to relocate their tent from the median to somewhere safer. By the looks of all the tents, chairs, and hammocks strung up along the full length of the median, Josh had a busy day ahead of him, rousting the birders from their makeshift roosts.

With another quick look, I darted across the street in front of Hodgepodge.

"Crosswalk, next time, Natalie!" Josh yelled, his big voice like a thunderclap.

Looking back at him, I said, "Sorry!" I noted, too, that the campers suddenly picked up the pace of packing their belongings, as though not wanting to be on the receiving end of his bad side. Smart people, those birders.

A bell rang out as I walked into Hodgepodge. I took a moment to adjust to the dim lighting, but only a moment. I was on break and didn't have much time to spare. Not that Anna Kate would mind if I was late getting back, but I would. I took pride in my work ethic.

Needlepoint sachets scented the air with balsam pine. Shoppers chattered loudly. Even though the small store had opened only fifteen minutes ago, it was at capacity.

Marcy had three people in line at the register,

so I didn't want to bother her. Instead, I signaled that I was going to set the grocery sack of headbands, bow ties, and hair bows behind the counter. There was an invoice in the bag based on our previous consignments, so I didn't feel the need to stick around and keep Marcy from her customers.

I was heading toward the counter when I spotted Cam Kolbaugh hanging a framed photo on a wall near a display of local pottery, so I detoured over to see him. I stepped up close to catch a glimpse of the photo without disturbing him and saw River lying near Cam's feet. His tail thumped against the wooden floor when he spotted me.

The photo was a shot of fireflies dancing in a moonlit meadow. Dark yet light, whimsical yet somehow somber. It was utterly captivating.

"That's beautiful, Cam," I said.

Cam startled, nearly knocking me over as he jumped back, mumbling, "Sweet Jesus," as he grabbed hold of me to keep me from falling over.

"Sorry," I said once I was steady on my feet. "I didn't mean to scare you."

"No, no." His hands squeezed my shoulders. "It's not your fault. I must be getting rusty."

River jumped up and pawed at Cam's foot with a whimper.

Cam's eyes had dimmed, and his arms were straight, locked. His breathing had quickened and his hands trembled.

"Rusty?" I asked, not quite following along.

"Once upon a time I was highly trained *not* to be snuck up on." He finally released his grip, and then gave my shoulders a friendly you're-good-as-new pat.

"Oh gosh, Cam. I'm so sorry. I wasn't thinking." My heart hurt for him and all he'd been through as a soldier.

"It's okay, Natalie." He smiled. "Old habits are hard to break is all."

"You sure you're okay?"

The light slowly came back to his eyes and River lay down, setting his head on his paws. "I'm sure. How're *you* doing, by the way?"

"I'm okay," I said, trying to be as honest as possible. "It comes and goes."

"I get that." He walked over and picked up another photo to hang. "Do you need a ride to your appointment this afternoon?"

As much as I wanted to take him up on that offer, I couldn't lie. "No, my father's loaning me his car."

"Check the hood for nests beforehand." He aligned the picture wire on the back of the frame with a hook on the wall.

I smiled. "I will."

I studied the newest photo, a doe drinking from a pool of water at the base of a skinny water-fall. Despite the fact that the sight of water usually gave me palpitations, this image radiated tranquility. "Is this near here?"

"Up near my cabin, well off public trails."

"No wonder you like it up there so much. It's so . . . peaceful."

"Even more so in person. If you're interested in seeing it, River and I'd be happy to show you and Ollie one day, as long as you promise not to tell its secret location. The last thing I need is all these birdwatchers up there, getting lost in the woods." At his name, River wagged his tail.

Suddenly, I wanted to see that spot more than anything. To *feel* it. But hiking with Ollie would be a challenge, and then there was the water situation . . ."Maybe one day." I checked my watch. "I should probably get going, since my break is almost over."

"It was nice seeing you, Natalie. Maybe . . ."

When he looked away and didn't finish his thought, I prompted him. "What?"

"It's nothing."

"You sure?" I asked.

He nodded.

"Then I guess I'll see you around." I bent and petted River's ears. "And you, too." He licked my hand, probably smelling bacon on it yet again.

As I turned away from them, two people in the far corner of the shop caught my eye. I blinked, wondering if I was seeing things. But no. Faylene Wiggins and my mother were in full conversation. Well, Faylene was. Mama, whose back was to me, seemed only to be listening.

I looked around, wondering where Ollie was, since Faylene was keeping her today. Suddenly nervous, I pretty much ran over, tucking around displays like I was a pro at obstacle courses.

"Natalie!" Faylene's eyes lit up when she saw me. "This is a surprise seeing you here."

My gaze dropped to the double-wide umbrella stroller beside her, and the smile came slowly as I saw Ollie and Lindy-Lou fast asleep side by side, their tiny hands clasped together.

"Aren't they the most precious?" Faylene asked.

The corners of Mama's eyes crinkled as she pushed a loose curl off Ollie's slack face. "They are most certainly that." Her gaze shifted to me. "Good morning, Natalie. I thought you had work today?"

"I'm on break." Who was this woman *smiling* at me, and what had she done with Seelie Earl Linden? Not a week ago, she'd been giving me the silent treatment for letting Faylene watch Ollie. Now, Mama was standing here, literally faced with my decision, and acting like it was no big deal. "I just stopped by to drop off some items for the shop."

"Marcy's already done sold out of what you brought by on Monday. She can't keep your handiwork in stock. They come in, they go out, lickety-split. You should consider expanding your line to clothes, blankets." She laughed. "Heck, you should probably open your own shop. Ooh, Lordy, don't tell Marcy I said that. I saw you over there talking to Cam. Everything okay? Looked kind of serious."

My head spun with trying to keep track of the twists and turns in her conversation. "Everything's fine," I said. "I was just admiring his photos."

Mama craned her neck. "Cam? The mountain man?"

"Yes, Mama. Cam lives in a cabin up the mountain."

"You and he aren't—" Mama cut herself off.

Faylene picked up the conversational thread Mama had dropped. She wiggled her eyebrows. "I heard he and you were snuggling on a bench out front not too long ago, and you two looked mighty comfortable with each other at the moonlight movie Friday night."

Mama's eyes flew open wide.

My cheeks flamed. "We weren't snuggling. I had a panic attack and he helped me through it. And no, we *aren't*."

"Bless your heart," Faylene said. "I'm glad Cam was there to help you out. He's a good one. One of the best." She dropped her voice. "His wife ran off with the cable TV guy while Cam was soldiering overseas. Broke his heart, she did. I think she's plumb out of her mind. You don't leave a guy like Cam, even if he was gone a lot. Men like him and Josh are hard to come by." She *tsk*ed.

I glanced over at Cam as he hung another picture. My heart hurt for him again. I'd known his marriage had fallen apart, but I never suspected exactly how hard it had gone down.

Mama slid him another look, but didn't voice any opinions about what kind of man he might or might not be. I was grateful she held her tongue.

"If you're asking me, Natalie," Faylene said, as she suddenly felt the need to examine her painted fingernails, "I think you and Cam would be good together. I'm just sayin' it's something to think about. Think real hard about."

"Thanks, Faylene," I said quickly. "But I'm not of a dating mind quite yet."

She patted my shoulder. "I understand, honey. But sometimes love has a way of sneaking up on you. Keep that in mind, so you're not startled when it up and taps you on the heart."

"Love," Mama said with a huff. "Natalie can't have known that man longer than a week."

I corrected her. "Actually, it's been almost three weeks."

"Love don't have no timetable, Seelie," Faylene said emphatically.

Mama looked to the heavens. "Lord have mercy."

I had expected more of a protest; after all, a fully bearded, divorced mountain man would never have been welcomed to supper, let alone into my life. But Mama, surprisingly, kept any further opinions to herself.

"Let me see what you've got there, Natalie," Faylene said, motioning to my sack. "I want first dibs, and I can afford to buy lots, now that I've rented rooms in my house to the birdwatchers. They're paying me a pretty penny to stay at my place. All three of my extra bedrooms have been snapped up, and when these guests leave, I'll take in others. God love those bird-loving tourists."

"You've taken in strangers while you're caring for Olivia Leigh?" Mama asked, shock and outrage punctuating the question.

"Calm down now, Seelie. I always watch the girls over at Marcy and Josh's house. I thought you knew that."

Mama raised an arched eyebrow at me. "No, I didn't know."

She might have known, if she'd been talking to me, so I didn't feel too badly that she'd been unaware.

"But still," Mama said, pursing her lips. "Strangers in your house, Faylene?"

"You don't have to make it sound sordid. Consider it more as a boarding house. I'm planning to sign up with Airbnb to help get the word out. Become official, so to speak," she said, using air quotes around the word "official."

Disapproval was stamped all over Mama's

face, in her narrowed gaze and those tightly pressed lips. "Don't you need a license to rent out rooms?"

Faylene set her hands on her hips. "No ma'am. I checked and Wicklow doesn't currently have any regulations for short-term rentals. I'm guessing that'll change real quick, once word gets out. Just got to make sure I pay all the proper taxes. Now, look at these booties. So dang cute!"

"Aren't they, though?" I jumped into the change of subject with both feet. "I found that vintage fabric at a thrift shop in Montgomery years ago, part of an estate sale that had come in that morning. I never bought something so fast in all my life."

Mama peered into the sack. "What is all this?"

"Consignments." I quickly explained my deal with Marcy.

Faylene said, "Aren't they wonderful? Natalie is one talented woman."

Mama reached in and pulled out a bib. She studied it, turning it this way and that, finally saying, "This is precious, Natalie. The ducks are a lovely print—timeless yet visually appealing. The stitching is very well done, and the striped piping is a wonderful touch."

Faylene clapped Mama on the back. "Well, she learned from the best, didn't she? Didn't you, Natalie?"

"I did. It's true."

Mama's gaze flew up to mine, as though not believing what she was hearing. And, Lord help me, I could have sworn she was blushing.

"Natalie's talent is all her own," Mama said. "I can see why her items are selling quickly. And I agree with Faylene, Natalie. You should expand. Perhaps some bigger-ticket items?"

Faylene's eyes went wide and she pulled a long face laced with surprise.

I imagined I looked the same. The old Mama would have taken all the credit, hoarded it away like a secret stash of chocolate.

"Thank you, Mama. Maybe I'll add in a few more things," I said. "Someday."

"If you start making dresses, you let me know," Faylene said. "I'll be first in line to buy one for Lindy-Lou."

Mama eyed the grocery sack I still held. "But perhaps . . ."

Ah, here it comes. The nitpicking, can't-help-herself-from-butting-in matriarch. It was almost a relief to have her back. Because I knew how to deal with *that* woman. The other one? Not so much.

". . . a more professional method of deliv—" Mama abruptly cut herself off. Then she laughed.

Looking as flabbergasted as I felt, Faylene said, "You okay there, Seelie?"

"Oh, I'm fine," Mama said. "Natalie, you do things the way you want. Don't pay me any mind, hear?"

I nodded. I couldn't believe what I heard, but I heard it just the same. With only a few minutes left to get back to the café, I couldn't help asking what these two were doing together—they weren't ones to associate during the day. Or ever. "What are you two doing over here, anyway?"

"Oh, I was just telling Seelie here all I know about Eden Callow," Faylene said. "You could have blown me over with a feather when Seelie came in and asked about Eden. Eden, of all people. I mean, whoever would have thought? Not me, that's who."

Mama caught my eye, and I was surprised to see humor in my mother's gaze.

Surely, my father had been wrong. Mama had to be medicated. In all my life I'd never seen her amused by Faylene's ramblings. "Eden?" I said.

Mama clutched her pearls. "I thought I'd try to get to know her, after all."

"Better late than never," Faylene added with a firm nod.

"The only way I can think to do that is through people who knew her." Mama dropped her pearls and added, "But I'm not having much luck. It seems Eden mostly kept to herself."

Faylene snapped her fingers. "You know, my cousin Mary Beth was a classmate of Eden's. She might have more information for you."

Mama said, "Thank you for your help, Faylene."

"Oh," Faylene said, her face lighting up. "You might want to talk to Aubin Pavegeau. He probably knew Eden best, after AJ."

Mama's cheeks sucked in and her lips tightened. AJ had been best friends with Aubin growing up—much to Mama's dismay. Aubin, with his family's backwoods background, hadn't fit the mold of what my mother had deemed appropriate to associate with the Linden family. Somehow, and I truly did not know how, AJ had talked her into letting him choose his own friends.

I waited for Mama to say something, wondering just how big of a change she was willing to make.

"I'll keep that in mind," Mama said stiffly. "Right now, I'm going on over to the library to see Mary Beth." She dropped a kiss on Ollie's head, then grabbed my hand and gave it a squeeze. "I'll see you later."

Faylene and I stood shoulder to shoulder as we watched her weave through store displays on her way out.

"Is she taking happy pills?" Faylene asked. "I hear they work wonders for some people. Or, in Seelie's case, miracles."

"Not that I know of. According to my father, Mama's not taking—or drinking—anything." Since he wasn't one to lie, I certainly had some suspicions he might not have all the facts. "He says she's had a breakthrough of sorts."

"Well, I don't know what she's done had, but

331

I have to tell you, honey, I like the changes I'm seeing."

I liked the changes too.

But I didn't trust them yet.

I wasn't sure I ever would.

Anna Kate

I stared at my fingers, thinking there was no way they'd ever return to a normal color. They were stained purple, and I suddenly had visions of turning fully purple, like Violet turned blue in the Willy Wonka movie.

"If you rub your hands with one of the unripe mulberries, the pinkish-green ones, it helps take off the stain." Summer crushed one, rubbed her hands together, then rinsed. To my amazement, the purple faded from her hands. "See?"

We'd finished our first harvest of the ripe mulberries and had washed five pounds of fruit. We'd let the berries keep in the fridge in the Harry Potter room overnight. Tomorrow, we would harvest again and start canning, repeating the process every other day for at least a week or more.

I'd worn old clothes, so the dye on my T-shirt and jeans didn't bother me, but seeing my hands a different color was slightly disturbing. I used her trick, and my skin went from purple to a soft pink that was barely noticeable. "Amazing."

She laughed as she dried her hands on a dish-towel. "It's a trick Zee taught me."

"Well, thank you for sharing it, because, even though I knew we were facing stains, I didn't realize quite how bad they'd be."

"Anna Kate?"

"Hmm?"

"I know it's none of my business, but . . ."

"What?" I asked, smiling.

"Why are you going through all the trouble of processing these berries if you're going to be leaving soon? There aren't going to be any pies to be made."

I wasn't prepared for the emotional punch to the gut that came with her question. It nearly knocked the wind out of me. I'd been stifling thoughts of what would happen when I left Wicklow and trying not to worry about the blackbirds. What was going to happen to them?

There'll be a whole flock of women there to help guide the way, that I can promise you.

Holding on to Zee's promise, I said, "If I'm being completely honest, I don't know why I'm doing it, other than it's what's supposed to be done. Does that make sense?"

"Zee would be happy to know they're being taken care of. She loved those trees and these berries."

With a sad smile, I said, "I know."

I went to get my wallet. "Let me pay you now

for your help before I forget. What's your going rate for mulberry harvesting? Whatever it is, I'm sure it's not high enough, so don't lowball." I planned to double the number, no matter what she said. I didn't know what I'd have done without her help. "I know you'll put the money to good use at college."

When she didn't answer right away, I faced her. "Summer?" There were tears in her eyes. I rushed over. "What's wrong?"

She threw herself into my arms, and after a stunned moment, I held on to her, and the sweet scent of honeysuckle filled my nose.

"I don't know what to do, Anna Kate."

"About what, sweetie?" *Sweetie?* Good God, this town *was* taking hold, but right now, as Summer sought comfort from me, I didn't find that such a terrible thing.

"College." She sniffled and pulled back. Swiping her eyes, she said, "I don't know if I can go after all."

"What? Why? Of course you can go. Is this about your father?" As strong as her desire was to go to college and further her education, she talked a lot about not wanting Aubin to feel alone when she was gone, despite his insistence that he'd be fine.

"No, it's about money." A tear leaked down her cheek. "I filed my FAFSA late and didn't get near enough in loans to cover what I need."

I knew from experience that the time to file for financial aid packages and scholarships was long past. By at least six or seven months. With a lot of the aid, it was first come, first served.

"I'm short eight thousand dollars." Her chin trembled, and she took a deep breath. "Which is mostly room-and-board fees."

I leaned against the sink, quickly trying to come up with a way to fix this. "Maybe you can find a cheaper place off campus, cook your own meals . . ."

"Not possible. It's a requirement for freshmen to live on campus. I've been saving up as much as I can, but it's not going to be enough, even with the school's payment plan. I'm starting to panic. I've waited so long to go to college, and now this . . ."

"What's your father say?"

A guilty flush made her cheeks turn red. "I haven't told him."

"Summer . . ."

"I don't want to worry him. He'll do something crazy like sell the house to come up with the money, and I can't let him do that. I'd rather never go to school than let him sell the house he and my mama built together. Maybe I should just defer this year . . ."

I sighed, trying to think of a solution. What would Zee do? She'd take over, that's what, and fix the problem. "Don't panic yet. How long do you have?"

"About a month. That's when I need to pay the first installment, which is a few thousand."

"Totally doable," I said, hoping I sounded more confident than I felt. "We'll figure something out."

"We will?" Her big blue eyes filled with hope.

"I'm no stranger to financial aid woes. I've been down this road before. It'll all work out. Have you applied for any on-campus jobs?"

A burst of honeysuckle scented the air as she shook her head. "Not yet."

"Then that's your homework. Get online and see what you can find. Let me worry about the rest for now."

She threw her arms around my neck again. "Thank you, Anna Kate."

I patted her back. "I haven't done anything yet."

"That's just not true." She gathered up her belongings. "I need to get home to tend to my nighttime chores. I'll see you tomorrow."

I watched her hurry off, wondering if she moved at any speed other than fast-forward. I already had two ideas on how to raise money, one that I'd put into action first thing tomorrow morning. The other, I needed to think about some more. Because for that plan to work, I needed to tell Aubin what was going on.

As I headed upstairs to take a shower, I could only shake my head at my strategy to keep people at arm's length.

    It had proven impossible.

    I'd done the complete opposite.

    I'd become a hugger.

18

Anna Kate

By Thursday night, I was exhausted from the busy week. As I tended the gardens, I tried to think of ways to change the café's schedule around to include a day off once in a while.

Contemplating schedule changes was easier than thinking of Doc, and how I'd told him when he stopped in for coffee this morning that I wouldn't be at Sunday supper this weekend.

I wasn't ready to go back quite yet.

Much to my surprise, Seelie had come into the café a few times this week. She never stayed very long, but went out of her way to make small talk with me. It was awkward, but not completely terrible. Natalie had informed me that Seelie was on a mission to find out as much about my mother as she could.

It was a sweet gesture. One twenty-some years too late, but I couldn't find it within myself to hold that against her anymore.

Not wanting to dwell on the Lindens, I went back to thinking of days off. Not just for me, but for Bow and Jena as well. I never knew anyone who worked so hard. I wanted to lighten their load.

Then it hit me that we only needed to tough it

out for another month, when the café would be closing. I'd set the date at July twenty-fifth. That would give me enough time to clean it up and get it ready for the real estate agents to come through before I left town. Which reminded me that I needed to check in with Gideon to find out how long he thought the whole real estate and probate process would take.

The humidity suddenly felt more oppressive than ever as I knelt down in front of the zucchini plants and pulled my weeding bucket closer. My lungs ached as I took a deep breath, and I wasn't sure if the thick air or the thought of leaving this place behind was to blame.

Because I suspected it was the latter, I shoved the thoughts out of my head and tried to focus on pulling weeds. But as I worked, I couldn't help wondering what was going to happen to Jena and Bow. And Mr. Lazenby and Pebbles. And Summer and her beautiful brown eggs. What was going to happen to the zucchini plants? Would anyone water them?

And what was going to happen to the black-birds?

I turned to look at the mulberry trees. Summer and I had been harvesting like crazy, and she would be here in a couple of hours to collect more berries and can them well into the night.

Without the love, the trees will wither and die.

My breath caught in my throat, and I choked

back raw emotion. If there weren't pies, the trees were going to die.

I couldn't let the trees die. I couldn't.

But I *needed* to go to medical school. I'd made a promise.

What I really needed was to find a solution that would include both. I turned toward the trees again. "I could use a little guidance," I said, hearing the naked plea in my voice.

The trees rustled in the breeze.

I pulled in another breath, ignored the squeezing in my chest, and knee-walked along the grass, counting the weeds I pulled to keep my brain occupied with numbers instead of things I couldn't change.

I was at forty-three when a pair of gray-blue eyes peered out at me from the patch of lemon balm.

I leaned back. "Hi, Mr. Cat."

He stepped out from his hidey-hole, stretching one leg at a time, and I reached out to rub his ears. He quickly put a good bit of distance between us.

"All right. Obviously, you like your personal space. I can respect that. Did you see I put out some water and food for you? It's on the deck." I pointed at the bowls. Bow had warned me that I was practically inviting every raccoon and possum within a mile's radius to stop by, but I hated thinking that this cat hadn't enough to eat or drink. Especially in this weather.

He flicked an ear, then took two steps in the direction of the gate and looked back at me.

"What now?" I asked. "Is Gideon stuck on the roof again?"

Mr. Cat took two more steps, looked back.

"I really need to get this weeding done."

He yowled, reminding me suddenly of Ollie when I made the mistake of not doing what she wanted immediately.

"Fine." I pulled off my gloves and stood up, thinking to myself that I shouldn't give in to his dictator-like behavior. I held open the side gate for the cat and let out a harsh laugh when I realized what I was doing. "Come along. I need to get back soon."

"Miss Anna Kate? You all right?"

"Hi, Mr. Boyd. I'm fine. How're you doing?"

Mr. Boyd was a constant presence in the side yard, while the other birding visitors tended to come and go.

"Good, good. How about that birding magazine wanting to do an article on the blackbirds?"

The freelance writer had called earlier, asking to observe the blackbirds and conduct interviews. He'd be arriving soon. "I'm not sure the blackbirds need any more attention."

I could've sworn the cat sighed as he sat behind Mr. Boyd's chair, waiting for me.

Mr. Boyd said, "I don't think you understand what a big deal these birds are. I've been studying birds for more than half my life, and I've never seen birds behave the way they do. They're special."

He didn't understand quite how special, but his enthusiasm made me smile.

He gestured toward the mulberry trees. "And the midnight singing? How'd you train them to do that?"

"I've been in town less than a month. No time to train anything."

"And the pies . . ." He trailed off as if debating whether to bring up the subject at all.

He'd scoffed when he first heard the legend of the pies and how extraordinary they were. Yet he kept coming back every day for another piece. "Have you been having unusual dreams?" I asked.

Frowning, he scratched his beard. "Funny you should say so. I've been hearing my mother's voice in my sleep. She's been lecturing me to find someone to settle down with and to write that book I've always been meaning to write. She always was one to nag. She thinks I'm lonely."

I wanted to laugh at his discomfited tone, but there was a tenderness to his voice that stopped me. "Are you?"

He shrugged. "I'm content enough. I have hobbies."

"Clearly," I said, gesturing wide.

"It's the strangest thing, those dreams. I've never had any like 'em. It's as though her voice is right there in my ear, talking to me." He pressed his lips together, then pushed them out in a sour pucker. "There's something else she said . . ."

Waving a fly away from my face, I waited, feeling like Mr. Boyd needed to get out whatever was on his mind.

"It's been a good twenty years since she's been gone. She'd fallen on a patch of ice and hit her head. I raced to the hospital, but she'd died by the time I got there."

"I'm so sorry."

He gave me a wan smile. "Since then I've carried a good bit of guilt for not being there, but in one of the dreams I've had this past week, she told me not to feel badly for not saying goodbye. That it had been her choice to go before I got there—because she didn't want me to see her suffering. She asked me to remember her the last time I saw her." The corners of his eyes wrinkled as he grinned. "It had been Christmas, which was her favorite holiday. She'd smiled and laughed the whole day long, singing carols and dancing around while wearing a Santa hat." Slumping, his chest puffed out as he exhaled deeply, lost in the memory. Then he blinked and straightened, standing tall. "Sorry, Miss Anna Kate. Didn't mean to tell you my life story. I must sound like a crazy man."

"Not at all. You sound like a man who loves his mother."

With a nod, he said, "I want to believe those dreams are messages, like the legend says. I truly do, but it's just so unfathomable."

"Reow!"

"Hold on," I said to the furry dictator.

Mr. Boyd looked around. "Hold on?"

"The cat is growing impatient."

"Cat?"

"He's right over—" But the cat was gone. I sighed. "I should get going. My advice to you about those dreams is to listen to your heart. It's as simple as that, Mr. Boyd."

"You and I must have differing opinions on the word 'simple.' "

"I bet you we don't."

With that, I left him standing by his chair. I walked among the tents, saying, "Here, kitty, kitty," but there was no sign of the gray cat. When I reached the sidewalk in front of the café, I looked both ways. Mr. Cat was sitting near the walkway leading up to Hill House's front door.

"You didn't have to run off like that," I said as I approached him.

I started up Hill House's walkway, thinking that Gideon was once again in need of some sort of rescue, but to my surprise, the cat kept going straight. I had to backtrack and jog to catch up to him. People on the sidewalk didn't seem to pay the cat any mind as he led me along. A few called out hellos to me, but didn't stop to chat.

As I walked along, I couldn't help but notice the NOW HIRING signs set prominently in many storefront windows, along with an abundance of blackbird merchandise. Hodgepodge had found blackbird plushies, and the next storefront down—a pottery gallery—was selling blackbird bowls and mugs. Another shop had blackbird artwork. Adaline's, an ice cream shop, had recently reopened and had added a blackbird flavor to the menu—blackberry with chocolate chips.

It warmed my heart to see that the town had embraced—and was capitalizing on—the blackbird brand, but it also caused me to worry. Right now the town was flourishing. There was an energy in the air, happiness. I didn't want that to end. What would happen if the mulberry trees died? Where would the blackbirds go?

Would they find another passageway?

Or would they stay in the Land of the Dead—for good?

I didn't have an answer to that—it hadn't been included in Zee's blackbird story. Not knowing bothered me. A lot.

It wasn't until the cat and I were almost upon the cemetery that I realized it was where he was leading me. The entrance was marked by a pair of stacked stone columns that supported a rusty metal archway. The cat went ahead, walking along a narrow paved road flanked by rows of tulip trees and a freshly mown lawn. He didn't look back, and eventually he disappeared around the bend that led to the graveyard.

I'd stopped at the columns—I didn't particularly want to go in. My grief was already too close to the surface today, bubbling up with thoughts of leaving the café and Zee's gardens soon. Seeing her burial plot might push me over the edge of despair.

Hot winds blew through the valley, and I picked up the scent of impending rain mixed in with the sweetness of cut grass. I leaned against a column, and heat from the stacked stones filtered through my shirt and shorts.

Tall ornamental grasses planted at the bases of the columns swayed. Robins hopped around, their heads tilted to the ground listening for worms. Cars with license plates from Indiana and Missouri drove past on their way into town. A truck from Florida went by, towing a camper. Birders, I assumed, arriving for the weekend.

The cat didn't come back.

I decided to wait five more minutes for him to return before going back to the café. Time was almost up when a flash of movement in the sky caught my eye. I squinted, wondering if I was seeing things. Because if my eyes weren't playing tricks, a blackbird had landed on a low branch of the nearest tulip tree inside the cemetery.

I didn't think twice. I went in.

Light bounced off the fluttering, glossy green

leaves of the tree and the eyes of the blackbird. In the daylight it was easy to see the blackbird's light, mottled chest, her orange beak, and the thin pale green rings around her dark pupils—green being the original color of her eyes. It was a trait that hadn't been noticed by the birders, but if they ever did spot the color, it was just one more oddity for Mr. Boyd to question.

"What are you doing here?"

She took wing, skimming low to the ground as she followed the curve of the lane leading toward the graveyard.

I hesitated only a second before following and kept my gaze averted from the freshly turned earth where Zee had been laid to rest. It didn't matter that I knew her spirit lived on as a black-bird—the visceral reaction to seeing that hole in the ground during her funeral services had nearly ripped me apart from the inside out.

My mother soared high, then swooped low behind the Linden family monument. I paused only a moment at my father's grave marker. It was also the place where my mother's ashes had been secretly scattered by Zee four years ago. It had always been my mother's desire to be laid to rest with him.

I glanced away from the granite stone and caught sight of the blackbird on the far side of the cemetery. She coasted, dipping out of sight as she landed in a maple tree. When she didn't reappear,

I broke into a sprint. Between the humidity and the exertion, I was out of breath by the time I reached the tree and stumbled to a full stop when I came upon Aubin Pavegeau. He was sitting in front of a headstone next to the tree.

Aubin looked up at me and said, "You best sit yourself down and catch your breath. Though I suppose if you're aiming to die, you picked a good place to do it. Take out the middleman of it all." He smirked.

I wasn't as amused, considering my lungs were on fire. Gulping air, I looked for the blackbird in the dense foliage above my head, but she had vanished. Instead, I saw the gray cat watching me from next to the tree trunk. His tail swished rhythmically in short bursts, as though he'd been impatiently waiting for me to arrive.

Honestly, I was surprised he wasn't out and out tapping his foot.

Between the cat and the bird I had no doubt I'd been brought here for a reason—a reason I hoped would reveal itself soon, because I had no idea what was being asked of me.

Sweat streamed down the sides of my face as I sat down in the grass next to Aubin. I swiped my forehead with my forearm, and decided now would be a great time for the clouds to move in and the skies to open.

"Just out for an invigorating afternoon jog on this lovely, ninety-degree afternoon?" Aubin asked. Wearing the same outfit he'd had on the first time I met him, he sat with his legs bent, his wrists resting on his knees. His walking stick lay in the grass next to him and a red Alabama ball cap shaded his eyes.

I pulled my ponytail up so the breeze could reach the back of my neck. The burning in my lungs was slowly starting to subside, but I'd have committed a felony right then and there for a drink of water. "I can't believe anyone runs for fun. I was chasing . . . a cat," I said, thinking it best to keep any mention of a blackbird appearance to myself. "A gray one."

Aubin's face flushed, and he began plucking blades of grass. His voice was tight when he said, "A cat. You don't say."

"You don't like cats?"

"Not particularly. Especially gray ones."

It seemed to me there was a story there, but I didn't press. My gaze went to where the cat had been, but he was gone. That cat was amazing at quick getaways.

I let go of my hair and finally took notice of where we were. The gravestone at our feet belonged to Frances Camilla Pavegeau, loving wife and mother. Sympathy twisted through me, stirring emotions I'd rather not deal with. I hesitated to leave, since I'd been led here, but I wasn't comfortable. "I should get going. I didn't mean to bother you."

Aubin went back to plucking grass. "Sit awhile, Anna Kate. Let your breathing get back to normal at least. I don't want you dying on my conscience. That dance card is full up." He tossed a grass blade at the headstone.

I didn't know what to say to that, so I said nothing. Even though it had been an accident, my mother suffered endlessly knowing she had been the one behind the wheel when my father died. I had the feeling that Aubin carried the same crushing culpability.

I bit back a half dozen questions that I ruled out as too personal or insensitive. Instead, I decided to switch topics altogether. "Thank you for the blackberry sweet tea recipe. I've started selling it at the café, and everyone's loving it. Aubin's Blackberry Tea."

"You didn't have to name it after me."

"Of course I did. It's your recipe. And because the recipe is yours, it's not right for me to earn money from it, so I'm setting aside all profits to donate to Summer's college fund. At this rate, she might have enough for the first installment of the tuition bill by the time I leave town. The rest, however . . ."

His fingers stilled mid-pluck. His eyes narrowed. "Tuition bill? Summer told me all the fees were covered with loans and scholarships."

A bee buzzed by, landing on daisies set in a wide bronze vase in front of the gravestone. "She didn't want to worry you. She didn't get quite the amount of financial aid she planned on. She's been saving, but doesn't have enough."

A gusty breeze blew through, and the maple branches groaned. I looked up but saw nothing but the silvery undersides of the leaves and gray clouds rolling in.

A storm was brewing.

He took off his cap, wiped his forehead, and put the cap back on. "Makes sense now why she's been runnin' herself ragged, taking on every odd job she can find."

"Like I said, there should be enough money from the tea to help her out with the first payment."

"I can't see how selling tea is going to bring in enough money."

I smiled. "You haven't been by the café lately, have you?"

"I haven't been there for twenty-five years."

I doubted the timeframe was coincidental. "When my father died?"

He let out a deep breath and glanced around. "You know, way back when, AJ and I used to sneak out of our houses to come here at night to play hide-and-seek. Scared the ever-living tar out of each other. Some days I sit here and expect to hear his 'Boo!' from behind me. It would be just like him to haunt me like that. He was full of jokes and pranks."

"He was?"

"Good Lord, yes. The best one? When he put a black rubber snake in his mama's toilet. Had to peel Seelie off the ceiling. I'd have paid good money to see that." He laughed. "AJ didn't see the outside of his room for nigh on three weeks afterward." His chest shook as he chuckled.

Smiling, I said, "If he'd done that to me, I'd have had a heart attack and died on the spot."

"Same," he said with a smile.

While I could sit and listen to stories of my father all day long, one thing was bothering me. "Why did you make it seem like you weren't that close to my father when I asked about him a few weeks ago?"

Aubin's hand clenched, released. "It's complicated."

"Uncomplicate it."

"It doesn't matter now, Anna Kate. It is what it is. I wasn't much of a friend at the end. That tends to taint everything else. Talking isn't going to change anything. I learned my lesson the hard way, changed some things about myself in turn, and I don't care to go picking open old wounds."

There was no mistaking the pain in his voice. "Seems to me, Mr. Pavegeau, that wound never fully healed."

After a long pause, he plucked more grass and said, "I don't want to talk about it all the same. Now, tell me how much money Summer needs."

I bit back the urge to fight with him to get some

answers. Not only because I wanted to know what had happened to cloud his relationship with my dad, but because I suspected it would do him some good to talk it out. Instead, I explained the payment plan and what Summer was up against.

He whistled sharply. "She's always worrying about me. No one worries more than that girl. She needs to go off to school, learn to be her own person and not my caretaker. But I don't see how we can afford it."

Grass poked the underside of my thighs as I crisscrossed my legs. "I'm not ready to give up quite yet."

He gave me a sad smile. "You're a lot like your daddy. He was the optimistic sort too."

"You say that like optimism is a bad thing."

"Hope brings nothing but pain."

I flicked a speck of dirt from my leg. "That's a sad way to live life."

"It's been a sad life to live."

We sat in silence a few minutes before he added, "I have some sticks I can sell." He picked up his walking stick and rolled it in between his palms. "I can set up a roadside booth at the end of our driveway to sell our products. Honey, vegetables, soaps. Might as well take advantage of all these tourists passing through."

"Speaking of them . . . How do you feel about boarders?" I asked, thinking of the idea I'd had for him to make quick money.

"Boarders? As in houseguests? I couldn't. I like my privacy."

"Boarders, as in *paying* guests. The birdwatchers need places to stay. The motel's full. Others in town have started renting out spare bedrooms and are charging as much as forty to fifty dollars a night."

His eyes flew open wide, and he tugged on his beard. "On second thought, I could probably stand some company. For Summer's sake."

Smiling, I said, "They're not long-term guests. Most stay a night or two to see the blackbirds, then move on. But more people come in their place. It's not forever, but short-term, there's money to be had."

His head bobbed. "I'd feel funny renting out the main house, but I do have a cabin in the back as well as an old hunting bunkhouse. The cabin has two small rooms, a kitchenette, a bathroom. Sleeps four. I've been using it for storage—stuff passed down from relatives that I can't bring myself to get rid of. The bunkhouse sleeps six. It's nothing fancy, so I probably can't charge much for those beds, but it's a place to sleep."

"How soon can you clean it all out? With this rain coming in, the birders will need somewhere dry tonight."

"Few hours, at least. I need to pick up some supplies, wash sheets, and do some scrubbing."

A trickle of excitement went through me that

everything was going to work out just fine for Summer. "I'll go back to the café and put the word out to everyone there. Then I'll come over to help you get things ready. Many hands make quick work."

"You don't have to do that."

"I want to."

"No. I couldn't let you."

I set my jaw stubbornly. "What would my daddy tell you to do? Because I'm betting he'd tell you to stop arguing with me and let me help."

He wagged a finger. "You aren't playing fair, pulling AJ into this."

Smiling wide, I blinked innocently.

Groaning, he stood up and said, "Fine. You and your daddy's smile win, Anna Kate. I'll be seeing you soon."

As I hustled back to the café, I thought of the gray cat leading me here. And my mother, too. I'd been thinking the reason was to rescue Aubin somehow or Summer.

But as the first raindrops fell, I couldn't help thinking this meeting hadn't been about them at all.

It had been about me.

19

"Sometimes you have to know when to give in. I mean, if he hasn't come around by now, he never will. Am I right?"

The reporter stared at the marvel that was the woman's hairdo. It looked a lot like white spun cotton candy. "Ma'am? I'm not sure if you're aware that I'm writing an article about the blackbirds?"

Pebbles Lutz waved a hand of dismissal. Her color was high, her eyes glassy. "I never read that kind of stuff. I prefer romance novels, if you want the God's honest truth. *Birds.*" She huffed. "Maybe I'll give him one more chance. Just one, mind you. I have my pride to consider. Ain't that so?"

Utterly perplexed, he said, "Yes, ma'am?"

"I think so too. Now, if you'll be excusing me, I'm feeling a touch under the weather." She patted his cheek as she passed by him. "You're a nice man."

He took a hand wipe out of his messenger bag, and as he wiped his face, the chair, and the table, he wondered what in the hell that had all been about.

Anna Kate

"I'm not happy, Miss Anna Kate." Mr. Lazenby folded his arms over his chest and harrumphed.

357

Early morning sunshine poured in the café's windows, and lingering raindrops sparkled on the glass. The storm the night before had blown through quickly, a blessing considering the roof on Mr. Pavegeau's bunkhouse had a leak. It was nothing a bucket couldn't deal with, but he'd vowed to get that hole patched today, and by the time I left last night, the birders staying with him were happy to be out of the weather.

It was a few minutes past eight and the café was packed. My hands and back ached from scrubbing wood floors at the Pavegeaus', and I was trying to hide my disappointment that Gideon hadn't come by this morning for coffee. In fact, he'd been absent a few days this past week.

I had been poised to take Mr. Lazenby's order when he'd voiced his complaint. "Why aren't you happy, Mr. Lazenby?"

His purple-and-silver-striped bow tie was askew, and there were dark circles under his eyes. "The pie I ate yesterday was broken."

He sat at the end of the community table, in what I'd come to know as "his" seat. Pebbles sat across from him, Faylene to his right, and I'd made sure to seat Mr. Boyd, Sir Bird Nerd, next to her. If he was lonely, Faylene was the perfect seat companion, since I was certain she'd never met a stranger in her life. They were talking a mile a minute about the blackbirds. Well, Faylene was doing most of the talking, but Mr. Boyd was nodding every time she paused for breath.

"Broken?" I tipped my head. "How so?"

His rheumy eyes narrowed in accusation. "I didn't get a dream last night."

"Rosemarie probably didn't have anything to say," Pebbles said as she sipped her coffee. "Might could be she's tired and wanted a night off from telling you what to do. All that talkin' must be exhausting. Besides, notes aren't guaranteed, Otis."

He frowned at her. "Don't be ridiculous. The pie was faulty." He glanced up at me. "I'm not fixin' to ask for a refund or nothing like that, but can you make sure I get a good piece of pie today?"

I knew there were mulberries in the apple pie he'd eaten yesterday, so there was only one conclusion I could come to. He hadn't been in need of a message. "Pebbles is right, dreams aren't guaranteed—they come only when there's something to be said or something that needs to be heard."

"Young lady, I have a hard time believing that Rosemarie suddenly has nothing to say after years of her telling me plenty. Uh-uh. No way. The pie was broken," he insisted.

"Maybe it's her silence that's saying something." Pebbles rubbed at the pink lipstick stain on her mug. "Did you ever think of that?"

Her white hair was stacked higher than usual

today, and she wore a lightweight floral top that had a floppy bow tied at the neck.

"Like what?" he asked her. "What could her silence possibly tell me?"

"Like maybe it's time to stop hanging on her every word and move on with your life?"

"Move on to what?" he asked. "I'm eighty-two years old."

"So? Doesn't mean life is over. Doesn't mean you couldn't find someone else to spend the rest of your years with. Maybe Rosemarie is trying to tell you it's okay to keep on living."

He snorted. "If she wanted to tell me that, she would have. *If the pie wasn't broken.*"

"Lord love a duck!" Pebbles huffed, reached into her purse, and pulled out three singles. She dropped the money on the table, threw her napkin on her plate, and said, "I've lost my appetite." With that she stood and stormed out of the café, stiff-arming the door on her way out.

Mr. Lazenby watched her go, then looked up at me and said, "I'll be having scrambled eggs, sweet potato hash, two pieces of bacon, and a piece of pie that's *not broken.*"

"You sure you don't want to try a zucchini frittata?" I asked.

"No. I most certainly do not."

I stifled a sigh as I jotted down his order. "Do you ever think you might be stuck in a rut, Mr. Lazenby?"

He set his napkin on his lap. "There's nothing wrong with routine, Miss Anna Kate."

I wasn't so sure. It was the first time I questioned whether eating a daily piece of pie was emotionally healthy.

Sometimes, like Faylene had said, in order to move on you had to let go.

Mr. Lazenby was clinging to that pie for dear life.

"Anna Kate, I'll take one of those frittatas," Faylene said. "You've got me hooked on them. Simply delightful. I'll also take a biscuit with sausage gravy, extra gravy."

"Ooh," Mr. Boyd said. "I'll have the same. Faylene, have you tried the zucchini fries? Also delightful. Just the slightest hint of heat from the cayenne pepper."

"I haven't, but I do like a little fire. Care to split an order?" she asked, tucking her dark hair behind her ear. "Maybe we can even get Otis to try one."

"Hmmph." Mr. Lazenby crossed his arms again.

"My treat," Mr. Boyd said, nodding.

"Thank you kindly, sir." Faylene looked up at me, a twinkle in her eye. "Order it up, please, Anna Kate."

"Will do," I said, turning toward the kitchen.

Jena moseyed over. "I still can't get over the sight of Seelie Earl Linden walking through that there front door like it's no big deal."

I swung around. Sure enough, Seelie was taking

361

the seat Pebbles had vacated. She eyed the napkin sitting on the plate in front of her with disdain.

Jena gave me a bump forward, toward Seelie. "Best go clear that setting before Seelie calls the health department about the lipstick on Pebbles's mug."

At my dark look, she laughed and went back to cutting biscuits.

I smiled as I approached the table. "Let me get these dishes out of the way, Seelie, and I'll be right back to take your order."

Mr. Lazenby's brows were furrowed as he said, "Pebbles might be coming back. We should save her seat."

I picked up the plate and set the mug and silverware atop it. "If she comes back, I'll find her another seat."

"But that's *her* seat."

"Is something wrong?" Seelie asked.

"Not at all," I said at the same time Mr. Lazenby said, "Yes."

I pointed at him. "You, hush up, or I'll slip a blueberry into your pie."

"You wouldn't!"

"Try me."

"What's got your goat?" he asked. "Sheesh."

"Seelie, you must try the frittata," Faylene said. "It's the special today, and Anna Kate outdid herself with that recipe. Zucchini, goat cheese, onion, fresh mint. Heaven."

I said, "Really, the zucchini is the star. There's two plants in the back that just keep giving and giving."

"I'll try the frittata, then. Thank you, Faylene, for the recommendation. Have you tried Anna Kate's zucchini cheddar jalapeño biscuits? Some of the best savory biscuits I ever tasted."

"I don't think I've seen them on the menu . . ." Faylene picked up her reading glasses and looked around for a menu.

"I haven't put them on the menu," I said.

"You must put them on there, Anna Kate," Seelie insisted. "Everyone would love them."

"Oh, I *know* I would," Faylene said.

Mr. Boyd nodded. "Me, too."

Mr. Lazenby turned his plate ninety degrees and said, "Not me."

"Maybe I'll add them tomorrow," I said. "The menu is already set for today."

"I look forward to it." Faylene slid her reading glasses on top of her head. "I've loved every single one of your new recipes, Anna Kate. Zee was a good cook, but you're a great cook. One of the best. I'm going to miss your food something fierce when you leave us."

I felt Seelie watching me intently, and my cheeks heated. "Thank you, Faylene. I'm going to miss creating new recipes."

"Will you be gone for long?" Mr. Boyd asked.

"A while," I said. As I rushed to the kitchen,

I heard Faylene explaining to Mr. Boyd about medical school. I dropped off the dishes and wiped my hands.

Jena said, "Was that a smile out of Seelie?"

"A few of them," I said.

"It's a daggum miracle."

"Order up!" Bow thumped the counter.

I picked up the plates, balancing one of them on my forearm. I was halfway to the table when a young woman motioned for me.

"Sorry to bother you, ma'am, but I was wondering if you sold T-shirts?"

"I don't," I said, and then smiled as I realized what a wonderful idea it was. "Not yet. Will you be in town long?"

"A few more days," she said.

"Check back with me then."

"I will. Thanks."

I walked away, my mind spinning. I needed to talk to Aubin to see if he wanted in on the project. It was another way to possibly earn money for Summer's college fund.

I set Mr. Boyd's plates in front of him, then went down the line, ending with Mr. Lazenby. I took Seelie's order and had to smile as Faylene peppered her with a million questions.

"Anyone need a coffee refill?" Hands went up left and right and I laughed. "And I'll be right back with your pie, Mr. Lazenby."

"No blueberries!"

I patted his shoulder and said, "Would you like a piece too, Seelie? Today we have peach, straw-berry rhubarb, apple, and blackberry."

"Oh no, none for me," she said, shaking her head.

"Is it the calories or the dream you're afraid of, Seelie?" Faylene asked.

Before she could answer, Mr. Boyd said, "Y'all don't really believe that the blackbirds are singing messages from people who've died, do you? They're just singing."

Faylene said, "Of course we do!"

I *tsk*ed. "What would your mother say about all these doubts, Mr. Boyd?"

His cheeks colored. "Those were just dreams."

"Ha!" Mr. Lazenby scoffed. "Dreams, my foot."

"Maybe you should cut Zachariah off the pie, cold turkey," Faylene said to me. "Save it for the believers. It's a precious commodity that shouldn't be wasted."

"No, no! Don't do that," Mr. Boyd said quickly. "I . . . like the pie."

"Then keep your skeptical opinions about the blackbirds to yourself while you're in this here café," Faylene said, poking him in the arm. "What would your mama say about your manners?"

His head came up sharply, and his eyebrows dropped low. "She'd say to mind them, and I know that because she said so in the dream I had last night . . ."

"See!" Faylene said. "If that there isn't proof, I don't know what is."

"Dreams," Mr. Lazenby mumbled, shaking his head.

Mr. Boyd, his cheeks pink, glanced at me. "Sorry, Anna Kate."

"Don't worry about it another second," I said.

Faylene beamed at him. "I do like a man who can apologize. Now, pass me one of those zucchini fries, if you please. I hear they're delicious."

My gaze went to Seelie, but her attention had turned to the writing on the soffit. When she finally looked down and caught me watching her, she looked away quickly.

But not before I saw the tears in her eyes.

Natalie

My therapy appointment this week fell on a Tuesday afternoon, and Lord help me, I was once again running late. The birders had kept the café busy and me on my toes right up until closing time. I had only a few minutes at home before I had to be on the road, or I ran the risk of having to reschedule.

The therapist would probably say my habitual tardiness was a result of me not wanting to go to the appointment at all, and she'd be right.

I didn't want to go.

But I needed to.

I knew the difference.

It was my third meeting with her, and while I didn't exactly enjoy our time together, I hadn't had a full-on panic attack in more than a week. We'd spent much of the last appointment talking about lies, and since I'd given no ground on the subject we would be revisiting the discussion today.

She was trying to convince me that lying wasn't always detrimental.

Right.

Clearly she'd never had a husband who lived a secret life, one who maybe, possibly, killed himself to keep from telling his wife the truth.

My lungs squeezed painfully, and I took a few deep breaths, focusing on calming myself down once again.

Avoiding looking in the direction of the pool, I ran up the porch steps of the little house. A large, thin, rectangular parcel wrapped in brown paper was tucked behind a rocking chair near the door. My name was written in dark ink on the packaging, and underneath that the word "fragile" was underlined.

I mused at the combination, wondering if the word "fragile" was describing the package or my state of mind. Both fit, I supposed, so I didn't linger on the intention.

Pulling out my keys, I unlocked the door, then pushed it open. Chilly air washed over me as I set the package on the kitchen counter, tore the paper, and gasped.

It was the framed photo of the doe and waterfall. A note slipped out onto the floor.

Natalie—
Thought that if you couldn't go to the waterfall, then the waterfall should come to you. Everyone needs a little peace in their lives.

—Cam

I blinked away a sudden rush of tears. *No crying.* But it was such a thoughtful, kind gift, I couldn't help the surge of emotion.

I needed to call Cam to thank him. Then I realized I didn't have his phone number. Marcy would, though . . . I reached for the phone, then dropped my hand. I didn't have time right now.

There was barely enough time for a quick shower if I was going to make it to the therapist's office in time. Skipping the shower was out of the question.

Fifteen minutes later, I was headed for the door when the phone rang.

Glancing at the ID screen, I recognized my mother's cell number.

Befores and *afters.*

Before Mama had decided to reinvent herself, I would have walked out without answering. *After* her personality overhaul, I grabbed the phone, hoping that the new her hadn't vanished. I kind of liked her.

"Hi, Mama. I was just on my way out to therapy."

"I don't have much time either," Mama said. "The Refresh meeting is having a short break, and I thought I'd take advantage to give you a call about a conversation I had a few minutes ago."

"About?" I kept an eye on the microwave clock. The blue numbers glowed at me accusingly. I turned my back on them.

"I was talking up your sewing and fabric choices to Patsy Dale Morgan when she mentioned she had an old trunk of vintage fabrics that you're welcome to, free of charge, since they're just collecting dust at her house."

I perked up. "I'd feel better if I could pay her for them, but I can't pay much . . ."

"She's not going to accept your money, Natalie. She says you'd be doing her a favor."

I recognized when it was pointless to argue. "That's awful nice of her. I'd love them."

"I'll tell her so as soon as I go back inside. And I'll have your daddy swing by Patsy's tonight to collect them."

"I can do that, on my way home."

"Oh, I know. I figured this way would be easier on you, what with your schedule lately. You know Patsy. Faylene Wiggins is a novice talker compared to her. You'd be there three hours at least, where your daddy has no qualms whatsoever about cutting off a conversation in order to make it home by suppertime. You know how he likes his meals."

The image of him poking at his roasted chicken and sweet potatoes at Sunday supper flashed through my mind, and the pit in my stomach widened. He could tell me all he wanted that he was fine, just getting old, but something wasn't right with him. I could feel it in my soul.

"Thank you, Mama."

"You're welcome, Natalie. And one more thing . . . when I was home earlier, I saw that burly mountain man leaving our driveway in his pickup truck. Had you been expecting him?"

"His name is Cam, Mama. And no. He brought by one of his framed photos. Left it on the porch." I didn't dare tell her that it had been a gift. No telling what she'd read into that.

"A gift?"

Shoot.

I couldn't out-and-out lie. "Yes, a gift. I'd been admiring it at Hodgepodge. You should check out his photographs next time you're in there. I think you'd like them. Now, I really need to get going."

There was a long stretch of silence before she said, "Then I'll let you go."

I could tell there was much left unsaid in that brief silence. I could practically feel her disapproval vibrating through the phone. But I had to give Mama credit—she hadn't voiced her opinions of Cam. It was a step forward. A baby step, but I was more than okay with that.

We said our goodbyes, and I took one look at the clock, groaned, and ran out the door.

20

Anna Kate

I looked out the side window. "Is it my imagination, or is it beginning to look like a tent city out there?" I spotted several trash cans and a sign with the word RULES written at the top of it.

"Not your imagination. Zachariah Boyd is doing his best to organize the chaos as more people arrive," Jena said.

Bow adjusted the heat on the fryer. "You could say the birders are *flocking* here."

"Ugh," I groaned.

Jena laughed as she gently kneaded biscuit dough. "That should be incorporated into Wicklow's slogan somehow. Wicklow, where people flock. Flock to Wicklow?"

"Wicklow, a flocking good time," I said, laughing. "We should put that on T-shirts too."

"I'd buy one," Jena said. "And wear it proudly. The sooner we can get them printed, the better. With the Fourth of July celebration next weekend, birders will be arriving in droves, making a weeklong vacation out of the trip up here. Not only that, but word is getting around about the hiking and biking. Wicklow will be a mountain resort town before we know it."

Biking reminded me of Gideon and his offer to take me riding one day. I looked toward Hill House and noted the lights were on. I hadn't seen him much lately. He'd only been by for coffee on Tuesday, and it had been a quick visit where we mostly discussed the zucchini and the bike ride he had planned.

I had the feeling he was avoiding me, and for some reason it was painful.

For some reason. I scoffed at myself. I knew why it hurt. I liked him. A lot.

Jena came over to see what I was looking at and poked me with her elbow. "Looking for Gideon? You do know he's sweet on you."

"He is not."

"Shoo-ee, honey, yes he is. Isn't he, Bow?"

"Sweet as this sugar," Bow said, winking at me as he poured sugar into waffle batter.

"It's why he's been keeping his distance." Jena put the pan of biscuits into the oven. "Yes, ma'am."

I tied an apron around my waist and saw that Mr. Lazenby was sitting on the bench by the door. "Why would he do that if he's sweet on me?" I dropped my head back and groaned. "That sounds so silly to say aloud."

Jena said, "I can think of a couple of reasons."

"Like?" I asked.

Dark eyes gleamed as she held up a single finger. "One being that you're leaving soon and

374

getting attached isn't the smartest thing to do."

That wasn't news to me. "And two?"

She stuck a second finger in the air. "He was Zee's attorney. He might feel it's inappropriate."

It didn't feel inappropriate, but I gave him the benefit of the doubt on that.

"And third . . . I can't help feeling he's keeping something from you. A secret."

Bow said, "I bet you're right about that."

Jena smiled at him. "I'm always right."

"I know." He grinned. "You already have that T-shirt."

She laughed. "I do, don't I?"

The two of them seemed to be in an especially good mood this morning. "A secret?" I asked, trying to rein them back on topic. "What kind of secret?"

So help me if he had been married all this time and conveniently forgotten to mention it.

"I don't know, sugar. It's just intuition," Jena said in that melodic way of hers. "I've been around this town long enough to know when people are keeping secrets." She sighed heavily. "I have to admit, I'm going to miss this place, though I'm looking forward to new adventures."

"Miss this place? Are you leaving town?" I asked.

Jena said, "We've been planning for a long time now to move along once you sold this place. We want to travel some, see the sights. Now, don't be looking at me with that long face. It's nothing to be sad about—it's been a long time coming. We were supposed to only be passing through here to begin with." She laughed. "And we ended up staying twenty-odd years."

I hated thinking of them leaving, though they had every right to move on with their lives. "Gideon says Wicklow has a way of holding on to you."

"He's flocking right about that." Bow crossed the kitchen and climbed a small stepladder to reach a roll of paper towels on a high shelf. He was wearing shorts today that showed off his skinny chicken legs, as he called them. It was the first time I noticed he had a jagged scar running down the back of his left calf. It looked familiar, the shape of that scar, though I knew I'd never seen it before. He usually wore pants to work.

"Where did you two live before here?" Though they were two of the kindest, gentlest souls I'd ever come across, they weren't very forthcoming with information about themselves.

"Here, there, and everywhere," Bow said. "We're gypsies at heart."

"Yet you've stayed here for more than two decades. Why?"

Jena suddenly busied herself with the muffin tin, wiping the metal edges with a damp dishtowel.

Bow's cheek twitched. "To right a wrong, Anna Kate. To right a wrong."

"Has it been righted?" I asked.

"Not yet, but we're workin' on it," he said, grabbing a knife to cut potatoes.

"For twenty-some years . . . ?"

"There's no time limit on trying to fix a mess you made." Jena came around the island, wiping her hands on the dishtowel. "But sometimes, well, honey, sometimes it's best to let the past settle a bit before you go stirring it up again. People see things differently through the lens of time."

"And is that what you're doing now? Stirring?"

"We're veritable dust devils," she said with a twinkle in her eye.

"And when that dust settles, you'll be leaving? Where will you go?" I asked. "What will you do?"

What was I going to do without them?

Then I gave myself a good, silent talking-to. I was leaving, too.

"Wherever the winds take us." She turned to check the coffee pots.

I wiped a counter. "I have to confess that I hoped you two would stay on and run the café."

"Are you rethinking medical school?" Bow asked.

"No, I'm going. My lease is signed—I move in August first. That gives me a couple of weeks to get settled before classes start." I stared at his arched back, trying to fight the sick feeling coming over me.

"Hmm," Jena said, her pencil-thin eyebrows raised.

I frowned. "What?"

"What?" she echoed.

"You're not one to beat around the bush, Jena."

Bow laughed. "No, she's one to perch in that bush and sing loud and clear."

"Hush." She swatted him. "It just seems to me, honey, that you belong right where you are. I see your heart here, plain as day. It's on that there specials board and the way you talk to the zucchini and it's in the pantry on the herbal tea shelf you created. It's out there on Mr. Lazenby's face, it's in the way you've taken up for Summer, it's in the love you have for Natalie and Ollie."

I wanted to make a snarky remark about how that wasn't much evidence at all, but I couldn't bring myself to joke.

I bit the inside of my cheek. "I have to go. I made a promise to my mom, and Callows don't break promises. I'd like to find a way to keep the café open while I'm gone. I'd become more of a figurehead, overseeing the operation from afar."

"And the pies?" Jena asked, as if knowing full well what would happen if there weren't blackbird pies.

It made me wonder exactly how much she knew of the blackbird legend and the secret of the mulberries. I suddenly suspected she knew it all.

"I haven't figured that out yet," I said. "Maybe

378

I can make them up in Massachusetts and over-night them." The mulberry preserves would be easy enough to pack up and take with me.

Jena *tsk*ed. "You're too smart to be thinking that plan would work in the long run. I'm going to say it plain as day: you can't have both. You need to choose: medical school or the café."

"It's not that easy," I said.

"Honey, nothing in life is." She took the rag out of my hand. "Best you open that door, before Otis picks the lock."

I looked up at the clock, surprised to see it was after eight. I hurried through the empty dining room to unlock the front door. "Good morn—"

"Don't you good morning me, young lady," Mr. Lazenby said, marching straight toward his seat.

People filtered in behind him, including Faylene and Mr. Boyd, and several other locals and birders I'd come to recognize by face, but not by name. Each gave me warm greetings, joking about the blackbirds or all the zucchini dishes on the specials board. But my gaze kept going to Mr. Lazenby. He was pouting.

I grabbed a coffee pot and headed his way.

He looked up at me and said, "It was broken again."

I left room at the top of his mug for him to add cream, just the way he liked it. "Another night of no messages?"

His lips pressed together stubbornly. Finally,

he said, "I did have one dream, but it made no sense."

"Was it from Rosemarie?" I asked.

"It was."

"What did she say?"

"She called me a blind old fool." He made a sour face. "That pie's gone bad. Rosemarie has never called me a name in her life."

As Faylene sat down next to him, she chuckled. "Not to your face, anyways."

"I don't know what to tell you," I said.

Mr. Lazenby scowled. "Where's Pebbles?"

Her chair remained empty.

"I'm not sure," I said.

"Me either," Faylene added, "but I did hear her mention yesterday that she planned to go to the moonlight movie tonight. You should call her, Otis, see if she needs an escort, since her knee's been giving her some problems lately. Arthritis," she said in an aside to Mr. Boyd. "You've always been so helpful to her in the past, Otis." In another aside, she said, "He drives Pebbles around to her appointments, takes her grocery shopping."

"Don't go making me sound like a white knight," Mr. Lazenby grumped. "I only did those things because Rosemarie nagged me to." He glowered and mumbled something about movies, old fools, and broken pies.

Faylene lifted her eyebrows. "I thought you said she didn't nag."

"Hmmph," he said, turning his back to her.

It was interesting to me that Rosemarie had asked Mr. Lazenby to look after Pebbles. And suddenly I wondered if Rosemarie's marked change in message-giving was her way of weaning her husband from the pie.

Faylene laughed and patted his shoulder. "You put Otis's breakfast on my bill, will you, Anna Kate? Seems to me he needs a pick-me-up. Poor old fool that he is."

"Don't forget blind," Mr. Boyd piped in.

"Oh, that's right. Poor blind old fool that he is. Nothing he likes better than a free breakfast."

"That's true. Thank you," Mr. Lazenby grumbled over his shoulder. Then his hand snaked out to pick up his mug and he slowly turned back to the table, but he didn't join in the conversation. He kept staring at the empty seat across from him.

As I collected orders, my gaze kept going back to Pebbles's chair too, and I thought that maybe, just maybe, Rosemarie had been playing matchmaker all along.

Natalie

I had slept fitfully the night before and was dead tired by the end of my shift. I'd planned to work on my sewing projects after work, but a long nap might be a better use of my time.

"You sure you're okay, sugar?" Jena asked me for approximately the hundredth time that afternoon.

"Yeah, Jena. Thanks. I'm mostly just tired and have a bit of a headache." I grabbed the pitcher of blackberry tea to top off glasses.

"I can do that," Anna Kate said, pointing to the pitcher. "And I can make you some willow bark tea for your headache—or you could take a short break at least."

"No, no," I forced a smile, "that's okay. It's good to keep busy."

Staying busy helped keep my thoughts at bay.

Anna Kate threw me a worried nod, then took two plates to a corner table. The café was due to close up in ten minutes, so I prayed those guests were fast eaters.

I hadn't lied to Jena—I was tired and had a headache—but I was also worried.

About Ollie and her swimming lesson this morning. Oh, how I hated those swimming lessons.

And about my father, too. I'd gone over to the big house to check on him last night, and he'd already been in bed, asleep, and it hadn't even been eight at night. Usually at that time he and Mama were on the patio sharing a cocktail.

On top of that, there were all the thoughts of Matt's death . . . and our life together. Therapy was causing me to pick the relationship apart, piece by piece. I turned over conversations in my head, regretting the times we'd argued, and wishing I'd been able to change what had happened. Some way. Somehow. All the while, Cam's talk about forgiveness rang in my ears, like an echo that just wouldn't quit.

Maybe it was true that I needed to forgive Matt. But I didn't know *how* to do that.

The therapist told me to be patient, but I was losing patience fast. I wanted to be . . . normal, even if I didn't know what that was anymore.

My thoughts were muddled, and all I wanted was a good, long sleep so I'd stop *thinking* for a while. I longed for silence. Peaceful, blissful silence.

I went into the pantry for more sugar packets. Bow and Jena stood just inside the doorway, their backs to me, their heads together. Before they noticed me, I overheard them say something about running out of time and desperate times calling for drastic measures.

"Oh!" Jena squeaked. She reached behind her and grabbed a bag of coffee beans. "Didn't see you there, Natalie." With a smile plastered on her face, she squeezed past me.

Bow busied himself by straightening cans on a shelf. "Need something, Nat?"

I wasn't sure what, exactly, they had been discussing, but by their guilty flushes, I deemed it better if I didn't know. "Sugar packets."

He reached for a box and two boxes tumbled off the shelf. He snagged both in midair.

"Impressive," I said, taking one of the boxes from his hand.

"Catlike reflexes come in handy once in a while."

As I went back into the kitchen, the front door swung open and Aubin Pavegeau walked in, a cane in one hand and a backpack slung over one shoulder. He was dressed in a pair of jeans and a gray Roll Tide T-shirt, and had what looked like a twig hanging out of his mouth.

Jena whistled as she spotted him. "Look what the cat done dragged in."

"I don't like cats much," Aubin said, tucking the stick into his back pocket, before giving Jena a quick hug.

Jena laughed and said, "No accountin' for taste. I see you're still chewing sweetgum sticks, Aubin. Some things never change."

He gave a sad smile. "And some things do."

"True enough." She pointed at me. "You know Natalie Walker? She's AJ's little sister."

Aubin's face paled as he looked my way, and for a minute there I thought he was going to turn himself around and march right out of the café. It wasn't a secret what he thought of the Linden family, but how we had managed to rarely cross paths in this small town was some sort of wonder. I'd only ever seen him from afar.

Finally, he stuck out a hand. "It's been a long time, Natalie. You and AJ have the same eyes. Same shape, that is. Different color."

I shook. "Daddy's eyes. No mistaking them." The thought of my father made my stomach start churning again.

Jena said, "It's good to see you out and about, Aubin. Isn't it, Bow?"

"Sure is. Real good," Bow said with a nod. "Take any table you want."

"Thank you kindly, but I'm not staying," Aubin said. "Just wanted to run something past Anna Kate. If she's got the time."

"Where *is* Anna Kate?" Jena asked, looking around. "She's disappeared."

Bow said, "She went out the back door a minute ago. Probably picking more zucchini. Here she comes now."

Sure enough, Anna Kate set two zucchinis and a bunch of parsley on the counter and smiled wide when she saw Aubin. "This is a nice surprise. Good to see you here, Mr. Pavegeau."

"I told you to start calling me Aubin."

"Old habits . . ." Anna Kate wiped her hands on her apron as she approached. "What brings you by?"

Aubin slid the backpack from his shoulder. "One of the items I pulled out of the cabin last week was a screenprinting setup my meemaw used way back in the day."

Bow said, "A little birdie told me your granny was one of the original artisans that put Wicklow on the map."

"That's right," Aubin said. "Her specialty was printmaking. Found some of her old print blocks as well, but what really caught my eye was her screen press. I cleaned it up, did some research, and . . ." He reached into the backpack and pulled out a folded tee. He flapped it open and held it up.

On the front of a white T-shirt was a blackbird sitting on a mulberry branch. The words "Black-bird Café, Wicklow, AL" formed a circle around the bird.

Anna Kate gasped and pressed her hands to her cheeks. "Oh my gosh, Aubin! This is wonderful. Absolutely perfect."

I said, "Did you do the artwork? It's lovely."

"Yes, ma'am. My skills are a bit rusty, but with a bit of practice, we can be sellin' these in no time."

"It's perfect the way it is," Anna Kate said, running a finger over the design.

"Let me see." Jena elbowed her way in. "Aubin Pavegeau, you're a talented man!"

Bow caught my eye and motioned to two plates sitting on the counter. I scooped them up to deliver and refilled water glasses while I was at it.

Glancing up at the clock, I saw it was closing time. Thank the good Lord above. As I went to

386

lock the front door, however, I spotted my mother and Ollie walking toward the café.

"Mama!" Ollie came running as soon as she saw me.

I caught her and swung her up to nuzzle her neck. Ollie squealed with happiness, giving me a moment of blissful peace . . . until I smelled the chlorine in her hair.

"How were swimming lessons?" I forced myself to ask.

Mama smiled. "Olivia Leigh will be a mermaid before we know it."

My stomach rolled. "Did you two come for lunch? We're just closing, but I can whip something up."

Mama gestured to her tote bag. "No, thank you. I brought some family photo albums to share with Anna Kate, then Ollie and I are going to get some ice cream from Adaline's. It's good to see Wicklow coming alive again."

As we went inside, I noticed straight off that Aubin Pavegeau was gone. The screen door slammed shut, and I looked toward the deck in time to see his head go past the window. I didn't blame him—I'd have avoided my mother if I were him too.

"Annkay!" Ollie said. "Hihi!"

I set Ollie down and she ran around tables until she reached Anna Kate, who bent down, her arms open wide.

"Hello, Ollie! Are you having fun with Grandma today?"

"Swim!"

"You went swimming?" Anna Kate made a fish face and tickled Ollie's belly. "Are you a little fishy?"

Ollie laughed and tried to make the same face. "Fishy!"

"Do you want some juice?"

Ollie nodded and Anna Kate went to the fridge.

"I'll get you some sweet tea, Mama," I said. "Have a seat."

The café quickly cleared out, and I busied myself with end-of-shift chores while Anna Kate and Mama looked at photo albums. Ollie was happy as a clam, charmed by a dustpan and hand broom.

So much for ice cream. Mama seemed to have forgotten she was going to drop off the albums and move along. By the looks of her and the photo albums stacked on the table, she planned to stay a good, long while.

"And this one," Mama said, "was when AJ was four and decided to make me a mud pie for Mother's Day. A bigger mess you never did see." Mama and Anna Kate had their heads together as they looked at the photograph. "He was so proud of himself, giving me that pie, smiling ear to ear."

There were albums upon albums at home featuring AJ. His short life had been well documented. There were only two albums of me. And I couldn't remember a time when Mama had ever shown me such love and attention as she was paying Anna Kate right now. I could only recall our heads that close together when Mama was giving me what for in that quiet, cold way of hers.

Jena hip-bumped me. "You still doing okay?"

"I'm all right," I said as Mama prattled on, detailing another one of AJ's triumphs.

"I'm not sure I believe you."

I said, "You know I don't lie."

"I got eyes. I see you're hurtin'. You know you can't hide it from me. Never could."

I had become friends with Jena and Bow one early spring night nearly fourteen years ago. I'd had a huge fight with my mother over something petty. In anger, I'd snuck out in the dead of night and had gone farther into the woods beyond Willow Creek than ever before. It was only when I decided to head home that I realized I was hopelessly lost. If not for some small cat prints that I followed by flashlight, I might still be in those woods. The prints had led straight to Jena and Bow's small cottage, and they seemed to be waiting for me when I stumbled out of the woods.

They'd taken me in, given me hot chocolate, and listened to me cry about the injustices of life. After that day, I'd spent a lot of time with them, helping them farm their homestead, listening to their tales of travel, loving them because they loved me for who I was.

"It hurts," I admitted. "But I'm all right. I know it's important for Anna Kate to see the pictures and hear the stories. They're her history."

"Seems to me the hurt isn't coming from the pictures or the stories, but you go right on telling yourself it is, if it makes you feel better," Jena said, patting my cheek before turning toward the dishes.

Wishing the day was over already, I sang the ABCs in my head to block my thoughts as I stacked chairs with painstaking efficiency. When there was a knock at the front door, my stomach bottomed out when I saw Josh Kolbaugh standing there in full uniform. Then he smiled and I remembered to breathe again. He wasn't bringing bad news about Cam. Thank goodness.

Anna Kate was already at the door to let him in. "Josh, hi."

"Got a sec?" he asked her, motioning outside.

"Sure." She followed him out.

Mama said, "What do you think is going on?"

"Don't know," I said as I turned another chair upside down and slid it onto a table. My gaze went to Ollie, to make sure she was keeping out of trouble. She was still playing with the broom and dustpan, and for a moment I wondered why I even bothered buying toys.

Whatever it was Josh had to say hadn't taken long. Anna Kate came back inside, her forehead furrowed.

"What's wrong?" I asked.

Anna Kate sat down and sighed. "I'd asked Josh for his help in finding a copy of the police report from the car crash. But he just told me the police don't have the records anymore—they were destroyed in a flood years ago."

Mama picked at the plastic on the photo page. "It's important to you, the police report?"

"I want to know what happened—just the facts. A police report would be the most impartial account."

Mama kept picking. "I have a copy of the report somewhere, filed away for safekeeping."

"You're serious?" Anna Kate asked, eyes wide.

Nodding, Mama said, "I'll try to find it in time for Sunday supper. That is, if you're going to be there this week. If not, I can drop it by here. No pressure."

"Thank you, Seelie," Anna Kate said. "I'll look at it on Sunday, at supper."

Mama beamed and turned a page in the photo book. "And this is when . . ."

I tuned her out, and tried to tamp down a growing bitterness. Because not only did I have to hear all about AJ's life these days, but now on Sunday I was going to have to hear about his death, too.

And suddenly, I couldn't take it anymore. Not one more minute.

I picked up Ollie, went into the kitchen, hung up my apron, waved to Jena and Bow, and went out the back door.

As the screen door snapped shut behind us, I glanced back inside.

Neither Anna Kate nor Mama had even noticed we'd left.

21

"Beautiful property you have out here," the reporter said.

Aubin Pavegeau limped toward the small cabin that was going to be the reporter's home for the night. A beautiful chocolate-colored dog raced ahead of them, and two goats bleated from a pen behind the main house. "Thank you. My wife and I built it shortly after we were married."

"I haven't had a chance to meet her." He dodged a chicken in his path. "Has she had any contact with the blackbirds?"

"If you ask my daughter Summer, she has. But you won't be meeting my Francie. She died some six years back."

"I'm sorry. Was it an accident?" He winced as soon as the words were out of his mouth. "You don't have to answer that—it was rude of me to ask."

"It's okay," Aubin said. "It was a car wreck that killed her. But most days, it feels like karma."

Natalie

It was a bit after seven o'clock when someone knocked on the door. I quickly crossed the room before whoever knocked did it again. Despite my best efforts to keep her awake to go to the movies tonight with Mama and Daddy, Ollie had fallen asleep early. Rather than subject them to her temper when she was sleepy, I'd put her to bed. There would be plenty more movies.

In the quiet, I'd been researching how to start an online shop, and had been pleasantly surprised to see that it was doable.

Very doable.

With a growing bubble of excitement, I thought I might just give it a go. A boutique of my own.

It was a goal I never even knew I wanted, until Faylene had planted the seed that day in Hodgepodge.

And then . . . I found I wanted it more than anything. Creating and sewing and running my own business sounded like a dream come true.

My bubble popped when I saw through the window next to the door that it was my mother on the porch. A tote bag dangled from her arm, and a big box that had a wrapped plate on top of it was in her hands. How she'd managed to even knock was beyond me.

Looking toward the heavens, I said, "Really? Now?"

Then I realized what I was doing—adopting Mama's method of coping—and I immediately vowed never to do it again.

Reluctantly, I pulled the door open. "Mama, it's late, I'm not feeling well, and I was going to bed soon . . ."

She walked past me into the house, tossing a questionable look at my pajama shorts and tank top. "I won't stay long. Your father is taking a nap before the movie showing, and I thought it was a good time to stop over." She glanced around. "Is Olivia Leigh already sleeping?"

I closed the door. "She is. I think she's going through a growth spurt. She fell asleep while eating her spaghetti, so I cleaned her up and put her to bed early."

"Have you eaten?" Mama asked, setting her load on the coffee table, and then picking up the plate on top. "I fixed you a plate of fried chicken and potato salad in case you're hungry. There's a slice of chocolate fudge cake there too."

I took the plate from her hands and felt a catch in my throat. "I ate with Ollie, but thank you for this. It'll be nice to have tomorrow."

"Are you feeling any better?"

I could still feel the headache pulsing near my temple, but pulsing was a sight better than pounding. "Much better. I'm sure I'll be fine tomorrow." I put the plate in the fridge, peeked in on Ollie, and said, "Has Daddy been feeling okay? Seems he's sleeping a lot lately."

Mama sat down on the couch. "He says he's fine."

"But?"

Mama worried a button on her sleeve. For a moment, I thought she wasn't going to say anything else, but then she said, "He hasn't been himself for a few months now. I keep nagging him to go for a checkup, but he's a stubborn old coot. What else have you noticed?"

"He's tired. He's not eating well. He winces in pain when he bends over or lifts something heavy." I sat in an armchair and tucked my legs beneath me. "Do you think it's something serious?"

Shadows swept across Mama's ice-blue eyes, darkening them. "Hopefully it's just old age. We're not getting any younger."

Your daddy is dying. "Hopefully."

"I'll try harder to get him to go to a doctor."

"Me, too," I said. "Power in numbers."

Fireworks went off in the distance, a series of loud popping noises. Around here fireworks generally started a good week before the Fourth of July and lasted a good week afterward. It was my belief that people just liked having a reason to blow stuff up.

"I brought over that fabric from Patsy"—she motioned to the big box—"and something else I wanted to show you."

Apparently Mama and I had differing opinions on what *not staying long* meant. It seemed to me she was here to stay for a while. I should have known this would happen, after she had done the same thing earlier at the café. "Do you want something to drink? Coffee? Tea? Iced tea? Iced coffee? A Coke? I have all the caffeinated beverage groups covered."

Mama said, "Do you have any gin? It's been a long week."

I couldn't hold back a laugh—it had been the last thing I'd expected her to say. "No gin. How about wine?"

"White?"

"Coming right up."

I found two glasses in the cupboard and pulled the wine bottle from the fridge. I poured, and carefully carried the glasses back to the living room, the wood floor creaking beneath my bare feet. If Mama had noticed my lack of footwear, she didn't point it out. She had better manners than I did.

"This is good," Mama said after taking a sip.

"It should be—Daddy picked it out. He gave it to me when I moved in. A housewarming gift."

"It was probably more of a dealing-with-your-mama gift."

"Maybe so," I said as I took a sip.

"It's rather amazing it hasn't been opened before now."

I laughed again, wondering when I'd last laughed like this with her. I couldn't remember a time. "This is the second bottle—Daddy gave me two."

Mama shook her head in amusement, and then set her glass on a coaster. She pulled a three-ring binder from the tote bag. "I was going through some of my old designs and thought you might like a few of the patterns. There are baby gowns and dresses, john-johns, shirts. Take what you want, if any. There are pictures of finished products to go along with the patterns." She handed the binder to me.

Flipping through the pages, I sat in awe as I took it all in. "These are incredible. I don't remember you making any of these things."

"I made most of them before you were born. I lost most of my passion for sewing when AJ died, but some of it has come back over the years. Not nearly like it used to be, however. Seeing what you've been doing recently is helping reignite that love. Suddenly, I want to create and design again. You see, I lost myself when he died, too," Mama added softly.

She didn't need to tell me. I knew. Oh, how I knew.

"In making all these life changes, I hope to find myself again, Natalie. A *better* me."

I also couldn't recall a time when Mama and I had sat and talked like this, sharing concerns and *feelings*. I didn't find it as awkward as I thought I would. "I like the changes so far. It's been good to see glimpses of the old you again."

"I wish it hadn't taken me so long to realize how lost I was. It wasn't until I saw Anna Kate that I realized how far I'd wandered. Here, hand that over, will you please?"

It made sense to me that in order to find herself,

Mama had needed to find a piece of AJ first. She'd found it through Anna Kate.

I passed back the binder. Mama flipped to the second page and set it on the coffee table. "This is the very first dress I ever designed, long before AJ was born."

I leaned forward to take a look. It was a darling pink and tangerine dress with the barest hint of gray detailing and delicate puff sleeves.

"All my life, I wanted to be a mother and to have a family. A big happy family. Four girls, four boys. A family of ten sounded just right. I had it all planned out in my head, certain it was going to happen. Which only goes to prove that I don't *always* get my way."

Good Lord, was she cracking a joke? My mama?

I realized with a start that this new mother of mine was going to take some getting used to.

She tapped a picture. "I made this dress for my first daughter, sure I was going to have a girl straight off."

I tried to imagine having seven siblings and couldn't fathom it. Couldn't imagine having any sibling, really. After all, I'd been raised as an only child, for all intents and purposes.

"It wasn't to be, of course. I struggled to conceive AJ, and Daddy and I tried for years after he was born to have another child . . . before we eventually gave up trying. So I spoiled AJ rotten. Absolutely rotten. I gave to him all the love I'd set aside for the big family I'd always wanted . . . I had the perfect little family, and tried to be happy with the blessings I had, but I never quite felt fulfilled. Then you came along. Perfect you, the prettiest baby you ever did see, with those big brown eyes and bow lips. We took you home from the hospital in that pink and tangerine dress."

"You'd kept it all that time?"

"Of course," she said simply. "In my hope chest. With your arrival, I had it all. I'd never been happier. But then AJ was taken away, and my perfect family was destroyed."

"*Mama,*" I said, a plea to make her stop talking right there. "Stop. Please stop. I don't want to hear any more." It wasn't likely to change a damned thing. There was no changing the fact that AJ was gone or how she'd treated me for most of my life. "What's done is done. Let's leave it in the past."

Her voice frosted over. "No, Natalie. It's time I've spoken up."

I knew that tone—she wasn't going to let this go until she said what she needed to say. However, if I was made to listen, *I* needed more wine. I collected the bottle from the kitchen and refilled my glass, then hers. I sat back down and sighed.

"So much of my identity was wrapped up in AJ that when he died, it was like I died, too. And oh my stars, how scared I was of losing you, too. Because if it could happen once, what would stop it from happening again?"

I set my glass on the table and wrapped my arms around my legs.

"I was so scared. All the time. It ate me up, day and night. I worried endlessly that something would happen to you. I loved you so much. All I wanted was to protect you. I cut your food into the tiniest pieces so you wouldn't choke. Made sure you washed your hands all the time so you wouldn't catch colds. I limited your time in cars. I walked with you everywhere to make sure you didn't get hit by a car or trip on a crack in the sidewalk. I didn't like you finger-painting because I worried the paint had lead in it. I didn't like you gardening because the dirt might have bacteria. I kept you out of crowds. I made sure you didn't play with kids who might be bad influences, ones who would eventually learn to drive and drive you right off the road . . ."

My chest hurt something fierce. "I've always known why you behaved the way you did. What I never understood was why you chose to show your love for me by being overbearing instead of affectionate. All I ever wanted was my mother back. The one who used to laugh and sing and play with me. The one who hugged and kissed me."

Her chin quivered before she locked her jaw.

It took her a moment to say, "The pain of AJ's death changed me, Natalie. I didn't realize I was showing you the wrong kind of love. I should have seen it, especially when your father pointed it out so many times, but I was too blinded by the fear to see the damage I was doing." Mama's eyes were full of remorse. "I worked so hard to keep you safe—to keep you here with me—that it's a slap in the face to know it was my actions that ultimately took you away. I understand now why you rebelled, and I am so very sorry, Natalie."

My chest squeezed. "I'm right here, Mama. I came back."

"I know, and that's all that matters now. It's like I said to Anna Kate. The past can't change, but people can. Going forward, I'm taking the lessons I learned from all that pain with me, but it's time to leave the pain behind. I promise to be a better mother, Natalie. Give me time."

I struggled to work through my feelings. It had been an overwhelming day, and I could feel my anxiety vibrating. My gaze went to the waterfall picture hanging on the living room wall, and I took deep, calming breaths. Pain changed people. I knew that firsthand—I'd said it about myself just recently. There was no going back to the Before. Not now, not ever. "You don't need time to become a better mother. You're already on your way."

22

Anna Kate

"Are you sure you're up for this?" I asked Natalie as we found our places at the Sunday supper table. She held a sleepy Ollie in her arms and didn't bother with the booster seat.

Natalie had called off work yesterday with a headache, and still looked like she was suffering. I was worried about her, especially after she left Friday afternoon without saying goodbye.

"I'll be fine," Natalie said. "Ollie's been watching a lot of movies, which isn't my finest hour of parenting, but it lets me rest on the sofa with a wet cloth on my head."

"Fine? Just fine? Absolutely fine?"

"Exactly."

The humor in her voice eased my anxiety somewhat. Jena had said Natalie was feeling poorly when she left on Friday, but I couldn't help thinking there was more to it.

Something to do with Seelie and those photo albums.

I knew Natalie hadn't had the best childhood, and seeing the way Seelie gushed over the photos had to sting. I wished I'd realized it while it was going on, but I'd been too swept up to notice much but the pictures. Guilt picked at my conscience.

As Doc set a heavy pitcher of tea on the sideboard, he grimaced.

"Daddy? Are you all right?" Natalie asked him.

"Right as rain," he said, heading back to the kitchen.

"I never did understand that phrase," she said, shaking her head.

Doc's color today was terrible, and I was surprised that neither Seelie nor Natalie had commented on it. Dark circles rimmed his eyes. He looked like he'd lost a good five pounds this past week, slimming down everywhere except for his stomach, which had bloated. His cheeks had hollowed, his neck had thinned.

He still hadn't told Seelie and Natalie of his ill health, even after he promised me he would. Apparently Lindens didn't hold promises to the same standards as Callows. I'd talk to him as soon as I could pull him aside, because it seemed to me time wasn't on his side. His health had taken a nosedive.

Seelie carried in a bowl of steamed carrots, took a look around as if taking stock of drinks and forks and napkins, then she sat. "Natalie, do you want help putting Ollie in her chair?"

Ollie. She'd used her nickname, and I glanced at Natalie to see if she'd noticed.

Emotion fell over Natalie's face, softening her eyes.

She'd noticed.

"It's best I hold her," Natalie said, rocking side to side. "She's still half asleep, and you know how fussy she gets when she's tired."

Doc came back with a basket of rolls, and Seelie's gaze followed him the whole time, her forehead etched with worry as he sat down.

Maybe she had noticed his coloring after all.

"Bankie," Ollie whimpered, barely lifting her head.

Natalie reached into the diaper bag at her feet and pulled out a quilt to tuck around Ollie. "Here's your blankie. Shh."

"That blanket . . ." I said, staring at it.

Natalie said, "Mama made it for Ollie's first birthday, using her newborn clothes as patches. It's Ollie's favorite—she has trouble sleeping without it."

Stunned, I turned to Seelie.

"What is it, Anna Kate?" she asked.

"I have a quilt . . . and I have trouble sleeping without it too. It looks a lot like Ollie's, except different patches, of course. I've had it my whole life."

Seelie gasped, and her hands went to her cheeks. "You must have AJ's quilt. It went missing after the car crash. He planned a picnic lunch that day and packed the quilt along with the basket. No one knew what had happened to the quilt, because it wasn't at the crash scene."

"I'll be damned," Doc said.

"How'd it get to you?" Seelie asked me. "It hadn't gone with Eden to the hospital. I know, because I checked."

"I have no idea," I said. "All I knew growing up was that it had belonged to my dad. I didn't know you had made it until right now."

"He'd be glad you had it," Seelie said, nodding. "I'm glad you have it."

Natalie reached for a roll, broke off a chunk, and offered it to Ollie, who refused it and tried to burrow even further into Natalie's collarbone.

Doc said, "Would you like some steamed carrots, Anna Kate?"

Seelie shifted toward me. "AJ hated carrots. The first time he tried them . . ."

I half listened as she recounted the story, because I was focused on Natalie and something she had said to me a while back.

Foods were the worst. If I said I liked carrots, I'd hear all about the time AJ tried carrots for the first time and spit them out on Daddy's tie.

As much as I wanted to hear more about my father, I had to keep in mind Natalie's feelings, especially since the guilt for hurting her on Friday was still weighing heavy. I hadn't known for sure that's what had happened until now—that she'd been hurt—but the truth shined in her eyes for all to see—if we looked.

I took the bowl from Doc, scooped carrots, and redirected the conversation. "Seelie, do you think there's room at the carnival next weekend for another vendor booth?"

"Certainly. Why?"

"Aubin Pavegeau and I would like to sell some screen-printed T-shirts."

"The Blackbird Café shirts Aubin designed?" Natalie asked. "He's quite talented."

I said, "Those, along with some new designs as well."

Seelie's lips pursed. "T-shirts?"

I explained how the project had come about and the various designs in the works.

"Flocking?" Seelie said, her hand on her pearls. "Don't you think that's a bit . . . risqué? I don't think it's appropriate."

"I think it's funny," Natalie said. "I'd wear one of those T-shirts."

"No, you would not, young lady," Seelie snapped. "It's tacky."

Every once in a while the old Seelie made an appearance. If Natalie's smile was any indication, she didn't take the admonition to heart.

"You're not thinking of the bigger picture, Seelie," I said. "The Refresh Committee should take note. Even though these shirts are being sold to supplement Summer's college fund, it's this kind of marketing that will attract attention. It'll lure people here. And once they're here, hopefully they'll stay around awhile. See the blackbirds, hike and bike the local trails."

"Spend their money," Natalie said.

"Exactly."

Seelie kept on pursing. "I still think it's flocking tacky."

Natalie laughed, nearly choking on her tea.

Seelie blinked innocently and reached for the rolls.

Doc ran his fork through his mashed potatoes. "If the café is shutting down in a few weeks, why make T-shirts? Seems a waste of time to me."

We all looked at him.

"What?" he asked.

Seelie said, "Anna Kate just explained that the T-shirts are a fundraiser for Summer Pavegeau's college fund."

"Did she? I didn't hear that part." He picked up his sweet tea and took a long sip.

Natalie looked at Seelie, her eyebrows drawn low in concern.

"About the café," I said, trying not to give Doc a lecture right then and there. He needed to let his family know what was going on with his health. It wasn't fair to them. "I've been brainstorming ways to keep the café open while I'm at school. Maybe I can hire a managing team. I'll still make the pies and overnight them down. Jena thinks it can't be done, but I think that where there's a will, there's a way."

Seelie said, "It seems to me you're happy in the café, Anna Kate. You come alive there—I've seen it with my own eyes. Why not defer medical school a year, give yourself some time here in Wicklow? Get the café on its feet again."

Ollie's hand wiggled out of the quilt and snatched the roll away from Natalie as she said, "I think that's a great idea. Give yourself some time."

"No," Doc said. "Absolutely not. Don't you two go planting ideas in Anna Kate's head just because you don't want her to leave town. If she defers, she'll never end up going. She'll get too comfortable here, and that will be that."

Seelie leveled him with an icy stare. "It's not our decision to make. It's Anna Kate's. It's clear she's unsure about selling the café. Giving her options takes away some of the pressure."

"She's made her decision already," he said. "Is she not starting classes in August?"

"That was before," Seelie said, her teeth clenched, "Anna Kate had other choices."

His chin jutted as his face paled. "The only choice she has is medical school. The sooner the better, so she can take over my practice sooner rather than later."

"Hold up now," I said, freezing. "Who said anything about your practice? I don't want it."

"It was supposed to be AJ's, which means it's supposed to be yours," he said.

409

Suddenly feeling sick, I clenched the napkin in my lap, twisting and turning it. Had I been blind to his true intentions all along? "Your speech about wanting to get to know your granddaughter . . . about moving forward. It wasn't about me at all, was it? It was always about you. What *you* want." I knew he'd been manipulating me, I simply hadn't realized the extent.

"Succotash!" Natalie yelled. "Succotash!"

"What on earth?" Seelie said, eyeing her.

Natalie reached for the diaper bag. "We should go, Anna Kate."

Doc's voice turned to stone. "Eden wanted you to follow in your daddy's footsteps—you said so yourself. His footsteps lead to me. My practice."

"Lord have mercy," Natalie whispered.

"Mercy," Ollie echoed from under her blankie.

My chest heaved with anger. "His footsteps, yes. *My* shoes. It would be nice at some point if someone actually cared what *I* wanted. You once asked me if I had regrets, and I told you I did. One. It was the day I promised my mother I'd become a doctor because I knew it was what she wanted and would make *her* happy. I made the promise. It's done. I'll see it through, but that's the end of it. The rest of the decisions are mine."

"You know how I feel about regrets." He shoved to his feet.

His words from the day I met him came back to me.

410

I've decided regret is like cancer. It eats you from the inside out, just the same.

The haze of my anger evaporated instantly. Had he told me straight from the get-go what was wrong with him? Did he have *cancer?*

Oh my God.

"I need some fresh air," Doc said. "We can continue this conversation later."

"Daddy?" Natalie said. "Are you all right?"

"James?" Seelie jumped up.

I saw Doc sway, and grabbed hold of him just as he collapsed.

Natalie

"He lied to me." I thought my heart might break clear open. "It was a lie of omission, but that's still a lie. I asked him flat-out if he was feeling well, and he evaded the question."

"I don't think he wanted to worry you," Anna Kate said, her eyes bloodshot.

"But it's a lie just the same, isn't it? Doesn't make it hurt any less."

Anna Kate reached out to hold my hand, and at the same time Cam's voice, once again, came unbidden into my thoughts.

Sometimes people lie to protect the ones they love.

Anna Kate and I sat side by side in the hospital waiting room. Faylene Wiggins, bless that woman, had come by to collect Ollie. She was taking her

411

to Marcy's house to play with Lindy-Lou until I could pick her up.

We'd been here a few hours now, and we were waiting on Daddy to be discharged against medical advice. He insisted there was nothing the hospital could do for him that couldn't be done at home, and there was nothing anyone could do or say to talk him out of it.

He was being sent home with information on hospice care.

Cancer.

Daddy had cancer. It was eating up his pancreas, affecting his liver function, and had spread to his lungs and his stomach.

He'd known for nearly six months now and hadn't said a word. Not a single damned word. There were no treatment options left. No cure.

He had a few months left, at best. If we were lucky.

My head swam, and it felt like the brightly colored walls were closing in on me. Every inch of my body ached, and I desperately wanted to go home and try to pretend this was all one big nightmare that I'd wake up from any minute now.

"I knew he was ill," Anna Kate said, her voice raw. "But I didn't know how sick he was."

My head was so fogged with emotion that it took me a minute to fully comprehend what Anna Kate had said. I shifted to face her. "You *knew* he was sick? How did you know?"

"I saw it," she said. "The color of his skin, the yellowing in his eyes . . . He told me he was seeing doctors."

As if I'd been burned, I dropped Anna Kate's hand. "How long have you known?"

Anna Kate winced. "Since the first time he came to the café."

"Why didn't you tell me? Or Mama? How could you keep something so serious to yourself?" I said, my voice sharp.

I sounded like my mother. The old one. I didn't even care.

Hurt flashed in Anna Kate's green eyes. "I didn't know how serious it was. And at first it was none of my business, and then he asked me not to tell. I made a promise."

"Some promises are meant to be broken, Anna Kate. I can't believe you didn't tell me."

"He promised me *he'd* tell you."

"Well, he didn't, did he? You should have, Anna Kate. *You* should have."

Lies, lies, everywhere.

Your father is dying. The voice suddenly rang in my head, and my stomach rolled.

I had known—someone had told me.

I just hadn't paid enough attention.

Why hadn't I paid enough attention?

Acid rose up my throat. I was going to throw up right there in the waiting room if I didn't get out of here. I jumped to my feet and ran. I headed toward the EXIT sign, thinking fresh air could only help.

But as soon as I stepped outside and sucked in a deep breath I knew nothing was going to help. The tears came hot and fast, and the more I tried to hold them in the harder they fell.

My father was dying.

23

The reporter was a virtual stranger in this town, yet even he'd heard of Dr. Linden's diagnosis. It was a popular topic of conversation among the diners.

"Dr. Linden, thanks for taking the time to speak with me."

"Please, call me Doc." He wrapped his hands around a takeout coffee cup. "I'm not sure I can offer any information for your article. While I know of the blackbirds, I've never had anything to do with them."

"Nothing at all comes to mind?"

Doc stared at the cup's plastic lid. "All I know for certain is that the blackbirds were here long before I was, and they'll be here long after I'm gone."

Anna Kate

"Where's Mr. Lazenby?"

I bolted upright in bed, and rubbed sleep out of my eyes as I looked around. I could have sworn I'd heard someone with a feminine voice asking me where Mr. Lazenby was. No one was around, but the window was open, and I saw the outline of the phoebe against the screen, fluffing her feathers on the windowsill in the morning light. Her crooked wing was a sure sign she was the bird that had been hanging around the café, but she didn't appear to be trying to get inside.

Which was just as well, because I didn't want to chase her around the apartment.

I lay back down. It was entirely possible I'd dreamed the voice, since I'd been thinking of Mr. Lazenby before I fell asleep. It had been five days since I'd last seen him, when he went home in a snit the day Pebbles didn't show up for breakfast.

I rolled onto my side and punched the pillow into a comfortable position. Usually this time of the morning I'd be dragging myself into the shower, but all I wanted to do was pull my quilt over my head and sleep the day away.

I stared at the walls, watching the morning light shift around. I could tell I'd been crying in my sleep. Hearing that Doc only had a few months left to live opened a gaping hole in my heart.

It had been three days since learning of his diagnosis. He was at home, resting, with Seelie keeping close watch over him. Natalie hadn't been in to work, either, missing two shifts.

She was angry. So angry. What she didn't understand was that Doc had lied not only to her, but to me as well. To all of us.

However, it was easier to be mad at me than him.

The expression on Natalie's face when she

found out I knew Doc had been ill had haunted my dreams. The scathing look of utter betrayal. It caused an ache deep in my bones and made me question why I'd kept quiet.

But I knew why. I made a promise.

Some promises are meant to be broken, Anna Kate.

Natalie's words cut like a knife, because I couldn't stop thinking that she was right. I'd made a bad decision, and I added it to my list of regrets, which had grown rapidly in these past few days.

I regretted not telling Natalie about Doc's health, and I deeply regretted coming to Wicklow altogether.

My mother had warned me to stay away, and I should have taken that caution to heart. If so, I'd still be in Massachusetts, happily oblivious to this charming little town.

Oblivious, anyway.

Because truthfully, I hadn't been happy up north. It wasn't until I'd come here that I found true happiness. I'd fallen in love with the café and Zee's garden and my neighbors.

My God, the neighbors.

Faylene, Summer, Jena, Bow, Gideon . . .

Flipping over, I punched the pillow again.

I sang the "Sing a Song of Sixpence" in my head and tried to fall back to sleep, but my brain wasn't having it. I tossed aside my dad's quilt.

It was time to get up. Get dressed. Get on with the day. I had a lot to do.

A day that now included checking in on Mr. Lazenby.

It was late morning when I left the café under the very capable control of Bow and Jena and headed across town. After checking in on Mr. Lazenby, I wanted to visit with Doc. I hoped I'd have a chance to talk with Natalie, as well. I didn't like the way things were between us right now, and I needed to fix it. Somehow. Some way.

On a narrow residential road, I found the house I was looking for. It was easy to see that the blue clapboard bungalow had been well taken care of over the years. The paint was fresh and bright, the lawn freshly mowed, and the flowers along the walkway full of blooms.

I walked under a wooden arbor and headed toward the front door to ring the bell. I heard it buzz inside the house.

"Go away," Mr. Lazenby said through the door.

"It's me, Anna Kate."

"Go on with you. Go away."

"I brought you some food from the café. Scrambled eggs, sweet potato hash, bacon . . ." The door cracked open, and I smiled as he scowled out at me. "Since Pebbles has been sick, I wanted to make sure you weren't ill too. I've missed you these last few days."

"Pebbles is sick?" he asked, reaching for the takeout box in my hands. "How sick?"

He might've opened the door, but it was clear he wasn't inviting me inside. "It's a virus of some sort. Fever, cough. Started up last week, according to Faylene. A little rest and she should be okay."

He scratched the white stubble on his chin. "Might could be why she missed breakfast last Friday."

It was interesting to me that her absence was still on his mind. "It's likely," I said. "She hasn't been around this week, either."

"I should probably check on her," he said, the wrinkles around his eyes multiplying as he frowned. "You think she'd mind?"

I tried not to smile. "No, I don't think she would."

He gave me a nod, and said, "We'll see. Thank you for the food, Miss Anna Kate." He closed the door.

I noticed he didn't ask if there was pie in the box. It seemed his priorities had shifted.

The blind old fool was finally seeing the light.

It was a quick walk over to Doc and Seelie's. She smiled when she saw me at the door. "I'm going to have to sedate the man to keep him in bed," she said by way of a hello.

She put an arm around me in an awkward embrace—she still wasn't comfortable showing me affection, which was just as well because I didn't know how I'd receive it. We were feeling our way through our relationship, one uncomfortable hug at a time.

"He wants to go golfing." Seelie looked like she hadn't slept well. Her eyes were shot with red, and shadows lurked beneath them. "Lord have mercy on my soul. Natalie and Ollie are upstairs with him now, trying to get him to eat something."

The foyer was filled with flowers, bouquets and arrangements of every shape and size. "I see word's gotten out."

"I have a dozen casseroles sitting in my freezer and at least that many loaves of cinnamon bread. The bread brigade is in top form."

I nearly laughed out loud at the term. It fit so well.

"Of course James doesn't want any of it. Maybe you could make him something? I bet he'd eat that, even if it's only so your feelings don't get hurt. I'm not above using trickery, Anna Kate."

"I'll bring something by later." And maybe an herbal tea as well. At this point it couldn't hurt. "How's Natalie today?"

"She's been good with James, but with me she's been quick-tempered and snappy. She's hurting."

I nodded, thinking we all were.

"Go on up. I must find some room in the freezer for a couple more casseroles, then I'll join you."

A carpet runner covered the wooden stairs, muffling my footsteps as I climbed. On the landing, I heard Ollie making *vroom*ing noises from down the hall, then Doc saying, "So help me, Natalie Jane, you're not too old to have a knot jerked in your tail."

"It'd be worth it if you'd eat something," she said. "Come on, it's your favorite."

I peeked into the room and saw Ollie driving her tractor along the footboard of a four-poster bed. Natalie sat in a chair, bedside, holding a plate of red beans and rice.

Doc, propped up in bed, spotted me and said, "Don't tell me you brought food too. If so, turn yourself around and come back without it."

"No food," I said, holding up empty hands. "Just me."

"Hihi! Annkay!" Ollie had learned how to wave properly, and I missed the way her whole arm used to flap.

"Hi, Ollie," I said, waving back.

Natalie set the plate on the nightstand and stood up. "Come on, Ollie. It's time to go."

"You don't have to leave," I said, aching at the detached look in her eyes.

"Natalie? You're leaving?" Seelie asked as she came into the room and stood next to me. "But you barely just got here."

Natalie picked up Ollie. "We'll be back later." She surged past us and out the doorway.

"I'll be right back," Seelie said tightly and strode out as well.

I sat in the seat Natalie had vacated and tried to think of something to say.

"She's angry," Doc said.

"I know."

"She's mad at me and taking it out on both of you."

"I know."

He laughed. "She'll come around."

I wasn't so sure. "You know, you really should eat something. You need nutrients."

"Months ago, when I declined the recommendation to undergo chemo and radiation, it wasn't a rash decision. It was because I didn't want to spend my last days going to and from the hospital, sick as a dog from the medicine that was trying to make me better. I want to *live,* Anna Kate. I do not want to be laid up in bed, being waited on hand and foot, being force-fed. So please knock it off."

I jabbed a finger at him. "Well, *we* want you around as long as possible. You've had *months* to deal with your diagnosis, but we're in shock, so let us fuss a few days. But what's going to happen if you don't eat? Or drink enough fluids? Stop being so stubborn trying to prove to us that you're doing fine. Because you're not."

With a heavy sigh, he said, "Fine. Hand me that plate. No need to get all fired up."

"I don't know about that. Seems to have gotten the job done."

I handed him the plate, and he picked at the food. "I behaved horribly on Sunday. I'm sorry."

"Stop that," I said. "It's in the past and we're focusing on the future, remember?"

"I remember, but I think I've been a little *too* focused. I've been getting my affairs in order these past few months, and it hurt to think of having to sell my practice, my legacy, to a stranger. When you showed up, and I heard you were planning to be a physician . . ." He set the plate aside and adjusted his blanket. "I got ahead of myself. It wasn't right of me, and it certainly wasn't fair."

I rubbed a finger on the chair's upholstery. "I've been thinking that maybe being a family doctor and carrying on your legacy might not be so bad."

His brown eyes shone with compassion. "I haven't been getting much sleep, and in those dark, quiet hours when it was just me and my thoughts, I came to realize that I'd been wrong. My practice isn't my legacy at all. It's only a place. A thing. Work. My legacy, who I am, the person I am, is my family. Long after I'm gone, I will live in you, in Natalie and Ollie, and Seelie. All of you will always be in my heart, and part of me will always be in yours. That's a damn good legacy, if you ask me. Don't you agree?"

Family.

I squeezed his hand and blinked away tears. "I agree, Doc. I agree."

Natalie

"Stop right there, young lady."

I had almost made it to the back door when my mother's ice-cold voice stopped me. I set Ollie down as I turned around. "Not now, Mama."

"Yes, now. I know you're hurting, but taking it out on Anna Kate isn't helping anything."

"So you're taking her side?"

"I'm not taking *any* side. There are no sides."

My heart hammered against my rib cage. "She didn't tell us Daddy was sick."

"It wasn't her place to tell us. It was *his*. It's his illness. If you're going to be mad, be mad at him. He's the one who deserves your anger."

"How can you say that? He's *dying*."

"That doesn't make him any less accountable for his actions. He made the choice *six months* ago not to tell us—a decision that had nothing to do with Anna Kate."

My chest felt fit to burst. "She should have told us."

Mama reached for me, but I stepped away. If she touched me—showed me affection—I might break flat open, and I wasn't sure I could ever be put back together.

"It's not Anna Kate's fault. It's no one's fault.

424

Don't you see what you're doing, Natalie? You're acting just the way I did toward Eden Callow all these years. You're needing someone to blame to help ease the pain. I can tell you from experience that it doesn't help. You're hurting because you love him. And the only way to get through the pain is to keep on loving him. Especially after he's gone."

I wanted to put my hands over my ears and sing *lalalala* at the top of my lungs. I needed to get out of here. Breathe. I couldn't get enough air. I was suffocating.

Drowning.

Picking up Ollie, I said, "I need to go." I pulled open the door and rushed outside.

"Bye!" Ollie yelled.

Mama's voice carried on the hot breeze. "Running away isn't going to help, Natalie. It never has. It never will."

I blindly walked back to the little house, wondering where I could go. Where I could hide. I needed space. I needed air.

I was halfway up the porch steps when I heard, "Natalie?"

"Hihi!" Ollie said.

"Hi, little darling," Cam said.

I blinked, trying to clear my raging thoughts. "Cam? What are you doing here?"

"I heard about Doc. Thought I'd come by to check on you. Are you doing okay?"

425

Was I okay? I wanted to laugh maniacally, but I was afraid all I would do is cry. "No," I whispered, trying to keep my voice from cracking.

"What do you need?" He put his hands on my arms. "What can I do?"

I needed . . . *peace*. My gaze rose to meet his. "Is your offer to take Ollie and me to the waterfall still open?"

"Of course. When?"

"Now," I said. "Right now."

His eyebrows dipped low. "You sure?"

"Absolutely. I just need to grab a few things."

Before he could talk me out of going, I handed off Ollie to him and went into the house. I quickly packed a diaper bag and grabbed snacks for Ollie and her blankie, too, since it was closing in on nap time. I put on a pair of hiking boots, and a minute later I was back outside, pulling Ollie's car seat from my hatchback to put into Cam's truck.

The whole time, I did my best to pretend I didn't see my mother watching my every move from the window. Or that the truths Mama had laid out to me in the kitchen didn't hurt more at that moment than my grief.

24

Anna Kate

Staying on task was proving to be difficult. I chopped mint, and its scent did nothing to soothe me this afternoon. I was worried about Doc, about Natalie, about me.

My gaze went to the mulberry trees as I contemplated the importance of legacies.

A stab of pain brought me out of my thoughts, and I dropped the knife. I'd nicked my finger. Blood pooled along the tip, and I cringed at the sight of it, which was another reason I wasn't much interested in conventional medicine. The sight of blood gave me the willies. I ripped a paper towel off the roll, dampened it, and pressed it to the cut.

I knew better than to handle sharp objects when I was distracted, but I'd gotten it in my head to take Doc some herbal tea to help him sleep. The stash of my favorite blend of chamomile mint, however, had been low.

On the counter, a dozen chamomile flowers I'd just harvested stared at me, their perky daisy-like faces fairly screaming that everything was going to be okay.

"I have my doubts, little ones," I said to them.

Checking my finger, I saw the wound wasn't deep. I washed my hands, rubbed some calendula salve on the cut, and put on a bandage. I washed the knife in case I had contaminated it and went back to chopping. When I had enough mint, I scooped it up and placed it on a tray along with the chamomile flowers.

As I slid the tray into the food dehydrator, I heard steps on the deck and looked up in time to see Summer heading for the back door, a cardboard box in her hands, not her usual basket.

The screen door slammed behind her as she came inside. "What're you cooking up now? Wait." She sniffed the air. "I smell mint. And apples?"

"Not apples. Chamomile," I said. The fresh flowers gave off a slight apple scent.

"Tea?" she asked, smiling.

"I can't help myself."

She laughed and set the box on the island. "My mama always said that when you have a gift you should use it."

Once upon a time, there was a family of Celtic women with healing hands and giving hearts, who knew the value of the earth and used its abundance to heal, to soothe, to comfort.

The dehydrator whirred as if in agreement. "Smart mama," I finally said. "It's for Doc. The tea. I want to help him any way I can."

Her eyes clouded. "I hope it brings him comfort." She was a sweet girl with a big heart. One

428

that was trying to forgive the Lindens—namely Seelie—for the way they'd treated her father, but was struggling. Time, I told myself. They just needed time.

Thinking of them reminded me that I still hadn't gotten my hands on the copy of the police report. There was always one thing or another to distract me from asking for it.

Summer motioned to the box. "I've brought by T-shirts for this weekend."

I cracked open the box top and smiled at the Blackbird Café logo that stared up at me. "Your dad has outdone himself. Between the T-shirts and renting rooms, is he getting any sleep?"

"He hired on a cousin, an artist who'd been working as a day laborer down in Fort Payne, to help out with the tees. Together they've come up with a couple more Wicklow designs, and they're already selling to shops all around town."

I smiled at her usage of "all around town." All the shops were located on one road, but seeing the storefronts open and busy felt like the whole town had spread its wings.

"He's in hog heaven, by the way, having guests around. He's started making them breakfast every morning. He said he likes trying out new dishes on a captive audience. It's been nice seeing him so . . . happy. He's really enjoyin' the bird-watchers staying with us, and he's even thinking of turning the main house into a bed-and-breakfast after I go off to school, making it official with licensing and all that."

"Really?"

"Really. And, Anna Kate, we have enough money now to make the first payment due on my tuition. If business stays like it does, we'll have plenty for the rest. Oh! And I got a job down at school, too. In the library."

"Summer! All that is fantastic news. Good for you."

"I can't thank you enough for your help, Anna Kate. We couldn't have done it without you."

"Oh no. I can't take the credit, Summer."

"Then who can? Because before you stepped in . . ." She grimaced.

I laughed. "I think the credit goes to Zee. It was her idea for me to stay here in Wicklow and run the café. If you didn't bring eggs every day, I might not have met you. If I didn't meet you, I'm not sure I ever would have found the Harry Potter room. It's almost like she had this all planned out."

As soon as I said it, I felt a prickle at the back of my neck. *Had* Zee somehow planned it?

Summer smiled. "I like thinking that. Well, thank you, Zee!" she said loudly.

With the back door being open, I hoped Zee, roosting somewhere near the mulberry trees, heard the gratitude.

"I know you only stayed because of Zee's will,

430

but I'm thankful you did, Anna Kate. After Zee died I thought I'd never eat blackbird pie again. When you came here, you gave me the gift of more dreams. I didn't take them for granted. I admit I'm sad that there might not be more pies, but they've already given me the lesson I needed to learn from them."

"What's that?" I asked, genuinely curious.

"That a person you love is never truly gone—they're always there, whether it's in a memory . . . or a dream."

Or in a heart.

All of you will always be in my heart, and part of me will always be in yours. That's a damn good legacy, if you ask me.

"And if that knowledge isn't the greatest gift of all," Summer added, "I don't know what is."

Natalie

"Are you feeling better?" Cam asked hours later.

We sat on a blanket at the edge of the waterfall pool. Ollie slept between us, using her blankie as a pillow. Small hands were thrown over her head, one of them gripping the green tractor. Her face was relaxed and angelic as her chest rose and fell rhythmically. River slept, too, snoring softly as he rested his head on Ollie's foot.

Taking a deep breath, I picked a pine needle off the ground and flicked it away. "I'm embarrassed."

431

"Why?"

"I've been acting a fool."

Mama's earlier words rang in my ears, echoing to the far reaches of my mind, where my deepest fears resided.

You're needing someone to blame to help ease the pain.

It's exactly what I'd been doing.

I wanted to blame Anna Kate for what was going on with Daddy.

And I'd wanted to blame Matt for his own death.

Because I *hurt.*

Good Lord, I hurt.

Because I didn't know how to cope, other than to run away. But in both of those cases, there had been nowhere to run.

There was no hiding from death.

"I need to apologize to Anna Kate and to my mother. And maybe to the staff at the hospital."

"That bad?" he asked.

"However bad you're thinking, multiply it by ten at least."

"I'm sure they understand." Cam leaned back on his elbows, stretching his legs out in front of him. "There's no rulebook on how to behave when blindsided with bad news, Natalie."

I closed my eyes, letting the sound of the waterfall soothe me, the crashing water, the gentle ripples against the creek bank. "I was terrible, taking out my grief on them."

432

If my mother hadn't given me that talking-to, I might not have come to my senses anytime soon. Sometimes the truth was hard to hear. Harder to accept.

Cam said, "I'm sure no one's judging you."

"I'm judging me."

"Quit it."

"Tell me how. Please. And while you're at it, I need a lesson on forgiving, too. I don't know how to do that, either."

He crossed his legs at the ankles. "For me, the first step was trying to understand the *why* of it all. I put myself in my ex-wife's shoes. I tried to look at our relationship from her point of view. Living alone, with me halfway across the world for nine, ten months at a time. I get that she was probably lonely."

"You were gone from her just as long. Did you turn to someone else?"

"No," he said, shaking his head. "But this isn't about *me*. It's about her. If you put yourself in your father's shoes, what would you have done if you received that diagnosis?"

Daddy had told me why he'd kept the cancer a secret—because he wanted to live as normally as possible, without people looking at him with pity and feeling sorry for him and bringing by a loaf of banana bread every week.

"I don't know." What Daddy had said resonated with me—I didn't like pitying looks and people feeling sorry for me, either. But I didn't know if that kind of diagnosis was a burden I could've carried alone.

This wasn't about me, however. It was about my father.

He was by far the strongest person I knew. The way he had carried our family after AJ died . . . carried me . . .

"I guess I can see why he did it." I picked up another pine needle, and bent it between my fingers. "I hate even admitting that."

"Why?"

"Because it excuses it. Him. And I'm still angry and not ready to let it go."

He took a sip of water from his canteen. "Angry because he didn't tell you? Or because he's dying?"

I stood up, dusted off my hands, and walked toward the water. Leave it to Cam to cut right to the heart of the matter. He had an uncanny ability to see straight through me. As I felt him come up beside me, I said, "It's not fair."

"Nope, it's not. For any of you."

Looking over my shoulder, I watched Ollie sleep, and my heart ached.

Ollie didn't know how much she was losing. Or how much she'd already lost. I didn't know if that was a good thing or not. At one point I thought it was, but now I wasn't sure.

Ollie would never know Matt's laugh or remember the way he'd smother her tiny face in kisses. And she wouldn't remember the way her grand-daddy held her just so when he read a book to her, all safe and happy and loved in his arms.

The spray from the falls blew against my legs. "How'd you forgive your wife?"

He picked up a rock, skimmed it across the water. "I don't exactly know. Forgiveness isn't a science. It's more of a feeling. Deep down, all I ever wanted was for her to be happy. She wasn't happy with me. I loved her enough to let her go."

I glanced back at Ollie. She hadn't moved an inch. "Weren't you angry?"

He skimmed another rock, and there was humor in his voice when he said, "I had my moments."

Rocks glimmered beneath the surface of the shallow water. "How'd you get over it?"

"It was a choice. I could either keep dwelling on what had happened, letting it define me, or take the valuable—and sometimes painful—lessons I'd learned from the relationship and move on. Maybe find someone eventually who loves me the same way I do them. It was an easy decision. I chose to move on. I came down here, to Wicklow, and started a new business, and here I am . . ."

Here he was.

"Do you still love her?" I didn't want to explore why that question hurt to ask.

"No," he said. "Falling out of love isn't nearly

435

as hard as you think when you know your wife ran off with the cable guy."

"I'm so sorry."

"Don't be. If she hadn't done that . . . then I wouldn't be here, would I?" He held my gaze and smiled. "With you."

I smiled too. "Why do I suddenly feel the need to send her a thank-you note?"

He laughed.

"Hihi!" Ollie yelled, and River barked.

I turned just in time to see Ollie running straight past my legs, into the water, screaming in delight as she fell forward. I lunged to catch her, and I fell hard on my knees. Water splashed in my eyes as Ollie slipped out of my grasp. No! I scrambled forward, reaching blindly. Suddenly a strong hand clamped my forearm, putting an end to my floundering, and Cam's laughter cut through my madness.

"It's okay, Natalie," he said. "Ollie's right here."

Thank God. Oh, thank God. My heart pounded in my throat as I sat up in waist-deep water, and wiped my eyes. I very quickly saw what was making him laugh.

Ollie floated on her back right next to me, her hair fanning out around her face, cheeks sucked in and lips puckered. "Fishy!"

Cam helped me up. "I didn't know she could swim."

As soon as I was steady enough, I lifted Ollie

out of the water, held her tight, sure I'd never, ever let go again.

"Fishy!" Ollie yelled as she wiggled in my arms. *"Pease."*

Ollie wanted back into the water. As she struggled against me, suddenly all I could think of was my mother and how she'd shown me that living a life in fear was no way to live at all.

It was a choice.

The only thing I could think to do right at that moment was choose to let Ollie *live*. Because if I kept stifling her with my anxiety, she was bound to drown without being near a single drop of water—just like me.

Swallowing back every fear I'd internalized since the day I received the shattering call about Matt, I slowly set Ollie into the water. I held my breath as she threw herself forward, face first, then quickly flipped onto her back. She shot skinny arms outward and giggled.

"She can't swim," I said to Cam, smiling so wide it hurt my cheeks. "But apparently she can float."

All because Mama had insisted on swimming lessons.

She'd been right. One hundred percent right.

About a lot of things.

25

"Hihi!"

The reporter waved to the little girl. "Your daughter is cute."

Natalie Walker finger-combed her daughter's hair, tucking soft waves under a turquoise-and-green headband. "Thank you. I think so too."

"I'm hoping you can help me with the timeline of all this"—he gestured around the café, incorporating the tents in the yard—"hullabaloo. How did the blackbirds become such a *thing?* Around town I'm seeing T-shirts, stuffed animals . . ."

A smile twitched the corner of her mouth. "It's all because of Anna Kate, sharing the blackbirds with us. With everyone."

He glanced toward the kitchen, to the young woman laughing as she dished up a piece of pie. "Yet she hadn't stepped foot in Wicklow until six weeks ago? What took her so long? Wasn't this a family business?"

Natalie wrapped her arms around her daughter. "You'll have to ask Anna Kate those questions, but it was inevitable that she came back, because she has Wicklow in her blood. It's my belief that all Wicklow girls return to their roots—and their mothers—at some point or another. It just takes some more time than others."

"Isn't her mother dead?"

Natalie held his gaze. "If you think that matters, you haven't been paying attention around here."

Anna Kate

Early the next morning, I saw Gideon step onto the back deck, dressed in his usual biking gear of athletic shorts and moisture-wicking tee.

"Well, hi, stranger," I said, holding open the screen door.

He gave me an uneasy smile. "I owe you an apology."

"For?"

"Staying away."

The door slammed as I let it go. "No need. I'm sure you had your reasons."

"Yeah, but—"

Frantic knocking cut him off. I glanced over my shoulder at the front door.

Mr. Lazenby.

"He's here early," Gideon said.

Mr. Lazenby's insistent knocking reminded me of my first days in Wicklow, when he'd woken me up to ask if there would be pie that day, desperate for a connection to his wife. I went to the door, pulled it open. "Is everything okay, Mr. Lazenby?"

When I saw the distraught look in his cloudy eyes, I knew it wasn't.

"Miss Anna Kate, I'm right sorry to bother you so early, but I need your help."

"Is this about the pie?"

Shaking his head, he said, "No, not pie. Tea. Do you recall offering me tea for my cough? Do you still have any on hand? Pebbles is doing poorly, and her doctors are telling her there's nothing they can do, that the virus has to run its course. She's having trouble sleeping, because the dry cough is keeping her up, and without rest, she's going to have trouble getting better. You can help her, can't you?"

"Come on inside. I'll get the tea for you. It's not going to work miracles, but it should help soothe the cough enough for her to rest."

"Any little bit will help," he said. "Thank you."

I heard him and Gideon talking as I went into the pantry and searched the shelf of loose tea blends I'd made. I found the licorice root jar, a pack of diffuser bags, and an empty jar and brought it all into the kitchen. "This licorice tea is *very* sweet on its own, so it doesn't need any sugar added to it. There's some cinnamon in here too, which is known to help the immune system, so it should help as well."

I made quick work of measuring out the dried blend and transferring it into the smaller jar. I wrote down brewing instructions using the diffuser bags, and put all of it in a Blackbird Café paper sack. I handed it over to him, along with a to-go box of zucchini cheddar biscuits. Apparently I'd jumped on the bread brigade bandwagon. "Give her my best, will you?"

"I can't thank you enough, Miss Anna Kate." His eyes softened.

"You already have just by coming here. Go on with you now."

He didn't need to be asked twice, practically running out the door and down the street.

"So Pebbles and Mr. Lazenby?" Gideon asked as I turned around.

I took the cup of coffee he offered. "It's been a long time coming."

"Speaking of a long time coming . . . I'll be starting the paperwork today to make Zee's will official. Technically, you have a couple of weeks left on the mandated timeframe, but it's just a waiting game at this point. Everything will be ready for you to sign when it's time."

He went on, explaining probate, but I barely heard half of what he said as I stared at the jar of tea on the counter. Its label, specifically. Licorice root.

For where your roots are, your heart is.

Zee had told me that once. Her roots were here in Wicklow. Mom's, too.

And mine.

It was breaking my heart to think I had to leave because of a promise I'd made.

"Anna Kate? Did you hear me?"

I looked up. "Sorry. Lost in my thoughts there for a minute. What were you saying?"

"I was saying that I'm torn, Anna Kate. Real torn."

"About?"

"A dream I once had."

I pulled a stool out from under the lip of the counter and sat down. "A dream, you say? It wasn't one you had after eating a piece of blackbird pie, was it?"

He pulled out the other stool. "It's time I told you, that pie is the whole reason I'm living in Wicklow. You see, the first time I was in town, I stopped by the Blackbird Café for something to eat . . . That night I dreamed of my grandfather. He told me I should stay in Wicklow, set up a law practice. I didn't think much of it, to be honest, other than it was nice to hear his voice again."

I set my elbows on the counter and propped my head in my hands. I could listen to blackbird pie stories all day long.

"Next day, same thing. I ate at the café. Had a piece of pie. Blueberry, if I recall. Later that night, Granddaddy was back. Told me to buy Hill House for my law practice." His eyebrows arched. "Granddaddy was never one to mince words."

"So he wasn't a lawyer."

Gideon laughed. "No, he was a building inspector."

443

I smiled and took another sip of coffee.

"By day three, I'd heard the rumors about the blackbird pies, and started thinking maybe there was something to the gossip. I was two years out of law school at that point, and a little lost, not sure what kind of law I truly wanted to practice. I worked at a big firm in Huntsville, and wasn't very happy. When Granddaddy mentioned setting up a practice here, it sparked my interest. For the first time in a long time, I was excited for the future. But when I inquired about Hill House, I was told it wasn't on the market."

"No?"

"Nope. I had to track down the owner and beg. By the end of that meeting, I had the strangest feeling that she'd been waiting for me all along. It was Zee."

Goosebumps went up my arm. "She owned Hill House?"

"Yep. The café used to be Hill House's carriage house."

I knew it had been a carriage house, but I hadn't put it together that Hill House had belonged to Zee as well.

"We became friends—she was like another grandmother to me."

"Do you still dream of your grandfather?"

"Not for a long time. I'd just moved into Hill House when I last dreamed of him." His long fingers wrapped around his mug as he lifted it to his lips. "He told me that Hill House and the carriage house belonged together, and to make that happen, no matter how long it takes."

"Wow," I said.

"I tried to talk Zee into selling the café, but she kept telling me that decision wasn't hers. That it was yours, and to talk to you when the time was right."

I ran my finger around the rim of the mug, reflecting on Gideon's messages. The dreams were supposed to be *loving* notes . . . This was more bizarre than Faylene's husband reminding her to pay the property taxes.

"I've been avoiding you lately, Anna Kate, because the last thing I wanted was for you to feel like I was using you when I finally worked up the nerve to ask you to sell to me. I swear, I didn't get close to you for your property. I . . . enjoy your company."

He blushed, and I smiled. "Then I hope you'll stop staying away. I've missed you."

Grinning, he said, "You don't know what you're asking. You might not be able to get rid of me."

I shrugged. "It's a risk I'm willing to take."

Gideon slid his mug back and forth between his hands. "About the land . . . I've come to believe I interpreted my grandfather's dream all wrong."

"Seems to me he was plenty clear."

"I thought so too, but maybe instead of me buying the café, maybe it's you who should buy

Hill House. There's plenty of money in Zee's estate for you to do so."

I put my mug down. "Oh, no thank you. Honestly, I have no idea what your grandfather intended, but I don't want Hill House. Don't get me wrong, it's a beautiful house, but it's yours. And I'm leaving town in less than a month."

"But, Anna Kate—"

I held up my hand to cut him off. "If you're about to tell me I should stay here in Wicklow, you can stop right there. I don't want to hear it."

Because I wanted to stay.

I wanted it more than anything I'd ever wanted in my whole life. Jena had said I belonged here, and I did. I was as rooted to this café as the mulberry trees were to the beyond.

But I'd made a promise, and though I thought a dozen times a day about breaking it, I couldn't. I simply couldn't. Callows did not break promises.

Gideon and I sat in silence for a few moments before he said, "I've been thinking about our time at the movie a few weeks ago, and how it ended so . . ."

"Terribly?"

"Abruptly," he said, laughter in his voice. "I think we should have a do-over. Do you have plans for the Fourth of July? You might have heard there's a big carnival and fireworks show . . ."

Glancing over at him, I saw a flash of that molten lava in his eyes before he hid it by suddenly looking away. He grabbed the coffee pot and refilled our cups.

"I'll be busy until three or so." I was going to close the café early and take a shift selling T-shirts.

"Would you like to have another go at a picnic dinner? Same terms as before. I'll bring the food, you bring the drinks."

"I never did get a piece of that fried chicken."

"You missed out. Truly."

"Faylene's been raving about it for weeks. I admit she's made me jealous."

"Then it's a date." He grabbed his mug and took it to the sink to rinse.

A *date*. I smiled stupidly at my coffee.

He left for his bike ride not long after, and I took the chairs off the tables, set up the cash drawer, and started the biscuit dough. The screen door slammed, and I thought Bow and Jena had arrived early, but it wasn't them.

Natalie stood by the back door, wringing her hands.

She wore a Blackbird Café T-shirt, a pair of knee-length twill shorts, and flats.

If she owned a pair of sneakers, I'd never seen them.

I kept on kneading the biscuit dough and said, "I wasn't expecting you until much later." In fact, I wasn't expecting her at all, despite the fact that she was on the schedule. With the way she'd run away from me yesterday, I thought she wouldn't be back to the café for a long, long time.

She stepped up to the counter. "I'm here for my shift. I came early because I wanted to talk to you."

The anger had faded from her eyes, but they still had sadness etched in their depths. Her shoulders were relaxed, her face soft, not hard like the last time I'd seen it. She seemed to be in a better place today, emotionally, but I wasn't sure I could handle any lingering coldness.

Where she and the Lindens were concerned, I was already too raw.

"About?" I was proud my throat didn't catch on the word.

"How sorry I am."

I bent the dough in half, pushed the heels of my hands into its softness. My chin came up, and I met her gaze and saw genuine remorse. "I'm listening."

"I run away. It's what I do when I can't handle the hard times. Not only do I run, I also push away people who care about me. My therapist says I do it to protect myself—I remove myself from the painful situation. It's taken me a long time to realize that running away doesn't protect me from anything—it just takes me that much longer to deal with the real problem. I've been working on new coping skills, but old habits are hard to break sometimes. You didn't deserve my anger, Anna Kate, and I'm sorry for the way I behaved. Please say you forgive me." She clasped her hands to her chest. "Please."

I stopped kneading and inhaled deeply. "The thing about families is sometimes they get angry and fight. Especially our family. But that doesn't mean the love isn't there," I said, paraphrasing words she'd spoken to me not so long ago. "The love is always there."

Natalie came around the counter and threw her arms around me. She gave me a noisy kiss on my cheek that reminded me of Ollie, and I didn't blanch at the show of affection.

In fact, I rather liked it. Floury hands and all, I hugged her back.

"Thank goodness for that," she said in my ear. "I have the feeling that our family is going to need all the love it can get over these next few months."

I hugged her tighter, but I didn't have a response for what she said.

I didn't want to think about the next few months.

At all.

Natalie

Ollie was upstairs reading a stack of library books with Daddy, while Mama and I prepped cocktails to take out on the patio to watch the lightning bugs dance in the twilight.

It had been a *week*. An emotional roller coaster, one filled with few ups and many stomach-dropping downs. I couldn't imagine that was going to change anytime soon, not with what we as a family were facing.

But we had each other to lean on. A month ago, I wouldn't have thought that possible.

Mama set a stack of dessert plates on the island and reached for the pie cutter. Anna Kate had sent me home from work with a blueberry tart she made at Daddy's request along with a jar of chamomile tea.

Mama easily slid the pie cutter into the tart, took out a piece, and set it on a plate. Plump blueberries glistened against the bone-white china.

"In case you're worrying," I said, "this tart has nothing to do with blackbird pie. It's just a tart, a mighty delicious-looking one at that."

"Did I say I was worrying? Were *you* worrying?"

"When am I not these days?" I said with a smile. "I mentioned it only because I know how you feel about the blackbird legend."

Mama lifted a shoulder. "I reserve the right to change my mind about the blackbirds."

My eyebrows went up. "You don't say."

"I can't say I understand it, but I see that Anna Kate wholeheartedly believes in the folklore. Why am I being so stubborn? It would be nice to dream of AJ." Her gaze drifted upward, to the room above us where we could easily hear the cadence of Daddy's voice. "Even if it's only a dream."

I put my hand on her back and gave it a gentle rub, a gesture that didn't quite feel natural even though I wanted to bring her comfort. All wounds took time to heal, especially when they'd been festering for so long.

"Have you tried the blackbird pie?" she asked.

"No."

Her gaze slid to me. "Because of the mountain man?"

"Did you know Cam was a Green Beret, Mama? Served two tours of duty overseas. He's a nice man. He's asked if Ollie and I will go with him to the carnival this weekend. I said yes. I was hoping you and Daddy would join us to watch the fireworks."

Mama's eyebrows shot upward and her hand froze mid-slice. "I—We—" She finished the slice and took a deep breath. "We'd like that."

"Did that hurt to say?" I asked, holding back a smile.

"A little bit," she admitted.

I did smile then. "Thank you."

She nodded.

"And to answer your earlier question, no, my decision on the pie has nothing to do with Cam. I thought I wanted to hear from Matt more than anything in the whole world. I wanted answers about his death, to put it to rest once and for all. I

451

put off eating the pie only because of Daddy. He didn't want me to, and I honored his wishes."

She set down the pie cutter and looked at me. "It shouldn't have been your father's decision. What do *you* want, Natalie?"

I set forks on the tray. "What I've wanted since the day Matt died. Peace. Daddy said I wouldn't find what I was looking for in pie, and he was right." I'd been doing a fair amount of self-reflection in the past few days. "I was so caught up in the way Matt died that I forgot how he loved me. He had his secrets and vices, yes, but all *I* ever knew from him was love. All Ollie knew from him was love. It's enough to carry us through our grief."

Mama's lips pursed as she set the pie cutter in the sink.

"For now," I quickly added before she said something snide about Matt's character, "I don't plan to eat any pie. I reserve the right to change my mind."

She glanced at me, and her lips fell out of their pucker. "Love can see one through many challenges."

She looked like she wanted to say more on the subject, but instead she went about setting napkins on the tray. There were many wounds still to be healed, but we'd get there. I was sure of it.

With a gentle huff, she threw the napkins down

and faced me. "I have something for you. Come with me."

"But the dessert . . ."

"It can wait. I saw that stack of books Ollie piled next to your father. We have plenty of time."

"What's this about?" I asked as Mama toted me into the dining room. "Do I need dealing-with-Mama wine?"

She put her hands on her hips. "No, you do not, young lady."

Her reprimands no longer made me want to run for the door, which told me exactly how far we'd come in the last few weeks.

"Not tonight, anyways. I have this for you." She gestured to a big rectangular box sitting on the dining table. "It's been a long time coming. Go on, open it." She nudged the box then lifted her hands, steepling her fingers under her chin.

Curious, I lifted the lid. As soon as I did, my hands started shaking. "Is this what I think it is?"

"It is, indeed."

Carefully, I lifted the quilt out of the box and spread it out on the table for a closer look. Through a patch of pink and tangerine fabric with the barest hint of gray detailing.

I saw a block from my baptism dress, another from the dress of my first daddy-daughter dance. One block held a monogrammed frog, and immediately I recalled wearing a dress with that frog on it the summer I turned five.

"I'm sorry it's late," Mama said. "For some reason, not long after you were born, I felt compelled to make your blanket from memorable events, not just from baby clothes. This," she pointed to a patch made of rainbow colors, "was what you were wearing when you lost your first tooth. This is your first Christmas, and this was the day you got braces, and here's the day your braces came off. And this one here was when you learned to ride your bike on your own."

I vaguely remembered that day. I'd been six, and Mama had made me wear a helmet, elbow pads, and knee pads—*and* had made Daddy run alongside me at all times.

"I've been working on it on and off for years. Picking it up, setting it aside. I could never bring myself to finish it, and I think that was due to us being . . ." She trailed off.

I waited for her to find the right word, curious to see what she'd come up with to describe our troubled relationship.

"Disconnected," she said. "The time finally came for me to finish it, which I did last night when I added this bit here." She tapped a quilt block.

I leaned forward. "Is that . . . is that the duck bib I made?" It sure looked like it. The colors were the same, and it even had the striped trim.

"I bought it at Hodgepodge."

"Why?"

"Full circle," Mama said. She tapped another

block. "This here is your first bib. I made it for you not long after you were born."

My eyes widened when I saw the pattern. Ducklings.

"We've come full circle, you and me. Right now seems like the perfect to time start a new circle. A new beginning. I love you, Natalie Jane. Always have, always will. Y'hear?"

I wiped away tears. "I hear, Mama."

26

Anna Kate

Much to my surprise, Gideon showed up at the café on Saturday for coffee. I hadn't thought I'd see him this morning, because of our *date* later tonight.

It was hard not to smile just thinking about it.

"You cannot possibly cram one more person in that side yard." The screen door slammed behind him, and he went straight to the mug shelf.

I grabbed a coffee pot. "I think there are people willing to challenge that theory."

Eventually, I was going to have to start easing the birders out to reclaim the yard. I had a dozen recommendations for places to stay, with the Pavegeaus' homestead at the top of the list.

Gideon set the mugs on the counter. "How's Doc feeling? I heard he went back to work yesterday for a few hours."

"He's holding steady. He missed his patients, and being cooped up was suffocating him. He's started the search for someone to take over the practice and already has a few good candidates."

I barely heard footsteps on the deck before Jena and Bow came in the back door. Jena wore a red, white, and blue tunic and had flag barrettes in her hair. "I do so love this holiday," she trilled as she flew around, putting her purse away and grabbing an apron.

"I'm sure they couldn't tell," Bow said, an eyebrow arched.

"The sass with this one." She smiled fondly at him, then turned on Gideon. "Nice to see you here this morning. I was startin' to forget what you looked like."

He said, "I've been around. I was here yesterday."

Jena faced me, then smirked. "Is that so?"

"Don't let him get off so easily," I said. "That was the first time I'd seen him in a good week."

Bow slipped an apron over his head, then clapped Gideon on his back. "Don't go giving the boy a hard time. You know he was nervous to ask Anna Kate about buying the café."

"Wait, you knew he wanted the café?" I asked.

Jena checked on the biscuits in the oven. "Of course, sugar. He asked Zee to sell at least once a month since he had that dream to reunify the properties. Only made sense he was going to ask you, too."

I lifted an eyebrow. "So much for your *intuition*."

Her musical laughter filled the kitchen. "It wasn't my place to tell you. It was Gideon's. Since he's here, I'm assuming he's made an offer?" She tipped her head, eyebrows raised with anticipation.

"I made one," he said.

"And?" Bow asked, looking between Gideon and me.

"I asked if Anna Kate wanted to buy Hill House."

Jena comically stumbled to a halt. She put her hand on her chest. "What's this now?"

He shrugged. "I think Anna Kate belongs here in Wicklow. My dream didn't say I had to be the one to reunify the properties. Maybe it was a dream meant for Anna Kate all along."

"What did you say to that, Anna Kate?" Bow asked.

"I said no, that's what. And I haven't decided what to do with the café, so don't ask. Technically, it's not even mine yet, so it's pointless to even be talking about this right now. I just want to focus on running the café until the end of the month, and then I'll go from there."

I had a little less than four weeks left here, and I didn't want to spend the whole time discussing the sale of the café.

Mostly because I didn't want to sell, but I hadn't yet figured out how to keep it.

I saw the worried look Jena shared with Bow, and sighed. I didn't expect them to understand the bind I was in. I threw a look out the window, toward the mulberry trees. I knew the trees would wither and die without the love in the pies, but I still wondered what would happen to the blackbirds if the passageway closed.

My chest ached as it swelled with emotion. I had the uneasy feeling that if the trees were left to die that the blackbirds would never return to Wicklow. Why would they? They'd have no songs to sing if there were no pies being made.

Blinking away a sudden sheen of tears, I wished for more guidance from the blackbirds. I wanted to know what would happen to them and not just guess at their fate. I needed to ask them—and could only hope they would somehow provide an answer.

Gideon rinsed his cup, put it in the dishwasher. "I'll pick you up at four, Anna Kate? That good with you?"

"Perfect," I said, glad my voice hadn't cracked.

"Pick you up?" Jena said, curiosity lifting her voice an octave.

"Anna Kate's been begging for a taste of my fried chicken," he said. "I thought I'd indulge her. We're going to have a picnic at the courthouse before the fireworks."

Bow nodded approvingly. "I've had your chicken. I can see why she'd beg."

I shook my head at their teasing and went for a coffee refill.

Jena said, "You know, Gid, I've been thinking on that dream you had."

"What about it?" he asked.

"What if the dream was meant for you *and* Anna Kate?" She took hold of my hand and dragged

460

me toward him, tucking me right up close to his side. She put my hand on his, then covered our hands with her own. "There's another way to unify these properties you two haven't given thought to yet." Clearly pleased with herself, she smiled broadly. "If I was a bettin' woman, I'd lay odds that your granddaddy was planting seeds in that dream, Zee watered them, and now it's up to you two to see if they take root."

Later that afternoon, I sat cross-legged on the stone bench in the garden, staring at the mulberry trees. A male cardinal, a wren, and the phoebe with the crooked wing picked at the ground under the trees, probably hoping to find a wayward berry. What Summer and I hadn't harvested had eventually fallen to the ground. Squirrels, chipmunks, and birds had feasted. The remnants had eventually broken down and seeped into the earth, spreading love back to the roots of the trees.

Now it's up to you two to see if they take root.

I wished Jena had kept her comments to herself. As soon as the words had come out of her mouth, Gideon and I had jumped apart as though poked with a cattle prod. We bumbled goodbyes and he left quickly. It had taken everything in me not to lash out at Jena.

As much as she was only trying to help, I had enough pressure on me without throwing my feelings for Gideon into the mix.

"I don't know what to do," I said to the mulberry trees. "How do I decide?"

If I stayed, I'd let down my mother.

If I left, I'd let down Zee and the blackbirds.

"What happens to *you* if there's no pie?" I had the awful image of the tips of the blackbirds' wings browning and curling. Suddenly queasy, I banished the image forever.

The leaves of the lemon balm shuddered, catching my attention. I glanced over and saw Mr. Cat sitting there, flicking his tail back and forth. I immediately grew concerned for the birds under the trees, but he seemed disinterested in them. His focus was on me.

"I don't suppose you have any answers, do you?"

The phoebe flew over and landed on a lemon balm stalk and started singing.

Mr. Cat tipped his head, looked at the bird, then turned and walked away.

I heard a creaking noise as Gideon came through the back gate, a basket in his hands. He called out a hello to Mr. Boyd, who sat by the back fence, his nose in a book. Mr. Boyd lifted his head and waved. He had plans to join Faylene later on to watch the fireworks. I'm not sure they needed to watch, because there were plenty of sparks shared between them. They'd been spending a lot of time together, and it had been sweet to see them falling for each other.

"How'd the T-shirt sales go?" Gideon asked me as he came closer.

"Sold out within an hour."

"An hour? That's amazing. Which one went first? Come on, it was the 'Flock Off' tee, wasn't it?"

I laughed, thinking of Seelie's horrified expression when she'd seen that particular logo. "Actually it was the Blackbird Café shirts."

He dipped his head in acceptance. "I shouldn't be surprised by that." He held up the basket. "Are you ready to go? The sooner we leave, the sooner you'll see what I packed."

"There's more than chicken in there?"

"So much more."

I quickly grabbed the cooler that I'd left on the deck, bid goodbye to the zucchini plants, and said, "Then let's get going."

Out on the main street large groups of people walked toward the courthouse with blankets and coolers and folding chairs. There was an electric energy in the air, one full of excitement and anticipation.

Most of the shops along the street had closed early, but colorful awnings flapped in the breeze, adding to the joyous feeling. Most of the awnings were new—added during grand openings and reopenings. There were two new restaurants and at least a half dozen shops, including a book shop, a candle shop, and a yarn store.

"You're quiet," Gideon said.

"Just thinking."

"About what Jena said earlier?"

I practically gave myself whiplash turning to face him. "No, about the town. How it's come alive. It almost feels like it's exhaling a sigh of relief."

"Oh."

I set my hand on his arm. "Did you want to talk about what Jena said earlier?"

"I mean, we don't have to. She was just hypothesizing."

"Right. Exactly. Hypothesizing."

Fireworks went off in the distance, a high-pitched whistle followed by distinct popping noises—people were overeager to get the party started.

"But . . ." He looked at me. The molten lava was back in full force. "All I'm going to say is if Granddaddy and Zee were matchmaking, they did a really good job."

I went as warm as that lava in his eyes. "I—"

A flash of quick-moving light on my left snagged my attention, and I stepped aside near a row of knee-high shrubs separating two storefronts.

"What is it?" he asked, following my gaze.

"Did you see that?"

"See what?"

"This is going to sound crazy, but I could have

sworn I saw Mr. Cat run behind those buildings with a sparkler in his mouth."

Gideon didn't hesitate to jump the shrubs to take a look. I waited for him on the sidewalk, and a moment later he was back. "I took a good look around, but I didn't see anything. Are you sure it was Mr. Cat?"

"Hard to tell because of the building shadows," I said. "Do you think we should go look for him? I mean, that can't be safe."

Gideon said, "A cat isn't going to hold on to something that would burn him. He'd drop it real quick if the sizzle got too close for comfort. Wouldn't he?"

We were still debating whether to form an all-out search party when we saw Mr. Cat walking toward us on the sidewalk, no sparkler in sight. About ten feet away, he took an abrupt right, turning up a narrow alleyway that ran between the ice cream shop and new arts and crafts store.

"I guess there's no need to worry after all," I said as we turned toward the courthouse.

Gideon looked over his shoulder. "That is one strange cat."

I laughed. "He is, but I've grown fond of him."

Ahead, four food trucks were parked at the curb in front of the courthouse, and at least two dozen booths had been set up on the lawn, selling everything from popcorn to fresh vegetables. A firework whizzed into the air, exploded, and filled the sky with colorful glitter that would have been much prettier if it were dark.

Gideon and I took our time browsing booths, lingering over small talk with the vendors, who were excited by the turnout. We didn't pick up our earlier conversation on what Jena had said, and I was grateful for the reprieve.

As we made our way toward the amphitheater, I spotted Faylene waving her arms, trying to get our attention.

"Yoo-hoo! Anna Kate, Gideon! Over here!" she yelled.

"Annkay!" Ollie shouted, mimicking Faylene's tone of voice.

I was happy to see that Natalie and Ollie shared a blanket with Cam. Natalie hadn't spoken too much about the mountain man, but I knew she was fond of him. Whether it was only friendship between them or something more, it was nice to see her smiling.

Ollie jumped to her feet as Gideon led me toward Faylene's landing zone.

"Hi!" Ollie said as I scooped her up to give her a hug.

I looked at Natalie. "Don't tell me she's dropped the second hi."

"It vanished a day or two ago," Natalie said.

I rested my forehead against Ollie's. "First the full-arm wave and now this. I can't handle you growing up so fast, Ollie."

She cupped my face with her soft hands and smiled. "Hi!"

"Hi, Ollie." I hugged her close and didn't let go until she started wiggling.

She'd grown so much in only six weeks. How many of her milestones was I going to miss while I was away? In a blink, she would be graduating high school. I glanced at Natalie, and she immediately stood up when she saw the tears in my eyes.

She was on her way over to me when someone yelled my name.

I turned.

"Anna Kate!" Mr. Boyd huffed and puffed with exertion as he beckoned. "Come quick."

"What is it?" I ran toward him.

"The café's on fire!"

27

"The fire came as a shock," Jena Barthelemy said. "But maybe, on closer look, it was a blessing in disguise."

"How so?" the reporter asked. Mesmerized by her lilting voice, he'd long stopped taking notes.

Dark eyes full of wisdom held him captive. "Sometimes, it takes almost losing something to realize exactly how important it is to you."

Anna Kate

My heart pounded as my gaze went to the sky. A skinny plume of black smoke rose above the café.

Gideon took hold of my hand, and we started running. Sirens wailed in the distance.

I stumbled on a crack in the sidewalk, but Gideon held me steady.

Please let the trees be okay, please, I silently pleaded. The café was a good distance from them, but fires could spread easily. And please let all the mulberry preserves be okay.

Please, let it *all* be okay. Because I wasn't ready to say goodbye. Not to the customers who'd become friends, not to the café, and not to Zee's garden. Not to any of it.

Not yet.

Please, not yet.

Gideon kept tight hold of my hand as we weaved around families and friends on their way to enjoy their night, while I ran toward home.

Home.

Steeling myself, I looked ahead to the café. From afar, it didn't look like anything untoward had happened, and I half expected to see Mr. Lazenby waiting on my arrival, but the bench in front of the café was empty.

A fire truck idled at the curb, and a small crowd of people had gathered.

I didn't see any flames or anything unusual at all. The café looked . . . fine.

"Where's the fire?" I asked, breathing hard, my lungs stressed from the exercise. I wiped sweat off my face and looked around.

A firefighter, a young man who'd eaten at the café a few times, stepped forward. "It was in the backyard, ma'am. It's out now. Mr. Boyd saw the flames, and he and a bunch of other bird-watchers banded together to put out the flames using a garden hose and blankets."

Small towns. I was growing fond of them, too. How else would this firefighter even know Mr. Boyd?

As the young man led us around the café, he added, "Due to their quick actions the damage was limited to the deck."

The gate was open and as we went through it, my gaze went first to the mulberry trees. Branches waved in the breeze as if telling me they were just fine.

I let out the breath I'd been holding and turned toward the deck.

Inky puddles pooled along the pathway and the café's foundation, and I did my best to dodge them as I carefully inched forward, trying to take it all in.

There was nothing but blistered, blackened blocks of wood where the stairs had once been. The deck itself was blackened, too, but that looked to be more from soot than fire damage. All in all, it wasn't too bad. The deck and brick could be power-washed. The stairs replaced. I could fix this. It could have been so much worse.

Relieved, I let my gaze wander. That's when I saw the zucchini plants. I ran over to them and dropped to my knees in front of their remains. There was little left. Charred stems and a wet, soggy pile of ash and sorrow.

I gulped air. They'd been doing so well . . . thriving, even, giving me so much of themselves. Now this.

"I'm so sorry," I whispered to them, my voice breaking. Tears welled up, then flowed free. I couldn't stop them.

Not even when I felt someone sit down next to me.

Gideon.

He put his arm around me, pulled me in close to him.

And let me cry.

Gideon handed me a cup of coffee early the next morning. "If you didn't want to sell the café to me, you should have just said so. You didn't need to try and burn it down."

"It's too soon to joke about it," I said with a groan and a grimace.

My eyes felt like they'd been rubbed with sandpaper as I looked at the deck. It turned out there had been more damage to the deck than met the eye. The inspector who had come by last night told me I couldn't reopen the café until the deck was replaced. Something to do with egresses. Honestly, I had tuned him out after he said I couldn't open.

I'd been wanting a day off, but not like this. I needed to get in touch with the insurance company to see how long it was going to take to file a claim.

Gideon pulled out a stool for me, then went around the kitchen gathering ingredients. "I can only joke because no one was hurt and there was minimal damage."

"What are you doing?" In the kitchen, other than a smoky scent that reminded me of camping, there was no evidence there'd been a fire at all. None of the soot had made its way into the building, and I was beyond grateful for that small miracle.

A sparkler had been found near the deck, and the investigators had labeled it the cause of the fire. No one knew how it had found its way there, but I had the funny feeling Mr. Cat had dropped it when it had gotten too hot. Why he'd picked it up in the first place, I'd never know. I was glad he hadn't been hurt—I'd seen him lurking near the mulberry trees earlier this morning.

"Making breakfast. You look like you could use some sustenance."

"You're right. I could. Thank you." It was barely seven in the morning, and I'd hardly slept at all. I tried to think of the last time I'd eaten. It had been early yesterday afternoon. No wonder I was starving. "Just nothing with zucchini, okay?"

With a sad smile, he came over and pressed a kiss on top of my head. "Deal. How about pancakes?"

"Sounds good."

Gideon measured flour, sugar, and baking powder into a large bowl. I wasn't surprised he was good in the kitchen, but I hadn't anticipated how nice it was to watch him cook.

I tried to let go of my worries as I kept an eye on him. "You know you're making enough to feed an army, right?"

He glanced back at me. "Because I am. I should put some bacon on."

"I'm hungry but not that—"

The front door swung open and Jena rushed in. She ran right up to me and wrapped me in her arms. "Good Lord, child. You look like you've been chewed up and spit out."

Bow came up behind her and said, "What Jena means to say is we're real sorry about the fire."

"That's exactly what I meant, bless your heart."

Behind them, more people filed inside. Aubin and Summer, Marcy, Josh, and Cam, and Mr. Boyd along with several other birders. Seelie and Doc and Natalie rounded out the pack.

They were all wearing Blackbird Café T-shirts, and had smiles on their faces and a hammer, saw, or other tool in hand. Seelie's was a pink tape measure.

My gaze fell on Gideon, who had fired up the griddle. "I'm dreaming, right?"

He said, "About time you finally admitted I'm the man of your dreams. I never thought this day would come."

Jena faux swooned and fanned herself with her hand, while Bow rolled his eyes at her theatrics.

Faylene came over and put her arm around me. "I knew you and Gideon had something going. Ain't no man cooks fried chicken just to be friendly."

"Twice," Marcy called out.

"Thank you, honey, for reminding me. *Twice*." Faylene held up two fingers to emphasize the statement. "Pebbles and Mr. Lazenby send their best. They're not here, on account of them volunteering to keep the little ones for the day—Summer's going to go over and lend them a hand after breakfast."

I squeezed my eyes closed tight, then slowly reopened them, one at a time.

"If you need a pinching, I bet Gideon would volunteer," Jena said, waggling her eyebrows.

I glanced at him. "Look what you've done, Gideon."

He shrugged. "Jena's not wrong."

"What's going on?" I stood up. "What are all of you doing here?"

"Why, what do you think, child?" Jena said. "We've come to tear out the deck and build a new one. It's not going to build itself."

"Someone pretty special once told me that many hands make quick work," Aubin said, his voice carrying.

"Hear, hear," Bow echoed.

Tears pooled in my eyes. "But the insurance . . ."

"Pshaw," Faylene said. "We ain't got time for that. There's a café to reopen."

"But it'll only be open a few weeks more . . ."

"Sweetie," Jena said, "we see how happy you are working here, and we didn't want you to miss out on that these next few weeks. We love you and want you to be happy. You're here now and we're gonna enjoy every minute we can get with you. Understand?"

"Yes, ma'am." Unable to stop myself, I hugged her.

Good God. I'd become a hugger and a ma'amer. How in the world had this happened?

But . . . I knew how.

Wicklow had gotten hold of me but good.

"Group hug!" Faylene yelled, throwing her arms around Jena and me.

Before I knew it, everyone had gathered around, hugging and laughing.

I was so overwhelmed with their love that I barely even noticed the soft brown feather sticking out of Jena's hair.

28

Anna Kate

A few days had passed since the deck had been rebuilt. The café was closed for the day, and as I'd already made the pies, I should've been weeding. Instead, I found myself once again sitting cross-legged on the stone bench in the garden, having a one-way conversation with the mulberry trees. So far, all of my questions had gone unanswered.

"Hello? Anna Kate?"

I turned and saw Seelie waving from the gate, the silk scarf around her neck blowing in the mountain breeze. I motioned her in, and she gave me an awkward hug before joining me on the bench.

She sat and brushed imagined dirt from the front of her knit shift dress and said, "James practically kicked me out of the house. Apparently, I 'hover,'" she said, using air quotes.

"Do you?"

"Of course I do." She laughed, and sunlight glinted off her light blue eyes, infusing them with warmth. "How could I not?"

"Hovering seems perfectly reasonable to me."

"Thank you," she said pointedly, then smiled. "I shouldn't grump. James did me a favor kicking me out—I've been meaning to come talk to you."

"Oh? About?"

"Two things. The first is this." She opened her leather tote bag and pulled out a manila envelope. "It's a copy of the police report you were wanting. Look it over; let me know if you have any questions."

I took it from her outstretched hand, wondering if I even needed to see what was inside. It wouldn't change anything. But, I had to admit, I felt a spark of curiosity ignite, wondering once again if it was possible to finally put to rest all the questions surrounding the accident. "Thank you."

Next, she lifted a leather portfolio from the tote. "You're welcome. And secondly, I know you've heard by now that I've been on a quest to get to know Eden better."

"I've heard one or two people mention it."

Or a dozen. Small towns held few secrets.

"Yes, well, my interviews were mostly fruit-less—Eden kept mostly to herself. Then I came upon the realization I already had every-thing I need to know at hand." She opened the portfolio, revealing a blank note page.

I waved away a gnat and said, "There's nothing there."

"That's because it's all right here." She gestured to me. "Who's a better reflection of Eden than you? In you, I've seen kindness in the way you stepped up to help Summer afford college. I've seen generosity in the way you've allowed the birdwatchers to stay on your land. I've seen creativity in your recipes. I've seen fairness, in the way you turned profits from the blackberry tea back to the Pavegeaus. I've seen strength in the way you've taken on running the café after suffering personal tragedy. I've seen forgiveness with me, with Natalie. I've seen a heart of gold in the way you care about Mr. Lazenby. I've seen humor in the T-shirt slogans. And I've seen love, especially in the way you look at Ollie. Now," she said, taking my hand, "some of that is all you, Anna Kate, but I'm betting you learned a lot of those characteristics from your mother. And that tells me all I need to know about Eden. I believe the car crash was an accident, plain and simple. I'm sincerely sorry for treating her terribly. I'm ashamed of myself."

I glanced at the mulberry trees. I hoped Mom had heard the apology. It had been a long time coming. Moreover, I hoped she accepted it, because it seemed to me it had come straight from the heart.

Sunbeams glinted off Seelie's pearls as she pulled her hand away. "I, of course, cannot speak on Eden's behalf, but as a mother who's learned some valuable lessons of late, I cannot help but think that Eden would want, above all else, for you to be happy, promise or no. You mentioned once that no one ever asks you what you want, Anna Kate. I'm asking you now. What do *you* want to do?"

I squeezed my hands into fists. "I don't know."

"I think you do. I think you've known since the first day you came to Wicklow. You need to own that truth, Anna Kate, or you'll never be truly happy." She stood up. "I'm going to head on home. I have hovering to recommence."

"Do some hovering for me, too, will you?"

"Absolutely."

With a wave, she was gone. I sat, thinking about what she'd said.

I knew what Zee wanted.

I knew what Mom wanted.

What did *I* want?

I glanced back at the café, then over to the birders, and Hill House.

I wanted to see where Mr. Lazenby and Pebbles's relationship was headed and listen to Faylene's gossip. I wanted to know how Summer fared at school and see Aubin's B&B plan come to life. I wanted to know if Ollie would be swimming on her own by the end of summer and if Natalie would allow her heart to love again. I wanted to hear Mr. Boyd's stories of his mother. I wanted to see Seelie continue to find her new self, and I wanted to hear Doc tell me every story he could remember about anything, including my dad. I wanted to get postcards from Bow and Jena. I wanted to have coffee with Gideon every morning.

I wanted to create tea blends.

I wanted to make pies and listen to the black-birds sing.

I wanted to be here, right where I was, in Wicklow.

"I've made my decision," I said to the mulberry trees. "I choose . . . me. I'm happy here. I want to use my gifts to heal, to soothe, and to comfort the people here, in Wicklow. I belong here."

It was then that I noticed a blackbird among the mulberry branches, watching me. She dropped to the ground, and I could see the green in her eyes. Mom.

She hopped around, pecking at the ground. I thought at first she was scratching for mulberries like the other birds, but her pattern wasn't random.

It was a message for me, her own love note.

I watched with a smile as she repeated the route, over and over again, following the path of mulberry tree roots.

"For where your roots are, your heart is," I said, repeating Zee's words.

She bobbed her head once and then flew back into the tunnel, disappearing out of sight.

Blackbirds only made daytime appearances on the rarest of occasions.

Today it had been to welcome me home.

Fluffy clouds swept across mountaintops in the distance as I walked under the rusty metal arch-way of the Wicklow cemetery.

This afternoon it wasn't a cat or a blackbird I was following. It was my heart.

The leaves of the tulip trees fluttered in the breeze, and I kept my gaze straight ahead, so it wouldn't wander over to where Zee had been buried.

Passing the Linden family monument, I said hello to my dad, and kept on going.

I found Aubin Pavegeau exactly where I expected to this time of day: in front of Francie's gravestone under the big maple tree.

He glanced up as I cleared my throat. He took the sweetgum stick out of his mouth and tucked it into his back pocket. "Anna Kate. What's doing?"

"Mind if I sit down?"

Apprehension came quickly into his eyes as he patted the grass. I sat down and set a manila envelope between us.

"What's this?" he asked.

"The police report on my parents' car crash."

His eyes went big and round as he lifted his cap, wiped his forehead with the back of his hand. "I've been waiting twenty-five years for this day to come. The day of reckoning."

"You were there that day, in the car when it crashed, weren't you?" I worked hard to keep the hurt out of my voice. He had to have some sort of reason for keeping quiet all this time.

"How'd you know?"

I opened the envelope and pulled out one of the photographs taken after the wreck. It was of the backseat, which had been littered with broken glass . . . and a sweetgum stick. "Freshly chewed," I said, pointing to the white, pulpy end.

I had to assume the police hadn't recognized what the twig was or considered it important in any way. But the moment I saw it, I knew. And I'd known who it belonged to.

"What happened that day, Aubin?"

Aubin plucked a piece of grass and rolled it between his fingers. "You know some of it already. We took a ride down to Tuscaloosa to see AJ's campus. He and Eden were so in love, those two, it was like to make a man feel sick with the gooey way they talked to each other." He glanced at me. "I didn't understand love at that point, because I was years away from meeting my Francie."

I had a hard time picturing my mother talking sappy at all, but the thought of it made me smile. "They weren't fighting? I've heard they had been that summer, because of Seelie's ultimatum."

"They hadn't been fighting that day, because AJ had made his decision."

"Did he pick my mother?" That certainly would have put an end to their squabbles.

"Kind of. Mostly, he chose himself. He decided he was going to do what he wanted—not what other people wanted for him. He loved Eden and wanted to marry her. And he wanted to go to college, so that's why we were going down to the school. He was meeting with a counselor to figure out how he could pay for college on his own."

He chose himself. A burst of pride brought tears to my eyes. I'd followed in my father's footsteps after all.

"AJ was nothing if not charming," Aubin said as he flung another piece of grass, "and by the time he left campus, he had financial aid in place. Plus the school had married housing options, so he and Eden decided they'd bump up their wedding date to Labor Day weekend. We'd stopped for lunch on the way home, a celebratory picnic, and AJ and I indulged in a few drinks."

"But I read that alcohol hadn't been a factor in the crash."

"It hadn't been for Eden. She didn't drink at all that day and insisted on takin' the keys."

I supposed that would have been all the police cared about—after all, she'd been the one driving.

Aubin's head dropped, and he stared at the ground as he said, "It had been a great day. We laughed a lot. We were near the bridge that crosses Willow Creek when—"

He cut himself off, and I gave him time to collect himself.

Closing his eyes, he said, "When out of nowhere this gray cat comes darting out from the tree line, chasing a bird. Eden swerved, clipped the cat *and* the bird, lost control, and hit the tree. She didn't even have time to brake, it happened so fast. When I came to, I saw Eden was alive but knocked unconscious at the wheel. AJ had been thrown from the car." Aubin swallowed hard. "He'd died on impact."

"And you?" I asked, my throat tight.

"I'd smacked my head good on a window, and my arm was cut up pretty badly from flying glass. I used the blanket in the car to staunch the bleeding, and ran from that crash as fast as I could."

I bent my knees, wrapped my arms around my legs. "Why'd you run?"

"Part of it was fear. I'd called off work that day, and I knew if word got back to my boss, I'd be fired. My mother was countin' on my paycheck to pay our bills and put food on the table. And I was scared about the drinkin', thinking the cops would put me in jail . . . The Lindens didn't like me, and they had sway with the police. It was stupid to run, because I knew Eden was likely to say I'd been there, but it was instinct, pure and simple. By the time I came to my senses and decided to turn myself in, word came 'round that Eden didn't have any memories of the crash."

"So you let her take the blame?" I asked, choking back emotion.

"I was going to, yes, but I couldn't bring myself to do it. I thought for sure the police would find evidence of cat fur or feathers on the car and realize what happened, but nothing like that ever came out. Guilt was eatin' me alive, especially after Seelie started accusin' Eden of causing the crash on purpose. I cleaned up AJ's blanket real good, and I went by the café to talk to her, to tell her what I planned, and to give the blanket back. I told her everything, and I cried like a big ol' baby. I promised her I'd make everything right."

A maple leaf fluttered to the ground. "But . . . you didn't."

"Eden stopped me from going to the police. She said she forgave me, said I'd done *her* a favor by keeping quiet, because it had showed her the Linden family's true colors. She made me promise not to tell anyone what had happened, that there was no point and would only cause me a world of trouble. She said we'd keep it between us. Next thing I knew, she'd left town. I've never told another soul what really happened that day. Until now."

Mom and her promises . . . I hugged my knees even tighter. She hadn't broken her word to Aubin, either—while she insisted she knew the crash had been an accident, she'd never once explained *why* she knew.

I suddenly wondered if Zee knew the truth. The hair rose on my arms, and instinctively I knew

486

she had. Now it all made sense. The terms of her will . . . and the connections to Summer. Zee *had* planned it all, because without Summer, I wouldn't have met Aubin.

Through her will, Zee had gifted me time to find the truth about the accident.

And to find myself.

She'd been a nurturer until the very end.

"I was such a coward. I let Eden down. I let AJ down. I let myself down. And even though Eden forgave me, I'm still working on forgiving myself." He glanced at Francie's headstone. "I don't know what I would have done if someone had accused me of killin' Francie on purpose. I don't know how Eden survived it."

Honestly, I wasn't sure either. I put the photograph away.

He reached for the envelope. "I'll go see Josh Kolbaugh right now, get this all sorted. It's long past time for the truth to come out and to clear Eden's name once and for all."

I put my hand on his arm. "No, it's not what she wanted then, and she wouldn't want it now."

He let that sink in, and then said, "Anna Kate? I'm real sorry about what happened. I wish more than anything you could have known your daddy. And that you could have seen Eden and him together. Seen their love."

"I wish that too," I said softly. But all wasn't lost—every day I was in Wicklow, I learned more and more about the people who'd given me life. I learned it through Aubin. Through the Lindens . . . And I'd keep on learning, because I wasn't leaving.

"I hope you can forgive me, too, Anna Kate."

I reached out for his hand, and he rested his palm on top of mine. "What is friendship, Mr. Pavegeau?"

He lifted up our joined hands. "I think it looks a lot like this, Anna Kate."

"I think so too."

But to my eyes, it didn't just look like friendship.

It also looked a whole lot like healing.

29

Anna Kate Callow stepped up to the table, her coppery-colored hair shining in the sunlight streaming through high windows. The room was awash in light, the woodwork gleaming, the atmosphere warm and friendly. A heavenly scent filled the air. Something sweet yet spicy.

She said, "I thought you'd be done with that article by now. You've been at it awhile."

He thought he'd have finished too. But he was having trouble trying to come up with a way to explain to his editor that his blackbird article had devolved into an existential essay on life, love, loss, and forgiveness. "I shouldn't be here much longer. Maybe another day. Or two."

She smiled sweetly at him as she tucked her hands into the pockets of her waist apron. "I probably should have warned you when you arrived that Wicklow has a way of holding on to you once you're here."

A drop of condensation slid down his glass. "One of the first people I interviewed told me this wasn't any old ordinary town. She was right."

Laughing, Anna Kate's green eyes sparkled with pure happiness. She turned toward the kitchen, then stopped to look back at him. "You stay as long as you want. You're always welcome here at the Blackbird Café."

Anna Kate

"Yoo-hoo!" Faylene Wiggins yelled, waving her arms. "We're over here! The movie's about to start, so get a move on. Hey, y'all, Gideon and Anna Kate are here."

Gideon looked over at me and said, "Third time's the charm for the fried chicken?"

"It better be. I'm starting to think I'm the only one in this town who hasn't tasted it yet."

"Don't worry," he said, squeezing my hand. "I know where you can get plenty more. All you've got to do is ask, Anna Kate."

"Is this all part of your grand plan to reunify our properties?"

"Yes," he said with a smile, "yes, it is."

"I approve."

Faylene's eyebrows went into the stratosphere as we approached and she spotted the hand-holding, but much to my surprise, she didn't call attention to it.

Marcy and Josh were there with Lindy-Lou, who was, as usual, asleep. Mr. Boyd gave a sheepish wave from his spot next to Faylene. Doc leaned against the magnolia tree as he read a book to Ollie, who was nestled in his arms. He gave me a wink and kept on reading about a little blue truck.

"Finally," Natalie said when she saw us. "I swear Mama bribed someone to keep the movie from starting until you got here."

Seelie glanced at me. "It was hardly a bribe. Ten dollars and a What the Flock T-shirt. Pittance, really."

"I don't know about that, Seelie," Cam said from his spot at Natalie's side. "Those shirts are a hot commodity."

"They're selling faster than Aubin can make them," Marcy said. "Please tell me you brought your fried chicken, Gideon. I've been dreaming of it."

"Poor Josh," Pebbles said. "Losing out in Marcy's dreams to chicken."

She and Mr. Lazenby sat next to each other in matching lawn chairs. It seemed Gideon and I weren't the only ones doing some hand-holding tonight.

"Don't feel sorry for me," Josh said. "I've been dreaming about it too."

I smiled at that as I spread a blanket in the empty spot between Natalie and Seelie.

"What's this about chicken?" Mr. Lazenby asked, eyebrows raised with interest.

"It's your favorite kind," Faylene said. "Free!"

He tried to scowl but it quickly turned into a wheezy laugh that filled me with happiness.

As Gideon passed around the plate of chicken, I pulled mason jars of blackberry tea from the

491

cooler to hand out. Jena had helped me pack them as she told me of her and Bow's plans to travel around the country. They were leaving as soon as I hired on more help. When I fairly begged her to stay on, she patted my hand and told me she'd been grounded too long and was ready to fly once again. She vowed they'd be back for Christmas, however, and I was going to hold them to that.

"Hi, Annakay!" Ollie said when she looked up from her book and spotted me.

She'd added the extra *a* this past week. Before I knew it, she'd be saying my full name with perfect enunciation. I was over the moon that I'd get to see her grow up.

I walked over and kissed the top of her head, then Doc's as well. "You two look cozy over here."

Doc winked. "Not as cozy as you're looking with Gideon."

Seelie swatted him. "Oh, hush now. You'll embarrass her."

"I come from hearty stock," I said. "I don't embarrass easily."

"That's good to know," Doc said, "because Seelie's planning family photos. In matching outfits."

"They're not matching," she corrected. "They're *complementing*."

"My mistake, dear."

I laughed as I sat back down. My gaze slid to

Natalie and Cam, who were playing tug-of-war with a chicken leg, then back to Seelie to see how she was reacting to the obvious date.

She slowly smiled and leaned into me to whisper, "If she likes him, then I suppose I like him too. We must get him to shave that beard, though. Good Lord."

The amphitheater lights dimmed, and quiet fell across the crowd. Gideon sat next to me, pushing in close to press a kiss to my temple. He'd been extra early for coffee this morning—because he'd stayed the night.

If Zee and his granddaddy had played match-maker as we suspected, then I owed them a debt of thanks.

The movie screen lit up, then went dark a second later.

The crowd groaned.

The screen lit up again, and cheers erupted as the opening of *Finding Dory* came on.

Then boos erupted, because the characters were speaking in French.

Despite the language barrier, the movie kept rolling, but many people started to pack up and leave.

Faylene said, "What do y'all say? Should we leave or should we stay?"

"Fishy!" Ollie bounced on her toes as she pointed at the screen. "Fishy!"

"Stay," we all said at the same time.

Faylene laughed. "Stay it is. You got any of those hand pies this week, Gideon?"

I smiled as I looked around at all the faces I'd come to know, and the people I'd grown to love.

Wicklow might have taken hold of me, but I was never letting it go.

Acknowledgments

I'm enormously grateful for the encouragement of my agent, Jessica Faust, who believed in this story from page one—and has always believed in me and my writing. Jessica, I simply cannot thank you enough for all that you do.

Amy Stapp, thank you for trusting me to tell this story. Your insightful wisdom and steady guidance took this book to a whole new, wonderful level. I'm excited to see what the future holds for us.

To the amazing, hardworking team at Forge Books, I'm incredibly thankful for your help in bringing the magic of Wicklow to life.

To Sharon, Shelley, Cathy, and Hilda, thank you for the friendship, hugs, advice, and endless enthusiasm for my crazy ideas.

Readers, you inspire me to write. Thank you so much for choosing to spend time with my stories.

Lastly, to my family—you are the magic in my world. Thank you for *everything*.